TRINITY

Nigel May

Bookouture

Published by Bookouture

An imprint of StoryFire Ltd.
23 Sussex Road, Ickenham, UB10 8PN
United Kingdom

www.bookouture.com

ISBN: 978-1-910751-04-6
EBOOK ISBN: 978-1-910751-05-3

ACKNOWLEDGEMENTS

Here come the girls! To Louise (the best proof-reader and friend a man can have), to The *more!* Girls for inspiration, ideas, tunes and love, to Belinda and Tammy for literary guidance, to Gen for tea, toast and titillation, to Cazz for design, to Steph for being wifey, to my gorgeous TV Trinity Lottie, Vix and Nush, and to Juliet for initially knocking me into shape.

Let's Hear It For The Boys! To Mikey & Marcy and James & James for a lifetime of laughter and to Wayne for an explosive intro into the world of publishing.

To the incredible people at Book Outure for joining Team Trinity. Total respect.

To everyone who has crafted my life and made my World Ideal. And to Al, quite simply my everything. Words are not enough.

PROLOGUE

Five years ago …

'You can take this place and stuff it where the sun don't shine.
Me and the girls are outta here for good!' It was with these not
so subtle words that 18-year-old Regan Phoenix flicked a finger
to the row of stuffy tutors at the front of her school assembly
hall and marched towards the exit.

Flanked by her two best mates, Anoushka Silvers and Evie
Merchant, the girls loosened their ties and strutted out of the
building. Three people united as one, fierce to those around
them yet inwardly fearing of all their dreams, insecurities and
aspirations for the future. 'The Trinity Of Beauties', as the three
of them were known across campus.

From today, they were out of here. Three girls who hoped
that they were individually and collectively strong enough to
walk into the big, wide world and have it become their play-
thing because they were ready to try and grab it by the balls.
As the faint odour of their combined signature perfumes still
lingered in the air after their departure, their fellow classmates
could only look on and stare enviously. To them, Regan, Evie
and Nush, as she was known by those close to her, were the three
luckiest females around. They had the looks men lusted after,
and the effortless style that only mega riches and an innate following of fashion could buy. They were the clique that every girl

aspired to join. The Trinity was tight. Three wasn't a crowd – it was, in this case, perfection.

Or at least it was at face value. If the other boarders at Farmington Grange could really see inside the minds of the three young women, they would have seen a knotted mass of anxieties, and self-doubts ricocheting through each of their thoughts.

It was the last day of their final ever term and the Trinity were no longer part of the most exclusive ladies' college in the country. Fashionable and ultra-expensive, Farmington Grange was famed as a place for the crème de la crème of the world's young ladies. But now it was over and uncertainty about what waited them in the outside world loomed heavy. Despite their swagger, the three of them not only shared a deep friendship but also a bond of vulnerabilities – a worry about not being able to live up to their own expectations or the expectations of those who had moulded their very lives. Not that they would have ever shown it to those around them …

—

'C'mon girls, I need a drink!' said Regan. 'I have a Lipsy top with an ultra-low neckline calling my name! Let's hit Diamantes in town – and if one person dares to mention my bitch of a mother, I swear I will hit them harder than a piñata.'

The 'bitch' in question was LA-based actress Montana Phoenix, Regan's mum, who was regarded as the uber bitch of the small screen thanks to her pivotal role as Sienna Revell in the worldwide smash soap opera, *Peregrine Palace*. A role that had brought her the money to purchase a dream home in the Hollywood hills, as well as countless chi-chi stop-off pads around the globe.

It had also allowed her to offload her only daughter, a mistake from a seedy tryst with a man whose name she'd never cared to share with Regan when she was on her way up the industry ladder. When her hindrance of a daughter was barely out of designer baby wear, she'd shipped her back home to England.

Montana had later claimed it was for Regan to gain *the best possible education megabucks could buy,* but it was more a case of getting her out from under her feet and preventing her from becoming the ball and chain that an actress of her social stature could do without.

How was an actress heading to stratospheric success supposed to schmooze and entertain Hollywood's glitterati with a screeching brat under her roof? Her idea of being a good mother had amounted to little more than making sure Regan never wanted for cash, and giving her the odd trip to some riches-drenched location in between filming seasons of *Peregrine.* This wasn't out of love, but served purely to gain press as the 'adoring mother on vacation' when Montana needed an offspring accessory.

'Thank God she's a looker,' Montana would tell friends. 'If she'd been hit by the ugly stick, I'd never have her near me again, it could kill me professionally.'

To say Regan was a 'looker' was an understatement. She had her mother's piercing jade green eyes that appeared feline to look at, but she also had an exotic plump-lipped mouth and full olive-skinned features that could turn a man's head from across a crowded room. It was these looks that had always given a deeply insecure and unloved Regan the one thing she knew she had in her favour – power.

Power to flutter her eyelids at any man she desired and draw him into her web like a seductive spider. In her mind, she hoped it would give her the power to get whatever she desired now that college was a thing of the past. All she really craved from life was a feeling of worth. Because despite her beauty on the outside, Regan had always felt far from beautiful on the inside.

Montana was deliriously happy to just glide around in her pampered LA world pretending to be blissfully unaware of anything when it came to her own flesh and blood. No amount of teen angst, underage partying and drug taking from Regan would ever register as cause for concern on her 'mum-ometer'. Regan was on the other side of the Atlantic so why should mother dearest lower herself to care …

———

Nush sashayed up to the mirror-polished bar at Diamantes, adjusting her Moschino dress as she did so. This was a night to celebrate and all three of the girls were dressed to impress.

They'd been coming to the plush watering hole for years, despite their age. It was the hottest bar in town frequented by the in-crowd from the surrounding counties.

Anoushka caught the eye of barman, Alejandro, admiring the way his black v-neck T-shirt clung tightly to his gym-enhanced pecs, revealing an inviting layer of thick black chest hair. She swooned inwardly as his thick accent erupted. 'Hey, pretty little Nush, looking good *muy sensual!*' It floored her every time. A hint of an accent and she could feel herself melting. *Whoa lady, drinks first* she thought to herself.

'Hi there, chico, school's out for good and we're in the mood for drinking ourselves *available!*' She chose the last word carefully, giving Alejandro the hint that it could be a jalapeno-hot night if he played his cards right. The thought of his strong, caring arms wrapped around her enveloped itself around her brain, sending a wave of comfort right through her. The harbour of a man's arms, protecting her with their love was something that had always been missing in her life. Maybe one day …

'Three large Alamo Splashes and a round of tequila chasers, if you please,' she smiled.

'Coming up, baby!' he grinned, flashing his pearly white teeth and turning to mix the drinks. As he walked away, Anoushka found herself taking in the glory of his tight buttocks, granite-strong and packed expertly into his trousers. Very horny. Not that she could trust him of course, she could never trust any man to give her the kind of love she craved. She blamed her father for that – yes, her damned father – he'd made her like this. If you couldn't get love from your daddy, then how could you ever hope to get it from a complete stranger? *God, I'm such a total cliché*, she critiqued herself.

Her father was media mogul, Lawrence Silvers. An East End rough diamond who had found his way into the heart of the nation by launching one of the first mega-successful glossy magazines to feature, as he put it, 'tits 'n' ass and a bloody good read to boot'.

Having left school with no solid qualifications he had worked his way into the publishing industry via the post room. His first job was sorting out the mail, and he made his first million a few years later in his early twenties from making sure males across the land got sorted as well … at least in their masturbatory fantasies. At last count, he owned more than a dozen 'flash-the-flesh' mags worldwide. Nush knew he was switched on and razor-sharp when it came to business, but as a dad he had always been a dud, leaving her with an empty, emotionless and seemingly permanently-barricaded heart.

At first she'd been daddy's little angel, the blonde little sweetie-pie first-born cherub that Lawrence had been proud to show off. Lawrence was a man's man and appeared to have it all – money, fame, a hugely successful empire and a model wife, Lysette, the former beauty queen with long blonde hair and a heart of gold.

To the male population, Lawrence was a God. Nush thought the same at first, idolising every moment spent with her rough 'n' tumble dad and spectacularly glam mother.

But when Nush turned three, Lysette fell pregnant again. Nush's memories of the time were of her mum constantly being ill and losing the bright shine that life had given her. Her once flawless skin seemed sallow and sunken, her spun-gold hair turned lank and lacklustre.

It was a terrible pregnancy with a tragic outcome. After giving birth to a baby boy, Lysette's body seemed to give in. Haemorrhage and high blood pressure caused her life to ebb away. As one life arrived another had been taken. Nush's princess of a mother was gone, replaced by a baby brother whom she couldn't help but blame, no matter how irrational that seemed.

The boy, named Harry, became the focal point of her dad's life. Lawrence finally had a son to kick a ball around with, a boy to talk girls with, and eventually a man to be heir to his empire. Anoushka felt she had literally been discarded to one side, left to grow up in the charge of a pinch-nosed nanny whose idea of youthful fun was no TV, no music and endless hours of dull educational tests. Meanwhile Harry got daddy's attention in the form of mini Quad bikes, toy helicopters and bouncy castles in the grounds of their manor home. It was a feeling that she had attempted to live with ever since.

As the years went by, her time with daddy became less and less, amounting to the odd bedtime story, a kiss, forced affection and …

'Here you go, gorgeous!' The sound of Alejandro's voice announcing the arrival of the drinks brought Nush back from her thoughts. *C'mon, this is supposed to be a night of celebration*, she mused to herself. 'Stick it on the tab' she flirted. Nothing was going to spoil her special night with her two best friends … nothing.

—

Licking the trail of salt from the back of her hand, Evie Merchant knocked back the tequila, feeling the liquid slightly burn her throat as she did so. The warm feeling spread across her small and exquisitely pert breasts, which she had maximised with a Verde Veronica bra and a loose-fitting shift dress. She'd teamed it with killer Christian Dior heels, a slight trace of make-up across her unblemished skin, and her russet Kidman-esque locks were tied back off her face in a ponytail. It accentuated her doll-like beauty even more.

She would miss college. Unlike her two best friends she hadn't been forced to go there by an overbearing father or an uncaring mother. It had been her choice, her wish, her sanctuary and hopefully her springboard onto her ultimate dreams.

Ever since she could remember, Evie Merchant had dreamt of being a famous Hollywood star. To be one of the glamour pusses lighting up Tinseltown – the talented ones tipped for Oscars, Emmys and Golden Globes and the beautiful ones adorning the covers of the thick glossy magazines. She knew that many of the world's best actresses had attended Farmington Grange at some point, which is why she'd begged her mother and father to send her there. But would she one day be able to follow in her Hollywood idols' red carpet footsteps? Evie wasn't sure.

The fact that she had always been the star of every end-of-term production was a point in her favour. Those in the know had said her Ophelia was the best Farmington had ever seen. And her voice in the musical *The Umbrellas of Cherbourg*, was something to rival Deneuve. She was good – the Knightleys and the Diazs of this world had better watch out. Could she ever be that good? Only the future could tell.

Evie would have moved heaven and earth to have a mother like Montana Phoenix ... just mentioning that name could open doors to the plushest of audition suites. No need to screen test if you were blood-tied to the biggest soap star in the world, but she wasn't, was she? Regan didn't know how lucky she was. But she'd never dream of asking Regan to pull favours. There was no mother-love there.

Evie couldn't bear it that her own parents were so conservative. Stinking rich, sure, but there was no glitz, glamour or celebrity connections at home – she'd have to try and work those options herself.

Evie's parents were both successful in their own right. Her father was Donald Merchant, the hot-shot investment banker who had been a multi-millionaire, maybe even a billionaire, for as long as she could remember. He was famed for lending expertise to flailing companies to raise debt or equity capital. Even the thought of it all turned her off. Where was the spotlight, glamour and buzz with all that?

Sure, it meant yachts in the Cote D'Azur, chalets in Aspen and beach houses in Cape Town, but Evie wanted to hang out with the entertainment in-crowd, not a bunch of old bores in suits. She wanted her talk of 'Ledgers' to be about drinking with the late, great Heath, not purchase ones and spreadsheets.

Her mum, Molly Merchant, was no more use. Her expertise lay in furniture design – big chunky slabs of weather-weary wood shaped into tables and chairs. It made Molly a fortune, but again, her clientele was hardly the A-listers of the entertainment world. It was Duke this or Countess that – old money families. Why couldn't Molly have been a fashion designer instead – creating haute couture frocks and diamond-encrusted accessories? At least then mother could have served some purpose come Oscar day.

Her parents lived at Hadleigh Hall, one of the biggest stately homes and tourist attractions in the country, which they shared with countless servants, two Great Danes and a muster of peacocks. Warm and cosy it wasn't, to Evie it had always seemed like a grey and lifeless prison with no joie de vivre.

Evie's childhood years there were not happy ones. She would spend hours sitting in her bedroom window watching the families of tourists wandering around the topiaried gardens secretly willing them to be her friends. She felt alone and unloved, with no friends of her own and her parents constantly away on business. Her only joy had been acting out scenes from films she'd watched on TV in the privacy of her own room to an 'audience' of precious porcelain dolls. Evie had been keen to leave for the nirvana of Farmington as soon as she could. Acting was all she cared about, but would it be enough to help her survive in life?

On meeting Nush and Regan, she knew she had finally found friends for life. They both had a thirst for excitement and a showbiz savvy that she idolised. They, in turn, loved Evie's innocence and charm and were in awe of her evident acting talent. Three flawed girls, forming one flawless Trinity.

———

Regan drained the last of her drink and slammed the glass onto the table, another lined up and ready to go. The girls were warming up nicely and were attracting glances from virtually every man in the bar. *The only ones not looking must be gay,* thought Regan, *and if they knew who my mother was they'd be over here in a shot asking about plotlines. Why does my mother always manage to invade my thoughts?*

'We're looking mighty fine, girls … may I propose a toast?' she cried, pushing all thoughts of Montana from her mind and turning to Nush and Evie. 'Here's to us, the *Trinity of Beauties* … may we party hard, get all we desire from life, both inside and outside of the bedroom, and never let life kick us where it hurts! Cheers ladies!'

But what would the future hold for them? Would one or all of them achieve their dreams and overcome their insecurities? The only definite was that soon the three of them would be mercilessly torn apart. Betrayal, jealousy, deception and death would attempt to destroy the Trinity – maybe for good.

CHAPTER 1

Now …

'You taste sweet, baby. Making *love* to you is *bad*.'

The voice was coming from between Regan's spread-eagled legs. It belonged to the shaven-headed rapper currently licking his, so he thought, *expert* way around Regan's tender flesh.

He'd been there for the last ten minutes as Regan stared absently at the hotel chandelier hung above the bed. He was demonstrating, to quote him, 'The alphabet of *leurve*'. It was a technique taught to him by LA's premier sexologist. As his tongue licked each letter of the alphabet onto Regan's exposed clitoris, she was supposedly guaranteed to cum by the time he reached 'H'. It hadn't worked.

The only thing that felt *bad* right now, in the true sense of the word, was the inside of Regan's skull. She felt like her brain had been rubbed down with a sanding block.

She was used to the feeling. She's had the same empty, cranium-pounding experience after nearly every night of meaningless sex she'd ever encountered. Time to fake yet another orgasm.

'Oh yeah, bad boy, that's it! You're the man! I'm there …' She knew the lines off by heart. How to raise her voice with forced excitement seemingly climaxing into a girlie satisfied squeal. Another testosterone-filled man feeling that he'd written the book on female satisfaction.

Known as Daddy O to the CD-buying public – real name Norris – the rapper laid back on the bed, placing his hands behind his head. He gave out a gold-toothed smile, looking at Regan and said 'Who's your big Daddy O?' Regan knew it was time to leave.

———

Ten minutes later Regan stumbled along the Holland Park Road leading from the hotel looking for a black cab. She felt woozy and still smelt of the previous night's excesses – her clothes impregnated with the odour of stale sweat from frenzied dancing. Her throat felt dry from hours of cocaine.

'Why the hell do I do it?' she said to no-one. One party just seemed to roll into another and they all ended the same way. Tired, cranky and lonely.

You could guarantee that Nush and Evie wouldn't be in such a state. Nush with her famed gossip column and Evie, the shining hope of the British film scene. People seemed to care about them and, more to the point, they seemed to care about themselves. Who gave a shit about Regan? Father – unknown. Mother – selfish cow. Best mates – doing very nicely, thanks for asking.

It was hard to believe that the Trinity had left Farmington half a decade ago, but what exactly had Regan achieved? Nothing to get her out of Montana's shadow. So far life had amounted to several loveless escapades and a liver on the verge of collapse.

She wasn't even that good at partying anymore. She used to have the reputation as the girl who could light up a dance floor all night long. She'd always looked flirtily fantastic as she bared her ass to the waiting paparazzi outside some happening nightspot.

But the last 18 months had seen Regan's star quality turn from 'dancing queen' to 'has-been'. Any magazine photos of her these days featured glazed eyes, ripped tights and the look of the late Winehouse or Hollywood's Lohan at their worst. The captions usually featured the words 'tragic' or 'out-of-control' and painted her as the antithesis of mother's pride.

Montana herself had ordered her own publicist to ban journalists from asking questions about Regan's exploits during interviews. The shame was too damaging. When one intrepid TV hack had dared to grill Montana live on TV about a wild night out that ended in Regan having her stomach pumped, she'd stormed off the show in disgust.

—

Regan's head was still banging by the time she got back to her London Bridge home. As she climbed the steps to the fourth floor river-view apartment her phone rang. It was Nush.

'Hello, doll, I hope you feel as crapola as I do,' Regan answered, turning the key in the door.

'So where did you end up *then*? Was it Daddy *O for orgasmic*?' taunted Nush.

'Pumped him dry girlfriend. Left him wanting more after satisfying my womanly needs,' lied Regan. 'I'm just back home.'

She collapsed onto the sofa, checking out the display on her answering machine as she did so. One message flashed. *Way to go, Ms Popular* … she thought to herself. 'What about you … get a slice of man pie?'

'I bit the *Bullet*, honey, literally. Jake Saunders, TV warrior and father of Mae-Ling Ch'en's child was mine for the night. You'd have seen it coming had you not been so off your face with the blingmeister!' Nush replied, not totally enjoying the bragging sound of her own voice.

'So another celeb shag each to add to the list then?' said Regan. 'You seeing him again?'

'No way, I don't think he'd want to. And I'd be very surprised if Mae-Ling wants to see him again either after today's *Staple* column hits the streets,' stated Nush.

'Especially if they bed a bitch like you,' smirked Regan, only half joking. 'Listen babe, I'm shattered. Need some shut eye. I'm going to pop a Zopiclone and crash out. Bell me later if Mae-Ling hasn't gunned you down first!' Again she was only half-joking. That woman had a reputation.

After hanging up, Regan threw off her clothes and enveloped herself in the fluffy towelling robe hung on her bedroom door. It felt comforting. A sleeping pill would be the perfect end to a far from perfect night. She stuck her mouth under the bathroom tap and glugged back the water to swallow the white oval tablet.

Falling onto the sofa again she pressed the play button on the answering machine. A man's voice broke the silence. 'Hi there, Regan. I got your number from a friend, hope you don't mind. My name's Leo Weiss. I'm a TV producer at Minted TV. I'd like to speak to you about a new project I'm working on. Any chance we could meet to discuss it?'

Regan vaguely heard him leave his telephone number as she drifted into the darkness of sleep. Some things would have to wait.

CHAPTER 2

As Anoushka Silvers finished her conversation with Regan, a ripple of discontent stitched itself across her thoughts. She'd done it again. Another night and another repeat performance of scandal and self-prostitution in order to satisfy her readers and satisfy her odious father. She cast her mind back to how it had happened yet again …

That morning she'd opened her eyes and run her manicured fingers along the cotton sheets she'd been sleeping under. *Okay, this is not my bed as I only have silk sheets,* she thought, *so I am not at home.* The next question, a mandatory one for Nush most mornings was – *am I alone?* The answer came as no surprise as she turned to survey the other side of the king-size bed: no. Lying alongside her was Jake Saunders, the muscled former athlete who had now found fame as a TV warrior on the hit TV show *Sporting Spartans.* His face adorned the postered walls of teenagers across the land and last night it had been adorning every inch of Nush's body in a hotel bed.

She'd done it again – tricked a man into bed just to satisfy a professional need and deep-seated longing to please her father. Although Jake had definitely provided her with a few wondrously divine moments of warmth and totally fantastic sex. At least this guy was hot, which was something Nush had not always been able to say in her quest for a good story. And Jake seemed nice too, which was such a pity …

They'd met at the launch party for *Sporting Spartans'* latest season, held at the Crystal Members Club in London's Fitzrovia. Nush was there in her usual capacity, as the number one must-have guest for any party organisers. She was the country's premier gossip columnist and if she wasn't on the guest list, then a celeb-filled bash was *not* worth going to. In the ritzy tittle-tattle of the gossip world, Nush's take on celebrities could make or break today's top names. Her praise could see someone's career ascend to dizzy heights overnight. But one caustic putdown and the same celeb's name could be mud, their career pretty much over.

She was famed as Britain's youngest ever columnist, having secured the role at the age of 20. Her boss was her father after all and the man that she had to keep constantly happy. When Lawrence Silvers had acquired *The Daily Staple* newspaper to add to his empire, he had literally cleared out the old staff in minutes. Much to the seething annoyance of Clarissa Thornton, *The Staple's* former gossip girl, Anoushka was given the column straight away, despite having no real experience.

'Keeps you off the bloody streets' her father had barked at Nush. 'You party all the time, you may as well earn a crust while you're drinking my account dry.'

It was true. If there was one thing Nush had revelled in since leaving Farmington it was partying. And writing a must-read newspaper column detailing the debauched nightly activities of the high-flyers frequenting those parties was the ideal excuse to hang out with the celebs with a cocktail in her hand night after night. She didn't really care about any of these people. Half of them were famous for having no particular talent other than appearing on some godforsaken reality show. As far as Nush could see, if they were shagging someone behind their spouse's back in some secluded corner of a VIP area then it was fair game for her to tell the world in every lip-smacking detail. Especially if Lawrence demanded nothing but the best stories. If it secured her daddy brownie points then a celebrity's professional loss was her family gain.

Her sharp-tongued approach had made her the acid queen of daily newspapers. It had also earned her a team of superstar-spying sources around the globe. They made sure that any celebrity dirt from Monte Carlo to Mustique would be aired first under her newspaper by-line. Even daddy was vaguely proud of her for getting *The Staple's* readership rocketing sky-high in weeks. If you wanted the ultimate in scandal then Nush's column was the place to head for the dirt on salacious celebrity frissons. It was indeed a dirty job, but her father had chosen her to be the one to do it. And even if, unbeknown to her readers, she was constantly riddled with ripples of guilt, Nush knew that she had those readers, and more importantly her father, to please.

Talking of dirt … Jake Saunders had a girlfriend and baby girl back home didn't he? Somebody was being a naughty boy here. He was currently seeing make-up artist to the stars, Mae-Ling Ch'en. Nush and Regan had spent hours poring over the tacky 16-page 'at home' welcoming baby Famke into the world in *Blaze* magazine some months back.

They'd laughed together at the party last night about how they'd taken the magazine and ringed with black marker any unsightly nasty *objects* around the couple's Kensington home. Adding a penned *ring of shame* to Mae-Ling's clawed toes, grabbing for dear life onto her ill-fitting Manolo Blahnik's, as she stood adoringly alongside the Cleopatra Palace scalloped crib. Money did not always buy class.

What the hell happened to Regan at the party anyway? The last Nush remembered was her disappearing into the night. She'd been on the arm of some foul-mouthed rapper who was

currently sitting pretty in the album charts with a CD formed
almost entirely from expletives. *Would Regan ever stay away from
bad boys?* mused Nush.

Anyway, who was she to talk? She was lying in bed with
somebody else's boyfriend, the father of a six-month old child.
The sex may have been earth-moving, but work was work and
she needed to craft a story here. Yep, a tasty piece about how
one half of celeb-land's hottest couple had proved that he was
just as athletic in the sack as his warrior alter-ego, Bullet, was on
his TV show. That would make a great lead for today's column.

Naturally, she'd leave out the fact that it was she herself who
was the 'mystery woman' on the receiving end of his rather impressive manhood. Some things close to home always stayed secret. That's why she'd insisted they leave separately from the club
last night and that he pay for the hotel on *his* credit card. For
a moment the devious necessities of her trade scratched at her
mind, but she pushed them aside as she'd trained herself to do.

Nush slid out from under the sheets and retrieved her Kiki
De Montparnasse underwear from the floor along with her dress
as she headed for the door. The tattooed torso of Jake Saunders
stirred softly, rolled over revealing a sizable erection and then
drifted off to sleep again.

The pill's still working I see, thought Nush, remembering the
Viagra she'd slipped him last night. She'd needed to make sure
he was fully working to maximise column inches, so to speak.
She was tempted to climb back in bed and climb back on board,
*but my work here is done. Sweet dreams, Jakey, you'll need it. By the
end of today I'm going to serve you one heck of a nightmare.*

CHAPTER 3

Evie was beside herself with joy. She had just stepped out of the sumptuous lobby at the Hostellerie Tros Marets and into the Mercedes convertible waiting to take her to the set of her latest movie. *Things couldn't be better*, she considered, taking her place behind her chauffeur.

She admired the scenery as the car sped along in the sunshine, blowing fresh country air through her long red locks. She reached for her Prada Butterfly sunglasses and basked in the heat.

The hotel was situated at the border of the majestic Ardennes in the southeast corner of Belgium and had been her home for the last three weeks. She loved its tranquillity and refined air. It also helped that the food was delicious, which, for a girl who never had to worry about her weight, was indulgently divine.

The main thing that impressed Evie, though, was that it had been rumoured that Jennifer Aniston and one of the Olsen twins had recently stayed there. Let them add Evie Merchant's name to that list. Plus, after 18 months of filming everywhere from Honolulu to Hong Kong, it was nice that Belgium was close enough to be only an hour or so away from the sanctuary of her London home.

At 23, Evie was still young enough to get giddy about her meteoric ascent to fame. She'd made it, her dreams had come true. She was a formidable actress but her rise into the multi-million dollar league over the last few years had been beyond even her wildest hopeful expectations. It only seemed two minutes since she'd been corseted-up doing Shakespeare at Farmington. And here she was, the envy of and inspiration for millions of girls worldwide.

Not that it stopped her getting completely tongue-tied around her fellow actors though. Give her a script and she'd be word perfect. But put her alongside George Clooney or Robert Pattinson in on-set catering and her mouth would just not connect to her brain. Random words spilled out in no particular order.

The movie she was shooting in Belgium was a rom-com called *The Bouquet Catcher*. A typical 'always the bridesmaid never the bride' affair, which her agent, LA ball-breaking hotshot Stephanie Love, had said Evie would be mad not to take. Steph figured that playing the ditzy unlucky-in-love heroine had worked wonders for Drew Barrymore and Katherine Heigl over the years and now it was Evie's turn.

A successful comedy could set you up as the perfect all-rounder, and seeing as Evie had already earned her 'Streeps' when it came to serious drama – she was already tipped for an Oscar for her performance in period drama, *Pengelly Manor* – comedy was the next genre to conquer. It was hard-talking Stephanie who called them 'Streeps' as an homage to Evie's idol, Meryl.

'Jesus, look at that woman's career,' she'd snap to Evie. 'She's frigging amazing … *Kramer vs. Kramer*, *French Lieutenant's Woman*, *Silkwood* … spot on, heart-wrenching, tissue-filling drama. Then she's splitting your sides in *Death Becomes Her*, *She Devil* or *The Devil Wears Prada*. Next she starts singing in *Mamma* freaking *Mia*! A-ma-zing! You wanna be like Meryl, you gotta earn your 'Streeps'.'

The other reason Stephanie had pushed Evie to do the movie was because of her male co-star, Jeremy Pinewood. If there was one male star who could pretty much guarantee backsides-on-seats at cinemas around the world it was the totally wholesome Pinewood.

He'd been a child star in his native Australia from way back, working his way through countless hit series. He'd even managed a short-lived but nevertheless multi-platinum singing career. With his lean, muscular frame, winning smile and floppy-fringed charm, he was the ultimate dude from down under. But whereas countless cloned counterparts had left the dizzy TV heights and then sunk without trace, Jeremy had always seemed to make the right move and stay one step ahead.

First move was to LA. Within weeks of moving to America in his late teens he'd bagged the same agent as Hugh Jackman and Matt Damon and a season finale part on *Peregrine Palace* as Montana Phoenix's toy boy. Evie remembered watching the episode with an intense interest, wishing that it had been her lips caressing Jeremy's chiselled features.

From there he'd fronted a couple of big bucks slice 'n' dice movies before turning his hand to musicals in a reworked Hollywood version of the *Joseph* story called *Dreamcoat*. This earned him the nickname 'The Dreamboat from *Dreamcoat*'. By the age of 22, he had already managed to grace the covers of virtually every magazine around the globe – from teenage girl thru to style icon thru to gay. He was huge.

And today, in a church in a quaint town in the middle of Belgium, was the day that she would finally get to meet her co-star. *How excitingly weird is that*, thought a gleeful Evie.

—

As her car pulled up at location, she heard her Blackberry Curve sounding inside her shoulder bag. A missed call from Anoushka, no doubt phoning for the low down on Jeremy. She would have to wait until the day's shooting was over. Didn't that girl ever switch off from the need to garner gossip?

Evie was desperate to speak to Stephanie to see what the latest industry buzz was about her and Jeremy teaming up for a movie. Indications before had been that it was the match many fans had been waiting for. The serious English rose alongside Australia's sexiest export. Due to the time difference between Belgium and LA, though, it was still far too early to call without rousing a snarling Stephanie from her slumber.

Heading to make-up, Evie nodded to the various crew members she saw. One thing she always tried to remember was to be courteous to all around her. A runner one day could become a fashionable new writer with the most sought-after scripts in town the next.

Seeing as Jeremy was the other major player in today's scenes, she'd expected him to be sitting in make-up when she arrived. She was surprised to see that the room's sole occupant was Mae-Ling, the make-up girl. It was the award-winning cosmetic connoisseur's first job since the birth of her baby girl. She'd chosen the movie because, like Evie, it meant getting back to her London home easily.

'We on our own then?' said Evie.

'Oh, yes, darling!' exclaimed Mae-Ling. 'Have you not heard? Mr Pinewood has brought his own make-up artist. Seems that I'm not good enough to lay my hands on his Antipodean features. I was good enough for Daniel Craig and Christian Bale sweetie … I ask you!'

Strange? Evie had met a few stars who had their own 'staff' with them on various sets. However, the ones who were choosy with their make-up were not usually the 20-something guys. It was normally the aging has-been divas who needed their own expert *maquilleur* filling in every etched wrinkle.

'Vanity kills, darling… thank Christ he can act,' purred Mae-Ling.

———

The next half an hour saw Mae-Ling expertly applying make up to Evie's features. A skilled dusting of foundation, a light caress of eye-shadow, a slick of lip gloss and Evie was done. As Evie rose from her seat, she looked into the light-bulb-framed mirror at her own 'film-star' reflection. It was true, things couldn't get better than this.

As Evie went to leave, the fax machine in the corner of the room started to beep. Mae-Ling, used to receiving faxes for Evie from Stephanie at all hours of the day, sauntered over to check out the offering. The fax wasn't for Evie. It was addressed 'urgent' and marked for Mae-Ling. Evie couldn't help but look. It was from Mae-Ling's London agent, Vera O'Connor. The cover sheet read 'Dearest Mae. Thought you'd better see this horror before you get wind from elsewhere. Tried phoning but you're obviously busy. Sorry darling – hugs – V x'

The sheet that followed was Anoushka Silver's latest column. The headline read 'JAKE MAKES-UP FOR MAKE-UP-MAE'S ABSENCE IN DRUG-FUELLED ROMP'. Mae-Ling's jaw dropped and her stomach turned in nauseous spasm. She turned to Evie. 'Isn't this bitch your best friend?' Evie didn't know where to look. One piece of paper and suddenly the air in the room was frostier than the glacier blue eye shadow she was sporting. Sometimes having a gossip columnist as a best friend was a real downer and as she stared at the trembling, hatred-filled face of Mae-Ling glaring at her, this was definitely one of them…

CHAPTER 4

As another copy of *The Daily Staple* hit the newsstands, Nush couldn't help but smile. Today's scandal-laden column was out in the public domain. It was a nasty business but her six-figure salary and need to succeed more than made up for any ripple of bad karma she felt.

Sat at her office desk, Nush considered her options for the evening ahead. A gallery opening on the South Bank for some trendy Brazilian artist? A workout DVD launch at The Lanesborough Hotel from some Z grade celebrity? Or a night in front of her plasma TV with back to back episodes of vintage *Desperate Housewives*?

No contest, thought Nush, *Wisteria Lane all the way*!

As she logged off from her PC, her desk phone rang. It was her father. Nush groaned inwardly. What did he want? *Please don't let him kick off at me again.* She gingerly picked up the receiver.

'Anoushka, your brother's back in town. Your stepmum wants to push the boat out for him. Welcome him back with a bit of a bash. Quite right too. Harry's been up some bloody mountain for months,' Lawrence snapped.

So, the prodigal son returns and out comes the bunting, eh? Nush was beyond annoyed. Harry had spent the last 18 months skiing and snowboarding his way around the black runs of Europe, choosing to spend daddy's money on overpriced hotel suites and deluxe chalets for him and his piste-mates. Lawrence said that Harry was 'building up character before taking the reins of the empire'. Like hell he was?

Harry lived for speed, hi-energy excitement and the thrill of the chase when it came to both sport and women. On the publishing front, the closest he'd ever come to getting involved with his father's magazines and newspapers was jacking off over the pages of one of Lawrence's top shelf publications.

'So, we'll expect you Saturday at the house. Bring that totty actress friend of yours, the Merchant girl. Harry's always banging on about her. About time he got a decent girl on his arm. Mind you, can't blame a lad for playing the field and sowing his oats. He's got his father's blood pumping through him after all.'

Nush cringed at the thought of Harry being a sleazy chip off the old Silvers block. She cringed even more at the thought of Saturday. Harry, Lawrence and evil stepmother Sadie all in the same room. *Better paint that gritted teeth smile on now and hope it has dried set by the weekend*, thought Nush. She'd need it for Sadie. If there was one woman on earth who could get Nush's temper racing from nought to sixty in record time it was low-rent Sadie Silvers.

———

Sadie had been married to Lawrence for the last four years. They'd first met when she'd jumped out of a huge cake at Lawrence's 40th birthday party at the private park in New York's Hudson Hotel. Her first words to Lawrence as her cream-covered body erupted through the top tier were 'Hey soldier, which bit of tasty little me you wanna eat first?' Trash didn't come any trashier.

———

Sadie Lee Bolan was born in the swamplands of Louisiana, in the city of Baton Rouge. About an hour from New Orleans, it was the place that first sparked her curiosity for the spotlight of fame.

Her home life was ramshackle, her parents not much more than hillbillies, but Sadie always knew that there was life beyond the swinging garden chair on their mosquito-infested veranda.

She'd seen it. Numerous movie crews who would come to the swamp areas around Baton Rouge to film. Its hidden little rivers, boats and dense greenery were the perfect setting for jungle-like vistas.

She'd seen lots of today's top stars filming crappy B movies there when she was a teenager. Hammy tales of killer monsters from the deep, flesh-eating fish and giant radioactive spiders. Her favourite had been watching scream queen Montana Phoenix running along the banks of the Pearl River, shrieking banshee-like into the air.

Sadie had wanted to be part of it all. She wanted to be the one falling into the arms of the marble chested male lead. She wanted to be the one who would return to her Winnebago at the end of a day's shooting for a massage and manicure. She wanted to be the one who mattered.

The one thing she never wanted to do was stay at home with her folks for the rest of her life. After saving up enough money from a job at a local burger joint, she quit Baton Rouge and headed to LA. She was just eighteen.

Life in LA was not the hotbed of passion she'd read about in her Jackie Collins novels. With hardly any cash to her name, she took a job flipping burgers at Bob's Big Boy diner in Burbank. Same shit, different city.

The place itself was great, with its jaunty umbrellas and flashy neons, but not even the constant diet of succulent fried chicken and gooey hot fudge cake could satisfy her aching ambition.

It was only after a chance encounter with Stafford James, an LA photographer, that her luck started to change. At first she'd pissed him off, dripping sauce from his chilli spaghetti onto his Old Navy cargo shorts as she cleared the plates from the booth table where he was eating with a male friend. From the moment Stafford raised a carefully shaped eyebrow in her direction, Sadie knew she was in trouble. This man looked fierce.

'Gee, I'm sorry, sir. Silly old me, let me get the manager for you, I'm sure we can sort something out,' said Sadie, turning on the Louisiana charm. It worked. Stafford smiled, seemingly forgetting about the big red blob on his lap.

'No worries, sweetheart, I'm sure you can make it up to me. And before you think I'm going to try and slip you a length honey, I bat for the other team. Queer, friend of Dorothy, shirt lifter.'

Sadie was taken aback by his in-your-face honesty. 'I'm a photographer, and a pretty well-known one at that. I shoot loads of girls for the glam rags. You ever modelled?'

A cheesy line, but it worked. A few days later, Sadie had shot the first of many glamour shoots. Thoughts of following in Montana's kitten-heeled footsteps went out the window. Stafford loved her butter-wouldn't-melt nature, plus she had a great set of tits. And for Sadie it was easy money.

Within a few years she had graced the pages of *Maxim*, *Hustler*, *Barracuda* and *Blender* magazines as well as bagging the ultimate prize as a *Playboy* cover girl.

It was the photo of her covering her pussy with a toy alligator on the cover of *Playboy* that had first gained Lawrence Silvers' attention. The photo was a tongue-in-cheek reference to Sadie's background and became one of the most memorable *Playboy* covers ever.

Lawrence had wanted to recreate the image for one of his mags and was determined to meet Sadie, but she was too busy to fit the shoot into her schedule.

Lawrence decided on a more direct approach. If the mountainous peaks of Sadie wouldn't come to him then he would go to them. Hence the decision to hold his 40th celebrations in America.

A lucrative lure of $300,000 was made to Sadie for an evening's work, jumping out of a birthday cake, cream covering her ample proportions for the European magazine mogul. How could she refuse?

It had been love at first sight, or maybe that should have been 'bite' given the circumstances, and within a few weeks Sadie had left LA for good to start her new life with Lawrence at the Silvers' Palladian home, Kingsbury Mead Estate.

Within six months the same home was the venue for one of the tackiest weddings the world had ever seen. Sadie had spurned the advice of teams of dress designers from Badgeley Mischka and Sassi Holford in favour of her own mini-skirted lacy concoction.

Exquisite lines and sumptuous fabric it was not. It was a puffball skirt pom-pom teamed with a nipple-hugging bodice. And at Lawrence's suggestion, she'd trimmed her veil with alligator teeth, in-keeping with her swamp roots.

Nush could have died watching Sadie totter up the aisle of the Kingsbury chapel. She was gaining a step mum only five years her senior. She'd said a silent prayer to her real mother, hoping that the hideously low-rent union wouldn't last.

Four years on, she was still hoping…

CHAPTER 5

Matsuhisa restaurant on North La Cienega Boulevard in Beverly Hills buzzed with the energy of a celeb-heavy crowd. At a corner table sat agent to the stars, Stephanie Love.

She currently had a dozen big names on her books, with four of them, including Evie Merchant, tipped to be featured in the next batch of Oscar nominations. Not that there wasn't always room for another high-rolling name on her client roster.

The quest for knowledge about who should be the object of her next plan of strategic attack was the purpose of today's lunch with Clarissa Thornton.

Stephanie liked Clarissa. First off she was a Brit now based in the States, so she had her ear to the ground both sides of the pond. Secondly, she reminded her of herself. Not afraid to speak her mind, not afraid to tread on people's toes, and not afraid to bitch-slap them into next week if need be.

Clarissa used to work at *The Daily Staple*, pre-Lawrence Silvers days. Her bitterness about being turfed out overnight and being replaced with the new boss's daughter was famed.

Not that it mattered now, as she tucked into jumbo clams amongst the cream of Hollywood society. She'd turned her life around by booking herself a one-way ticket to Los Angeles the day after getting the boot, putting her London flat up for rent, and finding herself a new bijou pad not far from the 'Hollywood' sign.

She'd then used her considerable US contacts to bag herself a job. Her business card said it all: Clarissa Thornton, Showbiz Editor, *Hollywood Daily*.

Hollywood Daily was one of America's must-see TV shows, fronted by the annoyingly handsome Carson Roberts. As Showbiz Editor, it was Clarissa who got to travel the world grilling the glitterati.

And for Clarissa, lunch today was all about digging deep into the life of Evie Merchant. *Not that Stephanie needs to know that*, she thought, contemplating her next course – *maybe the buttery Kobe beef or the black cod in miso.*

'So, how's Evie doing on her new movie, Steph?' enquired Clarissa. 'She's working with the fabulous Jeremy Pinewood isn't she?'

'It's perfect isn't it? She should stick her hands down his pants as soon as look at him. Now that would be my idea of a spot-on career move. The boy is hotter than the Kalahari right now. She could do with some kind of frigging love life for God's sake. She's been as dry as the bloody Sahara for as long as I can remember.'

'So, has anything happened between them yet?' probed Clarissa, a little braver with her questioning now that the lunchtime drinking seemed to be loosening Steph's tongue. A romance between two of the sexiest young stars around would make for blistering editorial. And if she could break the story before her nemesis Anoushka, then so much the better.

'That would be telling,' teased Stephanie loudly. 'But their first scenes together are this week. The sooner they get it on the better, and I say that as her *tenpercentary*. The money-spinning opportunities could be huge.' Steph clapped her hands together with glee and returned to her sashimi salad.

—

Interesting, thought Stafford James, two tables up from Stephanie and Clarissa. He and his dining partner, a weak-voiced but thankfully well-hung Puerto Rican model, were just finishing their main courses. He continued to mull over all he had overheard from Stephanie about Evie and Jeremy. So, they might be getting it on, eh? Nush would definitely love to break that story first.

So what if it wasn't his gossip first-hand? In Hollywood, you either dug up dirt or you stole it. Time to make a phone call. With the LA/London time difference Anoushka should still be at work.

Stafford had been Nush's eyes and ears in Hollywood pretty much ever since she started her column at *The Staple*. It was Sadie who had initially recommended him after knowing how well connected Stafford seemed to be with all levels of LA society. From the movers and shakers on the way up to those stars whose 'fame flame' was still worthy of burning column inches, Stafford had more or less photographed them all.

Many of the male ones he'd also slept with, a fact known to Nush. She had promised Stafford that one day she would get him so shit-faced on a night out that he would spill the beans and bring a few of the star-name macho-men of film-land crashing down on their sorry sodomised arses.

When Anoushka had first approached him about snooping for her, he'd told her where to get off. 'I do have a reputation in this town, young lady,' he'd sniped at her. 'And it won't get soiled with the skid marks of your unbridled nastiness.' This reluctance hadn't lasted long, though, after Nush's promises of big dollar payouts for every story.

As for his reputation? Well, as a giddy gay gossip to hang out with at the *Vanity Fair* party or backstage at Lady Gaga's secret gig, he was very much in demand. But as a photographer, jobs were leaner than ever. Glossies were shooting in house or choosing only to use top names like LaChapelle and Von Unwerth.

He'd needed to pay his bills, and a constant stream of lovers with not a nickel to bounce off their young buff butts had made life more expensive. But thanks to him driving the gossip train for Nush, Stafford was now half way financially solvent again.

And that meant money for the odd nip and tuck here and there. So far his ill-gotten gains from *The Staple* had paid for rhinoplasty, countless face peels, cheek implants, liposuction and a pair of age reversing pec implants.

Anoushka answered her work phone after two rings. 'Hey, Staffs, what you got for me today then?' Talking to Stafford made her mood immediately lighter than it had been seconds before when she was talking to her dad about brother Harry's return. 'A Montana Phoenix sex tape?' she sniggered, imagining how Regan would react to that.

'No, sweetness, it's about your other best pal, Evie,' whispered Stafford. 'A not-so-little loud-mouthed bird sat two tables down from me at Matsuhisa has just been telling Clarissa Thornton that Evie might be getting it on with Jeremy Pinewood on the set of her latest film.'

Nush hated gossip involving either Regan or Evie but she did feel a tickle of excitement deep down. A call to Evie was needed, or even better, maybe a little set visit. She could be with Evie in Belgium in two hours or so.

Plus the thought of Clarissa being on the other side of the Atlantic while she got the scoop made it all the more appealing. After hanging up, she reached into the drawer for her passport.

———

Five and a half thousand miles away, Stafford paid the bill and slipped out of the restaurant with his model at his side and a throbbing dick in his pants. Dancing with the devil always made him horny. 'C'mon, sweet cheeks,' he leered. 'Back to mine. My cock doesn't get sucked on its own you know.'

CHAPTER 6

Now, if Stafford had not been so busy concentrating on the pleasures of the flesh as he exited Matsuhisa he would have spotted his dear friend Montana Phoenix drive by.

Immaculately garbed in the back of her pure white open-top Rolls Royce Corniche, she was on her way to the offices of Coeur Cosmetics. It was the company she had chosen to help with the worldwide launch of her first designer eau de toilette, *Babylon*.

She had wanted the scent to be named after herself, but of course someone had already snaffled *Montana*. But *Babylon* was the right name for the fragrance that she was branding as *the odour of opulence*. Like her it was sexy, sensual, puissant and completely irresistible.

Her meeting was with her international agent, Bradley Roderick, the man who was, as far she was concerned, destined to stretch Montana's supremacy in the media world beyond her wildest dreams. He was also the latest object of Montana's affections.

Despite the general rule of thumb about never mixing business with pleasure, Montana had been swept into the whirlwind of his gallant charms from the moment she signed with him.

Bradley was a man in his mid-forties that no woman could resist. He had remained unmarried, but his list of exes included at least four Emmy-winning actresses and a series of the world's top models.

Montana was hoping she would be the one to tame his bed-hopping ways. She was also convinced that, alongside him, her glamorous empire, or 'Glampire', as Brad called it, would be unsurpassable.

As her driver pulled up outside the Coeur offices, Montana checked her make-up in the mirror of her vintage Tiffany sterling silver compact. *Looking good, sweetie*, she said to herself. Montana was of the Dolly Parton/Joan Collins school of thinking, believing that a star should never be seen without immaculate clothing, full foundation to lip-liner make-up and hair that was spotlessly coiffed.

Adding a quick mist of *Babylon* across her ample cleavage, Montana stepped out of the car and into the building.

After taking the lift to the fourth floor, Montana clicked her Dior Extreme sandals along the marble floor of the corridor, before sweeping majestically into the boardroom. A good entrance was everything.

Bradley beamed a wide smile as Montana entered. She adored his smile, the lines it caused to crease heroically around his eyes melting her heart.

'My angel' she simpered, as he held her face in his hands and kissed her gently on the lips. She would have willingly let Brad take her there and then, but they were not alone.

The other party in the room was Jean-Luc, the man that Coeur called 'The nose'. It was after extensive meetings with Jean-Luc that Montana had decided on the ingredients of *Babylon* in the first place. A Herculean mixture of deep, ravishing floral tones that she felt would leave any man begging for sexual mercy.

'Bonjour, cheri,' she gushed. 'Just how much am I loving *Babylon*! So are all of my friends, darling. People on the set of

Peregrine can't wait for the launch. C'est magnifique, n'est ce pas?'

The three of them sat and talked business. *Babylon* would first be launched in America with an exuberant designer party at the Crown Bar in West Hollywood. Brad felt that its 1940s vintage film set elegance would be perfect for Montana.

A trip to Europe for a launch at Soho's Kingly Club would then follow. It was there, in its former Pinstripe Club days, that Christine Keeler had met and started her clandestine affair with John Profumo, a fact that Brad thought would be perfect to give *Babylon* an even sexier edge.

From there it would be onto the Venice Film Festival, where a select gathering of the world's press would join Montana for a weekend of jaw-dropping abundance. Then back to LA in time for the new season of *Peregrine*.

A squealing Montana could barely contain her excitement. 'It all sounds stupendous,' before adding cautiously, 'and *who's* paying for all this exactly?'

'Coeur Cosmetics will outlay all costs for the trip,' said Jean-Luc. 'We will then recoup the expense from worldwide sales, which we are sure will be phenomenal. We have an entire *Babylon* range ready to go, featuring everything from silky body lotions through to invigorating sea salts. With you pushing the right buttons worldwide, we feel that the range can appeal to all.'

'That's a good point, actually,' continued Brad. 'You'll be required to appear on shopping TV in the UK. It's worked wonders for the likes of Kathy Hilton and Joan Rivers as the channels appeal to an eclectic mix of people, especially the mothers. You need to capture that market, sweetie, so make sure that unruly daughter of yours lies low and keeps her nose clean... literally. The last thing we need is poor publicity.'

At the thought of relying on Regan, Montana's lip-lined smile faded.

———

Having been sat in the reception of Minted TV for the last forty minutes, Regan was not in the best of moods. To be kept waiting was one thing, but to be kept waiting when you have no idea what you are waiting for was maddening.

Leo Weiss, rising hot-shot producer, had been cagey on the phone when Regan had got back to him. She knew that he was making a TV show and she knew that he wanted her for something. He'd promised that it wasn't one of those stupid shows about 'The real woman behind screen legend Montana Phoenix', desperate to get her only daughter to ooze home truths about childhood beatings and behind-closed-doors torment. She'd had enough offers of that kind before. When she did eventually decide to mudsling Montana's image, she'd do it with gravitas, but until that day, she'd stay quiet.

No, Regan really hoped that this was something that was about her. Not about family connections, not about back-stabbing. Something that would prove to the world that she was more than just Montana's embarrassing daughter.

———

'Hi Regan, what we'd like to do is prove to the world that you're more than just Montana Phoenix's embarrassing daughter.' These were the first words that Leo said to her as she relaxed into the plump leather chair situated in front of his office desk. Regan couldn't help but smile. If ever an opening gambit was going to get her undivided attention, he had hit the bull's-eye.

'I'm listening,' she replied.

'How do you think the world sees you at the minute, Regan? You've not exactly got the best press over the past few months, have you?' With that, he placed a folder on the desk, inviting Regan to look inside. 'This is how Minted TV views your profile.'

With a hint of trepidation, Regan opened the folder in front of her. It contained an inch thick of press cuttings, all detailing her party-loving activities.

'REGAN'S HOSPITAL DASH' read the headline above a photo of Regan in the back of an ambulance, her eyes rolling upwards into the back of her head. That was the night she'd had to have her stomach pumped due to alcohol poisoning.

Other features, accompanied by equally damning photos of a shambolic Regan, read 'THE PHOENIX WHO WILL NEVER RISE FROM THE ASHES' (her smoking dope at Glastonbury), 'REGAN'S ROYAL RANT' (her trying to punch a minor royal in the face at Annabel's in Berkeley Square) and 'REGAN BOOBS AGAIN' (no prizes for guessing which of her bodily assets she was showing off in the back of a cab that time).

Those were just some of the UK press cuttings that she'd seen and had tried to blot from her mind. The folder was also piled with cuttings from American reads such as *The National Enquirer* and *US Magazine*. In the land where Montana's status was on a par with royalty, the headlines were even more pointed.

'MONTANA'S HEARTACHE AT THE CHILD WHO REFUSES HER HELP' read one. The photo of an angst-ridden Montana clutching a toddler photo of Regan, alongside yet another shot of her egregious daughter off her face at some party was enough to give Regan bile reflux. Help? Since when had her sodding mother tried to give her anything of the kind? With an angry bang, she slammed the folder shut.

Leo Weiss stared directly into Regan's cat-like eyes for a good ten seconds. *God, they were a beautiful hue of green. A man could get lost in those quite easily*, mused Leo. He thought he spotted the tiny bubbles of tears forming in the corners of each of them. He was right.

Regan's lip started to quiver. Before she knew it, long wet rivulets of despair ran down her cheeks. Tears dripped onto the figure-hugging Ramones T-shirt she was wearing. She'd chosen it, hoping that it gave her a kickass edge for a TV meeting, teaming it with an above-the-knee preppy look skirt.

'Sorry, crying in the office of some high-brow TV exec is *so* not a good look,' she blubbed as Leo handed her a box of tissues. 'I guess it's just that when I see all that shit written about me, it makes me wonder where it went wrong.'

'I reckon we can change all of that,' continued Leo. 'The world sees you as an out-of-control airhead who lives to fall out of clubs night after night. It knows that you drink, it knows that you get twatted, it knows that mummy payrolls it all. What it doesn't know is how much you're hurting and the potential you have to shine in your own right. True?'

It was more than true. Regan had never really had a job other than the odd day helping out fair-weather clubbing pals in their boutiques. She'd never needed to. Having a multi-millionairess as a mum kind of made you lazy.

As for the nights out? Her best ones had been spent with Nush and Evie giggling about corny chat-up lines from city slicker chancers on the pull in some cocktail bar. That, or the Trinity having a *Grease*-style sleepover in their PJs. That was when Regan was truly happiest.

The drug-heavy, hedonistic star-studded bashes had left her empty. A commodity for pussy-crazed men to hump and dump as she searched for something meaningful. Someone for the press to label as a girl who had it all but used none of it wisely.

'So, how are you and Minted TV going to change that then?' quizzed Regan.

Leo walked out from behind his desk and moved towards a flip board on the other side of his office. Regan noted that he was wearing a beautifully fitted Merc suit. It gave him an air of retro-cool. Under it he wore a black roll neck top, adding to his overall sexy mod look.

He turned the front page of the board revealing the words *From Wild Child To Rothschild*. They were written in swirly holographic, gold calligraphy and glittered as if dipped in diamond dust.

'This is the TV show that will turn you into a star. A star who will be standing on her own two feet and not in anyone else's shadow. This is the show that will gain you respect.'

Respect? The one thing she had always deemed out of her reach. She allowed herself to smile. Regan knew that she was very, very interested.

CHAPTER 7

Despite having more money in his various bank accounts, both on-shore and off-shore, than most men could dream of, Lawrence Silvers was still rather tight with his purse strings.

So he wasn't overly forthcoming when Anoushka had phoned him asking if she could have the use of one of his private jets for a few days.

Had it been Harry wanting to use it for one of his mates' stag parties or to nail a tender piece of female flesh into the Mile High Club then he'd have said yes straight away, but what the hell did Nush want it for?

'It's actually for Harry's benefit,' she fudged, half telling the truth. 'I need to fly to Belgium to visit Evie on the set of her movie. I've been tipped there's a decent story there about her getting it on with her co-star and I want to scoop it. Plus, while I'm there I can coax her into coming to Harry's party on Saturday.'

She didn't think for one minute that Evie's schedule would allow her to. But years of practice had taught her how to play her father.

'Well, what are bloody waiting for then? I'll phone the pilot now and get him to meet you at the airfield.'

Two hours later, Nush was touching down as close to Malmedy in Belgium as air traffic would allow. She'd phoned ahead to arrange both a hotel room at the Tros Marets and a hire car, which was waiting for her as she landed.

She'd tried to phone Evie both before takeoff and after landing, but it had clicked through to the messaging service. *Maybe she was already practicing her sex scenes with Jeremy*, she surmised, breaking into a smile.

It was going to be late when she got to the hotel. Nush wondered if she was going to be interrupting something beautiful.

———

Beautiful was the last word Evie would have used to describe her day on set. In fact, in the three weeks she'd been there, today had definitely been the most difficult. Thank God she had a few days off lined up soon. She needed them.

After the appalling fax incident this morning, which had turned Mae-Ling into a tearful demon all day, things had gone from bad to worse. *What the hell was Nush thinking? Didn't she know that Mae-Ling was working with her on this movie? Sometimes that girl could be so insensitive.*

Mae-Ling had spent practically all morning crying hysterically at the side of the set. Often it was so loud that filming had to be halted. When Mae-Ling had been chastised for this, her response had been to point at Evie and scream 'Blame her and her fucking stupid friend'.

Evie had managed to laugh off the first couple of outbursts and tell the exec producer that Mae-Ling was 'Still a touch postnatal'. But after the fourth or fifth time, shooting was halted for an hour while Evie was forced to explain exactly what had caused Mae-Ling's misery.

Even though it was nothing to do with her, Evie was being made to feel as if she were to blame. Inconsolable about Nush's column, Mae-Ling was sent back to the hotel to pull herself together.

To add to Evie's feelings of woe, all of this had happened in front of Jeremy Pinewood.

Evie had started the day thinking that he would be a dream to work with, but a few hours together and she'd caught herself muttering 'Snooty little git,' and worse under her breath with alarming regularity.

Jeremy had sauntered onto the set alongside his make-up artist, Mario, who had worked alongside Jeremy since his days down under.

So neither Jeremy nor Mario were overly pleased when the executive producer had requested Mario to be on hand for everyone's touch-ups after Mae-Ling had been retired for the day.

Jeremy was just as eye-poppingly beauteous as Evie had hoped. His hair tumbled down across his forehead forming perfect little curls that Evie was itching to run her fingers through. His lips were plump and full-bodied, and his body… wow. Evie would have had to have been blind not to spot that he'd been working out quite spectacularly.

His arms and back rippled in muscular waves underneath the tailored suit he was wearing for the scene. At one point, he stripped off his suit and shirt to change after sweating under the set's torrid lighting. Evie couldn't take her eyes off him.

His chest stood rigid and proud, his nipples perfectly formed as they nestled in a light sea of swirling chest hair. The hair grew down across his taut stomach, weaving across the dips in between his abs and then descending below his trouser line.

Idyllic didn't even start to describe what Evie thought about his body. He seemed the ultimate man, sculpted in the shape of a demigod.

Evie had to catch her breath and turn away swiftly when Jeremy caught her staring.

But, as celestial as he was, Jeremy had basically been a stand-offish prick all day. After an initial cursory 'Hello' snapped at Evie, they'd hardly shared a word.

Admittedly, the Mae-Ling fracas didn't help the atmosphere on set, but when Jeremy chose to return to his trailer for lunch, it was obvious that mingling with his associates was not his favoured way.

He delivered his lines perfectly, and in the scene where their characters first meet, he shot Evie a wide movie star smile so delicious that Evie's mind went blank, making her forget her line. His snide tutting at her mistake, however, made sure that the smile didn't have the same effect on the second take.

As they wrapped for the day, Evie tried her best to find good in Jeremy, convincing herself that he was either fastidiously private or, like her, still young enough to get nervous about the pressures of fame.

But no, it seemed simple. Looks were deceptive. Despite his ambrosial looks on the surface, Evie had to face the fact that Jeremy was plainly an ugly, nasty piece of work on the inside, and filming this movie for the remaining few weeks was going to be hellish.

But God damn him, why did he have to be so darned sexy to look at…?

———

The knock on her hotel room door snapped Evie out of her dozy slumber. She'd drifted off watching an episode of *Peregrine Place* dubbed into Flemish. *Montana even sounds sexy dubbed*, she thought.

'Who is it?' she questioned, praying that it wasn't Mae-Ling. The last thing she needed now was a slanging match about why Evie chose to be best mates with, to quote Mae-Ling, 'a low-down, venomous gutter snipe like Anoushka Silvers'. Anyway, the rumour going round was that Mae-Ling had flown back to London to confront Jake about the sordid goings-on. Heaven help the girl he'd been shagging around with.

'Room service,' said a muffled voice in a ridiculously over-exaggerated Manuel *Fawlty Towers* accent. 'What on earth…?' puzzled Evie, opening the door.

'Surprise!' Nush appeared, holding a huge bottle of Dom Perignon and two glasses. 'You alone? Or am I smelling the flames of a hot new superstar romance, missy?'

Wide-eyed and stunned by Nush's arrival, Evie attempted a broad smile. She was relieved to see a friendly face, yet panicked by Mae-Ling's potential close proximity.

'Girlfriend,' Evie exclaimed, 'You have no idea. You had better come in…'

CHAPTER 8

Kingsbury Mead Estate looked like a huge fluffy meringue, covered inside and out in a huge mass of white.

Esteemed and noble architectural experts throughout the ages would have looked down at the elegant grace and understated classic nature of the building and turned in their graves. Every corner, from the imposing uniformity of the symmetrical Palladian doors to the glass-domed conservatory, was covered in fake snow and party foam.

Even the immense grounds, stretching all the way to the magnificent bridge crossing the babbling river at its furthest point were covered. Huge machines pumping out confetti-like snowflakes whirred away in between fairground rides, marquees and makeshift bars. The country estate had become a total state – and Sadie Silvers was elated with how it looked.

Ever since Lawrence had announced that Harry was coming back home, Sadie had been beavering away night and day to make sure that this was the event that every merrymaker talked about all season.

Seeing as Harry was returning from skiing, Sadie had decided on a white theme to remind him of all the snow he'd left behind. You could be forgiven for thinking it was deepest winter at Disneyland. It was in fact, May in rural England.

The party wasn't for another two days but Sadie had decided that today was dress rehearsal day. She had seen all the rides in operation, from the dodgems to the Ferris wheel. She'd made sure that there was no chance of the bars running dry as 500 guests and no alcohol was tantamount to social suicide. She'd even phoned the Knightsbridge caterers four times to make sure that everything was as she desired.

She'd also inspected the monumental dance tents where various big name DJs would bang out tunes throughout the night. Harry's crowd would doubtless love the rock tent spewing out classics from Aerosmith to Foo Fighters. Lawrence and his associates would make the most of the funky classics at the disco tent. And she had also created a special chill zone – a massive, kaleidoscopically-lit area with scatter cushions covering the floor and ambient, velvety smooth tunes playing in the background. Very Café Del Mar.

The focal point on the front of the house was a gargantuan photo of a smiling Harry, dressed in salopettes on some alpine mountainside. He looked the epitome of youthful vitality.

'Is this major league cool or what?' said Harry, joining Sadie as she stared at the photo. 'My mates are going to freaking love this!'

'That's the idea, honey, I'm not having a son of mine coming back home without putting on a display for the neighbours.'

'Actually, the nearest neighbours are about five miles away, Sadie, so strictly speaking, they'll see bugger all,' argued the 20-year-old.

'That's why I've organised end-of-night fireworks, you fool. That way, people in different time zones will know that Sadie Silvers knows how to throw a party. It's razzle-dazzle time.'

Even though Sadie wasn't truly Harry's mum, over the last few years she had become the closest thing he was ever likely to get. She made his dad happy, she made Harry smile and she got right up Nush's nose. So, as far as he was concerned, she ticked all the boxes.

'Anyhow, how long you sticking around here, Harry? You back for good, ready to help that father of yours with his empire yet?' she continued as the two of them walked inside. 'I could do with him back home you know. He's no spring chicken anymore and mama needs a little more lovin'!'

At 45, Lawrence was 14 years older than Sadie. In fact there was less of an age gap between Sadie and Harry. 'I'd like to turn your father into a daddy again and heaven knows I'm not going to get pregnant with him working twenty-four-seven. My eggs will be fit for diddly before too long,' she joked. 'When I start my hot flushes I'll be ready to poach them all!'

'*Urgh*, too much information, thanks! No, I'll stay for a week or so and then I want to head back to Europe. There's a pretty wicked ski run in Austria I've got my eyes on. I reckon dad can hold off for a year or two, eh?'

'Right, well while you're here hot-shot, you can help me unpack this lot,' Sadie grinned, pointing to a pile of cardboard boxes stacked up in the Kingsbury ballroom, now transformed into an avalanche of white.

'What the hell are these?' queried Harry, pulling some black and white fabric from the first box.

'Penguin costumes. Your party is going to have the cutest set of waiters ever. See, your mama thinks of everything.'

———

Nush and Evie had eventually fallen unconscious at about 4am. There was loads to talk about and one bottle of champagne had rapidly become a second, then a third...

Evie had filled Nush in on the Jeremy situation, much to Nush's disappointment. 'I can't believe he's such a wanker,' she'd cried. 'This would make such great copy.'

'Please don't, you've got to promise me that you'll write nothing about this. He thinks I'm a jerk as it is, and if he sees his antics splashed all over my best friend's column, he's going to know it's me.' Evie was serious.

'Hey, calm it, lady,' quipped Nush in return. 'You know my golden rule, never dish the dirt that could hurt my girls. I could have made a fortune out of Regan by now! She'd have kept me in column inches for months on end. Now tell me about Mae-Ling?'

Evie retold the day's events. The fax, the rows, Mae's storming off set and the supposed flying home to Jake. 'So, who was the girl he did the dirty with? She should be quaking in her bed-hopping boots.'

The rouging of Nush's cheeks gave the game away. She could hide the facts from *The Staple's* readers, but Evie was one person who could see right through her.

'You have *got* to be joking. Are you a masochist? The woman is savage. She could rip your head off. The last person who crossed her ended up in casualty. You're in enough trouble as it is having written the column. If she finds out it was you who slept with Jake as well, I'll be coming to your funeral.'

'Well, thank God you look great in black, darling.' The alcohol was making Nush flippant. It often had that effect. 'Anyway, she won't find out, will she? There's only you and Regan who know, so I'm safe. Plus let's not forget it was Jake who was doing the dirty. I'm a free agent who just happened to think he was cute and also highly useful. And now that *Little Miss Eyelash Curler* is back in the UK, she'll never know I was here, so I'm sorted.'

'What if Jake tells her it was you? Then you're stuffed.'

'He won't. He'll want the whole thing to blow over as quickly as possible in my opinion. He won't want to lose his place as warrior numero uno on *Sporting Spartans*. He'll do what the named and shamed always do. Go on TV, say sorry to the kids and TV bosses for being a bad boy and then get loads of extra press. Look at Beckham and all that alleged personal assistant stuff years ago. Never did him any harm, did it? Plus, Jake said I was the best he'd ever had. Evie, I kid you not, the man has a dick of death. It's like a baby's arm and he so knows what to do with it. He was flipping me over like a tiddlywink.'

The girls laughed and drank until they crashed out, Evie gasping at Nush's graphic details of her exploits with Jake. Alcohol definitely made Nush loose-lipped.

———

Evie woke up face down, still fully-clothed, to hear a forceful banging on the door. Her head pulsated with pain in time with the knocking. She turned to see Nush, also fully dressed, laying on the couch, her face squashed up against the cushions.

Her lipstick-smudged mouth opened. 'Tell whoever it is to come back later when the drummer in my brain stops playing,' she slurred. 'What time is it?' On checking the LCD on the bedside table clock she saw it was 9.53am. Her call time was at ten. She was due on set in seven minutes. The set that was a half-hour drive away.

Ignoring the clang of her sozzled brain as it rattled inside her skull, Evie ran to the door. The commotion at the door didn't stop until she turned the handle.

'I'm coming now. I overslept. Is the driver outside? Tell him I'm on my way. Can someone phone the producer please?' She fired off the list without looking up, her head feeling too heavy to lift.

When she did look up, she wished she hadn't. The fist banging on the door belonged to Mae-Ling. So she hadn't gone home after all. 'You thinking of joining us today?' she barked, like a snappy terrier.

Without answering, Evie slammed the door shut, praying that Mae-Ling hadn't seen the body still slouched on the couch behind her.

CHAPTER 9

Leo Weiss and Regan sat opposite each other in the Trattoria at Fifteen London. It had been 24 hours since Leo had pitched the idea of *From Wild Child to Rothschild* to her, and despite already knowing her answer, Regan had left the meeting saying that she wanted to 'sleep on it' before committing.

'So, what's it to be then, Regan?' Leo's tone was stern yet slightly flirtatious. 'You in… or out?'

'I'm in. You had me at the title yesterday – I just wanted to see you sweat!' Regan teased, chasing the remains of her baked aubergine around her plate.

It was true. The show seemed perfect for her. From what Leo had said the day before, it would give Regan her own identity.

As the title suggested, the show would aim to turn Regan from a cocktail-swigging club-whore into a strong and independent woman who could stand confidently side by side with the Rothschilds or any of the world's elite families.

Leo had thought of the idea after reading about the former black sheep of the Rothschild banking dynasty, Nat. The one time bad boy had shed off his image as an all-round hell raiser to become one of the most respected and shrewd businessmen on earth. As far as Leo could see, the young Rothschild's success was due to five crucial factors – an innate style, dynamic organisational skills, unfaltering self-control, team working ability and formidable business acumen.

Regan would be required to complete a task demonstrating each of these ideals. The programme would pit her against a fellow wild child, one-time girl band member Grace Laszlo. Grace had been one third of America's raunchiest female trio, Sexalicious, before getting the boot for snorting coke backstage at one of their concerts. The actual act itself was pretty *de rigeur* for the music world, but Grace's fall from favour had come due to the fact she was snorting the coke off a fan's cock while his mate filmed the entire episode. The footage hit the net and Grace was substituted immediately with a lookalike replacement. Like Regan, her current media image was in tatters.

The show would be the saga of Regan versus Grace. One would be crowned the ultimate victor – the girl who would shed her debauched past in front of millions of viewers – going from a serious wreck to being taken seriously in just a matter of weeks. Their fate would be judged by a team of experts.

'Just think what *The Simple Life* did for Nicole Richie,' said Leo. 'It turned the whole dynamic of the Richie family on its head. She lost the tag *Lionel's daughter* and he suddenly became known as *Nicole's father*. The whole spotlight of fame went from him to her. As soon as this show hits the airwaves you'll be over every magazine and paper out there… for the right reasons.'

'So why has it got to be a competition? Why can't you do wonders for both Grace and I?' probed Regan. 'Not that she stands a chance anyway. I was staying at my mother's in LA when the coke story broke and that footage is way beyond anything that I've ever done. Well, on camera, anyway. That girl's a liability that you don't need on the show.'

'But that's just it, Regan. Minted TV does need Grace. All of our hit shows recently have a competitive edge to them. The public loves to see someone win, but the ratings really explode when people tune in to see someone lose. It's classic car-crash TV.'

'So you're hanging one of us out to dry?' sneered Regan, suddenly not relishing the programme's premise so much.

'Not exactly, but one of you has to lose, and how she copes with failure is just as important as who wins. Plus, the failure will be on a massive stage. Once Grace confirmed, ABC in the States picked up the show like a shot. Knowing that Montana Phoenix's daughter was potentially the other girl in the mix, they agreed to simulcast the show. We're talking about a show of Simon Cowell-esque proportions here. Now, if you're in, young lady – sign here,' concluded Leo, winking cheekily. Regan felt a ripple of desire course through her veins. *Charismatic and forceful – a potent mix*, she thought.

Leo placed a contract bearing her name and a pen on the table in front of her. Contemplating the fact that *From Wild Child to Rothschild* would be beamed into millions of homes worldwide, including her mother's, she signed.

'Okay, business over. I'm all yours, Leo. Let's go celebrate. I don't know about you, but I could do with a bloody stiff drink.'

CHAPTER 10

The on-set gym was another of the perks that Jeremy had insisted on before signing on the dotted line for *The Bouquet Catcher*. But as he stood, bare-chested, admiring his deific body pumping bicep curls in the full-length mirror, it was the last place he wanted to be right now. He should have been on set opposite Evie, except that she was late.

How dare she? What's the point of me being on time if she can't be bothered to turn up? he cursed inwardly. Jeremy had only been in Belgium for less than 48 hours but already Evie was top of his dislikes list.

He admitted she could act, he admitted she was fairytale stunning, but nobody, not even a red carpet darling like Evie, kept Jeremy Pinewood waiting.

After the happenings of the day before, Jeremy had woken up feeling that he'd done what he had set out to do. He'd come to the set to make sure that Evie knew that he was top dog on this film. It may have been a pairing made in film producer heaven to have two of the sexiest names on the planet together, but there was only one name that deserved top billing as far as Jeremy was concerned and that was his. Which was why he'd treated her with derision all day.

So her brazen disregard for her call time this morning had wound Jeremy up like a coiled spring. Word had reached the set from Mae-Ling that Evie was running late due to getting hammered in her hotel room. Mae-Ling had described Evie's eyes as being like 'two stabs in a voodoo doll' and her breath as '40% proof'. Jeremy could only surmise that Evie wasn't as sweet as she seemed.

Maybe the pressure of stardom is getting to her, he speculated, checking the impressive mounds of his triceps as he raised the weights above his head. *Some people can take it, others can't.*

—

Having left Nush still semi-comatose on the couch, Evie finally made it to the set at 11.30am.

As she arrived, a hushed silence spread like a rolling mist. She spied Jeremy. '*Afternoon*' he offered, deadpan.

Evie knew that an apology was in order. 'Can I say to everyone that I am so sorry for being late. It's never happened before and you all have my word that it will never happen again,' she said, her bottom lip quivering. 'A friend of mine arrived at the hotel unexpectedly last night. We had a few drinks and I forgot to set my alarm. No excuses, but I'm here to work. Let's get this scene done.'

'There was me thinking you'd got drunk all on your own,' needled Jeremy in a hushed whisper. 'How tragic would that be? At least you had company. I hope he was worth it.' Evie chose not to answer.

—

Looking down at the English coast from the plush comfort of the private jet's soft leather chair, Evie knew that she was glad to be flying home. Having finished her stint on the film in Belgium, she now had a few days off before she was due to join Jeremy again at London's Ealing Studios to start filming the majority of their scenes together.

The three weeks away had been good, filming countless 'church scenes' in her character's quest to find a possible groom, but the remainder of the film would be cosy love scenes between her and Jeremy.

Her hours on set with him earlier that day had been pretty insufferable. His constant sniping and the fact that her head was still numbly revolving in a whirlpool of hangover were a lethal combination.

'Hair of the dog?' ventured Nush, returning to her seat in her dad's plane with two gin and tonics. 'You look like you could do with it.'

Taking the drink, Evie replied with a smirk, 'Well, unlike you, you old lush, I haven't been able to spend virtually my entire day sleeping!'

It was true. Having been warned by Evie that Mae-Ling was in fact still working on the film, Nush had decided that sleeping was the safest way to spend the day. Her daily column could be dealt with by her team of juniors, all hungry to get their stories in print.

The icy freshness of the drink felt shivery as Evie swigged it back. She felt the stiffness of her shoulders and upper back ease as the spirit seemed to wash away the rigours of the day. 'I hope there's plenty more where that came from for tomorrow night,' she enquired, licking her lips.

'I'll say one thing for my wicked stepmother,' replied Nush, 'she may be the tackiest bimbo God ever put breath into, but she would rather date Hannibal Lecter than run out of booze at one of her parties. I'm sure she's having Kingsbury's river drained and refilled with Veuve Clicquot as we speak.'

Evie was beyond happy that Nush had invited her to Harry's welcome home bash. A few days off, a private jet back to the UK and the promise of a good night out would soon help her forget about her on-set woes.

As the jet landed on terra firma, Evie downed the rest of her drink. Exiting down the steps to find their awaiting Mercedes, the girls hugged. Falling into the cosy comfort of her ride home, Evie's phone rang. It was Regan. 'Whatever you're doing tomorrow night, missy, cancel it... you're coming to Nush's family party as my plus one,' instructed Evie.

CHAPTER 11

The off-the-shoulder white linen Paul & Joe robe draped seductively across Regan's body as she stared at her reflection in her full-length bedroom mirror.

Irresistible, she thought. Seeing as the theme of tonight's party was white, she had decided on a look that would give her a heady mix of ice queen meets Aphrodite. A pair of Prada Napa clogs and a tiara of white hawthorn blossom added to the look. *May blossom for a May party.* Regan was elated with her seasonal choice.

Things were on the up. Her quest to make it big in the TV world was due to commence in a matter of days and she had a new object of desire in Leo Weiss. A somewhat lingering kiss on her lips as they'd parted company the night before had proven that. He wanted her, Regan was sure. Who could blame him? She was oozing self-confidence.

Regan couldn't wait to tell Nush and Evie her news and finally prove to them that she had the potential to stand tall in her own unique way. They seemed to be succeeding in life despite all of their inner insecurities, maybe now was finally her turn.

Shutting the door behind her as she left her apartment, she felt the balmy afternoon air on her face. Walking to her Aston Martin DBS, Regan looked out over the river at the flock of tourists swarming around London Bridge, watching them as they posed for photos and snapped their cameras. *Soon, they will all be watching me*, she thought to herself. She loved the idea.

—

'So what time did you tell Regan to get here?' enquired Nush. 'She is going to freak when she sees what Sadie's done to this place. I feel like I'm at the winter Olympics.'

Surveying the surroundings as the two women stood in Kingsbury's grounds, Evie had to admit that Nush was right. Ever since she arrived at the Silvers' family home earlier that evening Evie had been mesmerised by the transition the classic mansion had undergone. She felt like she was walking through the set of a Tim Burton movie. In between the marquees and the fairground rides stood huge sculpted ice statues of reindeers and polar bears, giving the whole place the feel of a cartoon Gotham City landscape. There were stilt-walkers, jugglers, circus clowns, fortune tellers, plus Sadie's troops of 'waiter penguins'. The place was ablaze with colour. It made for an intoxicating mix alongside the tableau of fake white snow everywhere.

Evie had chosen a figure-hugging embroidered silk dress from Armani for the evening. The classic skin-skimming curves of the smooth ivory fabric felt good against her flesh. She'd pulled her hair into a loose sexy chignon high on her head, leaving two Titian swirls of hair to cascade romantically down either side of her face.

'She should have been here by now. She messaged me to say she was en route. You know, Regan, she'll be here when she decides. So who else is on the guest list tonight?' enquired Evie.

'The usual bunch of suited and booted letches from *The Staple*. I'll put money on at least one of them trying it on with either you, me or Regan tonight,' replied Nush. 'Investors, advertisers, football wife bimbos, the odd porn baron, some names from the telly, Harry's bunch of sweaty-palmed ski pals… a befitting pot pourri, darling. Mind you, there could be a few stories for the column tonight if I dig around discreetly. I do have daddy to please.'

'You never stop, do you?' Evie laughed, her eye catching sight of a rather handsome waiter adjusting his penguin feet as he tried to serve drinks. 'But no work tonight, let's concentrate on the man front. I could do with some love at the moment. I'm even starting to fancy the ones dressed as flightless birds!'

Although Evie was joking, Nush thought that there was an air of tristesse about the comment. Evie deserved a good man. She'd succeeded in so many areas of life, but finding love was still not one of them. Nush was fully aware that Evie's love life was as pitted and flawed as the cheeks of an acne-ridden teenager. *That's a mission for me*, she contemplated. What were best friends for, after all, if it wasn't for lending a helping hand when it came to the affairs of the heart? Even if her own heart has been mercilessly looted more times than she cared to mention, Nush was determined to help Evie avoid yet another *woe-mance*.

A screech of tyres blistered onto the driveway in front of Kingsbury, flicking pebbles and fake snow into the air. The door of the car, a powerhouse of mechanical muscle, opened and out stepped Regan.

Spying Nush and Evie, she threw her hands euphorically above her head, announcing her arrival. 'Evening ladies, Regan Phoenix is ready to party… care to join me? Now, what in the name of total tackiness has happened to this place?'

———

An announcement had been made for all off the party-goers to gather in the Kingsbury ballroom. The Trinity stood together, clutching their flutes of champagne, deep in conversation. Whispers of 'Isn't that Montana Phoenix's daughter?' and 'Can you believe Evie Merchant is here?' seemed to follow the women wherever they went.

Regan had brought the girls up to date with her news about the TV show, while Evie had filled her in on the whole Mae-Ling and Jeremy situation. Nush had been busy scanning the room looking for a potential beau for Evie. No-one appeared good enough, but the night was only just beginning.

A fanfare of music thundered from the skyscraper-like bank of speakers either side of the ballroom, followed by a cheesy game show host voice. 'Ladies and gentlemen, welcome to Kingsbury Mead Estate for Harry's welcome home party.' Nush visibly cringed as a group of young lads, all dressed in white *Saturday Night Fever* style tuxedos cheered at the mention of Harry's name.

'Will you please put your hands together for your generous hosts this evening, Lawrence and Sadie Silvers.'

The lights dimmed and a spotlight illuminated the top of the staircase at the far end of the ballroom. Frosted faux icicles hung from every part of the banister. Lawrence and Sadie appeared to hearty applause. Lawrence wore a crisp Alexander McQueen suit, which even Nush had to admit took years off her father. Sadie's outfit was, unsurprisingly, nothing short of a travesty. The bottom half consisted of a frilly-looking mini petticoat made from two layers of soft tulle. The top layer had been ruffled with extra frills to give the petticoat extra slutty bounce as Sadie tottered around on her high heeled white leather boots. The top half was a sequinned boob tube clinging for life to her cleavage. It was fastened at the back with an oversized ribbon bow. The vision was completed with a wand comprising of a glittery star and curling tendrils of sparkly foil.

'Now *that* outfit is class,' sneered Regan. 'Very *readers' wives*!'

While Sadie squealed and waved her wand around at the crowd below like a demented fairy, Lawrence began to speak. 'The reason we're here tonight is to celebrate our boy Harry coming home.' Lawrence reached out to hold Sadie's hand as she gave a dainty curtsey. Nush could feel her throat go tight and dry as a wave of vomit-inducing nausea washed over her. It was only outweighed by a sudden feeling of complete worthlessness at the words which followed.

'Harry has spent the last few months doing what every young man dreams of doing. He's been living life in the fast lane and has become our very own Action Man. The son every father desires. He has made me and his mother Sadie very proud. I count myself lucky that someday soon, when I decide to step back from the hard work of running my empire, it will be Harry who takes the reins and proves to me, yet again, what a true chip off the old block he is. Tonight's all about him. My son, my life, my Harry…' With that, Harry ran to join Lawrence and Sadie, hugging his father and kissing Sadie with a playful squeeze. The crowd erupted again.

Nush went over what she'd just heard. It was as if *she* didn't exist, somehow erased from Lawrence's mind. Harry was *daddy's little Action Man…* well, boarding down pistes doesn't put cash in the family account. *All we ever wanted in a family…* what did that mean? Was Nush surplus to requirements? Good enough to employ but don't expect any father-daughter bonding. Was she just another payroll number to him?

What made the speech even more cutting were the words *he has made me and his mother Sadie very proud.* Sadie was not his mother, how dare he? What about Lysette? His former wife whose body lay buried in the Kingsbury estate chapel. The woman who had always stood by him and who'd endured the cut-throat ups and downs of business. Who had given life to his precious son and given hers in exchange. At that moment she wished it had been Harry that had died. That would have been so much fairer. Life never was though, was it?

As she watched Lawrence backslapping Harry yet again, Nush had never felt more detached from her own father and brother. Blood was supposedly thicker than water, but the link between her and the two men was thinner than a human hair. Feeling herself fade into the background yet again, the first hint of a tear pricked at the corner of her eyes.

CHAPTER 12

The party was in full swing. Having downed yet another champagne cocktail, Regan could feel her head starting to spin. It was time for a little pick-me-up. And the packet of powdery goodness in her bag would be just the ticket. Well, it was a *white* party after all.

Regan kept a drunken eye out for Nush and Evie as she made her way back to the house. She hadn't seen either of them for over an hour. Nush had last been seen telling Sadie in no uncertain terms what she thought of her outfit, a move that hadn't been particularly well-received by her stepmother. As for Evie, she'd last seen her on the Ferris wheel, laughing with some man in a white shirt.

Walking into the marble-floored entrance hall at Kingsbury, she knew she had to find a quiet spot to take the coke. It had been a while since she last visited Kingsbury but she remembered it well enough to know that the house was filled with offices, libraries and studies. One of them would doubtless be free for her requirements.

After what seemed like a good ten minutes of stumbling around, Regan spotted a large oak door. She didn't remember ever venturing this far into Kingsbury before.

She turned the door's ornate brass handle and pushed it open. With a slight creak, the door opened into a dimly lit study. A superb mahogany writing desk filled the centre of the room, papers and files spread across the desk. Filling the wall behind it were row upon row of books. It reminded Regan of the huge library in Disney's *Beauty and the Beast*, one of her favourite films.

Flicking the desk light on, Regan moved over to the shelves. Stiff leather-bound books lined up against one another. Charles Dickens, William Shakespeare, Francis Bacon, Thomas Kyd, the list of classic names continued. *And there was me thinking Sadie would be curled up at night with some erotic fiction*, mused Regan, giggling at her own thoughts.

She followed the line of books with her finger, until she came to a stacked pile of albums. She picked up the top one and opened it. It was full of family photos.

Flicking through the pages, Regan recognised that the photos must have been taken a good fifteen to twenty years ago at least. One photo featured Lawrence sporting a seriously dated outfit and a frizzed curly perm, proudly standing with Harry in a football kit. Another featured Harry and Lawrence larking around in an inflatable dinghy. Another of Harry and his dad proudly displaying a trout he'd caught on a fishing trip.

Regan was determined to find some of Nush at the same age. If she could dig out some embarrassing shots of Nush with a Farrah Fawcett flick or a gappy-toothed smile in pre-Harley Street orthodontist days, then this trip down the Silvers family memory lane would be well worth it.

She could only find one photo. It was of Nush as a toddler, sat lovingly on a beautiful blonde woman's knee. Nush's head was leaning against the woman's bosom, sucking her thumb. It was a cherubic picture of togetherness. From Nush's descriptions to her before, Regan knew that the woman in the photo was Lysette, her mum.

You could look for a million years through the Phoenix family albums and never find a photo as pure and loving as that, thought

Regan. They were just full of Montana on the arms of countless Romeos.

Regan went to place the album back on the shelf. Still a little wobbly on her feet from the drink, she knocked one of the other albums down from the shelf. It fell open on the floor.

Picking it up, Regan again looked at the array of photos. Lawrence with the lads at work. Lawrence alongside a Silvers helicopter. Lawrence sat on board a yacht in some sun-drenched marina, his arm around a woman in a tiny bikini. All the photos epitomised his playboy lifestyle. Something disturbed Regan about the photo on the yacht. She looked at it again. With a blinding flash of realisation, she recognised the woman as Montana Phoenix. *Why were her mother and Nush's father together? They didn't even know each other... did they?*

Regan's head swam with confusion. The more she stared at it, the less she understood. She needed to find out the story behind it, but in her current alcohol-sozzled state, she knew that now was not the time. Taking the photo from the album, she placed it in her bag.

—

Looking up at the petrol blue sky, dotted with glittery stars, Evie felt warmly enveloped by her surroundings. She was loving her night at Kingsbury and had to admit she was having a ball. She'd been whirled around the floor at the disco tent. She'd eaten frosty-coloured candyfloss, laughed at clowns and even been cajoled onto the dodgems, something she'd never done before in her life. Her insurers on *The Bouquet Catcher* would have had kittens at their leading lady risking whiplash and broken bones, but Evie didn't care. Because she was experiencing it all with a man by her side, and a very attractive one at that... much to her surprise she was enjoying the company of Nush's younger brother, Harry.

Evie had been more dumbstruck than anyone when she found herself looking at the 20-year-old in a flirtatious way. If she had a type, then she'd always thought Harry was certainly not it. Plus he was Nush's younger brother! She'd met him before, but back then he'd been an annoying pipsqueak of an acorn, but a physical lifestyle had obviously turned him into a rather mighty oak. And his boyish, roguish charm and slick line in patter had made her crumble at his advances from the moment they'd met that night.

'I bet you can't believe you're talking to *the* Harry Silvers,' had been his opening gambit. 'It's not every day a *lowly* actress like yourself gets to meet a true king of the business world like me,' he'd winked. His cocky allure proved magnetic. Plus the crisp white polo shirt and linen trousers he was wearing appealed to Evie's fashion radar. The T-shirt succeeded in flaunting his muscular arms.

It had been Harry who suggested they dance. 'We'll go to the disco tent. It should suit you down to the ground, seeing as you're old enough to remember the retro tunes they're playing in there.' His sideways dig at her *advanced years*, even though she was a mere three years older than him, made her smile. 'God, you're even more gorgeous when you smile,' he said, reaching out to stroke her cheek. Evie had been surprised that she hadn't pulled away from his touch. 'Let's go dance.' She'd gone willingly.

After dancing, Harry had taken her to the Ferris wheel. As they spun silently around, Evie felt the slight May breeze weaving through her hair. She shuddered momentarily, not so much due to the breeze as to the frisson of the situation. Harry stretched out his arm and placed it around her, his touch masculine and comforting. She allowed herself to sink into his body, placing a hand on his chest, enjoying his warmth.

Harry stroked the back of her neck, teasing her nape with his feather-light touch. 'Did you know that in traditional Japanese culture, the nape of a woman's neck held a strong sexual attraction for many men as it was one of the few areas of the body left uncovered.' he said.

Evie looked up in to Harry's eyes and before she had time to rationalise, her lips were on his. His mouth felt moist and inviting, his kisses sweet and tender. That was it – like the ice statues in the warm night air of the Kingsbury grounds, Evie's heart had just melted. She had fallen for Nush's younger brother, an awkward thought that she managed to conveniently push to the back of her mind.

——

As far as Nush was concerned, the party had been a complete disaster. Crashed out on the scatter cushions in the chill out tent, she reflected on the evening and slurringly recounted it back to Ashley Erridge. Just days off his 27th birthday, Ashley was the eldest son of Lawrence Silvers' most trusted friend, Johnny Erridge. Johnny had worked alongside Lawrence within his publishing empire for most of his working life. The two of them had been sparring partners in the boxing gyms of the East End back in their teenage years. As soon as Lawrence hit it big, he employed the straight-talking cockney to be his right hand man. Without Lawrence, Johnny would have probably ended up doing time at Her Majesty's pleasure for a life of crime.

Whereas Johnny was harder and rougher than a bricklayer's handshake, Ashley was the complete opposite. Mild-mannered, quietly spoken, pencil thin and, to be honest, a touch creepy. He adored Nush and tonight he was the only person who was prepared to hang off her every word and listen to her woes and to Nush that suddenly seemed all-important.

'So, I've had a bit to drink tonight and I decided to tell Sadie what I thought of her ridiculous outfit and then dad goes mad at me and says she's more of a woman than I'll ever be. I hate that woman. Thinking she can take the place of my dead mother and spend the family money on parties for Harry. Did you see her tonight, dressed up like some fairy *Bride of Chucky*?' Nush finished the rest of her cocktail and signalled a passing waiter to bring her another, before continuing. 'Your dad and mine are like peas in a pod – all machismo rubbish. Unless you're a sporting powerhouse and have your dick in every passing bimbo, they don't want to know you. Must be worse for you, Ashley, because you're actually a guy.'

Nush drunkenly laughed, without realising just how close to the truth she was. Johnny had never paid any real attention to Ashley, he was his dad's biggest disappointment. Not like Ashley's younger brother, Seth. With a natural flare for sports and with muscles harder than Popeye, Seth was everything that Ashley would never be. He was currently a star figure in the National Football League in America and engaged to one of the winners of *America's Next Top Model*. Ashley had never even had a decent girlfriend. Ashley despised him.

'See, the thing is…' Nush picked up. 'You and I are like the runts of our families, Ashley. We're both the oldest, but we've both been callously shoved aside for our favoured siblings. I used to think you were a right loser too. I even fancied your brother to be honest, but d'you know what… I should have seen it really. You and I are both outcasts. We're kindred spirits,' she slurred.

'Harry seems to be having a good time though,' pointed out Ashley, finally speaking. 'Didn't I see him with that actress friend of yours earlier? They seemed to be getting along very well.'

The coupling of Harry and Evie pricked Nush greatly. She'd seen the two of them as they tumbled off the Ferris wheel, and had shot Evie a disbelieving stare that had not gone unnoticed by her friend. Nush had spent all night looking for a decent man for Evie. Why did she bother? She should start looking out for number one. Evie was off with Harry, Regan was doubtless in the arms of some sweaty-haired rock fan… what about her?

Finishing yet another drink, Nush looked directly at Ashley. *Needs must*, she thought. 'You're sad and single. Do you fancy a shag? No strings, just two rejects getting off.'

Ashley couldn't believe his luck. The woman he'd always fantasised about was suddenly asking him if he wanted sex with her.

Five minutes later they were stood inside Nush's old bedroom at Kingsbury, her gown discarded on the floor. Jettisoning her tiny thong she lay back on the bed, instructing Ashley to remove his clothes. As he did, she looked at his body. Skinny but well defined in a sinewy jockey kind of way. As his boxers came off, his penis sprang forth, long and thin, reflective of his body as a whole.

Beyond excited, as he climbed onto the bed, his evident excitement seemed to get the better of him. Without even touching himself he shot a stream of milky sperm across the sheets and onto Nush's thigh. The moment was dead before it had even had chance to bloom.

'I'm sorry,' he whimpered. 'I'm too excited. I'll be better next time.' Embarrassed by his action, Ashley hurriedly dressed again and turned to kiss Nush on the lips. She turned her head away as he did so. Unsure what to do or say next, he left the room.

As he shut the door behind him, Nush burst into pathetic tears as she thought about just how ludicrously tragic her evening, and indeed her life, had become.

———

Having stashed the photo of her mother in her bag, Regan had snorted a huge line of coke. As she walked back outside into the fresh garden air, she felt her lips start to numb and the sweeping effect of the drug hitting her system. She looked around, seeing where the evening could take her next and spotted a small tent decorated with bunting. A sign outside read 'Madame Anselina, Fortune Teller to the stars.'

This could be fun, pondered Regan. *I could find out if the TV show will be a ratings winner, whether I win or not and when mother's success will crash and burn.*

Pushing back the flap of the tent, Regan walked inside. It was decorated with swirls of purple and pink chiffon, giving the room an air of sophisticated mystique. Sat in the middle of the tent was Madame Anselina, eyes closed, with her hands placed on a large crystal ball. Regan shivered on seeing her, her skin rising into goose bumps. The air wasn't cold but there was something about the fortune teller that spooked Regan. Maybe it was the coke making her paranoid. Without opening her eyes, Anselina beckoned Regan in.

'Come, my child, you are welcome. Allow Anselina to look into your future. I feel there is money around you,' murmured the psychic.

'Go figure, lady, every partygoer here is moolahed to the max.' Regan spoke out loud without thinking. As Anselina opened her eyes and fixed Regan with a piercing, punishing gaze, she wished she had kept quiet.

Her worry increased as Anselina's eyes opened wider and became transfixed on Regan's hair. Swaying back and forth, Anselina screeched. 'Foolish child. You wear hawthorn blossom in your hair! You dare to bring it here into the sacred place of

Anselina. Do you not know the folklore and mythology of the hawthorn? Bringing it to me signifies that illness and death will follow.' Her voice escalated in volume with every word, rooting Regan to the spot. The dryness in her throat from the coke was beginning to make her feel sick.

'I feel it, I see it around you. Death is wrapped around you like a coat. You hapless child, your innocence at bringing the hawthorn has set the wheels of destruction in motion. Suffering will occur and the outcome will be inevitable. Someone close will leave this earth forever. Now go!'

Anselina collapsed forward onto the table, her hands splayed either side of the crystal ball, her breathing deep and uneven. 'I said *go!*'

Tears running down her cheeks, Regan ran from the tent.

CHAPTER 13

Montana Phoenix cordially invites you to join her for the world launch of her exquisite new perfume, Babylon.

The invitation was just how Montana had imagined it. Deckle-edged, scripted in an elegant font with a vignette of chic colour running behind the copy. All placed inside a tanzanite-coloured envelope, reflecting the shade of *Babylon's* shapely bottle.

Placing it back in her bag, Montana smoothed down her dress and pulled open the changing room door, back into the main area of the boutique, Balenciaga on Melrose Avenue, which was deserted except for Montana, Stafford James and an attentive assistant, catering for Montana's every need.

The designer store, with its space age cool was normally packed from mirrored wall to mirrored wall with LA's hippest shoppers, but Montana had requested some privacy whilst undergoing her final fitting for her frock for that night's launch. In true megastar style, they had shut the store just for her.

'Oh, my darling, that looks divine!' cooed Stafford as Montana stood before him. 'It takes years off you... 21 again, sweetie!'

The flouncy cocktail dress would not normally have been Montana's chosen style, but her younger female co-stars on *Peregrine Palace,* every one of them a fashion aficionado, had been raving about the store's latest collection and she had to admit they were right. She looked like a woman half her age.

'Bring on the paparazzi, Stafford. This is the look I want all over the papers tomorrow morning!' Montana twirled round, looking at her reflection. 'All we need now are the diamonds, honey… let's hope those nice people at the House Of Cartier have done me proud!'

———

Bradley Roderick ran his lips across Montana's naked shoulders as he fastened her diamond Cartier necklace into place. His soft touch plus the feel of the multi carat masterpiece against her skin made her tingle. She turned to face him, returning his kiss, running her fingers through his hair as she savoured his lips. Tonight was her night and Montana was going to enjoy every moment of it.

The anticipation for *Babylon's* launch was immense. According to Brad, pre-orders at Fred Segal were already astronomical, as they were at nearly all stores across the States. TV advertisements for *Babylon* had been beamed across Europe, creating huge interest. As for tonight, Stafford had phoned her from the venue, the Crown Bar, to say that the place was already rammed with people awaiting her arrival.

Montana wanted to make them all wait. She wanted to wallow in her own glory. She felt justified in doing so. She'd worked damned hard for moments like this. The days of schlepping to some godforsaken backwater location to make some crummy straight-to-video movie were well and truly behind her. No more bowing down and going down on the film and TV bigwigs to get parts. No more working her teeth and tits at every available soiree to try and impress. Those days were history.

'Come on, angel, that *glampire* of yours needs building,' teased Brad. 'There's a red carpet in town with your name on it.'

Clipping her chandelier diamond drop earrings into place
and slicking on a film of lipstick, Montana was ready for her
evening.

———

The flashes from the rows of paparazzi outside the Crown Bar
were still twinkling in her eyes as Montana sashayed up to the
club's bar, Brad by her side. The look of the place was Hollywood glam meets 1940s gentleman's club and every corner
was filled with cool and powerful industry people – all there
to see Montana. Scanning the milk chocolate-coloured ban-
quettes around the room she could see stars from stage and
screen, fashion designers and sports stars, all hoping to attract
her attention. Mingling alongside the beauty editors from all
the leading magazines were a million dollar mix of the young
Hollywood It Crowd, who seemed to see Montana as a cool
mother figure.

Shame her own daughter didn't feel the same. Mind you, Regan
was the last person Montana wanted to see right now.

The next two hours were a blur for Montana. She skilfully
worked the bar, guided by an ever-attentive Brad, making sure
that no-one of any importance was ignored. Journalists were
talked to and mini-interviews given, fellow celebs were fawned
over with promises of 'doing lunch'. The whole evening was a
performance of which her on-screen persona, Sienna Revell,
would have been proud.

Towards the end of the evening, as the mass of guests began
to leave, clutching their Babylon goody bags, Montana heaved
a sigh of self-satisfaction. Luxuriating in the calm of a private
banquette, she allowed herself to relax. Flanked by Stafford and
Brad on one side and the two co-owners of Coeur Cosmetics
on the other, Montana was grateful that they had declared the

launch a success. They were paying for it after all. Needing a drink, she ordered bottles of Krug for the table. Mingling all night was thirsty work.

The table was in full conversation about the next stage of 'Team Babylon's strategy' when two women approached the banquette. A touch peeved to have to stop drinking, Montana perfected her painted-on smile and looked up. She recognised the woman in front of her as Clarissa Thornton. The other looked vaguely familiar.

'Hi there, Montana. Clarissa Thornton, *Hollywood Daily*, mind if we chat?' enquired Clarissa.

'Actually, Ms Phoenix has given all the interviews she intends to tonight. If you'd like to contact *Babylon's* PR I'm sure we can arrange something very soon.' Brad had piloted into work-mode again.

'No, Bradley darling, don't worry. I've always got time for the viewers of *Hollywood Daily*. Of course we can chat. Where's the camera?' Montana may have been the wrong side of 40, but she knew how important a show like *Hollywood Daily* was. It was coast-to-coast coverage in one easy interview.

'Oh, there's no camera, Montana. I'd just like to introduce you to someone. This is Grace Laszlo.'

Montana knew the name instantly. *She was the little tramp whose sluttish antics had been splashed all over the press a while back.* Scanning Grace's tiny T and micro mini outfit from head to toe, Montana could feel her lip curling in disgust. *She wears that for my perfume launch.* From her constant twitching, Montana guessed that she was completely off her face. 'How lovely to meet you, Ms Laszlo,' she feigned.

'Likewise,' responded Grace, noisily chewing gum as she spoke. 'I'm mad about your perfume. I'll be sure to wear it when I see Regan in Britain this week.' Her tone was sarcastic.

'Oh, *you're* a friend of dear Regan's, are you? How charming. I had no idea that she knew someone *like you*.' Montana's words were clipped and emphasised, leaving no doubt as to her meaning.

'She doesn't, we've never met. But that badass daughter of yours and I have a lot in common. A bum image in the press for one and our new TV show for another.'

For once, Montana was lost for words. *What TV show?* She was sure Clarissa was trying to hide a smile. *Smug cow.* Thinking as quickly as her Krug-soaked brain would let her, Montana curled the sides of her mouth upwards and spoke through gritted teeth.

'I've been so busy with the launch of *Babylon* that darling Regan and I haven't had a chance to speak in a while. Is it one of those wonderful biography shows about living with a famous mother? Do you have one too?'

Grace rattled off her response like gunfire. 'Not even close, grandma. It's a reality show contest. Me against your whacked out loser of a daughter to see who can save their garbage reputation first. I'll whip her ass *and* get her to dish the dirt on life with TV's biggest bitch. Your ivory tower is coming down.' Grace banged her hand down on the table as if to stress the point. She did it with such a force that Montana's glass of champagne wobbled back and forth before falling over, spilling its contents over Montana's Balenciaga.

Montana's forced composure snapped. She saw red. Ignoring Brad's attempts to stop her, she rose to her feet, grabbing his full glass as she did so. Throwing the Krug into Grace's face, she launched her attack, bearing her teeth as she snarled. 'Listen to me, you skanky coked-up piece of trash. I've spent most of my life having to deal with my embarrassment of a daughter, so I know exactly how to deal with a ten-a-penny lowlife like you, missy. If you go spreading any of the shit that comes from Regan's mouth, you'll be hit with a law suit quicker than you can wrack out your next line.'

'That's enough, Montana. We're leaving!' Brad's words were stern and stony. Grabbing her by the arm, they pushed past a smirking Stafford, who was loving every minute of the drama. Looking back at the table as Brad manhandled her towards the door, Montana could see the two scandalised expressions of the Coeur co-owners. Mortification was etched deeply across their faces. She knew there would certainly be humble pie to eat come the morning.

On the other side of the bar, an angry and sodden Grace turned to Clarissa. 'So, I hope you got the story you wanted. You sure ain't paying enough to justify me getting a soaking from that bitch.'

Elated with her night's work, Clarissa gloated, 'You keep grabbing me the headlines and I'll keep the cash coming your way.' Reaching down into her bag she clicked off her digital recorder.

CHAPTER 14

Evie and Jeremy's week on set had been strictly business, systematically filming scenes with no small talk or chit-chat.

Despite his initial dislike of Evie, Jeremy couldn't help but be somewhat intrigued by the change that had occurred in his co-star during her few days away. If was as if someone had turned her into the 'queen of smoulder'. Her skin seemed softer, her hair more rubicund and her eyes were embossed with a sultry desire. But he knew it wasn't for him. She'd fallen for someone. The crew was small enough for word to have filtered around. And Evie's eyes being focussed on someone else other than him was something that, much to his surprise, scored an irksome groove right to Jeremy's very core. Why did he suddenly seem to care?

It was a situation he was keen to discuss with the ever faithful Mario. 'Oh yes, Miss Merchant is sporting the look of love,' deadpanned the Italian, adding a final swish of powder to Jeremy's face as he talked to his employer's reflection in the dressing room mirror. 'But you know she finds you… *allettante,* shall we say. Any fool could see from the looks she gave you last week. She finds you, how you say… alluring.'

Jeremy knew that Mario was right. Despite his brusque treatment of her, Evie had still been doe-eyed putty in his hands last week. But now? He'd watched her sitting on the edge of the set between takes, chatting animatedly on her mobile, smiling the most appetising of grins and playing coquettishly with her hair, as she did so. She'd met someone, it was clear. She'd grown in confidence, even having the backbone to tell Jeremy what a bigot he'd been to her at first and how she didn't deserve to be treated in such a truly offensive manner. Her matter-of-fact heart-to-heart had really taken him by surprise. He'd never expected someone of his kudos to be spoken to in such an honestly blunt way. He rippled with discontent as he took in Evie's words and knew he would have to do something about it. Because strangely, her mettle made her seem much more attractive.

At first, the bad air between them had stung Evie like a scorpion. But the jubilation of the ecstatic evening she'd spent with Harry at the party and his constant courtship ever since had changed everything. Hardly an hour had gone by without a phone call professing his desire to see her. Suggestive texts had peppered her day. Countless bouquets of long stemmed red roses arrived at the studios, all wrapped with bright organza bows. Three times since the party he had been waiting outside her house as her driver dropped her off, ready to escort her inside. It wasn't until the third time that the young couple had finally made love.

Her longing for Harry had made any feelings she had had for Jeremy and his matinee idol looks ebb somewhat. She could still see his beauty but it was like looking at a poster. She found him two dimensional. She had tasted a different fruit, one that was mouth-wateringly sweet and didn't come served with a huge portion of sour arrogance.

Away from the set though, in the outside world, there were rumours that her relationship with Jeremy was more than just on-screen. It didn't surprise her. Virtually every Hollywood starlet was linked with their dashing co-star at some point during their professional time together. It was how the press machine rolled.

A rough cut of a scene from the film with Evie and Jeremy kissing had leaked its way onto YouTube, with the film company behind the flick promising that the kiss was just the 'tip of the amorous iceberg' that would be witnessed come the film's release. There was even talk of the movie being rushed into cinemas to capitalise on the press intrigue between the pair. The press had already gone wild with false speculation. Evie was too loved up to care.

The only fly in the ointment had been the constant phone calls from Nush. As one of the few people who actually knew about Evie's affair with Harry, she had played every discouraging card in her repertoire to try and end it. Harry was too young for her, too selfish for her, too much of a player for her.

Evie had tried explaining to Nush how Harry made her feel but she refused to listen. She was adamant. Harry was no good. After days of her protestations, Evie had stopped taking her calls. If her friend couldn't be happy for her, then so be it. Waters between the three girls in the Trinity didn't always flow smoothly.

CHAPTER 15

Regan's first day of filming on *From Wild Child to Rothschild* was also riddled with angst.

Angst over the photo she'd found of her mum with Lawrence and also about the deadly prediction of Madame Anselina. But the hugest slice of angst was about every tabloid headline in the country bludgeoning Regan with the fact that her mother considered her, to use Montana's exact words, 'an embarrassment of a daughter'.

The story of Montana's poisonous outburst had first broken on Clarissa Thornton's *Hollywood Daily* – a recording of the conversation between Montana and Grace has been played out the day after the *Babylon* launch party. It had been carefully edited to make the entire dialogue totally one sided, portraying Grace as the poor victim on the receiving end of Montana's forked words. Within minutes of the show playing the tape, entertainment news desks across the globe were clamouring to run the story. A photo of a sobbing and sodden Grace, clutching a bottle of *Babylon* to her chest as thick black rivers of mascara corkscrewed down her face mysteriously hit the world's internet, credited to an anonymous launch goer. Another stroke of genius on Clarissa's part. Five minutes work at the Crown Bar had landed her with a worldwide scoop. Montana Phoenix, the biggest bitch on TV, was proving to the world that she was just as nasty in real life.

The coverage in the press that the *Grace vs. Montana* spat had produced for *Wild Child* was immense. As Grace had been ushered through the departure lounge at LAX, dark glasses covering her face, the gathered paparazzi and reporters had gone crazy. Raising a hand against the constant popping of the camera flashes, Grace had delivered her prepared reply, dotting her voice with cracked strain and upset.

'Let me just say that Montana was someone I had always admired, respected as a fellow artiste. I was a true fan. But her evil words about both me and her very own daughter have left me numb with disappointment. I am just glad that I can be there for Regan at her time of global humiliation and bitter rejection. We have a lot in common, but sadly I must now add the hatred of Regan's mother to that list. I shall be a shoulder to cry on throughout our time together.'

Regan liked Grace as soon as she met her in the makeshift green room of their first location, the Dexter Berlin fashion house in London's East End. They were there to film their first challenge. It was the 'elegance and style challenge', in which they both needed to create and model their own red carpet dress.

Regan's first meeting with Grace was being filmed for the show, which Leo had said would make for explosive watching. Prepared to do whatever the cute-as-a-button Leo wanted of her, Regan had readily agreed to the access-all-areas approach to filming.

Because of the hype it was generating, the show would be aired mere days after its recording. Both ABC in the States and the UK network had moved their schedules to shoehorn the show into a prime-time slot. Now that Montana had involuntarily gotten involved in the show too, the volcanic bubbling lava of expectation enveloping *Wild Child* was fierier than ever.

Grace had burst into the green room with the force of a Florida hurricane. Dropping her Anya Hindmarch day bag to the floor, she embraced Regan in her arms, making sure the cameras were catching her every move.

Her hold was tight and warm around Regan. Kissing the side of Regan's face with a loud m'wah, Grace whispered in Regan's ear loud enough for the overhead boom following her to pick up the sound. 'You poor sweetie. What a dreadful week you've had what with all this yucky publicity about your mum. She was vile, honey! But you and I are going to show her just what you're made of.'

Regan liked her style. Because of the rather public dispute between Grace and Montana, Regan had assumed that Grace might have been completely against her from the word go. But, she had certainly come out as Regan's ally, not afraid to say what she really thought about Montana.

Their attempts at dress-making and learning how to sashay up catwalks were a liberating experience for both of them. It was Regan who had actually *won* the first show, her monochromatic flapper-style frock being deemed much more elegant than Grace's paint-splattered print dress by the judges.

Feeling jubilant at her first success, Regan invited Grace out to The Ivy for dinner. It was the perfect press opportunity to show the world that they were genuinely getting on with each other. Posing together outside the London restaurant, they linked their arms, moving their bodies to flaunt their curves, giving the cameramen the shot they wanted. Grace was inwardly seething at losing on the show, but as far as she was concerned, the war was far from over and the battle had only just begun.

The two women spent most of the meal talking about the many men who'd weaved their way in and out of their lives. Regan was enjoying having a fresh pair of ears to share stories with. Regan laughed wildly at Grace's snort-by-snort account of the naked backstage antics that had ended her Sexalicious career.

Just as they were finishing their desserts, Grace smiled at Regan across the table. 'Mind if I say something to you. All this talk of men... I kind of knew you'd been... er... popular, shall we say. Your mum said as much.'

Swallowing a mouthful of ice berries, Regan sat back in her chair. 'Excuse me? My mum said what exactly?'

Stroking her hair away from her face, Grace stared directly at Regan. 'What you heard in the press was only half the story. *Hollywood Daily* couldn't use most of what your mum said. I'd only gone up to say hi to your mum because of this show and because I love her on *Peregrine Palace*. She was ripped on the champagne, honey, probably high on something else.'

Loving the sound of her own lies, Grace continued. 'She may have called me a slut because of the whole fan thing, but she hinted the same about you too. All the guys you've been with, drugs, drink, everything. For a mother who doesn't give a flying fuck about you, she sure is quick to judge. She let it all out. If it wasn't for fear of million dollar law suits, Clarissa and the *Hollywood Daily* crew could have snowballed that story for weeks.'

Sat across the table from Grace, Regan felt her rancour rise and flood into her brain. 'She started calling me a slut? That's rich coming from the woman who's had more men in her life than most hookers can dream of. There's not enough hours in the day to tell you how many horny sad old men have wandered in and out of her life... provided their bank balances were big enough of course.'

Regan was unstoppable. Grace thought to herself *like mother, like daughter, these broads know how to get angry*. She let her continue. 'Do you know the Eartha Kitt song *Where Is My Man?* It was big back in the 80s and was all about a woman who's constantly looking for a rich man. My mum used to play it all the time at the house in LA. It could be her theme tune. I always remember one particular line she'd sing – *You know I've tried some other men, the kind with zeroes less than ten, but every time I grab the ring it's always brass.* That's Montana to a tee. If the men didn't have the Coutts private bank account with millions in it, she didn't want to know. I can only assume my dad didn't reach the megabucks benchmark, otherwise he'd still be around.'

Grace relished the information. A few more dinners like this and she was sure she could have all sorts of defamatory dirt tumbling from Regan's lips, which would guarantee a hefty payday from Clarissa.'

She curved her lips up, amused by the dollar signs in her head. 'I don't know the song, but I'll be sure to download it.'

CHAPTER 16

Nush was proud of her London home. It was the first one she'd bought since leaving Kingsbury. The house at Plantation Wharf was her own little oasis of relaxation.

Her home was arranged over two floors and housed a bright reception room, a spacious master bedroom with a Thames view balcony and a self-contained studio flat for when people chose to stay over. Tonight it was Regan's turn.

Nush hadn't seen Regan since the party for Harry at Kingsbury, a night she had chosen to obliterate from her memory. What with Evie falling for Harry's schoolboy charms and Nush attempting to seduce creepy Ashley it had been, for her, an unmitigated disaster.

The thoughts of that night ran through Nush's head as she reached home. She needed a drink. Work at *The Daily Staple* was over for another day, and as usual, her father had spent most of the day moaning about Clarissa Thornton's Montana scoop. Lawrence's machine-gun words still rang in her head as she walked past the Square's leafy trees. 'I didn't fire that silly bitch to employ an even stupider one from my own family!' He knew how to make her feel useless and inferior.

'Every newspaper out there wants dirt on Montana and you miss out on her slagging off her own daughter to the entire world.'

Nush had tried to argue with him that she would never write stories that involved Regan and Evie. It was her unwritten code of

Trinity honour. It was another argument that had fallen on Law-rence's deaf ears. 'If it wasn't for Harry not wanting to upset his lat-est bit of stuff, I'd write a story myself about Evie getting shagged by my own flesh and blood!' snapped Lawrence. 'The minute Har-ry bins her, you'll be writing his kiss 'n' tell whether you like it or not, lady. Your friends have got to be of some fucking use to you.'

The thought of Harry and Evie being together in the first place picked at Nush's skin like a heat rash. She could certain-ly do with a meaty story to outdo Clarissa, but the last week's worth of columns had been filled with nothing juicier than a camp thespian outing himself and a children's TV presenter flashing her hairless pussy as she departed a taxi. Nush needed to up her game to prove she hadn't lost her touch.

———

Regan was heading over to Nush's to watch the first episode of *Wild Child*. She was due to start filming the second show the next morning and the hefty schedule was beginning to take its toll on her energy levels. She'd not even had a chance to make a proper move on Leo as yet.

The thought of a night crashed out with Nush watching the show, gossiping about Evie and discussing the photo she'd found was just what she needed. Plus she wanted to tell Nush about Madame Anselina's prophetic vision.

It was just before nine when Nush opened the door. Nush had already changed into a pair of cotton pyjama bottoms and a spaghetti strap top. She clutched a large glass of Chilean Char-donnay in her hand. 'Hey, wild child,' she said, smiling. 'Your debut show is on in ten minutes. Dinner's on the lap trays and the wine's chilled to perfection. Have I missed anything? Other than the biggest Montana Phoenix scoop ever, of course!' Nush's words were jokily derisive.

'No, I think mother's said enough for this week, don't you? Now, make way, *embarrassment of a daughter* coming through,' she laughed.

They watched the show while eating, Regan surveying it with fingers over her eyes. As the credits rolled, she swivelled herself around on the sofa and looked at Nush. 'Well…?'

'My honest opinion? You came across really well. Funny, charming, the person I know and love. It'll be great for the public to see you that way. Plus I'm glad you beat that scrubber Grace. She's a real piece of work.' Nush necked her glass and reached for another bottle. 'But anyone who hangs out with Clarissa Thornton is bound to be.'

'She's alright, you know,' replied Regan, not bowing to Nush's bitterness. 'I'm really getting to like Grace, you should meet her. We'll all go out one night.'

Nush was quick with her comeback. 'Whoopie-doo, can't wait. Anyway, enough about her, how are you with the whole *mother mouthing off about you* thing? Have you spoken to her?'

'No chance, she knows about the show anyway so I have nothing to tell her for the minute. She's doing her perfume thing. She's due over here in a week or so, so doubtless we shall be running into each other then. But I needed to speak to you before I speak to her.'

Regan began to fill Nush in about finding the photo at Kingsbury. It was obviously as much a shock to her as it had been to Regan. 'Your mum knows my dad? I suppose they could have just bumped into each other in days gone by. Let me see the photo…'

Scanning it, Nush considered the options. 'Maybe they had mutual friends. Or met on the European party circuit. I certainly don't recognise the yacht. But this photo must be at least twenty years old. I'll have to ask him.'

'Can you leave off until I speak to Montana. I want to see what she says first. She knows you're my best mate so surely she would have mentioned your dad if they'd known each other. If she denies ever meeting him, I'll produce the evidence.'

Regan's voice was cut short as the two girls screamed, Nush dropping her glass to the floor. They both leapt from the sofa. The huge reception room window about five metres in front of them had smashed. A large brick landed on the floor, a sheet of paper wrapped around it with two elastic bands.

'What the hell was that?' shrieked Nush. Both girls ran to the window, looking out into the courtyard at the front of the house. A figure, dim in the night, was running away from the house. The figure seemed large and bulky.

Shaking, Regan picked up her mobile. 'I'm phoning the police.'

'Hang on, there's a note attached,' motioned Nush. She reached down to grab the brick, removing the bands as she did so. Unfolding the paper, she saw a row of cut out letters from a newspaper that had been stuck together. They formed a sentence 'You deserve to die'.

Both women froze as they read the words. Regan phoned the police and then perched herself down on the sofa again, alongside Nush. Shaking with fear, she preceded to tell her all about Anselina's deathly prediction. Nush could only sit dumbstruck and listen.

CHAPTER 17

All couples have their ups and downs, but the last few weeks had been nothing but a constant downer for Jake Saunders and Mae-Ling Ch'en.

Ever since the story of his sexual treachery had been splashed in scandal-laden globules across the pages of Nush's column, the couple had tried unsuccessfully to put on a united front. Their star definitely shone brighter as a joyous partnership.

Both had kept busy – Mae-Ling working alongside Evie on *The Bouquet Catcher* and Jake with his appearances as alter-ego Bullet from *Sporting Spartans*. But Mae-Ling was finding it hard to balance her professional life and the role of mother. Despite trying to stay strong and remain outwardly happy for the people she worked with, behind closed doors she was a complete wreck. Despite Jake never actually admitting the name of the bed partner in his betrayal, Mae-Ling had banished him to their spare room. She couldn't bear to touch him.

Her mind boiled over with thoughts of hatred, shame, disappointment and insecurity. She had always considered herself a strong woman but she hadn't counted on just how much Jake's treachery would affect her.

Jake had tried to explain to Mae-Ling that his sleeping with another woman meant nothing to him. He couldn't blame her for not believing him. He didn't believe himself. He had no reason to… he knew it wasn't true. He had been ready to leave Mae-

Ling months ago, just before she had announced that she was pregnant. For him, their life together had become stale and dry. To the world, they were seemingly solid and like two pieces of a jigsaw, but Jake was finding their togetherness more and more mismatched. If it hadn't been for the fact that he knew the world would brand him an evil bastard for leaving a pregnant woman, he would have walked out the door there and then. To leave Mae-Ling at her time of need would have been career suicide.

He had felt trapped – things weren't clean-cut anymore. It wasn't simply a case of an *OK!* feature telling people how he and Mae-Ling had drifted in opposite directions, work pressures getting between them.

Oh no. As a father to be, he was suddenly burdened with responsibilities. He had decided that he would try and make their union work. They were soon to be three and although it was privately messy, Jake would attempt to play the family man that his image demanded.

Not that he regretted the baby one bit. Famke was a beautiful bundle of joy.

Jake was proud to be Famke's daddy and if putting up with a woman he'd fallen out of love with was the price he had to pay for cupping Famke in his arms every night, then he would ride the storm.

He had ridden it well until he'd laid eyes on Anoushka Silvers. He had never intended to cheat on Mae-Ling but one look at Nush and it had been inevitable. His time together with Nush had been short but it had been good. The kind of good that made him know that he would have to see Nush again…

———

Babies had been on the mind of Sadie Silvers for months. It was the one thing missing from her life. She had the rich husband, the house, the social standing and the money to visit any designer destination around the world. So why did she feel incomplete? Easy, there was a baby-shaped hole within her.

Falling pregnant seemed to be the one thing that money couldn't buy. Despite nights with Lawrence where their copulation had been fierce and adventurous, she still wasn't pregnant.

Sadie couldn't understand why. She had been fastidious as she knew timing was critical. Her military-like approach to getting pregnant had made her go virtually teetotal and she'd predicted her most fertile days. She'd made Lawrence cut out his beloved caffeine and cigars, and even stopped her vigorous fitness sessions with Marcelino, her personal trainer, for fear of putting a strain on her body. Sadie was lining him back up to shift the baby weight after giving birth. But to give birth, you had to get pregnant first. Sadie was very impatient.

The impatience was still niggling at her as she sat on her bed in the master bedroom at Kingsbury. Having stopped off at Harrods on the way back home, she opened the carrier bag in front of her and pulled out a box tied with a bow. Inside it was a matching set of leopard print Dolce & Gabbana bra and briefs. Tonight was the night. It was time for *Operation Seduction*. Lawrence was due back from the *Staple* offices in an hour or so and she was going to make sure that he couldn't resist her feminine charms.

Laying the underwear on her bed, she stripped and turned to look at her naked form in the bedroom's full-length mirror. She placed her hands on her trim, flat belly and pushed it forward, imagining how it would feel to be with child. She loved the idea, patting her stomach as she smiled to herself. 'Mama wants a baby, so a baby is what she's going to get.'

Tonight was definitely the night, she was sure. Call it woman's intuition, but everything felt right. It was as if her own body was telling her she was ready to conceive.

Sadie poured herself a small brandy from a crystal decanter, relishing its taste as it passed her lips. Reaching down into bedroom cabinet she located half a dozen scented candles. As she lit them around the room, the sweet infusion of honeysuckle, jasmine and rose filled the air. Bathed in candlelight she slipped her body into the briefs and bra and lay back on the bed. Looking at the bedside clock, she saw that Lawrence was due any minute. She relaxed, turned on by her own body, while the brandy made her head spin slightly with an anticipatory flutter of excitement. She was ready to make a baby…

CHAPTER 18

The Stein Terrasse in Salzburg was the epitome of hip. Situated on the seventh floor of the Austrian city's Hotel Stein, it was an ice-cool melting pot of laid back snowboarders, wannabe Olympic skiers and trendy young bucks from the four corners of Europe who flocked to its restaurant and bar.

Sat on its open-air terrace looking across the Salzach river at the snow-capped frosted peaks in the distance, Evie sighed to herself. The morning air was unusually nippy for the time of year, and a swirl of her breath was visible against the brisk air. It was a sigh of torment. It wasn't just the air that was chilled, her heart was too.

Evie had been in Salzburg less than a day but she had a good mind to head straight back to the airport and fly home. She was there to be with Harry, but in the 24 hours since landing they had exchanged about as many words. With the change in geography had seemingly come a change in Harry's priorities.

In Britain, they had spent their time together as a young, fresh, exciting couple, but the trip to Salzburg was a weekend stopover on the way to Seefeld, where Harry was determined to master a black ski run as well as topping up his snowboarding skills. They had gone from being *two's company* in the UK to *eight's a crowd* in Austria, and Evie didn't like the feeling.

Harry had come to join his friends and suddenly she'd become the trophy girlfriend in front of them. The cocky laddish charm she'd fallen for at Kingsbury had turned into pure cockiness. Any air of gentlemanly romance and charm had evaporated. Every comment about Evie, not *to* her but *about* her, was *film* this or *movie* that. He'd even started referring to her as his 'Oscar-winning bit of stuff' despite the fact that she was no nearer to winning a gold statue than he was. In short, he seemed to be showing off about his prize – the prize of having Evie on his arm.

It wasn't even as if they could be overly loved up with each other anyway, as Evie was under the strictest orders from Stephanie that any relationship with Harry should not be visible to the outside world. After all, the word on the street was still that Evie was stepping out with Jeremy Pinewood thanks to the film teaser on the Net. Even though neither Evie nor Jeremy had confirmed the coupling, the fact they hadn't denied it had only managed to fan the flames. Stephanie had been adamant on the phone to Evie that the worldwide gossip-fest surrounding them was a hopefully lucrative money-spinner in the run up to the major movie awards season.

'It's wonderful news, darling!' she'd oozed down the phone. 'The film company obviously realise how good you two would be together. Your fan bases together are simply colossal. I've already had *Variety*, *W* and *Rolling Stone* on the phone wanting cover shoots with you both.'

But none of it mattered to Evie. She thought she'd fallen for Nush's brother, but the last 24 hours were beginning to prove otherwise. Harry's confidence-boosting passion for her had come along at just the right time, but now it seemed to be dissipating quicker than Salzburg's morning mist.

What had added to Evie's brain strain was the fact that since their heart-to-heart on set Jeremy had suddenly started texting her completely out of the blue. One text had become two and suddenly she was faced with a flotilla of text flirtations. That's what they were. But why now? Already this morning she'd had 'How's my lovely leading lady today?' and 'Movie-making's not the same without you… let's get together soon'.

Evie would have loved to have been able to ignore them with one press of a delete button, but something in her mind urged her to store them. To pore over them to try and decipher their true meaning. The fact of the matter was that she liked the idea that maybe Jeremy wasn't such an arrogant prick after all. Maybe there was the heart of a true gentleman beating away underneath that pumped-up flesh.

The sound of Harry and his friends laughing raucously bumped Evie from her reverie. She had no idea what they were laughing about, and cared even less. She couldn't even tell if Harry was looking at her from behind his mirrored Oakley sunglasses. Impatient for some attention, she reached out to touch his leg under the table.

'I was thinking we could take a trip up to the castle today, just you and I.' Having never been to Salzburg before, Evie was keen to visit the 11th century fortress which dominated Salzburg's skyline.

'Love to babe, but no can do. The gang and I need to get some new clobber for the slopes before heading to Seefeld. Can't be seen in last season's snow gear, eh guys?' He laughed, causing a contagious wave of mirth among his entourage. Evie felt more alone than ever.

'Why don't you get the funicular up to the castle yourself and we'll meet back here this evening for dinner.' With that, his conversation returned back to his companions.

For Evie, it was the final straw. Pushing back her chair with a loud scrape and shaking with wrath, she tossed some Euros onto the table and turned to walk back into the bar to catch the lift down to their suite. As she did so, she could hear Harry's voice crowing to the others. 'God, these arty types get a bit temperamental, eh?' prompting more hilarity from his flock of human sheep. She could still hear their mocking tones as the lift door closed behind her.

———

Safe inside their hotel suite, Evie stared at herself in the mirror and screamed, venting her rage. It made her feel better. The day was still young and for once Evie's time was completely her own. It was one of the few moments in the life of a movie star where she could damn well do as she pleased. Maybe the castle would be a good idea after all. Picking up the guide map she'd bought at the airport, Evie studied what Salzburg had to offer. The castle looked good but something much more appealing had caught her eye. Of course, that's why she knew the name of Salzburg – it was the setting for *The Sound of Music*. In her rush to cross Europe to be with Harry she hadn't even thought about the city's movie connection.

As an aspiring actress, Evie had spent every waking hour as a child transfixed to the TV revelling in the wondrous musicals that she longed to appear in one day. *Chitty Chitty Bang Bang, Carousel, Meet Me in St Louis, The Wizard of Oz* and, of course, the best of them all, *The Sound of Music*. Just the thought of Julie Andrews Do-Re-Me-ing her way up and down the steps with the Von Trapp children on either side made her smile. As far as Harry was concerned, for today it was a case of *So long, farewell, auf wiedersehen, adieu…*

According to the guide, the famed movie steps were just around the corner from the hotel in the Mirabell Gardens. She could be there within minutes.

As Evie entered into the gardens between the two muscle-bound classical statues forming an arch at its entrance, she felt as she had as a child on Christmas Day watching the opening scenes of the film as the novice nun Maria weaves her way across the lush fresh green hills before bursting into song. It wasn't just the hills that were alive, Evie's senses of nostalgia and innocence were too. Everywhere she looked there was a sweet souvenir of the film, reminding her of how its musical magic used to draw her into a serenaded world a million edelweiss-covered miles away from her horribly lonely home life at Hadleigh Hall.

Placed in the middle of the Baroque gardens stood a fountain with a statue of Pegasus, the winged horse, at its centre. It was around this that the Von Trapp children had marched their musical way. It was one of Evie's favourite scenes. As a young girl, she had stomped around in front of the television pretending to be Gretl, the youngest and most cherubic of the Von Trapp singers.

Then came the steps. Evie greeted them like she would an old friend, with a wide, cheek-curling smile. If it was possible for inanimate objects to fill a person with affection, then the steps surely did. Oblivious to the tourists milling around her, she jumped back and forth, up and down the steps, just as Maria had done in the movie. Taking her mobile phone from her bag, she directed the lens of the onboard camera at herself as she held out the phone at arm's length. Halfway up the steps, opening her mouth wide, as if mock singing, she took her photo.

Uploading the photo to a message she added the words 'To my favourite things – take a look at do-re-me in Salzburg'. Scrolling to Regan and Nush in her contacts book she added them as recipients and pressed send. *That should raise a giggle,* she thought to herself.

Just as she was placing her phone back into her bag, it beeped signalling the arrival of a message. Thinking it was probably one of the girls, she clicked on it without looking. It was from Jeremy and as she read it, her mind went blank. Unsure of what to feel, she read it over and over again. 'Hey Evie, I miss you and I think you miss me too.'

CHAPTER 19

As Nush sat on her own waiting for a detective to arrive at her flat, Evie's daft phone message had been as welcome as a drop of golden sun in the murky quagmire of her life. It was the only thing so far that day that had made her crack so much as a vague smile.

With no love life to speak of since her pitiful episode with Ashley, and a constant barrage of professional beatings from her father about Clarissa's showbiz scoop making her feel more worthless than ever, her existence had gone from high-end glitz and glamour to abject failure. As tragic as it all seemed at the time, it all now appeared trite alongside the horrific doom-laden death threat that had literally landed in her life the night before.

Thankfully Regan had stayed the night with her, but she'd had to leave at the crack of dawn for a day's filming. They'd both hardly slept as they'd been up most of the night answering the local police station's questions and organising for a glazier to do some makeshift repairs on the reception room window.

The police had asked all the typical questions but a shaken-up Nush was unable to make any sense of the situation.

'Have you got any enemies, Miss Silvers?' enquired the policeman who'd arrived on the scene minutes after Regan's frantic call.

'That is like asking Cher if she's ever been under the knife!' Nush had snapped, her patience stretched to breaking point. 'Of course I have countless enemies. I slag off people in the national press every bloody day. I'm the bitch who has to try and ruin lives, remember?'

The policeman obviously didn't, clueless about Nush's profession. He kept eyeing the glass of wine clutched in Nush's right hand, the bottle in the vice-like grip of her left. She had not stopped drinking since his arrival.

'So, Miss, is there anyone in particular who springs to mind who you have… er, *slagged off* recently?'

'Take your pick.' Nush started to reel off a list of likely candidates. 'The footballer with the super injunction, the pop diva with a secret lesbian lover, the reality show judge spending his millions on rent boys… need I go on, officer?' Nush was shivering both with rage and the coolness of the night air blowing in through the shattered window. She poured herself another glass of wine.

'Can I say something, too?' invited Regan, who had spent the last thirty minutes cleaning the glass from the carpeted floor. She told the officer about Anselina's prediction but, unsurprisingly, her story was met with an air of ridicule from the officer. Regan could sense his disbelief. 'You may think it sounds like mumbo-jumbo, officer, but how do we know the message was meant for Anoushka? It could have been for me, I could have been followed here tonight.'

It was true, despite being thrown through the window at Nush's flat, the note could have been intended for either or both of them.

Having concluded his questioning, the officer had promised that a detective would be round the next morning. As Regan and Nush had finally climbed into Nush's bed together, preferring not to be alone after their fright, an exhausted Regan had fallen into a deep sleep immediately. But Nush's brain kept turning over and over, fixated on the figure they'd seen running away from the house. *Who was the threat aimed at? Was it just an idle threat or was the person behind it as psychotic as the note suggested? Would they try and come back?*

Nush finished another bottle of wine before finally crashing out.

———

Throwing her mobile onto the sofa as a knock sounded at the door, Nush braced herself for another round of questioning. Her brain still felt fuzzy from the wine. Opening the door, she came face to face with a ruddy-faced man with a mop of dark shiny hair tumbling down across his forehead. He looked efficient yet friendly. She guessed from his youthful appearance that he wasn't much older than she was.

'Ms Silvers, my name is DS Oliver Cole. I'm here about the incident last night, may I come in?'

'Be my guest. I want you to find the crazed son of a bitch who did this.'

DS Cole invited Nush to recount the events leading up to the brick coming through the window, taking notes as he did so. He couldn't conceal a smirk when Nush mentioned Anselina's prediction to Regan. 'I'm sure that is no more than a coincidence, Miss, but we will be questioning Ms Phoenix too.'

'What about the brick and the note?' questioned Nush. 'Were there any fingerprints on it? The officer took it away last night and said you'd be testing it.'

'We drew a blank on that one, I'm afraid. The only prints on it seem to be from yourself and Ms Phoenix. Whoever threw it was wearing gloves when they did so.'

'Well they certainly seemed pretty wrapped up as they ran off,' replied Nush. 'I know this country's summers aren't exactly tropical but whoever it was certainly seemed to be overly dressed. It was like the person was wearing a thick hooded coat.'

'Did you get a good look at all? Could you say what colour the coat was? How tall the person might be?'

'Not a chance, he or she was virtually out of sight by the time Regan and I got to the window. If we'd have seen them closer to us then maybe, but it just looked like a dark smudge in the distance.'

'Do you have closed-circuit television? This kind of complex normally does.'

'Oh my God, of course, there's a CCDP camera up on the roof. My father made me have it fitted after a series of robberies around this area last year. It's some fancy megapixel digital one. Whoever threw the brick is bound to be on there and all the images the camera takes can be looked at through my PC!'

Rushing to her computer, Nush clicked on the photography desktop icon controlling the camera. 'It all works on some kind of time delay if I remember rightly. If I can get it to work, then I should be able to rewind back to last night and see if we can detect anything.'

A colour image of the area in front of Nush's apartment opened onto the screen. A numeric readout at the top gave the current time.

'You said the brick came through the window around about half ten last night. Can you get it to go back that far?'

Rolling the mouse over the 'rewind' button, Nush watched as the images time-reversed. DS Cole watched over her shoulder, seeing his arrival at the apartment. Then came snatched movement from Nush's neighbours, footage of Regan leaving in the early morning light, then the image got darker as night fell across the screen. Nush could feel her heart beating in her chest. 'Right, it should be around here…'

Suddenly it appeared. A dark shapeless figure loomed into vision. The figure was wearing a hooded top far too large for their size. It worked as a perfect disguise against the angle of the camera. With each click of the PC mouse, the figure reversed towards the house. Finally an image appeared where the figure looked upwards as they threw the brick at the window. As they did so, the movement of hurtling the brick caused the hood of their coat to fall away from their head. It was the perfect moment for the camera to capture their identity.

The photo might not have been crystal clear but Nush was in no doubt as to who the villain was. Looking DS Cole straight in the eyes, she coughed up the words, unable to take in what she was seeing on the screen. 'I don't bloody believe it...'

CHAPTER 20

At any one moment in time, Los Angeles International Airport will always be full of showbiz names. Which is why no-one was surprised to see Jeremy Pinewood walking along one of its nine terminals, two bodyguards symmetrically placed either side of him. Another day, another megastar.

Jeremy felt good to be back in the States, his work on *The Bouquet Catcher* in the can. Being back in LA gave him the chance to really work out his emotions for Evie. Okay, so she hadn't actually agreed to be with him as yet, but who could possibly resist his mesmerising charms once he'd whipped up a typhoon of temptation. He had once been described by a journalist as a 'sexual lumberjack when it came to felling women' and it was a tag he loved to believe.

Having given the obligatory heart-throb smile to a bank of photographers, Jeremy sank into the comfort of his limousine. He was ready to head home, to his retreat in trendy Beachwood Canyon in the Hollywood Hills. A little bit of bliss where he could close the doors and truly be himself.

Checking for messages from Evie as he did so - none so far – Jeremy dialled his agent. 'I'm back in the country. What gives? Are David Letterman, Clarissa Thornton, Jay Leno and Ellen fighting over me yet?'

Jeremy's agent laughed down the phone. 'Yes… Letterman and Co do want you, but they would rather you and Evie together. But she's in Austria right now with some friends of hers. Her gobby agent's been on the phone to me non-stop about the joys of you two working together. I have to say it would be rather fantastic if your doubtless charm had won her over. There's no chance of you two getting together for real is there… like soon?'

Jeremy could sense urgency in his agent's voice. 'Why the rush? The film won't be out for months and even if Evie's a tougher nut to crack than most women out there, she'll still be mine come premiere night.'

Jeremy's agent continued, laughing at his client's bravado. 'I've had the film company on to me today. The rushes for *Bouquet* look great, the buzz is immense and a potted version of the film is being put together at breakneck speed for an airing at the Venice Film Festival. They want both you and Evie in attendance, and they would love you there as a couple. They want the world to see what they saw with you guys on set.'

'But Venice is only a few weeks away. I'd love to go, but what if Evie won't do it?'

'You gotta be kidding me. With an agent like Stephanie Love firing orders at her like ammunition, she'll be there. Working that Venetian red carpet with you on her arm will steal the thunder from any other film there.'

Snapping his phone shut, the words of his agent kept swirling around Jeremy's mind. This movie could be the biggest of his career so far. His actor's instinct told him that both his and Evie's work on the film and the on-screen chemistry between them was on a par with many of his favourite rom-coms – *When Harry Met Sally*, *Sleepless In Seattle*, *Four Weddings*, maybe even as good as his ultimate favourites, the wholesome Doris Day and the ruggedly chiselled Rock Hudson in their movies together back in the 50s and 60s. Oh yes, if this all worked out as planned, Evie and Jeremy could be the Doris and Rock for a new generation. Teaming up with Evie could turn out to be the best move of his career. And she was an absolute head-turner in the looks department. It was win-win.

High up in the Hollywood Hills, it wasn't long before the wrought iron gates of Jeremy's LA home swung open. Stepping from his Limo, Jeremy opened the front door and headed straight for the outdoor rooftop patio at the top of the house. It was always his first port of call after a long journey as it housed his spa tub. The mass of hot bubbles popping against his skin seemed to unlock every knotted joint in his body, leaving them fluid and stress-free. His maid, Tasmina, always prepared it for him once she knew that he was back in the country and heading home.

Having plucked a beer from his kitchen fridge Jeremy discarded his clothes as he moved towards the patio. He admired his naked reflection in the glass of the patio doors as he slid them open. Overcome with narcissism he had to admit that his gym-pumped body and immaculate features were a combination that virtually nobody could resist. He smiled as he thought of Evie, powerless to his charms. The thought tickled him. She was a beautiful woman and any man, especially him, would be pleased to have her on his arm.

The plumes of steam rising from the effervescence of the bubbling tub soothed his flesh. Draining his beer, he stepped into the water, feeling the delicious heat of it seep into every pore.

Looking out at the nirvana of eucalyptus and pine trees surrounding the patio, Jeremy thought that life was good, but he couldn't help feel that it was about to become perfect.

CHAPTER 21

Seeing the face of Mae-Ling Ch'en staring up at her from her PC, hatred etched across her features as she threw the brick, had left Nush shell-shocked. She'd always been aware of the make-up artist's reputation for having the odd screw loose, but even Nush had been amazed at the lengths that Mae-Ling had gone to in the hunt for revenge.

Once DS Cole had left, promising that Mae-Ling would be taken in for questioning that day, Nush had done what she always did first at a moment of crisis… reached for a bottle. A glass of wine, despite it still being early afternoon, had made her feel more in control of the situation, and if she was honest, more in control of her life.

DS Cole had asked Nush not to mention their discovery until Mae-Ling was safely in custody, but the feeling of the wine flowing through her veins convinced her to phone both Regan and Evie. Regan would be wondering if the brick and note had been meant for her and Evie would be floored by the news that the woman who'd been applying her make up for the last few weeks was nothing short of a psycho.

Regan's phone had clicked straight through to the messaging system. She must have been filming. Next up she tried Evie. No-one answered. *Doubtless she's up to no good with brother Harry in Salzburg,* thought Nush. The thought of Evie wasting her time with Harry still left Nush with a nasty taste in her mouth. She couldn't help it. *He may be my little brother, but he's still a little shit. Why was Evie bothering with him? How naive could you be?*

Desperate to speak to Evie to tell her the news about Mae-Ling, Nush tried Harry's mobile. Maybe she could get through to Evie that way.

Harry's voice answered, 'Yo, sis'. Nush could hardly hear him as loud music played in the background. She could hear the sound of female voices. She didn't recognise any of them as Evie's.

'Listen Harry, is Evie there? I need to speak to her urgently.'

Harry's reply was slurred and distracted. 'Nope, not here right now. She's missing a good party. We're all having fun...' His voice trailed off as girlish laughter sounded in the background.

Concerned at what she'd interrupted, Nush persevered with the conversation. 'Are you drunk, Harry? Who's that with you? Look, will you tell Evie I rang?' She was starting to get annoyed.

'I'm a little high, I guess,' giggled Harry down the phone. 'Some of the gang are here. Speak later, yeah? Bye...'

Nush stayed on the phone, waiting for the line to go dead. It didn't. She was just about to click the cancel button on her phone when she became aware that she could still hear Harry's voice in the receiver. The loud music faded, obviously between tracks on Harry's iPod. The voices got clearer.

'C'mon girls, I wanna fuck while I'm still buzzing.' From the moans of pleasure that followed from Harry and the two females at the other end of the phone, you didn't need to have the investigative savvy of Miss Marple to work out what was going on. Harry was nuts-deep in some piece of trash behind Evie's back. Unable to bear listening to any more, Nush pressed cancel.

Staring into the bathroom mirror of her Austrian hotel suite, Evie could still see her disgust at Harry written across her tear-stained face. It was ponderous and painful.

Evie's mind was a storm of confusion as to just how quickly Harry's attitude towards her seemed to have performed a complete U-turn. He had shattered their union as easily as a rioter shatters a shop window.

After the frothy innocence of her day discovering her inner Maria Von Trapp, Evie had returned to the hotel suite she shared with Harry ready to forgive him for his earlier rudeness. She had decided that youth was to blame and that he was simply showing off in front of his band of impressionable playboys and simpering society girls.

It was the society girls she'd heard first, their moans emanating from the other side of their suite door as she went to slip her key card into it. You didn't need to be a pornographer to recognise the cause of the pleasurable sighs.

Their cries of carnality mixed with Harry's, forming a cocktail that left no doubt in Evie's mind as to what was happening. Gingerly she opened the door a fraction and peered inside. Three naked bodies entwined on the bed. From the spaced out looks on the faces of all three it was obvious that they were high. Empty beer bottles littered the floor around the bed, adding to the debauched scene.

Forbidding herself to cry, Evie shut the door again and walked to the rooftop bar and ordered herself a drink. When she returned to her suite an hour or so later and slowly pushed open the door again, the two girls had gone.

She'd found Harry half-dressed, stretched out on his back on their hotel bed, eyes shut and mouth open, breathing heavily. It was a pitiful, foolish sight.

Evie walked to the bathroom looking out of the window at Salzburg old town below. The distance between her and Harry suddenly seemed as wide as one of the mountainous valleys on the horizon. It was only when she had locked the bathroom door behind her that she allowed herself to cry. Another romance had ended in heartache and tears…

CHAPTER 22

In theory it should have been a good time for both Montana and Regan Phoenix. The sales figures for Montana's *Babylon* perfume had come through and she was outselling the likes of Lopez and SJP by two-to-one.

But no-one wanted to talk about that, every interviewer in the world just wanted to question her about her outburst concerning Regan. Montana only had herself to blame. After years in the business she should have known that her professional guard should never be dropped, especially when stood in front of reporters like Clarissa Thornton. But Grace's spiteful niggling at Montana had worked and before she knew it, her dislike for her own daughter had been splashed all over the TV. What really made her blood boil was that the story had been portrayed in a totally one-sided manner, turning trashy Grace Laszlo into a victim. Brad had tried to contact Clarissa about how the recording had been doctored, but his calls had remained unanswered.

———

On the surface, life should have been pretty good for Regan too. The first episode of *From Wild Child to Rothschild* had eclipsed American TV, with viewing figures of 30 million. It was a figure that most debut shows could only dream of.

In the UK, the figures had been equally as impressive with 9.2 million viewers tuning in. The show had received a 36.5 per cent audience share. Producer Leo had been deliriously happy when he heard the news, presenting both women with Tiffany bracelets as a thank you. But, just like her mother, the appetising wealth of media success Regan was currently immersed in was being overshadowed by gloomy greyness.

Regan was desperate to get to the bottom of the mystery of the photo. She'd left messages with Montana hoping to ask her about Lawrence Silvers, but she'd met with a wall of silence. To add to her woes, the episode with the note and Anselina's prediction were still sending a shudder of chills through Regan's bones.

She knew that it was affecting her concentration during the second week of *Wild Child*. Week two of the show was supposed to highlight Regan's organisation skills as a sharp business woman. Both she and Grace were put under the watchful eye of top PR guru Helena Fishburn. Helena was huge in her field, her list of successes including parties for London Fashion Week and the MTV Music Awards.

The day had started with Helena informing the girls that they would both have to organise a charity celebrity auction. As it stood, it was a ridiculously hard thing to orchestrate and execute given weeks of planning, but both Regan and Grace were informed by Helena that the auction would take place that night at fashionable London nightspot, Chinawhite. The winner would be the woman who made the most money for charity.

Grace rose to the challenge straight away, phoning stars from the world of music to turn up at short notice and bid on a range of items mostly from her own wardrobe. To quote her, they were either people she'd 'sung with or slept with'. Regan had the feeling she wasn't joking.

Grace had chosen to call her event the 'Goodbye to Grace' auction. Her idea was that she would auction off all of the clothes, shoes, bags, jewellery and underwear she had with her in a hope of saying goodbye to the *slutty* old Grace portrayed in the press. By the end of the evening she would be a new woman. Helena had loved the idea.

Regan was stumped. Grace seemed to have a network of contacts to ask favours from. Who did Regan know? Evie was out of the country, Nush was dealing with the break in and she considered Montana public enemy number one, so the three top names on her list were out of the question straight away.

Years of party-going were highly useful for making one night fair-weather friends, but people she could really rely on in a time of need seemed to be few and far between. Regan had to face the fact that, besides Evie and Nush, her life was one long list of ex-shags, anorexic 'It' Girls and models immersed in the world of heroin chic. Plus there was just the question of what to auction…

The auction was due to start in less than three hours and Grace had already left to pick up the Alberta Ferretti dress she had blagged for the evening's event. Regan hadn't even thought about her outfit. Her levels of concentration were beyond low. She needed an idea, a plan to see her through to hopeful victory. As time ticked away, a vague notion started to form in her mind.

———

The mass of cameras outside Chinawhite were split into two definite teams. There were the TV cameras filming for the show itself and then three rows of paparazzi photographers hoping to catch the perfect celebrity moment.

So far, a flurry of media names had been snapped posing their way into the venue. The biggest cheer had been for rapper Daddy O, still plugging his way across the UK media. Invited there by Grace, it appeared that he was a sexual conquest that both she and Regan had in common. Puffing on a cigar and followed by two buxom beauties wearing faux-fur coats and bi-kinis, it was a bling spectacle of 50 Cent proportions.

A Limousine pulled up outside the club. The cloud of smoke from another cigar rose into the air as the rear door opened, and out stepped Lawrence Silvers. Alongside him, wearing a skirt not much wider than a belt, a baby T and a fur shrug over her shoulders, was Sadie.

It wasn't that often the two of them ventured out for the night, but tonight was special. This was big exposure and Law-rence had his reasons for being there. Sadie, as ever, just lapped up the attention, twirling and pouting for the waiting crowds and photographers.

Regan's heart was in her mouth as her car pulled up outside the London hotspot. She was used to stumbling into and out of clubs high on coke and drunk on alcohol, but tonight was all about her. She had a job to do and it started from the moment she stepped onto the red carpet.

Stroking the fabric of the monochrome Ashley Isham dress she'd picked up at the designer's trendy London boutique, Regan took a deep breath and stepped from the car. Posing for the pho-tographers and smiling into the TV lenses, she said with confi-dence and poise, 'Are you ready to make some money, guys? I'm hoping that all my esteemed guests have deep pockets tonight. There's a heck of a prize up for grabs.' Running her tongue along her upper teeth she winked coquettishly into the lens and sa-shayed into the venue. 'Textbook entrance even if I say so my-self,' muttered Regan under her breath. 'Follow that Grace.'

Grace Laszlo had been planning her arrival all afternoon. This was one night where there was only one possible outcome in her mind and that was a victory.

She'd toyed with the idea of hiring some swanky car for the night, but seeing as her theme of 'Goodbye To Grace' had gone down so well with Helena and the team working on the show, she'd decided to layer on her transition from tramp to vamp with a trowel.

Having hired an Italian sedan chair for the evening, she'd seated herself in it just around the corner from the club. The front and back of the lavishly decorated sedan were being supported by four oiled male models, bodies like extras from *Spartacus*, naked except for silver skin-tight shorts and shiny silver boots. They held the chair, with Grace inside it, at shoulder height and marched their way gladiator-like round the corner and to the club. Another male model, equally sculpted from pure muscle, walked in front of them, a huge stereo system perched on his shoulders. The music blasting out from it was one of Sexalicious's biggest hits.

Sticking her head out of the sedan window as the models stopped outside the club, a flawlessly made-up Grace beamed her perfect-white smile to the crowd. 'Good evening London, may I present the former Grace Laszlo.' With that, she stepped from the sedan. Wearing what amounted to little more than Daisy Duke buttock-skimming hot-pants and sequinned strips of fabric tied around her breasts, Grace looked every inch the trashy pop star. 'Take a look because tonight is the night that the Grace Laszlo you see before you disappears for good. I shall be auctioning off all my Sexalicious belongings to the highest bidders. We're talking about pieces of music history here. The tops, the bottoms, the jewellery and even the underwear I threw off for a certain notorious backstage epic I'm sure all my internet fans will remember.'

The mention of her coke-snorting episode bought a cheer from the crowd. 'They're all coming out for the last time, because tonight I'm turning my trash into cash for charity. Boys, lead the way… it's time to say *Goodbye to Grace*.'

The inside of the club was heaving with people. Grace, Regan and Helena Fishburn were huddled backstage expectantly. Leo fluttered around dishing out orders. Regan had hardly taken her eyes off him since he'd entered the club. Decked out in head to toe Ben Sherman, he looked a true slice of retro style and the closer she worked with Leo, the closer she wanted to get. *Maybe tonight could be the night to work the Regan magic*, she mused to herself.

The lights dimmed and a hushed wave of anticipation spread across the crowd. The *Wild Child* theme tune gushed from the club's sound system and a voice boomed forth. 'Ladies and gentlemen, welcome to the *From Wild Child to Rothschild* celebrity auction. Will you please put your hands together for your host, PR to the stars, Miss Helena Fishburn.'

Taking her place on the stage, Helena, a vision of efficiency in her Chanel trouser suit, ran through her opening speech. Grace and Regan hovered in the wings. *Please let this work*, Regan begged, uncertain how the evening was going to pan out.

Helena ended her speech, 'So, let's welcome the lady who is first up to make you lovely people splash the cash, Ms Grace Laszlo!'

Walking onto the stage, dragging a rail of clothes behind her, came Grace. The shorts and hoochie sequinned top she'd worn earlier had been replaced by the Alberta Ferretti masterpiece she had borrowed for the night, drawing wolf-whistles from the crowd.

Grace began her auction. Regan could only watch in wonderment as hands flew into the air for lot after lot. Keen to be seen on such an international scale, it wasn't a night for shrinking violets.

As well as the gathered celebrities bidding for Grace's brassy back catalogue, phone bids were placed from around the world.

The Hard Rock Hotel in Las Vegas bagged an outfit Grace had worn on her first Sexalicious album cover for a cool £75,000.

The time came for Grace's last lot of the evening. Her current total stood at £160,000 but she was expecting big money for her ultimate item.

'I'm nearly at an end, and I feel honoured that so much money has been raised. As many of you know, I have been savaged by the world's press over the last few months, admittedly due to my own stupidity, but this show is proving to me that no matter what people, or certain *aging soap stars*, have said about me in the past, I can now become someone worthy of respect.' At the mention of the aging soap star, Grace threw a glance offstage to where Regan was standing and blew a puckered kiss. Regan, knowing the cameras were constantly on her, awkwardly blew one back.

Grace ventured on. 'Tonight is the night that I shed all of that negativity. I am not ashamed of anything I have done, but certain video footage recently gained me press for all the wrong reasons. It would be easy for me to attempt 'a Paris' and market the DVD for my own gains, but I would rather that something good and wholesome can come from the entire sorry affair. It is my wish that charity should be the victors and not I. So, I give you the panties I threw off at that time… as famed as the late Michael Jackson's white glove and Madonna's Gaultier bra. A sexy piece of pop culture history. Everybody… what am I bid?'

As Grace held up the thin wisp of lacy material that comprised her final lot, Regan had to admit that Grace's speech was worthy of an actress of Evie's standards. Her sincerity, genuine or not, had gone into overdrive.

A sea of hands shot into the air, shouting bids. Four figure bids from the D-listers were soon eclipsed by more meaty amounts. After a constant metronome of ever-increasing bids between the two parties, the eventual winner was the Las Vegas hotel with a dazzling bid of £90,000. Grace was ecstatic. Her total for the evening was a cool quarter of a million for charity.

'Thank you everyone. I'll see you all at the bar, but not before introducing my new best friend… the wonderful Regan Phoenix.'

Taking a deep breath, Regan walked centre stage. 'Wow, how do you follow a girl who's just shown the world her knickers?' A ripple of polite laughter circled round the club.

'My auction is called *Making Headlines*, something that all of us here seem to do for either the right or wrong reasons. Both Grace and I have a pretty shambolic reputation with the press. So, I thought that I'd like to give everyone the chance to make their own headlines with a once-in-a-lifetime prize. May I introduce to you all, one of my best friends, and a lady who has never written bad things about me… yet! I'm not sure if the rest of you can say the same. From *The Daily Staple* it's the fabulous Miss Anoushka Silvers.'

A cocktail of cheers and boos rose from the crowd. Lawrence and Sadie cheered and whooped as Nush sauntered up to Regan and held her hand tight. It had been less than 24 hours since the brick incident and they were both still shaken up about what had happened. Nush had explained that it was Mae-Ling who was to blame when Regan had phoned her that afternoon.

It was only when Nush had finished filling Regan in about Mae-Ling that Regan had proposed her idea for the auction, an idea that Nush was to now relay onto the crowd. Having steadied herself with a hefty drink before taking to the stage, she began to speak.

'Hello everyone. Yes, I expected boos – most of you have featured in my *Staple* column over the past few years, and I'm the bitch you all love to hate. For what it's worth, I feel guilty as charged. But, first off, check out tomorrow's papers, where you'll see that you're not the only ones who make headlines.' Her reference was to the headlines that would tell of Mae-Ling's attack in the tabloids the next morning. 'And, secondly, I'm offering you my job.'

A whisper of thrilled expectation passed over the crowd. 'That's right, you could be *Making Headlines* for charity tonight. My father, and owner of *The Daily Staple*, Lawrence Silvers, who's here with us this evening, would like to offer you the chance to replace me for the day. You can write my column and rename it as your own. As long as what you write gets past our lawyers, then the dirty, drunken, seedy celebrity world is your oyster. I'm sure there are lots of you here with products to promote and axes to grind, so all we need now is to see who's got the pounds to get yourself in print. Over to you, Regan…'

The warm omen of a successful night spread across Regan's body. She'd had no notion of whether the idea was even possible when she'd phoned Nush earlier in the day, but thanks to Lawrence giving it the green light, she was overjoyed that just one lot could hopefully win the second week of the show for her. Lawrence was naturally thrilled that *The Daily Staple,* and more so, his kind offer, would be getting huge free exposure both sides of the Atlantic.

'Okay everyone,' began Regan. 'Who are the budding journalists out there? Can we start the bidding at £20,000?'

Just as Grace's panties had prompted minutes before, a wave of bids crashed towards Regan and Nush. Keen to gain what was pretty much a free page of press for themselves in a national newspaper, the bidding got higher and higher. The cornucopia of celebrities out for the evening caused the amount to escalate. Glamour models wanting to promote their lingerie, reality show no-hopers hoping to extend their fleeting fifteen minutes of fame, celebrity chefs hoping to rustle up interest in their next cookbook. Everyone wanted to bid.

The bids started to slow as they reached £180,000. Regan started to panic, willing the bidding to get a little higher and surpass Grace's £250,000. Grace's invitees for the night had gone strangely quiet, obviously keen that it should be their friend who would win the night's action.

Looking around the crowd, one person shot a hand into the air. 'I'll bid £250,000!' It was Sadie Silvers. A loud intake of breath filled the club.

Lawrence nearly choked on the beer he was quaffing as Sadie's voice chirped across the club. The last thing he wanted to do was pay for his own press. The whole idea was to get someone else to cough up for charity and Lawrence still looks the good guy. He grabbed Sadie's arm roughly and pinched her skin, causing her to wince. 'What the fuck are you doing?' he spat between gritted teeth.

Onstage, Nush tried unsuccessfully to suppress a smile. *Go on Sadie, way to go! Spend the old man's money.*

'A fantastic bid there from Sadie Silvers,' said Regan, elated that there was now no way she could lose the challenge. 'Do I have any advance on £250,000?' She was pretty much sure that she wouldn't. 'Going once, going twice…'

It was then that another voice sounded from the back of the room. 'I'll bid £260,000 to make the headlines.' Everyone turned to see where the voice was coming from. Stood there, grinning from ear to ear, was Clarissa Thornton.

Nush stopped smiling immediately, as did Grace, who was watching from the wings. Regan could only stand and stare.

CHAPTER 23

The front page headline of *The Daily Staple* read *MAE-LING ARRESTED FOR ATTACK ON GOSSIP QUEEN*. The story made interesting reading. But to Ashley Erridge, as he read the paper at his Hackney apartment, the story was a nightmare. Someone, it appeared, had set out to kill his beloved Nush. Even if they hadn't gone through with it, the threat was there, and who knows what would have happened if the police hadn't pounced on Mae-Ling.

Running his finger over Anoushka's face in the photo as he read the story, Ashley couldn't help but think how lucky both he and Anoushka were.

Ashley had thought about nothing else since their brief interlude at Harry's party. Finally Nush had come to him to share her woes.

He knew that the night at Kingsbury had been the moment he had been waiting for his whole life. To finally get within tasting distance of how life with her might be. He was sure that night was just the start of things to come. She'd felt rejection from her own family, the hollow feeling of being an outsider. She'd said they were kindred spirits. If that wasn't an invitation for them to be together, then Ashley didn't know what was.

All of those school holidays he'd spent when he was younger watching Anoushka from afar. Tagging along with his dad and brother for visits to Kingsbury. Ashley had thought that he and

Anoushka could never be as one, that she wasn't interested. But the party had proven she was. He was the knight in shining armour to her damsel in distress. There were hundreds of people at the party, but Anoushka had chosen him.

CHAPTER 24

Harry had still been comatose on their hotel bed as Evie packed her belongings and left Salzburg. Evie wanted Harry out of her life. Where was the polite young man she'd naively fallen for?

As she hailed a cab she considered her options. Where exactly was she going? She'd been planning to spend the next week or so with Harry, living a winter wonderland life of Alpine cabins and après ski.

'Airport, please,' Evie instructed the cab driver, knowing that the one thing she definitely wanted was to be as far away from Harry as possible.

In times of need, time to call the Trinity, to see what the girls are up to, mused Evie. *They'll get me through this*. Reaching for her phone, Evie scrolled through the names in her contact book. Seeing Jeremy's name flash past the screen made her recollect his message from earlier. *I will never understand men*. Evie's head pounded. It was best to just forget about it. She had enough to think about. *How had things become so rotten so quickly? What had happened to old school romance? Was it too much to ask for a slow but sure affair to remember for all the right reasons?* At least Jeremy's recent advances seemed suave and gallant.

Pressing the call button for Nush, she heard the phone click straight through to Nush's messaging service. 'Hi Nush, it's Evie. Need to speak to you about Harry. Let's just say he's still in Austria and in a few hours I don't intend to be. Seems you were right…' Hanging up, Evie scrolled down to Regan's name. Again it went straight through to answering machine.

Staring at the Austrian countryside whizzing past her cab window, Evie felt as cold as the snow-capped mountains around her. The girls were busy, Harry was history and thoughts of Jeremy just left her perplexed. Wallowing in her own emotions, the sound of her phone ringing snapped her back from her thoughts. *Saved by the bell, please be the girls.*

It wasn't. It was Stephanie calling from the States. Her voice exploded down the phone before Evie could even say a word. 'Listen, honey, I know you're probably halfway up some godforsaken mountain right now, kitted out in designer salopettes, but I just thought I'd better fill you in on what everyone's talking about. It's all about you, you, you, sweetness.'

'Really, what are they saying…?'

'Well you, my angel, are off to the Venice Film Festival in a few weeks' time, and I'd very much love it if you and Jeremy could put on a united front for it.' Steph explained that *The Bouquet Catcher* would be a main focus of the festival due to the film company rushing its release. 'I've cleared your diary, sweetie, you're going to be there, and just think of all the positive press that you and Mr Dreamboat could bring in the run up to the Oscar announcements. With *The Bouquet Catcher* going into cinemas before Christmas and with you hopefully getting an Oscar nod for *Pengelly Manor* come New Year, the next twelve months could be orgasmic, darling. Talking of orgasms, how goes it on that front?'

Her spirit elevated by Steph's buoyant nature and dollar sign exuberance, Evie filled her in on the situation with Jeremy and her recent departure from Harry. She spared her the details, but made it clear to Steph that she and Harry were definitely over and she was heading to the airport. Steph couldn't have been more pleased.

'Darling, the man was no good for you anyway. You need a real gent the whole world's bloody heard of, not the snotty-nosed brother of one of your ridiculous friends. A celebrity A-list coupling is the perfect vehicle for huge megabuck success. Look at Brad and Angelina darling… or, more to the point, Brad and Jennifer Aniston back in the day. Did anybody really care about her once they split up? I don't think so. Reduced to acting with flea-bitten hounds! What about Reese Witherspoon and Ryan Philippe? Fabulous together, but when they fell apart, he dropped off the Hollywood radar. Who was Katie Holmes pre-Tom apart from some teen star from a teenage TV show? Him jumping up and down on Oprah's sofa raving about her like a freak did her the world of bloody good. All goes back to the days of Taylor and Burton of course. Together they were the sexiest *force majeure* in the world. You and Jeremy could be next.'

Evie felt amused at Steph's notion that Evie's life would be perfect overnight if she teamed up with Jeremy. *Was it the thought of Jeremy's sudden courteous courtship lifting her spirits?* She still wasn't sure. 'I'll think about it, I've told you… I'm off men!'

'What you need is a little *you*-time darling? I'm on the Net now. Take a plane to Zurich from Salzburg, change there and head to LA. You could be here by tomorrow. I'll book you into the Beverly Wilshire. Get some treatments at that wonderful spa of theirs, pamper yourself a little. Dip your fingers back into the world of glam, sweetie. All that hanging out in frosty old Europe is bringing you down. Let Stephanie show you a good time. My treat, no quibbling… I won't take no for an answer.'

'But, I'm really not sure…' Evie stuttered, 'maybe next week…'

Before she could continue, Steph cut her conversation dead. 'I said no quibbling. Text me your flight times when you know what they are and I'll meet you at the airport. Oh, and sweetie, thought you might just like to know, Jeremy's in town. Not that I'm trying to force you two together or anything. Bye for now.'

With that, the line went dead. Pulling up outside the airport, Evie stepped from her taxi. As she was paying, a young woman with a child stood waiting alongside her, keen to secure the cab. Evie smiled at the young girl, who was no more than about four years old. Her cheeks were rosy, dusted with a reddy hue from the cool Austrian evening air. A woollen beret sat angled on her head. The little girl looked up at Evie and smiled back, revealing a missing front tooth.

'Aren't you gorgeous?' Evie stroked the girl's face. The mere action made her sad, a feeling of emptiness running through her.

Taking her suitcase from the cab driver, Evie pushed the melancholy to the back of her mind and walked into the airport terminal. On autopilot, she sauntered up to the information desk and asked about flights to Zurich and connections onto LA.

CHAPTER 25

Clarissa Thornton's star was definitely in the ascendant and the bigwigs at *Hollywood Daily* were certainly taking note. They'd given her carte blanche to go wherever, spend whatever and scoop whoever to make sure that it was their show that broke the headlines. At this rate she'd be pushing the regular show host, Carson Roberts, and his nauseatingly good looks, off air and replacing him full time. There were mumblings that she might even be getting her own show, something to put her on a par with Tyra or Ellen.

But all of that had paled into insignificance alongside her latest triumph. The biggest buzz of all had to be outbidding everyone to get her by-line back where it truly belonged, on the pages of *The Daily Staple*.

Despite the butterflies in her stomach as she'd bid telling her that maybe £260,000 was too much carte blanche to be taking, she'd known deep down that the exposure her actions would bring both *Hollywood Daily*, and more importantly herself, on *Wild Child*, would appease her bosses. A lump-in-the-throat phone call to them after the auction had put her worries at rest. They were delighted she'd scooped the auction prize.

Regaining the job which had been cruelly snatched from her by Lawrence and replacing her bitterest rival, albeit for a day, was a revenge that Clarissa was going to wallow in. She wanted to call the shots about the page and have complete control of what was to be written. It was a point she was keen to stress the day after the auction as she sat in the offices of *The Daily Staple* opposite a grim-faced Nush and an equally peeved Lawrence.

'So, I see that apart from a lick of paint and the odd coffee machine, not a lot has changed here since you kicked me out, Mr Silvers.' Clarissa's tone was pointed yet exultant.

'Listen, honey, you know damned well you're the last person I want back here, but seeing as you won that bloody auction fair and square there's jack shit I can do about it. Just make sure that whatever you write is worth reading, okay.'

'Oh it will be,' purred Clarissa, smoothing out the sun-drenched print of her Matthew Williamson silk funnel neck dress. She was happy with her choice of clothing. If ever there was day to pull out the designer names it had been today. Despite Nush looking resplendent in an uber-modern Nicole Farhi, Clarissa still thought that she herself had the feel-good, look-good edge.

'You can do this Friday's column as I shall be out of the country,' barked Nush. She was not in the mood for dealing with Clarissa today. Her phone had been ringing constantly with people wanting to speak to her about the Mae-Ling scandal, which had broken in the papers that morning. The whole thing had shaken her up more than she cared to admit, but she just wanted to put it all behind her. Not that pushing it onto a mental backburner would be easy. The media was full of it. She wanted to get on one of Lawrence's private planes and fly away, hiding herself from prying eyes and busybody journalists. Ironic, considering her own job. *Maybe I'm getting a little bit of my own medicine* were the words that kept passing through her mind. *If I can't take it then maybe I shouldn't dish it out.*

She wanted to get away from Lawrence too. As ever, it had been her dad's reaction to Nush's life that had scarred her the most. What would most loving fathers do when their only daughter gets a death threat? His reaction had been to tell Nush to toughen up, that if she was going to go around dishing the dirt on people she should pretty much expect it back. Yet again, he'd let her down, made her feel worthless. The men in her life had a habit of doing that. They were out to hurt. Look at Harry. Just a few weeks into a relationship with Evie and already he was sowing his seed behind her back. She still had to break the news to Evie about Harry. But for all Nush knew, the pair of them were skiing themselves silly up some Austrian mountain, Evie blissfully unaware of Harry's infidelity. It was Clarissa's voice that brought Nush back from her thoughts. 'Actually I can't do this Friday because, as hard as you may find this to believe, Anoushka, I'm pretty in demand right now. There are several UK chat shows that want me to appear, and I shall be working closely with my dear friend Grace on *Wild Child*. It is the biggest show on TV right now and I want to be as close to Grace and Regan as possible to make sure I get all the stories. I'm surprised your boss is letting you go anywhere else when there's so much potential dirt on your own doorstep, dear. Oh I forgot, daddy's your boss isn't he, it's not like you had to *earn* your job, it was just given to you.'

Nush waited for Lawrence to defend her. To her annoyance, but not to her surprise, he didn't. In fact, quite the opposite. 'True enough, Anoushka, you're going nowhere until that series finishes and we know who's won. If someone so much as sneezes a hint of scandal on that show, I want to find out about it first on your page – alright?'

Having dealt with Nush, Lawrence turned his attentions to Clarissa. 'So when are you going to work for us, then?'

'When I get you the story you deserve, Mr Silvers. It will be bigger, better and more scandalous than anything you seem to have served up lately. I want the glory, I want the by-line and I want to be able to drop it on you at a moment's notice. You won't be disappointed, Mr Silvers. I'll get you the kind of circulation grabbing scoop that you won't be able to turn down. Are we agreed?'

Nush's blood boiled within her veins. 'Now just hang on a minute, you stupid cow...' Her words were cut short by Lawrence.

'Agreed. I don't pretend to like you, but you get me a story that grabs the world by the short and curlies, then we have a deal.'

'But dad...' Nush's exasperated voice tried to cut in, but to no avail.

'Shut it, Anoushka. Business is business. Now, if we're quite finished, I have an empire to run. Ms Thornton, I'll wait for your call and the story had better be big or else I'll know that I was right to send you packing.'

Rising to her feet, Clarissa strode towards the door. 'Oh it will be, you have my word. If you want the top story, then it has to come from the top person, and we all know who that is, don't we?' She smirked at a deflated Nush as she marched from the office. Lawrence followed her out.

Left alone in the room, Nush couldn't hide her anger anymore. Picking up a glass from one of the office desks, she flung it against the wall. As she smashed into a thousand tiny shards, she let out a scream. Nush needed a drink and she needed one now.

———

Clarissa could still hear Nush's scream as the doors of *The Daily Staple's* lift shut behind her. The shrill sound of it filled her with a warm satisfaction. *Maybe getting the push from this place was the best thing that could have ever happened to me,* she mused to herself as the elevator descended to ground level. *Today is a good, good day...*

As Clarissa walked past the uniformed security guards and towards the revolving doors in the *Staple* building's lobby, her mobile sounded. It was Grace.

Bracing herself for the conversation, she pressed the answer button. Grace leapt straight in.

'Thanks to you, missy I am now two-nil down on this god damned show. I could have evened things out last night if it wasn't for you and your £260,000 bid. Do you want me to lose this stupid programme or what? Because if you do, then you can shove me digging the dirt for you right up your pompous little Brit ass and go to hell.'

Clarissa was on such a high that no-one, especially trash like Grace, was going to bring her down. She let her have it with both barrels. 'Look here, Laszlo. Just remember who's paying you for that dirt, okay? It's only thanks to my careful editing of that tape from Montana's perfume launch that the world seems to think you've gone from coke-snorting floozy to poor put-upon victim. Unless you want me to tell the world that the tape was doctored, you'll do things my way. As far as the world will be concerned it had to be you who did the doctoring because there's no way I'm confessing to it. Work with me on this and you'll come out of *Wild Child* a winner, with a sparkling reputation you don't deserve and with cash up to your surgically enhanced, silicone-filled tits. Just get me the dirt on Montana from Regan. You understand?' With that, Clarissa snapped the phone shut.

Emerging from the revolving doors, Clarissa felt the warm summer air on her face and allowed herself to smile again. She may have been pissing off a lot of people, but Clarissa Thornton was definitely looking after number one, and she loved every minute of it.

CHAPTER 26

Stafford James had not really enjoyed his night, which had surprised him greatly. After all, he had spent it at his dear friend Montana Phoenix's palatial Hollywood home, dining with her and Brad. Normally this would be enough to guarantee an evening of the utmost glamour, backbiting bitchiness beyond Stafford's gayest ideals and the bubbliest champagne flowing from every corner. But despite Montana cutting no corners when it came to entertaining, the night had been as flat as day-old champagne, her fountain of fun and laughter as dry as a month-old grissini and the air between her and Brad frostier than gelato.

At the end of an excruciatingly painful two hours, Montana and Stafford had retired for a nightcap onto Montana's Kenyan-style veranda while Brad excused himself to finalise details for the forthcoming *Babylon* trip to Europe. It was the moment Stafford had been waiting for all night. Finally alone with Montana, he spoke as they both sank into the brightly-coloured cushions strewn across the veranda.

'Right, lady, call me a busybody old queen who should know to mind his own, but something tells me that all is not well in the state of Glampire. Care to spill the beans?' As he spoke he placed his hand on top of Montana's and gave it an encouraging squeeze.

'Why am I such a bloody fool, Staffs? Everything was going fine. I've finally found a decent man in Bradley. Regan was safely ensconced on the other side of the Atlantic doing whatever she does. The perfume is flying off the shelves. And I cock it all up with that bloody stupid outburst, making myself look a total bitch right the way round the globe. Brad is as mad as hell. We've been stony with each other for days.'

'Oh, we're getting maudlin, are we?' said Stafford, mockingly. 'Well, first off, cherub, you are a total bitch and I for one wouldn't have it any other way. It's the only way to survive in this superficial world we call our lives. Your fault has been to show it. But you're old enough and ugly enough, darling, to know that people soon forget about what you've said. Most TV shows are much more interested in that actress Merchant woman and that heavenly Pinewood chap. I still can't forgive you for getting passionate with him on *Peregrine Palace*. I'd scratch off your false lashes to get that one in the sack.'

Montana could pretty much always rely on Stafford's bluntness to lift her moods. She knew what he was saying was true. The outburst would normally have been forgotten 24 hours later, swamped by some other A-Lister's woes, but the trouble was that Regan's face was everywhere thanks to *Wild Child*. TV, magazines, billboards across town – it was bearing down on her from every conceivable angle. And Montana was finding it increasingly hard to deal with.

As the tears ran down her cheeks, Montana replied. 'Stafford, you've known me from pre-*Peregrine* days. Back then I'd take any shitty little B-movie role and turn up at the opening of an envelope if I thought I could make a decent contact with someone influential. The one thing I never wanted was a daughter getting in the way. But what if this programme is the start of worldwide fame for her? If she's got one iota of shallow Phoenix blood in her she'll crumble at the first megabuck offer to tell the world what a terrible mother I've been. I'll be the new Joan Crawford. It could ruin me.'

'What could she say exactly? She was over to Britain before she was knee-high. She never saw the countless men trooping their way through your home like toy soldiers, did she darling? You show me one top notch female superstar who's not pulled her knickers to one side at some point in her life to further her career.'

Despite his coarseness, Montana knew that Stafford was right. She'd been no angel in the past, working her way through a string of playboy suitors. They were more than welcome in both her home and her bed provided they were influential or blanketed in riches. Montana was fully aware that her rise to fame had been a carefully calculated and manipulative real-life game of snakes and ladders, played by using her femininity and sexual lure to avoid the snakes and head up the ladders.

'But that's all behind me now. I'm with Brad, a good man who loves me. But lately he doesn't even want to be in the same room as me. I think I've blown it, Stafford. I don't think he'll forgive me for what I said about Regan.'

'Brad is your manager too. He's probably worried about the effect the bad press is having on the perfume, but if it's flying out of the stores then what's he got to worry about? Even heart-less old me can see that he adores you. He loves you as a woman, just maybe not as a business woman right now. Your best bet is to just hold your head up high, ride whatever storm comes your way and do a lot of sucking up to Regan when you see her. Who knows, one day Brad could be Regan's stepfather after all.'

The thought of Brad and her one day being a union thrilled Montana. However the mention of the words *father* and *Regan* in the same sentence didn't.

'That's another thing,' she continued. 'Regan's been phoning up and leaving messages for me. She wants to talk. What do I say to her? I can't lie, Stafford. The whole world has heard what

I said. That bloody Grace woman wound me up, you heard her, and now she's probably poisoning Regan even more. I know I should phone Regan back but I don't know what to say. Something else is niggling at me too. Regan said she had something she wanted to show me from my past. I don't know what it is, but I know it's not going to be good. The less rooting around Regan does, the better.'

'Well, honey, it's not like she's got some father who can come out of the woodwork, is it? Wasn't she the result of some squalid casting couch moment? How fabulously low rent.' Montana was silent. Stafford was momentarily worried that he may have gone too far.

'Only you can get away with saying things like that, darling,' sniffed Montana. 'Regan's father is well out of the picture, thank the Lord. He didn't want to know her.' Something piqued at her internally as she finished the sentence. Bypassing her feelings she carried on. 'Anyway, so you don't think I've blown it with Brad?'

'Darling, there's no way you've blown it. You're Montana Phoenix for God's sake. But if I were you, just to be certain, I'd slip back inside and make sure you haven't blown things by blowing him good and proper. Us guys are governed by our groins and putting a sexual smile on Brad's face will soon make him forget about all this Regan nonsense. Now get yourself inside and turn on the passion. I'll let myself out. Mind if I use your driver to get home?'

Montana smiled for what seemed like the first time that evening. 'Well, that's certainly one thing I know I'm skilled at. So if that doesn't win him over then nothing will.'

As Stafford walked back inside from the veranda he turned to Montana once more. 'Goodnight, darling, and if you and Brad do decide to get married, then first off I want to be best man and my suit will be made by Ozwald Boateng. Secondly, don't forget the two words that no Hollywood wedding should be without…'

Without hesitation, both Montana and Stafford looked at each other and said 'Pre-nup!'

CHAPTER 27

The high-energy rhythmic beats of the Latin music ricocheted around the gym hall with a sexy passion. Carla, the ultra-fit, lycra-clad Zumba instructor, shook her mass of chocolate brown hair and screamed encouragingly into her headset at the sea of bodies gyrating in front of her.

'Come on everybody, Zumba means moving fast and having fun. I want to see you sexy people sculpt those bodies and burn off those calories.' Carla's enthusiasm was infectious, even for Regan, who had to admit that in the past her idea of keeping as fit as possible was to make sure that her drugs had come from a reliable source. But as she punched the air and shimmied her body around to the calypso beat, she had to confess that she was actually having fun.

Turning to Grace, who had dragged Regan along to the 'fitness-party', as she called it, in the first place, she couldn't contain her smile. It felt good to be happy. She was winning the *Wild Child* race, a fact that didn't seem to be overly bothering Grace, was making a name for herself beyond the manicured grasp of Montana and had found a new friend in her co-star on the show. It was euphoric for Regan to feel part of a success…

Pushing her hair away from her face as it bobbed up and down in time to the workout, Grace grinned cheekily at Regan. 'So, girlfriend, correct me if I'm speaking out of turn, but there was definitely a spark of electricity between you and our dear producer after the auction. Am I spotting the foundations of a little relationship?'

In between deep breaths Regan answered with a wave of non-commitment. 'I'm liking what I see with Leo, put it that way.'

It was true, Regan had been thinking about Leo a lot. She'd found herself checking him out in between takes on the show. Admiring the curve of his backside cupped snugly within his trousers and the way his fringe dangled across his forehead. She'd planned to make a move on him after the auction, but in the post-event fracas all opportunities had been lost. Lawrence had disappeared before she'd had a chance to investigate any connection between him and her mother, Nush had been feverishly downing cocktails in search of solace and Leo had been receiving endless back-slaps congratulating him on the show. When she and Leo had finally locked glances, there was definitely something more than just a shared interest in the programme. His eyes seemed to have an extra sparkle, his smile an added air of desire. Regan was sure that behind that seemingly innocent butter-wouldn't-melt façade there was a sexual desire that would erupt like Vesuvius, given half a chance. They would just have to get their timings right.

Having finished their Zumba class, both women headed off to the changing room to get out of their fitness gear and shower. Life at an all girls' school had knocked away any inhibitions Regan had about her body but stood next to Grace's naked form in the gym showers as the pummelling water washed away the rigours of the class, she couldn't help but admire Grace's lithe, toned, sculpted body. Regan couldn't help but feel a little jealous of her friend's sensational curves.

'Your body is incredible. How do you stay so fit?' Regan had voiced the question out loud before she'd even thought about it.

'Honey, they don't call me *Amazing Grace* for nothing! Personal trainers, fitness classes in everything from boxercise to dancercise and a totally vigorous sex life is all it takes. And if that doesn't work, then LA has more than its fair share of avenues to explore when it comes to getting procedures done. I'm up for anything if it means looking good. In La La Land you can get anything fixed from wonky teeth through to a flabby vagina. Surely you must have learnt that from your damn mother? She's had her skin lifted so many times she can wear her kneecaps as shoulder pads.'

'I'll tell you all over lunch… my treat. I don't know about you but all this jigging around has left me starving. Let's go eat. Sushi sound good?'

'Lead the way, sister. And for the record…' Grace looked up and down Regan's naked body. 'You have a body that is definitely made for sin, honey. You have curves that read like poetry.'

———

Staring at her own naked body in her full-length bedroom mirror, Sadie Silvers could tell that something was different. She could feel that something was growing inside her. It was an intuition that had been eating away at her for days. She hadn't been able to think of anything else. The signs were looking good and her period beyond late. Now was the moment that she'd been waiting for.

Lawrence was at work and she was alone at Kingsbury. She'd spent the morning heading to the nearest pharmacy to buy a home pregnancy kit. Even though she knew in her brain what the outcome would be, she needed to be certain before breaking the news to Lawrence.

An heir to the Silvers' empire would be the cherry on the icing of Sadie's sumptuous existence. Something solid that would be the binding eternal link between her and Lawrence.

She loved Harry but he was another woman's son – Lysette…
the woman who she'd never meet, but always felt she had to
compete with. How do you compete with a dead person? A
child between Lawrence and Sadie would make everything perfect. *Please God, let it be a boy.* That's what Lawrence would really want, a brother for Harry to dote on.

Taking the pregnancy kit from its packaging she walked into
the en suite and closed the door behind her. She didn't want to
be disturbed. Squatting over the toilet, Sadie did what she needed to do. Placing the kit on the marble bathroom cabinet once
she'd finished, Sadie forced herself to look away from it and
started to count. She needed to leave it three minutes. She could
feel her heart beating against her ribs. She was nervous. She'd
tried for so long to have a child but the timing had never been
right. This would be their first together… the start of a new era.
Plus Sadie wasn't stupid. Even if Lawrence decided to trade her
in for a newer, younger model, a child would secure megabuck
paternity payouts for Sadie forever. Indeed, there were many
other things riding on this pregnancy than just Sadie's maternal
longing.

Composing herself, Sadie stared at her face in the bathroom
mirror. 'Okay… let's see if my body has been telling me lies.' At
that potentially life-changing moment, Sadie looked down at
the pregnancy test. The result was spelled out loud and clear…

CHAPTER 28

From the moment that Evie switched her mobile phone back on at LAX airport it went into a constant state of vibration. The many hours she'd spent up in the air on her flights from Europe had been a haven of silence, giving her time to sleep and think.

Twice during the flight she'd cried about Harry. The idea of yet another fruitless romance made her sad. Two voice messages were from Harry. One was a sleepy hangover of a message with Harry wondering where she was, why her suitcase wasn't there anymore. Surely you didn't need to be a member of Mensa to piece the clues together.

The second message was more fraught with worry and despair, Harry's voice begging for an answer as to why she had apparently walked out of his life. Accompanying his voice massages were three texts. Two were simple 'ring me' texts, whereas the third was angry and spotted with venom. Evie deleted them all, not feeling strong enough to deal with Harry just yet.

The other texts were from Jeremy. The first one read *Am back home in LA. The distance between us has done nothing to cool my feelings for you. Let's not miss out. Call me.* The second one simply said *I hear you're closer to me than I thought, geographically and hopefully emotionally too.* It puzzled Evie. *So Jeremy knows I'm flying into LA then,* she mused. The penny quickly dropped. Doubtless Stephanie had been talking. The film world was suitably small enough for word to spread like a California forest fire in just a matter of hours, especially with a voice as loud as Stephanie's.

The other message was from her agent demanding she call her on arrival. Not wishing to talk just yet, Evie texted Steph that she'd landed and said she would wait for her at one of the airport coffee shops.

Having ordered an iced café latte, Evie waited for Steph to arrive. She picked up a magazine from a bundle of them squeezed into a rack on the coffee shop wall. The front cover had a photo of Regan and Montana on it. They were two separate images which had been photoshopped together. The headline read 'MUM'S NOT THE WORD FOR REGAN PHOENIX – TV'S NEWEST STAR'. Evie sipped her latte, opened the magazine and started reading. It was comforting to know that she wasn't the only one of the Trinity with relationship worries and making headlines.

—

Nush was desperate to forget her failings. Ever since she'd stormed out of the *Daily Staple* building, having left a note on her PC saying 'Gone home ill', and demanding that her deputies write the column, Nush had wanted to get blitzed.

In an attempt to hide away from prying eyes, she'd chosen a private members' club in the heart of London's Soho that she often used for interviewing celebrities. Nush sat in the furthest corner of the bar and ordered a bottle of vintage wine. She was on her third glass when she spied a handsome man of about thirty on his own at a table just along from hers. His appearance was one of success, a city slicker decked out from head to toe in the finest Patrick Grant Savile Row tailoring. It was a moneyed look.

Nush admired his chiselled features, broad set shoulders and shock of yellowy-blond hair slicked fashionably into place on top of his head.

Picking up the bottle of wine on her table to pour herself yet another drink, Nush clinked it noisily against her glass as she tried to steady her increasingly drunken movements. The sound made the stranger look in her direction. As Nush mouthed the word 'oops', the man flashed a drop-dead smile in her direction. That was it, as far as Nush was concerned, the deed was sealed... she knew how she wanted to spend the rest of her day, and it wasn't alone. She needed appreciation. With a flirtatious curling of her fingers, she beckoned the man to her table.

'Hello, you look like you're having a fun day.' His voice was deep and rich.

'Better now,' replied Nush. 'I was thinking of getting another drink, care to join me?' Her words were slightly slurred, a fact not lost on her new drinking partner.

'I'd love to,' he said, signalling the waiter as he did so. 'More of the same?' he motioned, pointing towards Nush's empty bottle. Nush nodded.

Holding out his hand as he sat down next to her he said 'My name's Rhys.'

'Anoushka. It's always pleasurable to meet a man drinking on his own, especially such a good looking one.' Nush was keen to step her flirting up a gear as soon as possible. She wasn't in the mood for too much small talk, the lascivious thoughts sweeping through her body told her that. The body under Rhys's suit and shirt looked tight and firm.

Time passed quickly, a blur of pleasantries with an underlying air of sexual tension. Nush had tried to keep up with the snippets of information Rhys had proffered about himself but none of it really lodged in Nush's head.

Draining the last drops of wine from her glass, Nush was ready to play yet another card in her game of seduction. Slipping off one of her Kurt Geiger heels under the table, she placed her foot against Rhys's shin and stroked it alluringly up and down his leg. He gave an encouraging smile.

A green light having switched on inside her head, Nush let her foot move higher, rubbing a finger suggestively across her bottom lip as she did so. Her foot kept moving, up past his thigh, until it found its desired resting place - the hard mound of aroused flesh between Rhys' legs.

Her action wasn't lost on Rhys. 'Shall we go? My car is parked not far from here. There's no-one at mine if you fancy. I'll get the bill.'

Nush nodded, pleased at where the rendezvous was heading. A man who was up for some bedroom action and eager to pay her somewhat hefty bar bill was definitely a bonus. It would save trying to prove yet more expenses to Lawrence.

The hours of drinking had left Nush wobbly on her feet and as she faltered her way out of the members' club, she steadied herself against Rhys. He placed an arm around her. It felt protective and reassuring and the feeling continued as he cupped her face in his hands and guided his lips to hers.

His kiss was ardent and bursting with lust. The feel of his five o'clock shadow against Nush's chin and his voracious nibbling of her lip as he hungrily pushed his lips into hers caused Nush to wince slightly. A ripple of anticipatory desire spread its way across her pussy.

The car park was old and grey, a forgotten deteriorated building that seemed out of character with the salubrious offices and apartments around it. The entrance was small and shabby, comprising solely of a ticket machine and an elevator.

'We'll have to get the lift down to the car. I always park it on the lower levels,' said Rhys. The clunky metal lift door opened, revealing a graffiti covered interior. Once the couple had stepped inside, Rhys made his move.

He pushed Nush roughly against the wall forcing her head to bang against it. She let out a yelp as she made contact, but remained turned on by Rhys's dominant strength, despite his brutal approach.

Positioning his mouth on Nush's neck, Rhys first nuzzled on her tender skin and then, unable to control his desire, began to bite down on the flesh with his teeth. His actions were almost vampiric and Nush's sexual rush suddenly changed to one of fright as she realised that the man in front of her was actually hurting her. She tried to speak, to object, but a cold chill of nothingness seemed to trap her words inside its vacuum.

Rhys pulled at the material of Nush's dress and the fabric ripped at the seam. He jammed his hand inside and mauled roughly at her breast. It was only then that he spoke. 'Is that what you want? You're a dirty little bitch, aren't you? You've been waiting for that.' The words tore into Nush's brain like barbed wire. Any attempts to scream seemed mute. Her senses numb, her throat as dry as unbuttered toast. This wasn't supposed to be like this.

The lift door opened, unveiling the dark empty space beyond. There were no cars, no sign of life. Just ominous shadows. The stark sight of it hit Nush like a battering ram, freeing her vocal chords. *How could she have been so stupid?* She started to scream, but there was no-one around to hear. As Rhys let go of her hair, Nush summoned all of her strength and took her chance. She ran through the opened lift door and stumbled into the shadows.

She kept running, the sound of her own heart beating wildly within her chest. She was determined not to let another man dominate her against her will. She was a survivor. She'd had to be. Men were savage beasts she would never understand. Why had this happened to her again? Why did she let herself fall prey to these situations?

Not daring to look behind her, she found herself at the base of a flight of stairs. Ignoring the pain in her body and the cloud of fear wrapping her brain she darted up the stairs, praying that the surrounding darkness would hide her from her attacker. Stair after stair she climbed, the breathing dry and hollow, the sound of broken glass crunching beneath her heels. After what seemed like an age she fell through a door and onto the pavement of the London street. Thankfully here was no sign of Rhys behind her.

She sat in the gutter trying to regain her breath. Nush was alone. It was feeling that was becoming all too common.

CHAPTER 29

The bottles of wine had been flowing copiously for Regan and Grace too, as had the cocaine. After their sushi lunch, the women had headed to one of Regan's favourite pubs, the Cittie of Yorke in London's Holborn district. She'd chosen it especially for Grace, wanting to show the American something typically British and steeped in history. Despite Grace not being that enamoured with the thought of a 15th century pub to begin with, Regan's promise of the best chocolate-orange flavoured vodka in London had won Grace over and by mid-afternoon the two women were holed up in one of the pub's booths. It was the perfect place to idly gossip and get girly. The conversation turned to Montana. Unsurprisingly, it was Grace who started it.

'So, have you spoken to everyone's favourite soap bitch lately, then?' she said, sniffing due to her latest line.

'No, she seems to be having some trouble registering the fact that I want to speak to her,' said Regan.

'The old bag's ignoring your calls.' As ever, Grace was blunt, but it was a bluntness that Regan had come to appreciate. She didn't feel that she had to pussyfoot around Grace. She'd spent her life watching what she should and shouldn't say about her mother, fearful of word getting back to Montana.

Regan carried on the conversation. 'Got it in one. She's obviously too busy with that infernal perfume of hers and trying to schmooze her way back into the hearts of the world's press. I come way down the list.'

Pouring herself and Grace another glass of wine, Regan continued. 'Mind you, if she's not glued to the TV watching *Wild Child* then I'll eat my Donna Karan handbag. If there's one thing that will irk my mother it'll be you and I together. I'd love to be a fly on the wall at her Hollywood slut-hut when we're getting bigger ratings than she's had in a long time!' The mention of the ratings made Regan stroke the Tiffany bracelet on her wrist. She smiled, longing to see Leo.

Encouraged by the loosening of Regan's tongue, Grace pushed her further. 'Slut-hut! From what I've seen of it in magazines, the Phoenix LA residence is a multi-million dollar property. You telling me it's a knocking shop behind those oak-panelled doors?' Grace laughed, but was highly excited at the prospect of sniffing out some juicy morsels of money-making gossip to feed back to Clarissa.

'Let's just say that the amount of traffic to and from that house over the years could make the Los Angeles Highway look like a country lane. She may seem to be settled down now but, if her history is anything to go by, it isn't going to last with Brad. She couldn't keep a man if she hammered his backside to her bedposts.'

Feeling a frisson of release from the coke rushing through her veins as she revved up to dish the dirt on her mother, Regan pushed on with her dialogue. 'I've seen it all over the years. Let's just say that she's never been a woman who was timid about getting down on her knees to beg for a job.'

'How do you know? Weren't you shipped off to England as soon as she could cut the cord? I'm surprised the bitch didn't shove you in a jiffy bag and have you FedExed as soon as you quit her womb.'

'You didn't have to be the sharpest tool in the box to connect the passionate moans coming from her bedroom and the constant line of men trooping back and forth. Before I was sent packing to the UK I guess I thought that was how all mums behaved. Our life was pretty glitzy even back then. It was parties most nights at Chez Phoenix. Wine would be flowing, silver plates would be piled high with coke and after a while mother would doubtless disappear off to a bedroom with some dirty old man with his tongue hanging out like an aging dog.'

Sensing that there was more to come, Grace egged Regan on. 'Surely you weren't part of all that? No woman in her right mind would let her child see all that going on.'

Regan couldn't wait to carry on. 'I'd have been sent off to bed by one of the maids hours before. But I defy any child to sleep through the racket from one of mother's parties. Music blaring, screams of hilarity, the smell of cigar smoke wafting through the house. I'd get up and sit at the top of the stairs, staring down through the banisters. If someone headed upstairs I'd run back to my room. It was pretty much the same story every school holiday.'

'You must have seen some famous names working their lecherous way up and down those stairs over the years?' prompted Grace. If she could get Regan to name drop a few big ones then the multi-dollar price tag on the story would doubtless go up in Clarissa's eyes.

'I'm sure I did, but I've no idea who they were. It was a world full of film types, politicians, tycoons, bankers. You see one suited, booted bigwig, you've seen them all… I'd be lying if I didn't wonder just who some of them were though. Mind you, I do think I might have a clue who one of them could have been…' She let the sentence trail off, waiting for an open-mouthed Grace to respond.

Jackpot. Here we go, mused Grace, feeling that she was on the verge of hearing something big. The dollar signs clicked into place in her brain like winning reels on a casino slot machine.

'I found a photograph at a party I went to recently…' Fired up, Regan told her the whole story of the party night at Kingsbury and the discovery of the photo of a young Montana and Lawrence Silvers.

'So, you reckon they knew each other way back when? You should have grabbed him at the auction and grilled him about it. You gotta ask, sweetie. If your mate Nush's daddy was getting low down and dirty with your mama then I really think you and your friend need to find out the truth, don't you? How kooky would that be?'

At the mention of her friend's name, Regan felt a chill run across her body making her shudder. Despite the comforting effects of the coke, she suddenly realised that maybe she had said too much. She was talking about the dad of one of her best friends after all, and as yet there was no evidence to suggest that the photo was anything more than guiltless fun from days gone by. Regan's face must have suddenly shown her worry as she stared at Grace.

Meeting her gaze, Grace knew just how to take away Regan's impromptu angst. 'Let's keep this party going. Another glass of wine, a vodka chaser and a line of coke coming up.'

As Grace headed to the bar, Regan smiled to herself. She was right to like Grace. She made Regan feel alive, full of fun, worthwhile. And what's more, she was definitely someone she could trust.

CHAPTER 30

If there was one feeling that Evie absolutely adored, it was the pampered luxury she felt when it came to staying in the world's finest hotels. And the majesty of the Beverly Wilshire, situated just paces from LA's glamour-coated Rodeo Drive, didn't disappoint.

From the moment Evie checked into the 10th floor Veranda Suite she knew that she had made the right decision in not heading back to the UK. Walking up the private stairs from her suite to her own exclusive garden terrace to check out the surrounding views of the Hollywood Hills, Evie couldn't help but suddenly lose herself in the soft, enveloping comfort of how far she had come with her career.

She remembered how, when she had first arrived in America after leaving Farmington, she had not known what the world was ready to offer her. She'd taken an acting job in a New York theatre production off-Broadway and shared a rather dank and dingy apartment with three other hopeful young actors: two boys and a girl. They had been good times, with the four of them talking well into the early hours, night after night, about their hopes and dreams. How one day they would all have their names in lights.

For Evie, success beyond her wildest dreams had quickly materialised. Chance meetings with casting directors, a clever agent pushing her in the right direction and her own effortless acting skill had seen her career flourish, leaving the hand-to-mouth days of the apartment behind her. But they were times she would never forget. Even though she could have tapped her parents for money anytime she'd liked, Evie had been keen to do things her way, surviving on the paltry wages she earned from the fringe production and not wanting to feast constantly on the privileges of coming from a family coated in riches. She'd wanted to be an equal with her flatmates. She had never even mentioned her family and upbringing to them, but instead pretended to be a wannabe actress who had been lucky enough to have a mum who had scraped together enough money from odd jobs to get Evie into drama school in London. It may have been a lie, but it made Evie feel worthwhile.

She had only turned to her parents in times of utmost emergency. The highs had been high, the lows had been low… they were times that she could now look back upon with chequerboard emotions. She'd lost contact with her three flatmates. She had seen one of the guys' names on the flyer for a New York musical. The girl had last been seen auditioning on *American Idol,* hoping to become the next Kelly Clarkson or Leona Lewis, but she'd fallen by the wayside into talent pool obscurity.

Evie never took her success for granted. Things could have been so different. Who knows where life would have taken her had she not made certain decisions or followed certain advice along the way? But looking out across the splendour of Tinseltown, an eclipse of satisfaction filled her. It was just what Evie needed to help her forget about the recent heartache with Harry. Her departure really was his loss.

Evie had arranged to meet Steph later that evening for dinner at Cut, the stylish hotel restaurant. It was a place she'd read about in countless magazines as a hangout for LA-based celebrities and she couldn't wait to sample the food there. Evie was keen to catch up with industry buzz – the upcoming Venice

Film Festival and, more importantly, any news on Jeremy. Her phone had been quiet since the airport and Evie was definitely curious about Jeremy's next move.

Seeing as she still had hours before meeting up with Steph, Evie decided to make the most of her surroundings and headed to the hotel spa for the afternoon. If anything could make her forget the impending jet lag, it was a good pampering.

It was hours later, after a series of skin-refreshing massages, that she finally returned to her suite. Evie's relaxed state of mind caused her to think of Jeremy. Did she want to see him? With her mind more uncluttered than it had been in weeks, she allowed herself to think rationally and clearly.

She started to tick boxes in her mind. *Was she warming to the thought of seeing Jeremy?* Yes. *Was she willing to forgive him for his rudeness towards her when they first met?* Yes. *Was he finally treating her as she deserved?* Yes. *Did she find him incredibly attractive?* Hell yes. *Could she see them together?* Not sure. Okay, so four out of five yeses isn't bad. Maybe she would text him and arrange to meet. What harm could it do? If he turned into a macho pig again then at least she would know not to waste her time. Yes, she'd text him... tomorrow. She needed the low down from Steph first. She wanted to trust Jeremy, she really did, but given her recent experience with men, there was still a protective part of her that chose to err on the side of caution.

———

Dinner with Steph was a sumptuously chic affair. The cocktail of the ultra-clean white-walled interior and the famed cuisine was a pick 'n' mix of pure perfection. Adding Stephanie's brash and breezy personality into the mix as the perfect dinner companion and the evening was a delight. To say that Steph was on good form was an understatement. She was cheerier than any of the Brady Bunch.

According to Steph, the buzz about *The Bouquet Catcher's* forthcoming 'showing' at Venice was immense. She had it on very good terms that Jeremy had already agreed to go and that he was keen, to quote Steph, 'To hook up with you as much as possible beforehand to put on a united front'.

'*Hook up?*' scoffed Evie. 'That is hardly very Barbara Cartland when it comes to trying to win me over in the romance department. *A united front?* I was kind of hoping from his text messages that he might be a little more... loving, shall we say?'

Steph immediately pounced on Evie's words. 'You were *hoping*! Hope springs eternal. You *do* like him darling, don't you? Steph's a happy little mama... I can feel you lovebirds tweeting together before too long.'

'We'll see. I'll text him tomorrow, alright? I'm in no rush to fall into any man's arms, even if they do have biceps to die for. Now, let's change the subject. Just how much are you paying for my stay here, because it must have cost you a fortune?'

Grinning smugly, Steph deflected the question. 'You're worth every dollar, baby, and, anyway, let's just say it's money well spent if it gets you and the delectable Mr Pinewood closer together. Just call me your Cashpoint Cupid.'

'I could think of other things to call you!' Evie was laughing again, enjoying the sensation of feeling carefree. 'Anyway, are you coming up to the suite for a nightcap? The view up there is breath-taking?'

'Mind if I don't, darling? I wouldn't want to spoil the moment. I'll settle up and be on my way. I'll phone you tomorrow, doll. Ciao... and give Jeremy my love, won't you?' With that, Steph was up and gone, leaving Evie agog at the table.

Perplexed, she stared up at the amplified moon shining through the restaurant skylight. *Talk about a quick exit, and what did Steph mean... spoil what moment?*

Evie didn't have to wait too long before realising. Stepping back into her suite, the scented smell of the air hit her, as did a blanket of vibrant, spectacular colour. Evie took a sharp intake of breath as she looked around.

Virtually every conceivable inch was covered in flowers. Bunches of pink and red roses, sprays of deep red carnations, huge spreads of purple and blue hyacinths. Elsewhere, Evie spotted irises, orchids, periwinkles, acacias, violets and zinnias all tied with huge sweeping bows.

Placed on the table in the middle of the suite was a lilac envelope with Evie's name written on it. Brimming with curiosity, Evie gingerly sauntered to the table, weaving her way in between the flowers. Picking up the envelope, she turned it over and lifted up the flap, revealing a sheet of matching lilac notepaper inside. Handwritten on it were the words, 'Dearest Evie, Welcome to Los Angeles. Forgive the intrusion but I figured your hotel suite could do with a bit of brightening up, so I've picked out some of the most romantic flowers I could find – hoping that, just like them, our relationship is about to blossom. How does dinner at 8pm tomorrow night at mine sound? I'll send a car to pick you up at the front of the hotel. Please say yes. I honestly believe we could have something good together. Love, J xx PS: Please don't tell me you suffer from hayfever or I shall be mortified.'

Laughing at the note, Evie felt her heart skip a beat. Jeremy had got in touch, and this was so much more than a text message. She'd agree to dine with him. What did she have to lose? But she wouldn't let him know until the morning. Keep him on his toes.

Looking at the sea of flowers around her though, Evie had to admit that it was one of the most romantic and noble gestures she'd ever experienced.

'Way to go, Jeremy. Take that Barbara Cartland!'

CHAPTER 31

If cloud nine was deemed to be the summit of ecstasy, then the feeling that Sadie had been experiencing over the last few days was a cumulonimbus way into double figures. The pregnancy kit and a follow-up trip to Harley Street had confirmed what she wanted to know, she was finally with child. All of her careful planning had paid off. All that remained now was to break the news to Lawrence and she was determined the moment would be picture perfect.

She had spent the day doing her favourite thing – organising. She'd arranged caterers for the night to come in and lay on a sumptuous *dinner-a-deux*. A starter of the finest Scottish smoked salmon and scrambled eggs was to be followed by a tantalisingly tender joint of South African steak with blueberry and coconut scones for dessert. They were all recipes handpicked by Sadie after hours trawling pregnancy advice websites. They needed to be rich in protein, yet still cater for both her sweet tooth – hence the scones – and Lawrence's pub-grub, meat and two veg mentality.

The caterers were already beavering away in the kitchen, putting the final touches to the food's presentation. Sadie had instructed them that dinner was to be served at nine, shortly after Lawrence's arrival home from work. She wanted the evening to run with the accuracy of a Swiss timepiece, giving Lawrence just enough time to get changed before dinner. She knew that she would have a job keeping the news secret until the end of the meal, but she was determined to try.

Staring into her bedroom mirror as she adjusted her flowing gown for the evening, Sadie had to admit that she looked the best she had done in ages. Her skin seemed flawless, glowing like porcelain. Her eyes appeared to have a sparkle worthy of a Disney princess.

Her phone sounded on the dressing table. She prayed that it wasn't a text from Lawrence telling her that he was to be late. With a sigh of relief she saw that the message was from Harry, doubtless raving about what a good time he was having with Evie in some enchanting log cabin. Sadie smiled to herself. She liked Harry. Evie was a lucky girl in her opinion. Harry would make a good catch for any lady. Reading the message, her smile disappeared. It was clear that things were not as rosy as Sadie had imagined. *Things have gone tits-up. Have you spoken to Nush? Has she heard from Evie? I don't understand women. Evie's gone. Silly cow. Ring me. Hx.*

Sadie was about to reply when she heard Lawrence's car pull up on the gravel outside the house. Harry would have to wait. Tonight was all about her and Lawrence and the fact that soon a new member of the Silvers' clan would be adding their name to the family tree…

———

Montana's skin was still glistening with a slick of sensuality from her latest bout of love-making with Brad. As he lay naked on his back alongside her, she nuzzled her face into the soft, warm crook of his armpit, enjoying the cushioning effect of his skin against hers. She swirled her fingers in a circular motion across his chest, forming whirlpools in his profusion of rich, masculine chest hair. She could feel that Brad was drifting into sleep, his breathing becoming deep and regular, but Montana was the happiest she had been for a long while. She was to marry the man she loved. Rewinding her thoughts back in time she couldn't believe how things had changed between her and Brad. She would certainly have to treat Stafford to an expensive gift or two next time she saw him. The old queen had definitely been right about how to win back your man…

After her heart-to-heart with Stafford, Montana had been determined to try and salvage the relationship she had with Brad. Stafford had crudely suggested that a horny dose of sex was the answer. As a bridge builder, it had definitely worked.

She'd found Brad hunched over his PC finalising arrangements for their forthcoming trip to the UK. He was tired and uncharacteristically tetchy, bashing at the keys with an air of impatience. Slinking in behind him, Montana had placed her hands on his shoulders and started to massage his upper back. Brad hadn't said a word, but his leaning back in his chair and sighing appreciatively at her touch showed her that she was having the effect she desired. Moving her hands around to the front of his body, she unbuttoned the top of his shirt and ran her hands down his pectoral muscles. Brad's head had tilted back resting against her own cleavage, allowing Montana to kiss his forehead. As she moved her lips away from him she whispered 'I love you Brad, I'm so sorry'. It was all that he needed to hear. They had discarded their clothes in an instant and moved to the bedroom.

They had spent the rest of the night making love. They had hardly spoken a word, not needing to. Their actions spoke for themselves. Their sexual union had been an olive branch to their recent upsets. Montana had experienced countless orgasms, revelling in Brad's technique as he performed oral sex on her, dipping his tongue gratefully inside her, savouring her taste as he flicked expertly across her clitoris. She had ridden waves of euphoria as he skilfully plunged his cock into her, moving her around the bed. For Montana, it was the best sex she had ever had. A million miles away from the loveless copulation she had experienced time and time again.

In between love-making, they finally felt able to talk to each other fully and without worry. All professional conversations about *Babylon*, sales figures, interviews and the dreaded Grace evaporated. The only talk was about the two of them, how they felt, what they wanted. Nothing else in the world mattered or at that moment, even existed. It had been a cathartic experience for them both as they simultaneously revealed what they wanted for the future... each other.

It had been Brad who popped the question. 'Montana, you know I love you more than I've loved any other woman.' His voice had been nervous and slightly faltering. Montana knew where the conversation was going as soon as it had started. She could feel her heartbeat quickening with excited anticipation.

Brad had continued, his lip trembling lightly as he did so. 'I love being with you, I love what you represent and I love who you are. The world sees this big Hollywood superstar who's completely in control. But I see someone who's vulnerable, who needs to share the love in her heart with someone. I want to make you my wife, Montana. Will you marry me?'

Montana had burst into tears as soon as the words had escaped Brad's lips. In an instant, all of the doubts she'd been feeling about their relationship had disappeared. She knew that being Mrs Bradley Roderick was what she wanted for the future. She had known it for a while, but now she knew that Brad felt the same.

Wiping away her joyful tears, Montana had replied 'yes' and kissed Brad tenderly on the lips. It led to another round of love-making.

From across the dining room table, Sadie watched Lawrence as he finished the last of his dessert. So far, the night had been a success. Lawrence had arrived home on time as planned and was pretty much taken aback by Sadie's announcement that caterers were about to serve dinner. He was used to Sadie's love of spending money for no apparent reason, but he adored her zestful spontaneity.

As the Kingsbury staff cleared the table, Sadie sauntered over to Lawrence and refilled his glass with champagne. Taking him by the hand, she bent down to kiss him, taking a few seconds to linger on his lips. The moment was finally here and she needed to steady her nerves before making her announcement. Lawrence spoke first.

'That was a fantastic meal. Just what I needed after another day in that bloody office. That sodding daughter of mine has done a runner again. No sign all day. Plus that Thornton woman is trying to run me ragged with her demands. Thank God Harry's alright. I never have to worry about him. Best son a man could ask for.'

Sadie was pleased that Harry had obviously not contacted his father about the situation with Evie. Doubtless he would, but at least it wouldn't spoil tonight.

'Yes, Harry's a good boy,' said Sadie. 'He'll make someone a great husband one day, and a good father no doubt if he takes after you, my angel. He'll also make someone a great big brother too.'

A wave of perplexity washed over Lawrence's face. Sadie's words didn't quite seem to compute in his brain. 'He's a good *little* brother to Nush, not that she appreciates it of course.'

'No, Lawrence. Harry will be a big brother soon. The thing is, I can tell you now because it's been confirmed by my doctor. Lawrence… you're going to be a daddy again, I'm pregnant.'

Sadie smiled. A smile that felt wider and more wonderful than any smile she had ever given before. Looking into Lawrence's face, she waited for his smile to reflect her own. It never came.

After what seemed like an eternity to Sadie, Lawrence let go of her hand and let it fall. Her news wrapped itself boa constrictor-like around his mind, squeezing out all thoughts from within.

Unsure what to do, Sadie repeated her announcement. 'You're going to be a daddy, Lawrence. I'm going to have our baby. Isn't it wonderful?'

What happened next would always remain with Sadie as one of the most horrible moments of her life. The feeling of rejection as Lawrence looked coldly at her, anger in his eyes. The sharp pain as he slapped her forcefully across her face, turned silently away and walked out of the dining room.

The next noise Sadie heard as she stood there, stupefied, was the sound of Lawrence's car on the gravel outside Kingsbury as he sped off into the night.

CHAPTER 32

When Mae-Ling Ch'en shut her eyes, it was because she wanted to block out the four walls of the police cell where she'd spent the last few hours. The drab, murky greyness that seemed to smell of despair served to remind her that her life had reached an all-time low. Quite how she had managed to let herself fall so low was a mystery even to Mae-Ling.

But as Mae-Ling contemplated the fact that her life would never be the same again, she knew full well the reason behind her demise. It was the betrayal by Jake, the man she thought would be her partner for life, and the subsequent revelation of his sordid romp through the words of Anoushka Silvers. A woman she had grown to hate. A woman she had come to blame for everything. *What gave her the right to try and destroy people's lives with her shitty little newspaper column?*

Mae-Ling was pleased she'd gone to Nush's house and thrown the brick through the window. She was pleased she'd written the note. As far as she was concerned, Anoushka Silvers would still get what was coming to her. All that was needed was for Mae-Ling to get out of this cell. She was sure that would happen soon enough. Until then, she would just keep her eyes shut as much as possible.

——

For Nush herself, keeping her eyes shut was the better of two options. The other was to open them and face what the world was bombarding her with. Since her savage encounter in the car park basement, Nush had holed herself up at her flat, not wanting to speak to or see anyone. Her body still hurt from the force of her aggressor's actions. Her mind felt as if it was ready to explode with the range of emotions ricocheting through it. Hurt, distrust, betrayal, pain, anger, self-loathing, failure. The list went on. She'd considered reporting the attack to the police, but that would just make her the centre of yet another front-page sensation. She'd had enough of those for one week. And deep down, she blamed herself...

She longed to be with her girls, to see Regan and Evie. But even that would bring complications. She'd listened to Evie's message about Harry. Things were evidently not good. Evie was a fragile soul when it came to men. How could Nush tell her about what she'd heard when she had spoken to Harry? As for Regan, she had enough on her plate with the TV filming and Montana's mysterious photo with Lawrence to investigate.

What could the girls say anyway? Nush does it again. Manages to get herself into yet another horrendous scrape with yet another random guy. She felt like a worthless victim, she didn't even feel worthy enough to be considered part of the Trinity anymore. Both Regan and Evie seemed to be on their way up. Success was knocking at their door. But for Nush there appeared only to be a one-way-street – and that one way was down. They'd be better off without her.

Momentarily opening her eyes, Nush looked at the bottle of pills she had placed on her bedside table. As she closed them again, encasing herself in the subsequent darkness, she thought to herself, *Yes, they'd be better off without me.*

CHAPTER 33

'Are you sure that's exactly what she said? That there's a photo of Lawrence and Montana together and that she thinks there might have been something between them in the past. This could be the biggest story of my career if you're right, Grace. And, if you can get me the photo to go with the words as proof, I'll make sure that you get a payday that will set you up for life.'

Snapping shut her phone, Clarissa could feel the snowball effect of her success escalating. A story that involved Montana, Regan, Lawrence and Anoushka all rolled into one would definitely bag her a network show. The only problem was that this was one story she certainly wouldn't be able to run in *The Daily Staple*. Lawrence Silvers may have been a fan of a reader-grabbing exclusive, but not when he would be the main thrust of the story. No, Clarissa would have to find something else for that particular moment of glory.

Just as Grace was dishing the dirt on her *Wild Child* colleague, Regan herself was chilling in one of her favourite bars in London's Soho, telling Leo Weiss just how much she had come to like Grace. The girls had just finished the first day of filming for the next episode of *Wild Child*. This instalment would re-quire them both to demonstrate self-control and intellect. They were to do this through the art of public speaking. The hope was that they could both speak coherently, intelligently and interestingly to a large crowd, proving that their airhead days were definitely behind them.

In order to try and achieve this, both Grace and Regan had spent the day with teachers from one of London's top public-speaking schools. It had been a major strain on Regan's brain with lots to digest and take in, which was why she needed a drink. Tomorrow she'd be learning all about the chosen topic for her speech and the talk itself would happen the day after. For Regan, it couldn't be over quick enough.

'It's alright for Grace,' stated Regan across the table to Leo. 'She's got the gift of the gab, having done loads of interviews when she was in Sexalicious. She's been grilled by any chat show host you care to mention and must have had media training through the record company.'

'It doesn't mean she can hold her own when it comes to speaking about a certain subject or cause. When she was doing the interview circuit she was talking about herself and the band. It would have been all about fashion, make-up, men and music. This is a whole different ballgame.' Leo's words were supposed to be supportive, but they didn't have the desired effect.

'I'm going to be awful. You heard Grace at the auction. She was magnificent. The whole world believed her every word. Anyway, where is this public speaking crap going to take place?'

Leo laughed. 'Now come on, you know better than that. I'm the producer on this show and if I told you what was happening and not Grace then people could say that I was giving you an unfair advantage. We're out of work now… coming out for a drink with you is not a professional meeting. I'm here with you because I want to be.'

His words were the first audible admission as far as Regan was concerned that maybe Leo was as interested in her as she was in him. 'So, this rendezvous is… er… personal, then?' en-

quired Regan, running one of her hands through her hair as she
did so. If this was a moment that required a hint of flirtation
then she wasn't going to miss the opportunity.

'I'm not supposed to have any kind of personal involvement
with the *talent*, but I figure I can make an exception. The show
will be over in a matter of weeks after all.'

'But we haven't even kissed yet, Leo. We might not be compatible. I know I'm a great kisser, but it takes two, you know.'
Regan was enjoying the thrill of seeing where the conversation
would lead.

'Do you normally chat up guys like that?' smirked Leo. 'Very
modern-day-woman, grabbing the bull by the horns.'

'I don't know, to be honest, I can't remember the last time
I did it sober,' replied Regan with a grin. Despite being on her
second cocktail, she felt remarkably clear-headed.

'Well, I guess we should find out if we are then, shouldn't
we?' As he spoke, Leo pushed back his chair and moved to Regan's side of the table. Running his hand through her hair, as she
herself had done moments before, Leo held the back of Regan's
head. His touch was firm and confident. He lowered his lips
onto hers.

At first, the kisses they shared were soft and inquisitive, their
lips brushing against each other with a feathery lightness. But
within seconds they embraced fully, Leo's tongue finding its way
into Regan's mouth. The hair from Leo's floppy fringe tickled
against Regan's face as their passion increased. Regan longed to
be somewhere more private and contemplated asking Leo if he
wanted to come back to hers, but any raunchy notions were cut
short by Leo's next words.

'I guess that means we're compatible then.' His cheeks were
infused with a rosy colour, flushed from their first embrace. His
smile spread wide on his face. 'I mean what I say though, Regan.

I can't take this any further until the show is over. It could cause real trouble for me.' He brushed his hand along her cheek as he spoke. 'The last thing I want is for anything to spoil this programme. It could be pivotal for both our careers. Look at you, two-nil up already against Grace. At this rate you'll be eclipsing your mother's fame sooner than you think.'

Regan listened intently as he spoke, lost in his eyes and his captivating charm. Regan didn't say a word, she didn't need to. She knew that she had bagged her man.

CHAPTER 34

Every time Sadie attempted to ring Lawrence about his violent outburst towards her, his mobile switched straight through to the answering machine. She'd left countless messages begging her husband to speak to her but received nothing in return.

She had been convinced that Lawrence would be happy to hear her news. But nothing in her worst nightmares could have prepared her for his reaction. It was like a bad dream, but the plum-coloured bruise on her cheek proved that it wasn't.

After Lawrence had sped away from the house, she had run to their bedroom and lay on the bed, sobbing, her mind a turbulent mix of rage, hurt and confusion. She'd not slept all night, redialling Lawrence's number on her mobile, listening out for his return. But come the early morning light, there was still no sign. He'd had a fair amount to drink throughout the meal and was well over the legal limit when it came to driving. *What if he'd had an accident? What if he was lying dead in a ditch right now?* Sadie would never be able to forgive herself.

Lawrence Silvers was sat opposite the Silvers' family doctor, Dr Pahal, at his private London clinic. Lawrence had woken the doctor from his bed in the middle of the night and had insisted that he see him straight away. Dr Pahal had known Lawrence long enough to know that there was no way he was going to argue.

Lawrence hadn't slept and had spent the night driving his car around in a silent rage. In the space of one evening his world had started to crumble. And it was the women he loved who had unintentionally smashed it with a baby-shaped demolition ball.

Rubbing the stubble on his chin and staring through blood-shot eyes, Lawrence began his tirade. 'Look, doc, this wasn't supposed to happen. When I had that vasectomy years back, you told me that that would be it. No more kids. Either there's been some kind of major fuck up here or my wife is doing the dirty on me. Could this kid be mine or not?'

Retaining an air of calm, Dr Pahal began to speak. 'If you'd had the vasectomy recently, Mr Silvers, then I would say that there could be a slim chance that the baby could be yours, but since the operation was performed over three years ago, then I would very much doubt you are capable of fathering a child. You brought me samples of your ejaculate to be tested at the time and you had a series of sperm-free samples. After two sperm-free samples it's considered that you are unable to get a woman pregnant.'

Lawrence could feel his skin turn cold as the doctor contin-ued. 'A vasectomy is considered to be the safest, most effective kind of birth control. The likelihood of you fathering a child now is pretty much non-existent.'

Despite what he was hearing, Lawrence was still finding it hard to believe that Sadie could be pregnant by another man. *Why would she cheat on him? Surely she had too much to lose? But if the baby wasn't his, then whose was it?* Lawrence knew that he had to learn the truth.

'What about paternity testing then? Is that a possibility or do I have to wait until the sprog is born? Is there anything I can do now to get this bloody mess sorted?'

'It's not generally done at this stage but it isn't out of the question. A DNA paternity test can be performed accurately before a child is born through amniocentesis and Chorionic Villus Sampling.'

'What the hell does that mean?' barked Lawrence.

'Chorionic Villus Sampling is usually performed at very early stages of pregnancy, normally around the eighth to thirteenth week of pregnancy. It's a sampling procedure that allows an obstetrician to obtain a small amount of matter which is used for a paternity test. Paternity tests conducted using CVS samples are normally just as accurate as tests performed after the child is born. It is a major and very expensive deal though, Mr Silvers. Plus, of course, your wife would have to agree to do it. There are risks.'

'Like what?' If she's been shagging around I want to know. She'll have no fucking choice in the matter.'

Ignoring Lawrence's machine-gun fire of expletives, Dr Pahal continued to share his knowledge. 'The baby could be killed as a direct result of the procedure. Roughly 1 in every 200 pregnancies in which the test is performed is lost as a result.'

'I know you can't tell me what to do, doc, and you know me well enough to know that I'll make up my own mind anyway. But in your opinion, speaking man to man, do you think the baby could be mine? That's all I want to know.'

Dr Pahal's answer was conclusive. 'Off the record, and speaking to you not as a patient but as a friend who's been coming to me for years, I'd say that there's no way that the baby is yours. I think you and your wife have some serious talking to do.'

Swallowing back his rage, Lawrence left the clinic and headed back to his car. Switching his phone back on, he dialled Sadie. She picked up immediately.

'Lawrence, where are you? I'm worried sick. What's going on?' Her voice was stippled with deep, frantic sobs.

Lawrence was in no mood for explanations. 'We need to talk. Meet me at The Dorchester. I'll book a room. Ask reception which room I'm in when you get there.'

Confused by his words, Sadie stuttered, 'But… but why aren't you coming home.'

'If you want to talk to me, then it's at The Dorchester. I'll see you in about an hour or so.' Lawrence hung up. He had other phone calls to make and he needed to make them as quickly as possible.

CHAPTER 35

In Evie's many jaunts to Los Angeles, she had never yet visited the ultra-swish Beachwood Canyon area. But tonight was the night when she was heading to the home of Jeremy Pinewood.

After another gloriously relaxing day of pampering herself, Evie felt on top form. Stephanie had been right - the impromptu trip to LA was just what Evie had needed to get over the upset with Harry. He'd left some more rambling messages on her telephone, but not wanting to let him spoil her excitement about meeting up with Jeremy, she'd switched off the phone.

It was only as Evie melted into the sheer comfort of the back seat of Jeremy's chauffeur-driven limousine as it picked her up outside the Wilshire that she actually thought about turning it on again. When she did, a series of frantic beeps signalled her missed calls and messages. One from Regan wanting to hear all about her 'man trouble', two from Steph wishing her 'good luck for tonight' and one from Jeremy saying how excited he was about their 'date'. Evie was still not sure if that was the right word, but had to admit she loved the sound of it. It was so classically romantic. Messages from Harry were conspicuous by their absence. Maybe he'd finally understood why she'd left Austria.

The journey to Beachwood Canyon was likely to be a fairly lengthy one, the Los Angeles traffic still being pretty heavy. Evie decided to pass the time by chatting to Jeremy's chauffeur.

'So, what's your name? I'm Evie…'

'I'm Robin, Miss, very nice to meet you.' He flashed a smile in the rear view mirror. It was the quintessence of Hollywood - white, wide, warm and welcoming. *Good looking chap,* thought Evie.

'So, do you work for Jeremy full time then?'

'I work for Mr Pinewood whenever he's in the country, Miss. He likes to surround himself with familiar people and I've been with him since he first came to Hollywood.'

'So, you must be forever taking girls to his home then?' Evie enquired cheekily, digging for information without wanting to be seen as prying.

'If Mr Pinewood is receiving visitors then I will undoubtedly be required to take them to and from his home. He's a very busy man.'

Diplomatic answer. When I get a chauffeur he will have to be this loyal and this handsome. Evie was enjoying the conversation. Robin seemed friendly and after a day of solitude and tranquillity at the spa she was ready to indulge in some idle chit-chat.

'So, tell me about Beachwood Canyon. It's up by the Hollywood sign, isn't it?'

'The upper area of it is the Hollywoodland that was originally advertised back in the 1920s by the Hollywood sign, yes. It's serene, it's scenic and it's an honour to be able to live there.'

'You live there too then, Robin? Chauffeurs must be getting well paid these days if you can afford that.' Evie giggled to herself, but then suddenly worried that she'd been patronising. 'God, that sounded awful, sorry.'

'Not to worry, Miss. I'll be the first to admit that there's no way I could afford anything remotely near Beachwood. I am lucky enough to get to live at Mr Pinewood's as a kind of house sitter when he's not there and as his chauffeur when he is. I thank my lucky stars for this job.'

'Must be lonely, though. Do you live there on your own?'

'Not at all, Miss, there's another live-in member of staff, Tasmina. She acts as housekeeper, so between us we make sure that everything is ready for Mr Pinewood's stays.'

'I can't wait to see it. Who knows, if I like the area, then you might be getting me as a neighbour in the near future, Robin.' Evie's skin shuddered excitedly at the thought.

'Well, you wouldn't be the first successful celebrity to live around here miss. Madonna's been here, the late Heath Ledger, Forest Whitaker, Anthony Keidis from Red Hot Chilli Peppers, even Peg Entwistle way back when.' As he said the last name, Robin looked expectantly at Evie, willing her to ask who Ms Entwistle was. Evie's response surprised him.

'Oh my God, I read all about her back in college. She was the actress who killed herself by jumping off the top of the Hollywoodland sign back in the 1930s. She was only 24. It's such a sad tale. She was born in Wales and moved to New York with her father. Then he was killed by a car and she relocated to Hollywood. She'd had a bit of success on Broadway in New York but when she moved here the work dried up and she became horrendously depressed. One day, she wrote a suicide note, walked up to the Hollywood sign, climbed a maintenance ladder on the letter H and jumped off. A hiker found her body. The really tragic thing was that a few days after her death one of her relatives opened a letter offering her the lead part in a play about a woman driven to suicide. It's such a bitterly tragic story.'

'I'm impressed,' said Robin. 'Most people have forgotten about her story.'

'To be honest, I haven't thought about it since I was at college. I have always said that a film should be made about her life. I'd love to play her myself, although Kirsten Dunst would probably be a more likely choice.'

'Well from what I've seen of your acting, Miss Merchant, you would do her story proud.'

'Thank you, Robin, and call me Evie, please.' Staring out of the window at the Hollywood sign in the distance, Evie felt a ripple of sadness pass through her body. Peg had been virtually the same age as Evie when she'd killed herself. She'd suffered so much heartache and felt the world would be better off without her. How awful that a person could be made to feel that worthless and low…

———

'Worthless' and 'low' were two words that Nush felt had been deeply branded upon her soul. As she had closed her eyes to block out the world around her, she had genuinely believed that never opening them again would be the most rewarding option. That leaving the Trinity and all those who knew her for good would be the easiest thing to do. Kill the lights on her life once and for all.

But before Nush had had the chance to stretch her arm out and grab the bottle of pills from her bedside table, she had fallen deep into sleep. As she slept, she dreamt …

She was outside a big top, huge red and white stripes streaking down the fabric. Bellyfuls of laughter rang out from within the tent and the jangle of music filled the air. It should have been a happy place but Nush could feel that there was something sinister about her surroundings.

The smell of the big top filled her nostrils as she entered, a heady mix of sawdust, popcorn and animals. The circus tent was full, a huge crowd of beaming faces looking down at her.

A pair of clowns blocked her path, one of them raising a bucket in her direction and throwing the contents towards her. Nush cowered, expecting to be drenched, but instead was show-

ered with ultra-fine glitter. The other clown squirted water from
a huge faux flower on his lapel. Their actions were exaggerated
and despite the laughter from the crowd, they seemed sad. Their
faces were painted, huge green crosses splashed across each eye
and a downturned semi-circle of red spread across their mouths.
Through their heavy make-up, Nush recognised their faces as
Sadie and Ashley.

A juggler crossed her path, a flurry of balls circling through
the air from his hands. Nush flinched as they whizzed past her
eyes. The juggler spoke. 'Mind you don't get hurt, Miss.' The
voice, belittling and condescending, belonged to Harry.

A large figure appeared, dressed in a red jacket, gold waist-
coat, black trousers, a pair of riding boots and a top hat. He
possessed the swagger of a champion. He was the ringmaster. As
he boomed to the crowd, it came as no surprise to Nush that the
voice full of machismo that thundered from underneath the top
hat belonged to her own father.

'Ladies and gentlemen, welcome to the Silvers' Family Circus
finale – the most dangerous stunt of them all. Without the aid
of a safety net, our intrepid and dazzling daredevil will fling
herself from a platform high above the circus floor. Behold our
very own soaring sensation, Miss Anoushka Silvers!'

The roar of the crowd was deafening. Nush tried to take in
Lawrence's words. *A dazzling daredevil? Soaring sensation?* She
looked down at herself. She was wearing a body-hugging sequinned outfit worthy of a burlesque showgirl. Most of it was
flesh tone in colour, giving the impression that she was naked,
vulnerable to the world. Her breasts and groin were covered in
a mass of shocking pink sequins. Taking in her new appearance,
Nush became aware of two people wearing similar outfits standing either side of her. Staring into their faces, it was with horror
that she recognised them as Clarissa and Mae-Ling.

Before Nush knew what was happening, the two women had roughly placed their hands on Nush's arms and were dragging her towards a ladder that stretched its way, skyscraper-like, to the uppermost point of the big top.

As the crowd whooped and cheered underneath her, Nush could feel herself being manoeuvred up the ladder. The three women climbed onto the small platform at the top of the ladder. Nush could feel tears streaming down her cheeks. The ringmaster spoke. 'May I have silence? The moment has come for our performer to take the plunge and fall to the floor. Will she go through with it? Will she be strong enough to survive?'

As the crowd fell silent, Nush became acutely aware of everything around her. She looked down at the crowd. Most of it remained a blur, but certain faces stood out. Gazing up at her from the audience, willing her not to jump were Evie and Regan.

Nothing made sense. The carnivalesque music of the big top danced inside Nush's head. A bright light shone from the crowd below. Looking at her friends again, Nush could see a ghost-like form sat behind them. The outlines seemed blurred but she could make out that the shape was female and possessed a mass of beautiful golden hair which wafted gracefully around her head. Focussing on the figure's face, Nush narrowed her eyes to focus. Suddenly it became clear. The image was Lysette, Nush's mother. She smiled, acknowledging Nush's recognition and held out her hands towards her daughter.

The vision of her mother blurred once more and then vanished, taking Regan and Evie with her. They were replaced by a gladiatorial man rippling with muscles, again holding out his arms to Nush. He wore nothing but a tight pair of shorts. His hair was slicked back against his head and a curly painted-on moustache wiggled comically beneath his nose. It was the image of a circus strong man, but the face was that of Jake Saunders. With his arms outstretched, he beckoned Nush to jump. 'I will catch you and keep you safe.'

As Jake encouraged Nush to jump, everything around her seemed to jumble itself into a whirlpool of sounds and images. The music, Lawrence's booming voice, the jabbing hands of Clarissa and Mae-Ling, the chilling faces of Sadie and Ashley... nothing made sense. *What should she do, who should she trust?* Unable to take any more, she began to fall, or was she pushed? Hurtling towards the sawdust below, Nush let out a gut-wrenching scream, a scream born in the pit of her soul.

It was the scream that wrenched her from her sleep...

———

As the immense metal gates swung open at the front of Jeremy's Beachwood Canyon home, Evie felt her heart skip a beat. Evie was actually nervous. The dynamics of their entire relationship had suddenly changed. Initially, Evie had admired Jeremy professionally and had secretly lusted after him. After their first few days on set she had begun to openly dislike him due to his bullish, brutish behaviour. Plus she had been busy with Harry.

But now that Harry was definitely history, and Jeremy's gallant likeability was soaring sky-high at a rate NASA would be proud of, things were very different indeed. Evie began to wonder what the night might hold. It may have been a meeting of two of the world's most influential media movers-and-shakers, but as far as Evie's pulsating heart and sweaty palms were concerned it was a date. A good old-fashioned *Shall I shan't I, what will I say?* kind of date.

As Robin opened the door of the car to let her out, Evie inhaled deeply and stepped out into the warm night air. As she looked up, Jeremy was already stood in the doorway of his house, immaculately dressed and looking just as deliciously seductive as she remembered. The smile beaming across his face showed that he was pleased to see her. 'You made it,' he gushed with the excitement of a puppy greeting his master. He bounded down the steps and took Evie by the hand. It felt wondrously civilised. 'You look amazing. Come on in, the food's almost ready and the Veuve Clicquot is chilled to perfection. The only thing missing is a beautiful lady to share it with me… and now you're here the picture's complete.'

God, he's keen, I'll give him that, Evie thought. *He's going to be hard to resist.* Not that she was convinced that she really wanted to resist anyway. She just didn't want to make things too easy for Jeremy and roll over in submission.

'Sounds divine,' she purred confidently, expertly hiding the fact that as they walked hand in hand into Jeremy's house, her stomach was nervously somersaulting out of control.

CHAPTER 36

The location was Speaker's Corner in the north-east corner of London's Hyde Park, a place where, for centuries, people had been allowed to indulge in public speaking, sharing their thoughts and wishes freely. It was there that the *Wild Child* team were preparing to film the remainder of the next episode.

Regan had spent the entire previous day researching, writing and revising her speech for the show. She had been told by her speech tutor that she should pick a subject that was close to her heart and after a whole morning of ruminating she had finally chosen 'The Changing Face of Modern Music'. Music was one thing she'd always been passionate about, and she'd grown up with her walls adorned with posters of her favoured idols – Bowie, The Smiths, Kurt Cobain, The B-52's. She wanted to speak about their influences on her as a person. How the chameleon-like changes of image from Bowie, the moribund downbeat lyrics from The Smiths and the moment that Cobain had blown himself away for good had coloured her world. She also wanted to throw controversy into the mix by highlighting the frothy bubble-gum nature of disposable music like Britney Spears and Jessica Simpson to prevent the whole speech becoming a self-indulgent fan-fest. They were Regan's pet hates and she wanted to ask why the world lapped them up. It was a chance for her to bring Grace into her speech as well, with her scantily-clad worldwide success with Sexalicious. Sex sells, but did it equate to talent? Regan didn't think so and was keen to say. She was sure Grace knew her well enough by now to know that it wasn't a personal dig. Anyway, hadn't Grace just publicly ditched her old sexed-up days during the previous show's auction?

But despite a day's research and writing, Regan knew that she was going into the Speaker's Corner task at half speed. Reading back her speech over and over again as she reworked it through until the early hours of the morning, she just seemed to end up with a jumbled mess of ideas. A mere four hours' sleep had left her tired and bleary-eyed, a fact that was not lost on Grace as they met in Hyde Park.

'Someone is going to be saying *praise be* to the make-up girls today, aren't they? Your face looks as washed up as driftwood, honey!' Grace's words were as direct as ever.

'I'd like to say the same for you, Ms Laszlo, but, as per, you look immaculate. Speech all polished to perfection? What subject did you plump for in the end?'

'Celebrities and Fur. Stars who have blood on their hands. I've got facts and figures that will shock the masses. By the end of today, PETA will be on the phone begging me to take on Pamela Anderson's crown in giving fur the cold shoulder. Bring it on, baby, bring it on!' Grace threw back her head and laughed, relishing the thought.

'Just how the hell do you stay so god damned perky, Grace? I'm bricking it about today.'

'A line or two in the back of the car on the way here helped a treat, doll. You want some? It'll lift those baggy eyes a treat.'

'No way, not in front of Leo. Anyway, my speech will be a rambling drivel as it is without the aid of coke.'

'Suit yourself. So how goes things with our sexy little producer anyway? Made your move?'

'Not as yet,' bluffed Regan, but the reddening of her cheeks revealed her fib. 'I'm still working on that one.'

Grace knew that Regan was lying. 'Now I know why you look so wrecked. Leo's been keeping you up all night, eh? Who's a lucky girl, then? Tell me about it later, doll, I'm off to get my speech outfit on. I'll ditch the moleskin trousers today… don't want to look too hypocritical after all.'

Annoyed that she was so blatantly bad at hiding the truth, Regan took her speech out of her back pocket and unfolded it, hoping that it would make a lot more sense than it had the last time she'd read it. Thirty seconds in, she realised that it didn't and headed off to make-up to try and achieve some kind of cosmetic camouflage for her baggy eyes. She already knew that today was not going to be her day.

———

Sadie walked up to the reception at The Dorchester Hotel and enquired about her husband's whereabouts. The uniformed man behind the counter answered. 'Mr Silvers is in the Mayfair Suite, madam.'

On the way there she stopped off at one of the hotel bathrooms, keen to check her appearance before meeting Lawrence. Staring at her bruise in the mirror, she could see that it had ripened, ever-darker hour by hour, the epicentre of it now a deep shade of aubergine. Sadie was sure that her meeting with Lawrence would be nothing short of horrendous, but if he could see how bruised she was, both externally and internally, then maybe he would be able to show some remorse.

Sadie entered the suite with a cocktail of trepidation and fear running through her veins. Since being with Lawrence, the man who she had always described as the man of her dreams, she had been the best partner she could be. There was just one doubt scratching away in Sadie's brain and she hoped against hope that she was wrong.

As soon as Sadie saw her husband she knew that his anger had far from quelled. In fact, it appeared to have escalated. Lawrence ordered her to sit. Unable to look him in the face at first, Sadie concentrated on the view of London's Mayfair rooftops through the hotel window. She was willing herself not to cry.

For about five seconds there was silence. To Sadie it felt like an eternity. It was Lawrence who spoke first. As he did so, he stared at the bruise on Sadie's cheek. Peppered in his anger, there were specks of disbelief and contrition. *How had it come to this?*

'You have no idea why I'm hurting, do you? Why I've been forced to hurt the woman I loved. The truth is… you've betrayed me. You know you have, you just weren't satisfied with what you had. You've ruined everything.'

She heard the words but their meaning didn't compute in her head. 'Lawrence… I would never betray you. I love you. I thought you wanted a baby. A chip off the old Silvers' block.' A nagging fear still swept through her mind.

Lawrence exploded with rage. 'Not with some slut who can't keep her hands off other men. I'd rather pull the plug on it than watch a baby of mine grow up with you as its mother.'

The maliciousness in his voice was too much for Sadie and she burst into tears. 'How can you talk like that, Lawrence? This is our own flesh and blood growing inside me.'

'But that's just it, Sadie, it's not *our* flesh and blood is it? Be honest… it's yours, yes, but it's not mine, is it? It can't be, not unless it's a fucking miracle. Whose is it then? Or don't you know, Sadie, too many blokes to choose from. Bet you've had them lined up as soon as my back's been turned. I'm out making enough money to keep you up to your eyeballs in Burberry and all the time you're dropping your knickers for the first piece of dick that comes your way. You keep your baby if you want but I'll have nothing to do with it or you. It can't be mine. I'll tell you why…'

Again Lawrence's words bounced around Sadie's mind. Despite her fears, Lawrence's tirade was much harsher than her wildest nightmares. *The baby couldn't be his? Claiming that it was over between them? That she was a slut?*

She listened with horror, colour draining from her face as he told her about the vasectomy and his conversation with Dr Pahal. Relentless in his verbal attack, he told her about the test that could be done to prove that he wasn't the father. Sadie sat open-mouthed trying to take in everything he was saying. It was only when his continuous bullet-fire of news had come to an end that she allowed herself to try and protest.

Her throat dry with shock, she croaked through her tears. 'I thought you wanted more children. Why didn't you tell me you'd had a vasectomy and that you couldn't have kids? Why keep it from me?' She felt betrayed too.

'More kids, Sadie… the two I have bleed me dry as it is. Harry and Anoushka are grown up now. Do you really think I'd want another baby crawling around, keeping us up at night with its constant bawling? You wanting to give it ballet lessons and horse riding classes. Sending it to the best school money can buy. I've done it, Sadie, and there was no way I was going to do it again. I have no need for another kid. I thought you and I were enough. But we're not are we, not for you? You get this test done and we'll see if I'm the dad. I know I can't be, the doctor says I can't be, but if you're so bloody sure that it has to be me, then you've got nothing to worry about, have you? But be honest, are you really telling me that's there's no possibility that it could be someone else's. Am I the only man who's shagged you? I reckon not, but what do you say? Who was it, Sadie, who the fuck was it?' As he shouted, he picked up the glass tumbler he'd been drinking from and threw it against the wall behind Sadie's head. It shattered into hundreds of tiny shards. Sadie let out a shriek of fear.

It was the question she'd been dreading. The one doubt that had been gnawing away inside. She'd always been faithful to Lawrence, ever since the day they had met. Or at least she had until that one time, that one stupid idiotic time. When her guard had been down and a weak-willed moment of madness had gone too far.

She remained frozen, unable to speak. Purple with rage, it was Lawrence who spoke. 'You take the test and prove I'm the dad and we'll move on. But I know I won't be, so we're through. I've booked the suite here for the night. Use it. Get your fancy man round if you want. Tell him your news. But don't come back to Kingsbury because you won't get in. The locks are being changed as we speak. Your keys are useless. Whatever you've got here is all you have. I'll get someone to pack your clothes and send them on. You can leave a forwarding address with my lawyer. Unless your body is rewriting medical history, Sadie, you've cheated on me. You've got another man's baby inside of you. Neither you nor that little runt will get a penny from me. I want a divorce and a quick one at that.'

With that, he was gone, slamming the suite door behind him. In the short space of half an hour, Sadie has lost nearly everything she held dear. Her home, her husband, her future happiness. All of it lost to one stupid mistake. She knew taking the test would be useless. Lawrence evidently wasn't the father. That nagging fear that she'd tried to bury was the reason after all. She'd known it.

Collecting her thoughts, a trembling Sadie dialled a number on her mobile phone and listened patiently to the rings.

'Hello there, you,' said the male voice on the other end of the line.

Sadie replied. 'Hi, it's me, listen we need to talk. I must see you right away…'

CHAPTER 37

The warm summer air felt good on Mae-Ling's face. She was elated at being out in the open air. Finally she wasn't cooped up in that police cell.

Being top of your field meant that money was no object and when money is no object then you can hire the best help there is. So after hours of police interviews with one of the most respected lawyers in the UK by her side, Mae-Ling was able to walk away from custody with the title of being 'mentally vulnerable' hanging over her head. Not that she gave a damn. It was a badge she was happy to wear, as it meant she could further pursue her revenge on Nush. So what if her conditional bail meant that she wasn't allowed to go within a few metres of that bitch? So what if she had a night time curfew imposed upon her? Fuck that. There would be no escape for Nush. She'd be made to pay for tearing her and Jake apart. Oh yes, for Mae-Ling Ch'en it felt good to feel the daylight on her face once more.

———

The daylight felt good to Anoushka as well, the warmth working its way through her pores and into her skin as she walked back home from the shops near her house. The last few days had been some of the darkest of her life and had taken her to lows she never wished to revisit. The lure of the pills on the bedside cabinet had been strong but her strange dream had made her look at things through different eyes. There were people who cared about her, who would be upset to find out that she was no longer around.

She had woken up with a newly found strength, a spark to survive. Strength she would thank the girls for when she saw them. They'd spent countless hours years ago at Farmington trying to analyse their dreams, so Nush knew they would all go into overdrive dissecting her latest hallucination. And Nush was certain that one of the cast in her dream would cause more discussion than any of the others – the appearance of Jake Saunders.

Placing the items she'd bought into a carrier bag at the checkout of her local delicatessen, Nush knew that she had a few decisions to make. Her work on *The Daily Staple* was bringing her down. She needed time out. Maybe a few days' holiday. One of the girls might be free for a trip away. That could be good.

What about the recent assault? She should really report it, but the last thing she wanted was to rake over all of the sordid details again. Then there was the business with Evie and Harry. If Harry was cheating then Evie should hear about it from Nush. But Evie could be such a delicate soul when it came to men and from her last message to Nush it had sounded like there was trouble in paradise anyway.

It was time to start a bit of life laundry. Nush headed to a bench, sat down and started dialling. There was no time like the present.

The hardest call would be to Lawrence. If she was taking a sabbatical from work then he would want to know why. She had to be strong. She was relieved when her phone clicked straight through to his messaging service. 'Daddy, it's Nush. Look, after all this business with Mae-Ling I need some *me time*. I'm taking some time off to get my head together. I'll sort the column and get the team to bust their asses for some scoops you'll be proud of. Hope everything's okay with you. I'll be in touch. Bye.' She heaved a sigh of relief as she clicked the off button. If Lawrence had been able to answer back she'd have crumbled.

The next call was to her team. Work had been the last thing on her mind lately and her reputation as the bitchiest columnist in the land had naturally suffered as a result. It was time to rectify that. She got straight through to her deputy, an eager-to-please, hard-faced girl fresh from university. 'I'm out of the loop for a while. You're in charge, so try and shine. Work your contacts, earn your money, get the dirt… or you'll have me to answer to. Remember the rules, too, no stories about my friends or else you'll be out on your arse.' Having enjoyed the trembling fear in her deputy's voice, Nush smiled to herself and hung up. *See, this old bitch has still got it*, she mused. *Now, who's next? The girls.*

She left a message for Regan to call her and then tried Evie. The international tone on Evie's mobile signalled that she was still abroad. Nush spoke after the beep, 'Hey, little Miss Hollywood, no idea where you are. Guess things are a touch awkward with Harry from your message. Sorry I've been quiet, I've had a rough time lately. I'm feeling a holiday is in order. Care to share a few days in Muscat on me? Body elixirs at the spa, cocktails around the infinity pool… you know how it goes. Ring me. I miss you guys.'

The walk back to her apartment was an uplifting one. Nush was pleased with how her day was going. It felt good to be finally putting herself first.

As she turned the corner into her street, Nush was surprised to see a black sports car parked right outside her apartment. The windows were also blacked out. Her first thought was *not more trouble, please,* but a quick scan of the number plate, which read

BULLET 1, and her mind started to race. Maybe this would be a welcome visitor.

The front electric window started to wind down to reveal Jake Saunders. Nush couldn't stop her mouth from falling open, both at her surprise and also at how good he looked.

Jake spoke. 'I know I'm the last person you expect to see right now, but after all that's gone on, I need to speak to you. That night we had together seems to have got a little out of control, don't you think?'

'Understatement of the year, wouldn't you say?' replied Nush. 'I try to wreck your life, your girlfriend tries to kill me and I end up being front page news. It turned out to be a little more headline-grabbing than even I'd first thought, yes.'

'I know you were doing your job and I'd be lying if I said it didn't hurt. But I enjoyed that night … and I think you did too. Mae-Ling and I were over long before you came along. You just proved what I already knew. What I didn't know is how much I'd think about you and want to see you again.' His words faltered as he spoke, giving him an air of boyish vulnerability which seemed to contrast with his air of muscular man power. Nush liked what she was hearing.

'Do you want to come in?' Nush had spoken the words before she had even had time to think about what she was saying.

'So, have you been thinking about me too, then?' offered Jake.

'Thinking about you…? You've crossed my mind,' Nush smiled, thinking back to her dream.

Walking into the apartment, Nush was unaware that no more than 200 yards away on the other side of the street stood another familiar figure watching her. It was Ashley Erridge. He'd been there all morning, scrutinizing Nush's every move. He'd followed her to the shops, watched her from afar as she made her calls and then followed her back home. It felt good to see her and he'd spent his time with a constant erection pounding against the inside of his trousers, imagining how it would be to feel the touch of her skin again. The erection had only subsided with the inconvenient arrival of Jake Saunders.

CHAPTER 38

Sexual attraction is a weird and wonderful thing.

For Evie, the feeling of sexual attraction she was experiencing was a piquant mix of high expectation and slight frustration.

Her evening at Jeremy's had been divine. She had been captivated by Jeremy's conversation, spellbound by his gentlemanly charm and had feasted on the most delicious food and drink. But every time she had thought that Jeremy might have made his move, he hadn't.

His words to her all evening had confirmed what she already knew, that he wanted them to be together. With the media frenzy of *The Bouquet Catcher* about to explode and with Evie still being hotly tipped for an Oscar nomination, there had never been a better time for the two of them to be together. But Evie needed to be sure that any union between them was genuine. She had only just suffered heartache at the hands of Harry and the last thing she wanted to do was fall headfirst into another loveless liaison.

Evie had tried to play things cheekily with Jeremy. She'd made enough mistakes in her life when it came to men already.

'So then, Mr Pinewood, big shot actor man…' Evie's words were playful, spurred on by the many glasses of champagne she'd already downed throughout the evening. 'How come you were so horrid to me at first then, if you fancy me? Not exactly the best way to wheedle your way into my affections, was it?'

They were sat on one of Jeremy's huge chocolate brown leather sofas. Evie had kicked off her shoes and was facing Jeremy, with her bare feet underneath her. It was a position that enabled Jeremy to slip his hand around her shoulders and play with her hair as he answered. 'I was just being ignorant. You know how vulnerable we actors can be. I just wanted to make sure that I was the star of the show. Stupid, I know, but it would have been very easy to be outshone by a talent as bright as yours.'

'But you and that make up guy of yours, Mario, were strutting around like you owned the place. I thought you were a right pair of prats.' Her own bluntness made her giggle.

'Guilty as charged, what can I say?' Jeremy held his hands up in defeat. 'I was acting like a prick. But please don't say I've ruined my chances with you. I am trying to make up for it after that telling off you gave me on set.'

'Flowers, delicious meals… yeah, I'll give you that. You certainly know how to treat a girl.'

It was then that Jeremy first kissed her, fully on the lips. It was a lingering yet somewhat soft and gentle kiss. Passionate yet polite. Evie felt her nipples stand to attention underneath her dress, anticipating what was to come. She knew that if Jeremy had offered to take her to bed, she would have eagerly followed. But he didn't. Jeremy turned to Evie and cupped his hands either side of her face. 'So, can we make a go of this and show the world just how great we are together? We're dynamite together and you know it.' There was something innocent and boyish about his words. Once again, as he finished speaking he placed his lips against hers.

'Yes… we can.' She laughed as she said it, excited that finally she'd admitted that Jeremy could be the man to potentially make her happy. 'Yes, yes, yes!' She repeated the word over and over to convey her certainty. Jeremy flashed his winning smile and started kissing her again. At that moment they tasted like the sweetest kisses on earth to Evie. She was ready to give herself to him, to lie back in his arms. But just as she thought Jeremy would sweep her into his muscular arms and carry her to his bedroom, the intensity of the situation again seemed to slow.

The kisses continued, but it went no further. Evie longed for Jeremy to place his hands against her breasts. She wanted to rip open his shirt and let her fingers dance through the chest hair that covered his carved pecs. To let her hands feel their way down his body. But it seemed that, for tonight, her fantasies would have to stay just that. A flash of thought within her actually appreciated the fact that he wasn't jumping to seduce her straight away. She found it intoxicating.

Jeremy was elated that Evie had said yes. In between kisses, he told her how she had made him 'the happiest man in Hollywood', how they would 'be invincible together' and how they could be 'bigger than Brangelina'. They weren't exactly the most romantic words Evie had ever heard but she still found Jeremy's enthusiasm infectious.

'This is the perfect end to the perfect night!' Jeremy exclaimed. 'Can we meet up again tomorrow? I'm going out for a run in the morning, but I'm free after that. How about I swing by the hotel to pick you up and we can spend the day together. Lunch at De Niro's restaurant, Ago on Melrose, and then see what the afternoon brings.'

'That sounds great. I guess I'll see you tomorrow then?' Evie's words were hesitant. She was happy that she and Jeremy were about to become an item, but somehow she had expected the night to end with more than just schoolboy-like excitement. Was she wrong to want to take it further with Jeremy so soon? Was it better for her to wait? Was the longing from between her legs the result of too much champagne? She'd given her all to

Harry readily enough and look how that had ended. Destination heartache. No, it was better to wait a little while and be sure before leaping into bed.

Slipping into the backseat of his waiting Limo, Evie couldn't help but feel her frustrations rise as Jeremy kissed her goodnight. If the sex with Jeremy was going to be as good as his kisses promised, then it would be mind-blowing.

'Did you have a good evening, madam?' asked Jeremy's chauffeur Robin from the front seat. Flushed from the evening's events, Evie grinned. 'Yes, wonderful thanks. It was truly perfect.'

She couldn't help but hope that tonight could be the start of something incredibly special.

Inside the house, Jeremy watched Evie from a downstairs window and waved her goodbye.

CHAPTER 39

'I shagged you for work, Jake. I went out to find a story and you were it. I didn't know what would happen afterwards. It's all such a mess. I'm not proud of myself. I have my reasons for doing what I did.'

Nush and Jake had been discussing the aftermath of their night together ever since they'd entered her apartment. There was something about Jake. The attraction between them was evident. Even Nush, in her complete distrust of the opposite sex, could feel a charge between them that would be sufficient to wake Frankenstein's monster.

'Can't you see, that doesn't matter. I can't stop thinking about you. I know we were both out of it, but from the memories and feelings I have about that night, I know it was good... very good. I was gutted when you weren't there in the morning. And as horny as hell!'

Nush recalled slipping Jake the Viagra that night. It was no wonder he was horny. He'd have probably been like it all day. 'But how can any man forgive me for what I did to you, Jake? Your infidelity was all over the press before you'd barely arrived back home to your girlfriend and baby thanks to me. Honestly, despite my hard-bitch exterior, that doesn't exactly make me feel particularly good about myself.'

'Will you listen to yourself? Stop putting yourself down. You're a gorgeous woman. I knew exactly who you were when I fell into bed with you. I knew I had a girlfriend and baby back home, but I also knew that I had a loveless relationship. Getting intimate with you was the best bit of sexual action I'd seen in ages even if there was a huge risk that I was playing with fire. I got my fingers burnt but I don't care. I want to see you, be with you again. You're stunning. Can't you see that?'

For once, Nush was taken aback. When was the last time a man had said such appreciative words to her? Could she trust what Jake was saying?

'It's not the first thing I see when I look in the mirror. No.' It was the kind of admission that Nush would only normally make to Regan or Evie. 'I don't know, Jake. After all the heartache I've caused, isn't it a bit messy to get involved with you. I like you, I like you a lot. There, I've said it. But until the business with Mae-Ling is sorted, what with her being charged and the papers all over us both like a rash, I can't think of complicating things further. I can't… I'm sorry.'

'I don't believe you. There's more to us than this whole sorry mess. But I won't pressurise you. Just think about it, please. Let's just spend some time together and see what happens. You're busy with work and I've got *Sporting Spartans* to contend with, but I really like you. I've thought of nothing else. I just want the chance to see what could happen. Please… you've got my number so ring me.'

Jake moved towards the door and opened it, ready to leave. Nush knew that she couldn't let him go without saying something, without showing some idea of how she was feeling. 'Wait Jake,' she heard herself say. 'Thanks for coming here and saying what you've said. I appreciate it. I'll ring you, I promise.' Walking up to him, Nush stood on tiptoes and planted a kiss against Jake's cheek. She let her lips remain there a little longer than normal. It didn't go unnoticed. Not by Jake, nor by the person stood right behind them on the doorstep. A crazed looking Mae-Ling watched on in horror. Both Nush and Jake caught sight of her at the same time. Screaming in horror, Nush tried to push the door shut, but Mae-Ling slammed into it and into the apartment before she could close it firmly.

'What the fuck are you doing here?' It was a dumbstruck Jake who spoke first.

'I could ask you the same thing, you bastard. Get away from her. That bitch ruined our lives. Now she's kissing you! What's going on?' Mae-Ling's whole body seemed to shake as she spoke.

Nush ran to the phone, fear mounting inside her. 'I'm phoning the police.'

'Don't even consider it, you bitch. Or I swear I'll kill you. Don't think I won't, because I will.' As Nush looked towards Mae-Ling she could see that she was holding a knife. The blade glistened in the rays of sunlight that streamed in through the open apartment door.

It was Jake who tried to calm the situation. 'Mae-Ling, put the knife down. Think about Famke. No-one meant for this to happen. Me sleeping with Nush didn't cause the end of our relationship did it? You and I had problems before. This situation has just made me admit we couldn't carry on as we were.'

It was only then that Jake realised what he had just said. Mae-Ling's sudden screeching stopped him from trying to rectify the damage. 'You slept with *her*… she's the slut in the story? I thought she had just written it, and all this time she was the woman in bed with you. The fucking irony. She tricks you into bed and then writes the kiss and tell without mentioning she's the one riding your cock.' The knife shook wildly in Mae-Ling's hand as she spoke. Tears started to roll down her face.

Nush was unable to move, rooted to the spot with fear. Jake had his hand out towards Mae-Ling, pleading with her to put the knife down. As he pleaded he edged towards her. Mae-Ling looked him straight in the eyes. As Jake looked directly into hers, all he could see was abject sorrow.

'How could you, Jake? With her... how could you?' Mae-Ling lunged towards Jake with the knife. Nush screamed as Jake tried to push the weapon out of the way, but he was too late, his reactions and co-ordination delayed by fear. The knife plunged into the flesh at the side of his stomach. Gasping, Jake slammed his hand to the wound as he fell to the floor. Blood started to run from between his fingers.

Mae-Ling turned her crazed eyes on Nush and cried 'You made me do this!' She was still holding onto the blood-stained knife.

'What have you done, you psycho bitch? I'm phoning for an ambulance.' Nush turned to grab the phone, oblivious to the danger of turning her back to Mae-Ling. 'Hang on, Jake, please, I'm getting help now. Just stay strong.' She could hear him moaning in pain.

Nush heard the voice answer at the other end. 'Hello, I need an ambulance please, now, someone's been stabbed. Please get here quickly.' She gave her address and hung up. Suddenly aware of the fact that Mae-Ling had gone quiet, she turned around. She was nowhere to be seen, but the blood-stained knife lay on the floor alongside Jake. He was still breathing, but only just.

CHAPTER 40

The blossoming friendship between Regan and Leo may have been simmering nicely at the start of the day, but eight hours of filming in Hyde Park's Speaker's Corner had certainly put paid to any kind of raunchy plans that Regan might have had for that evening. For Regan, the entire filming of episode three of *Wild Child* had been a total disaster. She had known it would be.

Her subject matter had been wrong, her levels of concentration were totally lacking and, when the cameras had started rolling at the beginning of her speech, she had dried up to drought proportions. Her mind had not been on the job and she had stumbled her way through twenty minutes before quitting her soapbox to lacklustre applause. As a result, Leo, whose major aim was to produce must-see TV, had not been happy. His last words to her as he'd stormed off set having witnessed Regan's shambolic attempt to captivate the gathered crowd were 'Let's just hope you take the next challenge a little more seriously, eh? This is not just your neck on the line here, this is mine too'. He was pissed off, no doubt about it.

Grace, on the other hand, had excelled with her anti-fur speech. Whipping the crowd up with her hard-hitting facts and pointing out audience members wearing fur and ridiculing them until they left red-faced. The fact that Grace had planted the people there for her own benefit in the first case was not even suggested. Grace had apparently won fair and square, bringing the score back to two-one. True to form, a euphoric Grace had headed directly to the nearest bar after her victory. As Regan was now at a loose end for the evening, any plans to cuddle up with Leo having evaporated into thin air, she had accepted Grace's invitation to join her.

Grace and Regan were downing cocktails in the social hub of Monroe's in Cavendish Square. It was a honey pot for the busy bee fashionable celebrities of the media world. It was Grace who was guiding the conversation. 'So what's the latest on mama Montana and Mr Silvers? Any goss to report?'

'Not as yet. I think that's why I was so all over the place to-day. I keep thinking about that photo. I carry it everywhere with me because I know sooner or later I'm going to have to confront either Montana or Lawrence about it. I guess I'll have to speak to Lawrence.'

'You have nothing to lose and everything to gain,' said Grace.

'Gain? Just what have I got to gain?' Regan was genuinely stumped.

'Knowledge about your mum. Knowledge is power and am-munition. You get one over on her and she'll be putty in your hands. Money, houses, cars, you'll want for nothing. Blackmail may be a dirty word, sweetheart, but it's a bloody lucrative one.'

'I don't need money. I have enough to buy whatever I want and this show should bring in big bucks for us both. What I do need is to know the truth. If she and my best friend's dad have history then I want to find out all about it.'

Draining the last of her cocktail, Grace eyed Regan across the table. 'Well, I tell you what I want, sexy... another drink with my new best friend. Same again?'

'Sure thing, but it's my round,' said Regan. 'I'm just going to take a trip to the little girls' room and then I'll get the drinks on the way back. Don't go anywhere.'

'Oh I won't,' whispered Grace as Regan walked away from the table. 'I'm hoping I've got everything I need right here.' She was scrutinising Regan's Dolce & Gabbana leopard print handbag, which was still sitting on the velvet seat Regan had just vacated. As Regan disappeared, Grace was quick to swoop. Unzipping the top of the bag, she rifled around inside. 'Make-up, diary, phone, sanitary protection… nice… where are you, Montana?' As she spoke to herself, Grace kept furtively looking up, checking for Regan's return. There was still no sign of her as Grace found just what she was looking for, the photo of Montana and Lawrence together. 'Ker-ching. Come to mama.'

Removing the photo, she quickly placed it into her own bag, zipped up Regan's once more, and placed it back where it had been left on the seat. It was seconds before a smiling Regan reappeared from the toilets and headed to the bar.

CHAPTER 41

As tough and as thick-skinned as she liked to believe she was, Mae-Ling knew that in a matter of a few short seconds, her life had literally crumbled around her into a million shattered pieces that could never be repaired.

Her trip to Nush's apartment had been foolish. It had broken the rules of her conditional bail, it would doubtless lead to a more damning case against her and could quite possibly lead to a heftier sentence when her time in court came.

But Mae-Ling hadn't been prepared for what she'd encountered. The last person she had expected to see there was Jake. On top of that, the last thing she had expected to hear from the man she had once adored was that Anoushka Silvers was the woman he had slept with. The thought of the two of them together made her sick.

Which was why she snapped – why she'd suddenly lost her composure and plunged the knife into Jake. She had dropped the knife in her panic, but as she fled from Nush's home, trying to see her way through tear-flooded eyes, she knew that she was in trouble. The knife was covered in her fingerprints. Guilty. Even if she'd removed the knife, there was a witness in the form of Nush. Guilty. The surveillance camera that had seen her throwing the brick through Nush's window initially was doubtless still working and had recorded her unlawful movements to and from the house. Guilty.

But guilty of what? Breaking her bail? Bodily harm? Maybe guilty of murder. What if she'd killed Jake? How would she ever explain that to Famke in years to come?

All of these thoughts crashed their way through Mae-Ling's mind as she lurched into a quiet side street around the corner from Nush's. Her breathing was hard and heavy. *What should she do? Where could she go?*

Leaning up against a wall, Mae-Ling tried to calm herself. As she leant there, she could hear the sound of sirens approaching closer. It would be the ambulance and police car rushing towards the apartment. *Please let Jake be alive*, thought Mae-Ling, the contemplation of a fatal outcome etching itself onto her brain.

Determined to distance herself from the apartment, Mae-Ling started to run down the road again. She vaguely recognised the area and thought that the banks of the River Thames were nearby. If she could get to the river it would be quiet and out of sight. She could collect her thoughts there and work out what to do.

In a matter of minutes she was looking down onto the river. From the pavement where she stood, a ladder led down to a pebbled area banking the Thames. She climbed over the wall and down the ladder until she felt the roundness of the pebbles beneath her feet. The bank was deserted. She walked to the edge of the water and stared out across the river. Seagulls squawked overhead and a boat rumbled past in the distance.

Mae-Ling shut her eyes, afraid of how the day had unfolded. *What would happen to her when the police caught up with her?*

It was a question that she never had to worry about. The next thing she felt was sharp blow with a heavy object to the back of her head. She tumbled forward, face down into the river, the water deathly cold against her skin. She never heard the urgent sound of footsteps running away from her lifeless body. She would never hear anything again.

CHAPTER 42

It had been a fruitful few hours for Stafford James. What he had assumed would be just another uneventful evening in front of the TV at his LA home catching up on *24* and re-runs of *Ugly Betty* had become so much more rewarding.

The evening had started with an exuberant Montana on the phone sharing the news about her recent engagement to Brad. 'Darling boy, if I hadn't have listened to your advice, who knows where I'd be right now. Brad and I have literally been making love ever since you left after that meal. I couldn't be happier, sweetie.'

Beaming a genuinely happy smile for his most lucrative fag-hag friend, Stafford was keen to get all of the details and offer his advice. 'Oh goody, time for a new outfit. When will it be? Please tell me it'll be a winter wedding, I look so much better in layers. I take it you won't be affronting the Almighty by wearing white? You should have it at the St Nicolas Greek Orthodox church in Northridge. Tom Hanks is forever there, so I hear, it's a celeb haven. Telly Savalas is said to haunt the place too, so you might persuade Jennifer Aniston to pop in. Wasn't he related to her?'

'Hold on there, Staffs, will you?' interjected Montana. 'We haven't even discussed any of the arrangements as yet, although I did let slip to Brad that I simply adore the Good Shepherd Catholic Church in Beverly Hills. It's where Sinatra had his funeral and I was there a few weeks ago with one of the girls from *Per-*

egrine Palace and it's simply divine. Nose-to-nipple with names. The Hiltons were there, although how Paris can sit in the house of God after that sex tape is beyond me. Reese Witherspoon had her head buried in a hymn book in the row behind me and that brutally handsome Mark Wahlberg was across the aisle. I could barely listen to the pastor's words for staring at that man's body.'

'I think you're beyond salvation darling, don't you? So, have you informed daughter dearest as yet?' enquired Stafford.

'No, she can read about it in the papers. I'm not even sure she'll be on the guest list the way we're going at the moment. Besides, she'll be too up herself with that darned show of hers. Anyway, enough of her, I have a little proposition for you. It's a gift to say thank you for being such a doll and putting up with me recently. I know I've been a complete bitch to be around.'

Stafford's eyes widened in anticipation as he listened. 'Fire away, I'm all ears.'

'Well, Brad and I are about to head over to Europe for TV promotion in the UK for *Babylon* and then we're moving on to Venice for a massively decadent junket with lots of magazine types. We treat them to the best things Venice has to offer and they write fabulous things about me and my wonderful perfume, you know how it goes. We're there at the same time as the Film Festival, so doubtless there will stars by the gondola-full. Fancy coming?'

'Darling, I'd love to, but we're talking mucho mucho Euros here aren't we, unless of course…?' Montana could hear the hope in Stafford's voice.

'That's what I'm saying, you daft old pooftah. It's a gift. All expenses paid. I'm sure that, given the way *Babylon* is selling at such a phenomenal rate, Coeur Cosmetics will be more than happy to cover your bar and rent boy bill. I'll just write you into the costings as another much-needed PA.'

Stafford was jubilant. 'Cherub, I'm eyeing my Louis Vuitton luggage set as we speak. When do we leave?'

As Stafford hung up the phone, he squealed with giddiness. 'Watch out, Europe, here I come. Those Italian men are bellissimo.'

———

It was the thought of what Stafford could do to those Italian men that put him in a horny mood. The offer of the free ride to Europe was a fantastic way to start the evening, but Stafford knew exactly what would round it off nicely. Getting his rocks off.

He picked up the little black book at the side of his phone. Now, which of his many conquests was he in the mood for tonight? Thumbing through the pages, he perused the names as if he were picking a meal from a menu.

Gavin, the sexy skinhead tattooed director? *Too rough, his stubble rips my face apart. I don't want a rash if I'm off to Britain.* Johan, the East-European model with a bubble butt you could spend days exploring? *Too costly and besides, Johan always wants to practice his English and I'm not in the mood to talk.* What about Vladi, the furry stud with the thick ten inches between his legs and the penchant for bondage. *No, the manacles can stay in the box under the bed tonight. I want a quick fix… no wining, no dining, just a good shag with an anonymous well-hung stranger.*

———

Forty minutes and a car ride later, Stafford was stood in the half-dark under a tree at one of LA's most famed gay cruising areas. If there was one thing that Hollywood's balmy nights were perfect for, it was a bit of alfresco cruising.

In the short space of time he'd already been there, he had witnessed countless men in different states of undress. Various bushy areas seemed to rustle with sexual activity. Stafford had contemplated joining in, but then a better offer had presented itself.

A broad-shouldered man wearing a black overcoat and a beanie hat pulled down over the top of his face walked in front of Stafford. *Bit overdressed given the time of year*, thought Stafford, but there was no denying that the man was incredibly handsome. The stranger flashed a coy smile at Stafford as he sauntered past. A moment later he stopped and turned round to look at Stafford once more.

It was obvious that both men were interested in the same thing. Stafford rubbed his crotch and watched to see if the stranger did the same. He did. The stranger unzipped his trousers and pulled out a thick, appetising cock.

There was no way Stafford was going to let this one get away from him and he swiftly moved towards the stranger and dropped to his knees in front of him.

The man unfastened the belt on his trousers and let them fall to his ankles. He wore no underpants. Stafford looped his hands around the back of the man, gripping onto his buttocks. They were as hard as steel. As Stafford ran his hands down the man's legs, the muscles there were equally as solid. This was a guy who looked after himself.

Stafford worked his lips frantically up and down the shaft, his movements becoming quicker. The man towering over him, his hands placed on Stafford's shoulders, started to moan as he fed his length into him. Stafford completed his task.

Standing to his feet, Stafford took out his own cock and watched as the stranger started to fasten his trousers again. 'Nice one mate, my turn now, eh?' he said.

The stranger continued to dress himself, ignoring Stafford's request. Undeterred, Stafford asked once again.

This time an answer came. 'Sorry, mate, I'm off.' There was a slight foreign accent to the voice which Stafford had trouble placing.

Not content to pleasure himself to completion, Stafford was hopeful that he could change the man's mind. 'C'mon, you'll enjoy it when you get going.'

As the man finished buttoning his trousers, Stafford placed his hand on the man's head and tried to force it in the direction of his cock. The man quickly flinched sideways causing his beanie hat to slide from his head and remain in Stafford's hand. Stafford's gasp was audible as he stared the stranger in the face.

Grabbing the hat back from Stafford, the stranger urgently slipped it back onto his head and ran off into the night. He was panicked and Stafford knew why. It wasn't every night that you got to grips with Jeremy Pinewood, was it?

'Bugger me,' declared Stafford. In his head he couldn't help but add the words, *I flaming wish*.

CHAPTER 43

Lying in a private ward at one of London's top hospitals, Jake Saunders knew that he was lucky to be alive. Yet despite the searing pain that still emanated from his stab wound even after painkillers – and the fact that the woman he once loved was responsible for his current bedridden situation – he still felt that a weight had been lifted from his shoulders. His relationship with Mae-Ling was well and truly finished. The truth was out. Mae-Ling finally knew that the woman he had betrayed her for was Nush. The same woman who was now sat holding his hand.

'It's been quite a day, hasn't it?' said Jake with gross understatement. 'Not quite what I imagined when I decided to drive to yours this morning. But at least I've spent the whole day with you.'

Nush couldn't help but smile at his deadpan demeanour. 'I could think of better ways to spend the day with a fit guy like you. Being threatened, watching someone getting stabbed, sitting in an ambulance and then waiting for hours in hospital are not exactly top of my list of date options. Oh, and being grilled by the police…'

'What did they say, have they arrested Mae-Ling yet? They'll throw the book at her for breaking her bail conditions.'

'They will when they can find her. There's been no sign of her since she fled my apartment. The CCTV saw her run off but once she disappeared round the corner she appears to have vanished. They tried your house but she'd not been back there. The nanny's looking after Famke.'

Jake scratched his head. 'I've asked my parents to come and stay at the house to look after the baby until I get out of here. Then, depending on what happens with Mae-Ling, I'll work out what to do about the house and stuff.'

'You're remarkably calm for someone who's just been stabbed by their ex. I don't even want to think about what might have happened.'

'It wasn't much more than a scratch. A few stitches and I'll be as good as new. I'm not exactly an innocent party in all of this, am I? As far as Mae-Ling was concerned everything was fine until I slept with you. I knew that it wasn't, but I didn't have the balls to tell her, did I? I could have stopped any of this from happening.' Jake looked sad as he spoke.

Nush was keen to try and elevate the mood. 'But if you'd have been single, then I might not have slept with you. That wouldn't have been much of a story for *The Staple* would it?' There was a bit of her that wasn't joking.

'I meant what I said today though, Nush, I think I could fall for you very easily. Just don't tell anyone what a romantic softie one of TV's hardest macho men really is. Okay?' Jake squeezed Nush's hand and chuckled as he did so.

'Your secret's safe with me,' she laughed back. 'Now, if you'll excuse me for a few minutes I have some phone calls to make and I could do with a coffee. I'll get one for you.'

'Please, and hurry back alright. It's no fun lying here on my own.' Jake patted the bed suggestively.

———

Sitting in the hospital reception, Nush checked her phone. She had expected there to be at least one message from Lawrence lambasting her for taking time off work, so she was surprised when her phone showed that she had no messages.

She phoned both Regan and Evie to fill them in on the day's events. She craved the understanding and support that only the Trinity could give her. At least she wouldn't be judged or blamed by them.

Nush had been on the phone to Regan and Evie for the best part of an hour. It would do Jake good to rest, but she had promised him a coffee, had she not? He must be wondering if she'd gone to Brazil to get the beans personally. Having bought two coffees, she headed back to Jake's room.

She was surprised to see that Jake wasn't alone. Stood at the end of his bed were three police officers. She recognised one of them as DS Cole.

Looking at Jake, she could see that he'd been crying, the glint of drying tears still apparent on his face. Nush started to shake slightly, spilling some of the coffee onto the floor.

'Good evening, Officer Cole. I didn't expect to see you again tonight. What's going on?'

'Evening, Miss Silvers. We thought you'd both like to know. A dead body has been found washed-up on the banks of the Thames near your home. It's been identified as Mae-Ling Ch'en. She appears to have been dead for several hours.'

'The silly cow drowned herself.' Nush had said it before she realised how heartless it may have sounded.

DS Cole continued, 'Actually, Miss, the cause of death seems to be a rather major blow to the back of the head with a heavy object. It would appear that Mae-Ling Ch'en was murdered.'

Nush dropped both cups of coffee causing a pool of hot brown liquid to run across the tiled ward floor.

CHAPTER 44

Leo Weiss was determined that the final two episodes of Wild Child would be riveting. 'Here's the story, girls. The first two episodes were dynamite TV. Both of you won over the viewers with your challenges, especially the nail biting nature of the auction. But despite viewing figures, as far as I'm concerned the last episode was dreary. Regan, your speech was not nearly hard-hitting enough. It was like watching a timid schoolgirl doing a show-and-tell in front of her class. Grace, yours was okay. Anti-fur, blah blah blah… yep, it's a sure-fire winner, and planting those fur-wearers in the crowd was good, if a little predictable. But the whole challenge lacked sparkle and fight. But I blame myself. The whole point about this show is that it's a competition. It could completely change the public's opinion of one or both of you. But we need you two to fight it out together on screen and to show people that you deserve to be seen as more than just a couple of spoilt bitches.'

'What are you suggesting, Leo?' teased Grace. 'Naked girl-on-girl wrestling. Last one standing wins?' Looking over at Regan she added 'I'm game if you are, Regan … Leo would love it!'

Leo's cheeks were reddening as he spoke, a tad embarrassed by Grace's impertinence. 'Our research shows us that one of the things that seems to be making the show such a success right now is the *British-ness* of it all. The viewers love the fact that we've got two girls from opposite sides of the Atlantic squaring up to each other but they also seem to like the fact that all the action takes place here in the UK. It makes sense if you think about it.' Leo paced around the room as he spoke. 'Think about your mother's show, Regan. Why is *Peregrine Palace* up there with the likes of *Dallas* and *Dynasty* as one of the most watched shows of all time in the UK? Escapism. It's total American OTT glamour. You're never going to get that from a British soap. The Americans love *Wild Child* because they get to see the UK, check out London's hotspots, see how life works here, visit places they've never been before. We're one of the biggest UK smashes in the States since *Benny Hill* for God's sake, so let's play up to it. For the next challenge we're going ultra-British.'

'Rule Britannia!' mocked Regan with a sideways smirk. 'What are we doing? Double-dating Princes Wills and Harry? I'm not sure what Kate Middleton would say seeing as she's marched one of them up the aisle.'

Ignoring her, Leo resumed his speech. 'The pair of you will go head to head in one of the most British sports of all. In order to highlight the skilled teamwork that any member of the Rothschild dynasty would most definitely demonstrate, you're both heading off to the west country to be taught polo.'

The mouths of both Grace and Regan fell open. 'Son-of-a-bitch,' muttered Grace. 'You're expecting us to knock seven shades of shit out of each other on horseback aren't you? And then hoping the royal family turn up to watch.'

'Believe you me, Grace. I would rip off one of my own balls to get royalty on this show, but seeing you two galloping around a park playing a royal sporting favourite is about as close as I can manage – unless your mother has any contacts at Buckingham Palace, of course, Regan? Do congratulate her on her forthcoming wedding, by the way.'

Mention of her mother's news caused Regan to flinch. It was the number two story of the day in every tabloid paper after the death of Mae-Ling and had even made some of the broadsheets. *The Times* had reported the news as 'AMERICA'S TOP TV QUEEN SET FOR FAIRYTALE ENDING' whereas *The Sun* had gone for the much catchier 'MONTANA TO BE TAKEN UP THE AISLE BY MANAGER'. Requests for quotes from Regan had been coming to her via the *Wild Child* marketing team all morning. Regan chose to remain silent.

'So, who's training us how to hit a small plastic ball around a field with a stick, then?' sneered Regan sarcastically.

'You'll each be coached by a different team. I want competition from the off. I know you girls get on with each other, but from now on it's war. May the best lady win,' Leo snapped back.

'That'll be me, then,' giggled Grace. 'I'm used to riding a Horse. Not of the animal kind though, the last time 'a Horse' got my legs wrapped around him he was a beauty of a bouncer called Brett, from a nightclub in Wisconsin. Horse was his nickname and he lived up to expectations.' As she strutted from the room, Grace looked at Regan and winked.

———

As soon as Grace left the meeting, she leapt straight into a taxi and went to The Hempel Hotel, the five star luxury boutique hotel in West London created by the British designer and former actress Anouska Hempel. Famed worldwide, the hotel was an iconic place to stay, favoured by celebrities, including currently, Clarissa Thornton. There was one purpose only for their get-together. For Grace to hand over the photo of Montana and Lawrence.

'So, do you have it?' grunted Clarissa as soon as Grace sat opposite her in the hotel bar.

'What's it worth?' snarled back Grace. 'It's a rich woman's world darling and here's where you keep paying.'

'Give me the photo, and I'll wire a good amount into your account later today. Say $10,000. If there's a good story to go with the photo then we'll double it. Will that keep you in cheap foundation?'

Despite loathing Clarissa's tone towards her, Grace was savvy enough to know to bite her tongue. 'Here's the photo, I'll dig around for the story with Regan and you do your worst. But it never came from me, understand?'

Clarissa took the photo and scrutinised the chemistry between Lawrence and Montana. With a smile, she said 'there's definitely some kind of history between our slimy newspaper man and Little Miss Wedded Bliss. We just need to find out what.' She flicked the back of the photo against the palm of her hand as she spoke, deep in thought. 'Did you get it copied?'

'Of course. First thing this morning at one of those colour copier places. The original is back in Regan's bag. I slipped it in there again before the meeting. She was too busy eyeing up the producer to notice. It's never left her bag, as far as she's concerned.'

—

Sinking onto the sofa at her riverside flat, Regan stared at the photo of her mother with Lawrence Silvers, oblivious to the journey it had been on over the last 24 hours. She was determined to keep it with her wherever she went as it was the key to finding out the truth. She needed to speak to either Montana or Lawrence and she needed to do it soon. The anxiety of not knowing what was behind the photo, if anything, was eating her up.

She picked up the phone and dialled Montana. Unsurprisingly it clicked through to the answer phone. A new message played out. It was Montana's voice, all chirpy and girly. *Hello, you're through to Montana and Brad. If you're phoning to say congratulations – then thank you. If you're phoning from a magazine bidding for the wedding photos – then we'll be in touch. If you're anybody else – then get off the line!*

Pleasant, thought Regan. As the phone beeped she left a message. 'Hi, it's Regan. Er … congratulations. Guess I'll see you when you come to the UK and you can tell me more. We have lots to speak about. Phone me if you can. Bye for now.'

Disgruntled at not being able to speak to her mother, Regan made a snap decision. She would try to confront Lawrence.

Scrolling through her phonebook she stopped at the switchboard number for *The Daily Staple*. Nush had given it to her once before. Taking a deep breath, she dialled the number and waited.

'Good afternoon, *The Daily Staple*. How can I help you?' said the girl at the other end of the line with an unnatural cheeriness.

'Er, hello there. Can I speak to Mr Lawrence Silvers on his direct line please?'

'I'm afraid everything has to go through his secretary. I could put you through to her. Who shall I say's calling?' The girl was nauseatingly effervescent.

'No, I … I need to speak to Mr Silvers personally. It's a delicate matter. My name is Regan Phoenix.'

'Really? Oh my God. What … the real Regan Phoenix from *Wild Child*? I love that show. Is this Vicky in accounts winding me up? Regan's so cool, I mean, you are. Is it really you? Your mum's just got engaged.' The girl became more and more flustered as she gabbled on.

In spite of her nerves, Regan loved the fawning her name seemed to evoke. 'Um, well, I'm sure Vicky in accounts is a nice girl and all that, but I have no idea who she is. This is Regan Phoenix, daughter of Montana, woman from *Wild Child* ... and I *do* need to speak to Mr Silvers pretty urgently.'

Regan heard the phone ring and then, just as it had with Montana, click into the messaging system. A ripple of relief ran through Regan. Lawrence's London twang boomed out. 'You've got my direct line so I must know you. I'm out being busy so leave a message and I'll bell you back.'

'Hello, Mr Silvers, this is Regan Phoenix, Anoushka's friend. I was wondering if we can arrange to meet up. I need to talk to you about something. It's about my mother. I believe you know her. I know you're busy, but if you could ring me on this number, I'd be really grateful.'

With her heart beating rapidly in her chest, Regan left her number and hung up. Her mind raced, wondering if Lawrence would ring her back and what she would say if she did. Indeed, what had she started? There was no going back now.

CHAPTER 45

Stephanie Love had spent the last few hours on her office phone. It was one of those glorious mornings where she had stunning news to tell the world about her number one client, Evie. A late night call from Jeremy's agent had confirmed what she had been wishing for. Evie and Jeremy had decided to become an item. To Stephanie, they were now a brand, a unit, a commodity and a million dollar money-making machine.

Immediately on entering her office, she had phoned the film company behind *The Bouquet Catcher*, ordering them to book a fleet of suites at the Westin Excelsior Hotel, Venice Lido for the forthcoming film festival. Barking her requirements with military precision, Stephanie ordered adjoining suites for Evie and Jeremy.

'I will also want suites for myself, one to house Evie's clothes and one for make-up,' she continued to rattle off her demands. 'And I mean nothing less than the best rooms, or else we don't play ball. If the agents of Scarlett Johansson or Megan Fox have already bagged the top suites, then get the hotel to cancel them. Evie's the queen bee now, got it? I trust I can leave everything to you.' Stephanie had hung up without saying goodbye; there was no time for pleasantries. She had too much to do.

Next up were calls to all of the major glamour magazines. Steph was determined for the bidding war to begin. They would all want Evie and Jeremy together on their covers to boost circulation. But it would all come down to money. Steph set their price at a cool $1 million. She then did the same with the TV talk shows. *Oprah, Ellen, Tyra, Letterman, Hollywood Daily* - again it was down to them to battle it out for the ultimate prize. An exclusive with Hollywood's sexiest duo.

It was as a mere afterthought that Steph actually contemplated phoning Evie.

'Darling girl, wonderful news about you and Jeremy,' gushed Steph. 'The word is out there with the magazines and the chat shows, so we'll see what gives next. I've ordered suites for us all at The Excelsior in Venice. Glorious hotel, a must-have for a festival starlet like you. This time next year you'll be the biggest box office draw in the world and there'll be an Oscar sat on your mantelpiece. God … does it get any better than this?'

Waiting for Steph's squealing excitement to ebb, Evie finally managed to interject. 'New travels fast then. We'll see what happens, but can we wait a week or two for the interviews, please. We've only just shared a kiss or two and there isn't a great deal to tell as yet. As the sharpest agent in Hollywood, surely you've got to admit that a few weeks of intimacy between Jeremy and I would make for much better editorial when we do decide to share the secrets of our relationship with the world.' Evie knew that flattery was always the way to persuade Steph to see things from her point of view.

'Of course, you lovebirds go off and coo together for a bit. Feather your nest, as it were. I'll keep the press eagerly hanging on. Any choices about which TV show you'd like to appear on, darling?'

'Not really, but can we attempt to avoid Clarissa Thornton on *Hollywood Daily*. She and Nush are bitter rivals and you know where my loyalties lie. Nush is one of my oldest friends and she needs me right now with all the bad press she's getting.'

'No worries. That Clarissa Thornton is a dreadful girl anyway. She never even crossed my mind,' lied Steph, secretly cursing as she had a sneaky suspicion that *Hollywood Daily* may have emerged as top bidders. 'I just hope she won't be in the frame for Mae-Ling's murder, darling. Bad press, even by association, is a definite no-no in the run up to the Oscars. I sometimes wish you'd ditch that Silvers girl as a friend. And Regan Phoenix. You are far too classy and important for the likes of them. Now, talking of Mae-Ling, just think, yours was probably the last face she ever had the joy of making up.'

It was evident from Evie's reaction that she was hearing about Mae-Ling's killing for the first time. Evie stumbled over her words as she spoke. 'Mae-Ling's been … er … killed. I didn't know. How? There's no way Nush is involved.'

'It's all over the Net. Apparently her body was found washed up by some river, her head pretty much caved in. It's like something from a horror film. *The Bouquet Catcher* was her last film. I wonder if they'll stick a dedication to her on the credits. I doubt it, she was a bit of a loose cannon, wasn't she? Nuttier than a Hershey's almond bar. It's bound to come up in interviews.'

Evie had to bite her lip to stop herself from blasting Steph's lack of sensitivity. She may not have been Mae-Ling's biggest fan and she certainly didn't agree with what she had put Nush through, but no-one deserved to end up dead on a riverbank. Stunned by the news, Evie brought the call to a close. 'I've got to go, Stephanie, Jeremy's picking me up in a while and we're out for the day. I'll speak to you tomorrow.'

'Fabulous, darling. Just make sure you two get your faces in the press. I want holding hands and romantic looks that Danielle Steele would write about. No sordid tongues-in-mouths or crotch grabbing in public. I always find that downright tacky.'

But Evie had already disconnected.

———

Jeremy was ravaged with worry as he pulled up outside the Beverly Wiltshire in his Tesla Roadster. He was unshaven, his eyes bloodshot and he was still shaky about the close call of the night before. Even though he couldn't be sure that he'd been recognised at the cruising ground, he knew that he had put himself in a perilous position. What if the man he'd been intimate with had identified him as one of the world's biggest heart-throbs? Jeremy hadn't slept at all and every time his phone had sounded, he had been convinced that it would be his agent with bad news about a scandal ready to rock the very soul of Tinseltown. Even though Jeremy relished the thrill of his alfresco escapades, he was aware that he was playing with fire. His sexuality was something that he had always tried to keep hidden from the outside world. That's why he needed to play the lady-loving boyfriend. If one of the hottest actors in the world couldn't play the role, then who the hell could? It was time for Operation Evie to be put into action, even more so than ever before. Whereas before he had known that a union would make for great press, now it could be career-saving.

An hour or so later, a still jittery Jeremy cast his gaze down the menu as he tried to relax on the patio at Ago. A pair of Marc Jacobs sunglasses shielded his eyes from the searing LA heat and also acted as a disguise for his tired eyes. Evie, casually weaving her finger down the menu as she perched opposite him, had already commented on his non-pristine appearance. He'd blamed his lack of sleep on the excitement of anticipation about their time together and the fact that he'd been up all night reading a script for a new movie he'd been approached for.

The restaurant was buzzing with activity. The chatter of industry news hung in the air. But the conversation between Jeremy and Evie during their meal was hardly what either of them would have called free-flowing. Jeremy was distracted, she could sense it. Determined to discuss them as an item, Evie waded in, feeling she had nothing to lose.

'Are you okay, Jeremy, you seem a million miles away. You do want to be here, don't you? You're not going back on what you said last night, are you? I know my agent has been telling the world this morning so we're going to make her look pretty foolish if we don't actually want to be together.'

Sensing that he needed to seize the moment and placate Evie's worries, Jeremy reached his hands across the table and placed them on top of hers. A camera clicked silently from behind the bushes at the edge of the patio capturing the moment. 'Are you mad? I love being with you. I'm just tired today, forgive me … you've seen my eyes!' Jeremy lowered his sunglasses below his eyes and winked at Evie over the top of the frames. The action caused a surge of delirium to pulsate through Evie. *Even when he's supposedly looking rough, he still looks as hot as hell,* she thought.

'It's just that sometimes I can't believe that I'm lucky enough to have a chance with a girl like you. There's a bit of me that's still the hick from the Oz outback who can't quite fathom how he's made it big in Hollywood. Believe it or not, I'm not that good at this romance stuff.'

It was textbook bullshit. Jeremy knew that with looks and a body like his, he could charm the underwear off any person he chose, but he needed to lay on the charm thickly with Evie today. His brain was elsewhere, still reliving the potential nightmare of the evening before. He knew that he had to treat this lunchtime encounter as a piece of acting. Let Evie hear what she wanted to hear, make sure the press obtained their photos and then get away pronto.

Evie felt herself drawn in by his story. 'Just be yourself, Jeremy, and you won't disappoint me.' Placing her hand on Jeremy's unshaven cheek, she ran it tenderly down the side of his face. Jeremy smiled as she did so. The camera clicked silently from behind the bush again. It would be one of the two shots that would appear in countless newspapers across the world the next morning. Jeremy's agent had done well in tipping off the paps to be there. But then he was merely following orders from Jeremy himself.

'I promise I will. Now, if you want me to be myself then I'm going to be honest with you. I'm knackered. Mind if I go back to mine and catch up on some sleep. I'd rather be firing on full cylinders when I'm with you. I should know better than to be up all night reading scripts when I've got a date with a beautiful woman the next day.'

The second photo was one of Jeremy kissing Evie fully on the lips as they walked away from the table. The eyes of everyone on the restaurant patio were upon them. Tomorrow it would be the eyes of the world.

———

The eyes of Stafford James were staring down at the photo of Jeremy that graced the latest issue of *People* magazine. He'd picked it up at his local newsstand, determined to study every line and feature on the actor's chiselled face. Forty minutes of peering at it had left him in no doubt. The man on the cruising ground the night before had definitely been Hollywood's Mr Dreamboat. It looked like Stafford had literally wrapped his lips around the biggest and juiciest celebrity story of the year. The questions now were, who should he tell and how would he prove it to them? Most importantly, what price tag did the story have attached to it?

CHAPTER 46

As far as Clarissa Thornton was concerned, it was all a matter of perfecting the publication dates. She had two potential major stories on her hands, both of them surrounding the million dollar lifestyle of Montana Phoenix.

Reclining onto the luxuriant bed in her hotel room, Clarissa scrutinized the photo of Lawrence and Montana in her hands. There could definitely be a story if she could find out some kind of meaty connection between the two of them.

The other headline-grabber concerning Montana was yet to be sealed, but one thing Clarissa was sure about was that it would be a no-holds-barred account of the mother/daughter relationship between Regan and her mother. The pieces of a very messy jigsaw puzzle of Phoenix family heartache were there – it just needed Clarissa to slot them all into place. And with Montana having just announced her engagement, there had never been a better time to bring the high and mighty queen of TV soap down onto her sorry grandiose ass. Yes, the timing had to be perfect.

––

'It was only a few months ago I was selling out arenas in countries around the world,' snapped Grace. 'Now look at me. Padding around a bloody field in the middle of nowhere, working out how to hit a ball into a goal from the back of a hulking great big horse. Somebody shoot me now. Thank God I have you guys for company.'

There was a modicum of truth in what she was saying, but most of her supposed moan had been beefed up with misery purely for effect. She was showing off to the guys in question, the three muscled men who had been looking after her since earlier that day. They had the unenviable task of trying to teach Grace the finer points of polo, ready for her *Wild Child* challenge.

By the end of the first day's training, both Grace and Regan were able to ride competently enough, but neither of them were actually able to swing the mallet and hit the ball with any degree of skill. It was a problem they were both discussing with Leo later that evening in the rustic charm of a Cotswold pub near their hotel.

'The only way we could hit the ball is if you painted a picture of Montana on it!' wisecracked Grace. 'Then we'd never miss it. It's a tough game. My entire body feels like I've been in the ring with one of the WWF. I have aches in places I didn't even know I had.'

In spite of the jibe about her mother, Regan was eager to agree. 'It's a freaking nightmare. My grip's all wobbly and the ball's too small. You'll be lucky if either of us actually get anywhere near it.'

'You've still got a few more days until the match,' smirked Leo. 'Now, if you'll excuse me, I have some work to do back at the hotel. Some TV network in America is chasing after me with a rather tasty offer for a show after *Wild Child* finishes. I need to email them my CV and some salary requirements. I suggest you two get an early night. Rest those weary bodies.'

'Yes, sir,' mocked both girls together. Regan felt a tremor of worry when Leo had mentioned about the potential of working in the States. How cruel would it be if they could finally be together after the show only for Leo to run off to the other side of the Atlantic?'

Being alone with Regan for the first time in a couple of days, Grace was anxious to truffle around for gossip. 'So, what news from Planet Phoenix?' she enquired light-heartedly.

'Seeing as I couldn't ask her about the photo, I decided to try another line of approach. I phoned Lawrence.'

'Good for you. So what did he say?' Grace was literally drooling with the buzz of expectancy.

'I left a message. I've now got to play the waiting game.'

Regan didn't have long to wait. As she was climbing into bed that night, her phone sounded, indicating a missed call. It had obviously rung while she had been in the bath soaking her tired physique.

Pulling the fresh cotton sheets up around her, she played back the message. Astonished at the voice she was hearing, she took in every word. 'Hello, it's Lawrence Silvers. I've told my secretary to book an appointment with me as soon as we're both free. Ring her to sort out a time. I know your mother. Or at least I did. I haven't seen her in years, apart from in that daft soap of hers. Bloody rubbish.'

CHAPTER 47

When it came to prioritising, Lawrence Silvers had to admit that a meeting with Regan to discuss her mother was way down the list. 'Why the hell would I want to get into a conversation about that silly bitch?' he'd mumbled to himself as he'd listened to the message. As far as he was concerned, even though the entire western population had fallen in love with the decadent Montana Phoenix and her bitchy TV alter ego over the years, she was somebody who was most certainly in his past.

Top of Lawrence's list right now was trying to set the balls in motion for removing Sadie from his life. It had been mere days since she'd dropped the bombshell about being pregnant. Suddenly all future plans of spending time in the Hamptons together or sailing arm-in-arm into a Mediterranean sunset were gone. No-one cheated on Lawrence Silvers.

Since meeting at The Dorchester, Lawrence's communication with Sadie had been zero. There had been no calls about collecting her belongings from Kingsbury, no talk about paternity tests and, most surprisingly to Lawrence, no pleas for forgiveness.

All the locks at the estate had been changed and all staff instructed not to let Sadie back onto the premises. Talks with his lawyer had proved that cutting Sadie out his life would be easy enough. The former model had signed a pre-nuptial agreement before their wedding, giving up any rites to a claim on the Silvers' family fortune. Sadie, in her sugary sweet southern belle naivety, had never envisaged that a day would come when Lawrence would want her no more. But the pre-nup and a lack of heirs to the Silvers fortune meant that cutting Sadie out of his life would be as easy as taking sweets away from a baby.

Lawrence was just hanging up on his lawyers when he heard a car pull up on the gravel drive at the front of Kingsbury. Curiously, he moved to the window to see who it was. A smile spread across his face as he saw the handsome features of Harry staring out through the windscreen.

'My boy returns.' Excitedly, Lawrence jogged as fast as his bulky frame would allow to the main entrance of the house to greet his son. Crunching the gravel underfoot as he stepped onto the drive, he arrived just as Harry exited the car. Straight away, he knew that something was wrong. Harry's boyish demeanour and fresh-faced childlike charm were nowhere to be seen. They had been replaced with a face that had fury etched across it like contour lines on a map. Spying his father in front of him, Harry raced towards him, screaming as he did so.

'You bastard, get off on hitting a woman, do you?' Before Lawrence could react he felt the full force of Harry's fist smack him squarely in the face. Taken completely by surprise, Lawrence stumbled, almost to the floor. Harry continued to punch him mercilessly, and Lawrence could feel the coppery taste of blood on his lips.

The onslaught only stopped when a piercing scream filled the air. 'Stop it, Harry, just stop it please.' The plea was dotted with sobs.

Looking up from where he lay on the gravel, Lawrence observed Sadie stepping out from the other side of the car, tears streaming down her face.

Lawrence stared up at his wife. 'What are you doing here? I've told you this isn't your home anymore. You're not welcome.'

Turning his attention to Harry as he gingerly stood back on his feet, Lawrence glared at him, unable to believe that it was the apple of his eye, the heir to his empire, who had attacked him with such force. Harry was shaking with rage as they eyeballed each other.

'Harry? Do you know what she's done to me, son? What's she told you? How could you bring her here? She's carrying another man's child. She's cheated on me. Don't let her turn you against me, Harry. No woman should come between a man and his son.' Wiping the blood from his chin, he held out his hand to Harry, searching for a reason for Harry's uncharacteristic rage as he did so.

Swiping Lawrence's hand away with his own, Harry was still visibly bristling with wrath. 'Don't fool yourself, old man, she's told me the truth. Sadie tells you she's pregnant, you get all macho and mad, belt her in the face and run off into the night. Next thing you're changing locks and filing for divorce. Smooth, dad ... really smooth. Hitting a woman, that's really something for me to look up to, isn't it?' His speech was backed by the sound of Sadie's sobs as she dropped to her knees alongside the car.

Lawrence could feel his anger swelling inside him. 'The child can't be mine, Harry, it's not possible. Ask the doctor. I loved that woman,' he spat the words, pointing at Sadie as he did so, 'but she's carrying somebody else's child. I wish I hadn't hit her, honestly I do.' His voice began to crack. 'But I saw red, I saw all trust I had in her just disappear. She's been with another man, I know it. I can't love a baby that's not even mine and I can't love a wife I can't trust.'

Crossing the gravel to be by Sadie's side, Harry bent down beside her. Fixing Lawrence with a steely look, Harry spoke. They were the words that would shatter Lawrence's heart for good. 'Both Sadie and the baby are too good for you anyway.' Placing an arm around Sadie's shoulders, Harry pulled her in close against him. 'It's not your baby, it's mine. I'm the father.'

Feeling as if all of the air within his body had just been punched from him, Lawrence fell, husk-like, to the floor again. A stream of tears rolled silently down his cheeks …

———

When Harry had received Sadie's call the previous day, he had been in the middle of packing his bags in his Austrian hotel room ready to head back to the UK. Harry had sensed the urgency in Sadie's voice and an air of eerie expectation had hung over him as he flew back to the UK. He knew that whatever Sadie had to say to him, the tone in her voice had suggested that it was not going to be good.

It was late in the evening when Harry eventually turned up at Sadie's hotel. When he'd asked her on the phone why they weren't meeting at Kingsbury, Sadie had evaded giving an answer. But seeing the bruise on her cheek as he walked into her hotel suite, he knew that the reason was because of Lawrence.

'How the hell did you get that?' Harry had fired off the question before he'd even hugged her welcome.

He could see that Sadie had been crying. Wrapped in the hotel bathrobe, she looked freshly cleansed from the shower, but her face housed a pain behind her eyes. 'Harry, sit down. I don't know where to begin so I'll just dive on in. I'm pregnant. I thought it was Lawrence's. He says it can't be, which is why I've got this,' she said, pointing to the bruise on her face. 'There's only one other person who could be the father, and that's you. I thought you should know … we're having a baby.'

As the colour drained from Harry's face, a kaleidoscope of emotions surged through him. First was fear, he was too young to have a child. He had a life of adventure and fun to lead before he wanted to start thinking about nappy changing and playing dad. Then his reaction changed to horror as he realised just what was happening here. He had managed to make his dad's wife pregnant ... his own step-mum. Wasn't that kind of sick? They weren't related, but hell ... it was like something from one of those crowd-whooping trashy American chat shows. Then, as he stared at the beautiful woman in front of him, his horror turned to anger. Sadie was a woman he'd always loved, maybe not romantically, but certainly as a mother figure in his life. And here she was, frail and weak, physically bruised and mentally scarred by a brute of a man. His own father. Without thinking, he cloaked Sadie in his arms. His warmth felt good to Sadie, the first comfort she'd known in days.

'I can't believe it,' whispered Harry. 'I'm going to be a dad ... but we only did it the once.'

Feeling his chest rise against her face as she nuzzled into him, Sadie answered. 'From where I'm from, Harry, it only takes the once ...'

———

The once in question had been the night weeks before when Sadie had waited lustfully for Lawrence to return home after work.

But as the minutes had past and turned into hours, Sadie had become impatient. She'd continued to sip on her brandy, waiting for her man to return. It was then that her mobile had sounded. It was a text from Lawrence. 'Am out with Johnny Erridge and the boys, don't wait up'.

Letting out a scream of annoyance, Sadie had thrown her phone across the room, watching it bounce off the wall.

There was a knock at the bedroom door and before she could answer, it had opened, Harry's face appearing around the doorframe. 'Hello, why the screaming? I thought someone was being murdered. Either that or you'd just found the mother of all spiders in your bathtub. Anything I can help with?' Despite being his step-mum Harry couldn't help but let his gaze run along the full length of Sadie's scantily clad body. She had curves that would put Nicole Scherzinger to shame. He'd felt a stirring in his loins straight away.

'There's no creepy-crawly, honey,' she joked, pleased to see her stepson. 'The only beast is your darned father. I'm annoyed with him as he's just announced he's out with the boys getting tanked while I had something a little different planned for tonight, as you can probably guess,' she said, showing off her outfit. 'Anyway, what are you doing home?'

'I've got some things to get ready for the big trip to Austria, but I'll join you for a drink if you like. Seems a shame to waste the ambience …' Harry had noticed the smell of the scented candles wafting through the air and the tea lights scattered around the room.

'I'm watching what I drink so I'm just sipping on mine, but there's plenty more brandy in the bottle if you want. Come on in.' Despite having drunk a minimal amount, Sadie could still feel the warmth of the alcohol flowing through her.

Pouring himself a glass, Harry had balanced himself on the edge of the bed. Sadie chose not to cover herself up as Harry placed himself alongside her. In spite of her maternal relationship with Harry, she felt sexy displaying her body in front of him. It was gratifying to be appreciated as a sexy woman. She was still unable to hide her shock, though, when she looked down at his lap to see a solid tube of flesh running down the top of one of his legs underneath his jeans. 'Harry, cover that up will you, you'll have my eye out with that thing.' An undercurrent of excitement between them seemed to run beneath her humour.

'Er ... sorry' replied Harry, draining his glass but making no attempt to hide his arousal. 'It's just that ... look at you, you're stunning. How can any man not give you exactly what you want? If I wasn't your stepson, I wouldn't have to think twice. You're everything a woman should be.'

His words melted like heated chocolate in Sadie's brain. 'But we're not related are we?' The words had tumbled from her lips before she could keep them in. Hearing them and the hint of inquisitive desire in her voice acted like a match lighting a fuse. Running his hand up Sadie's bare leg as he did so, Harry placed his mouth against hers. The heady smell of the brandy on their combined lips filled their nostrils. Sadie let out a moan of rapture as Harry let his fingers travel up her stomach and cup her breasts.

As an air of sexual urgency took the pair of them, Harry and Sadie relieved themselves of their clothes, tossing them onto the floor. Sadie gasped with joy as she placed her hand around Harry's proud erect cock, its girth way more impressive than she had been used to with Lawrence. Harry's breathing was short and feverish as she guided his cock swiftly into the wetness of her pussy, its size causing her to breathe in sharply.

Neither of them spoke as Harry buried his full length into her, their bodies rocking back and forth. Sadie abandoned herself to the complete pleasure of the moment, forgetting about any doubts she may have had at first. Harry's scimitar of flesh felt majestic inside her.

Determined to experience the young lover from every angle, Sadie guided Harry round until he was laying flat on the bed, her legs straddled either side of him. From that position she was able to expertly work her way up and down his shaft, savouring every inch as she desired. She raised her body up, letting the tip of his cock languish deliciously against her vaginal lips. Harry twitched with a carnal delight that raced through his core. Then Sadie lowered herself so that the lips of her pussy were pressed as far down his shaft as they could, engulfing the extent of Harry's weapon inside her. She repeated her actions, bringing Harry close to climax, allowing his cock to pulsate with waves of pleasure against her inner walls.

Unable to hold back any longer, Harry used his strength to manoeuvre Sadie around so that she was underneath him once again. Delving his cock right to the hilt for a final time, Harry unleashed his orgasm into her.

It was only then that Harry spoke. 'My dad's so lucky to have you. You were amazing.'

Harry's words were still ringing in Sadie's ears when a drunken Lawrence, stinking of lager and cigars, had climbed into bed alongside her later that night. Grunting about how horny he was, he had rammed his hand between her legs, brutally thrusting his fingers up her. Bringing the full weight of his sweaty body down on top of her, he had then placed his semi hard cock between her legs, forcing its way awkwardly into her. Ninety seconds and a few frenzied strokes later he had reached his climax and emptied his balls. They hadn't even kissed. Without saying a word, Lawrence flopped his cock out of her and rolled over. The heavy blast of his snoring filled Sadie's ears as she tried to go to sleep. Even in the dark, it was still Harry's face that filled her thoughts.

CHAPTER 48

As DS Cole stared at the array of horrific photos of Mae-Ling's dead body spread across his office desk, he clasped his head in his hands. As yet, he had no solid leads about her murder. A study of Nush's surveillance camera system had backed up everything that Nush had said about Mae-Ling's visit to her on the day of her death.

A study of the knife that Mae-Ling had dropped revealed only her fingerprints on it. There was no doubt who had stabbed Jake Saunders, but DS Cole had drawn a blank about Mae-Ling's murder.

He had questioned both Nush and Jake about who could possibly have wanted Mae-Ling dead. Mercifully both she and Jake had alibis. They had been at the apartment until an ambulance had arrived, as the CCTV footage had proved. From then on, they had been at the hospital, as hordes of witnesses could testify.

Nush had kept vigil at Jake's side in the hospital, watching through heavy eyes as he slept. Eventually she'd fallen asleep too, waking to find a doctor hovering over Jake inspecting the stab wound.

'You're a lucky man, Mr Saunders, there's no long term damage and the wound itself is not particularly deep. We'll dress the wound again and then you're free to go. A few days rest and you'll be as good as new.' As the doctor left to continue on his rounds, Jake looked over at Nush.

'Morning. Looks like I've got the all clear. How are you feeling?'

'The whole thing is a bloody nightmare, Jake. I just want to get away from it all. My place is bound to be swarming with reporters again. They'll want every last juicy titbit of gossip.'

'Then come back to mine, we can lock the world out and you can play nursemaid and mop my feverish brow.' Jake winked as he spoke.

'Your place is going to be equally besieged. We could both go back to Kingsbury, my father's place. There's plenty of room and the gates and guards will keep reporters at bay. Some fresh country air might do us both some good.'

'Inviting me back to daddy's already. You're a fast mover. But it sounds a perfect idea. Sure your dad won't mind?'

'I've been front page news for God knows how long now. I've taken leave of absence from work, and as far as he's concerned I'm in the frame as a potential murder suspect. I don't think turning up with you will be top of his list of worries, will it?'

'I'm surprised he's not phoned you, wanting to find out what's going on.'

'Jake, there's something you need to learn about my dad. I'm not his number one concern. Why would he need to phone? I suspect he can pick up any newspaper today, including his own, and read about us both on the front page. A murder case like this is hardly going to be swept under the carpet, is it?'

Nush's suspicions were right. A few hours later, the two of them headed to the rear of the hospital to catch a taxi to Kingsbury.

A crowd of reporters and paparazzi had been gathering at the hospital since the story broke, all hoping for a glimpse of Nush and Jake. Although the link between them still remained a mystery, the media had already surmised that perhaps there was more between the pair of them than had previously been known.

As Jake and Nush climbed into the cab together, a few sneaky photographers, who had cleverly guessed that an escape might be made from the rear of the private hospital, snapped away. Trying to shield their eyes from the flashes, Nush and Jake remained silent as one of the photographers shouted at them. 'So, are you two an item, then? Mae-Ling find out, did she?'

Nush could feel her cheeks reddening as she closed the cab door. She knew that it would only be a matter of time before the whole sorry story came to light. Squeezing Jake's hand as the cab sped off, she sighed. 'I guess we're going to make the front pages again tomorrow as well.'

CHAPTER 49

'Nike want you both to model their new sportswear. Emporio Armani have expressed an interest in a major billboard underwear shoot for you and Jeremy, and Pepsi are considering a huge tie-in with you both for the release of *The Bouquet Catcher*. Your photos will be all over their cans. My favourite offer, though, has to be Coeur Cosmetics wanting you both to do signature fragrances. Once Montana Phoenix's push on *Babylon* comes to an end they want yours to be the next sweet smell of success. You're a brand sweetie, a brand …'

The pairing of Evie and Jeremy was the talk of Hollywood and Stephanie was keen to share the news with Evie as they brunched at The Penthouse, perched high above the Santa Monica shoreline. With its stunning 360 degree views of West LA, it was the perfect place to indulge in some of the best food in town whilst staring down at the hapless minions drinking coffee from Styrofoam cups numerous floors below.

'Another Mango Bellini, darling?' I do feel we should celebrate, don't you?' roared Steph, oblivious to the curious looks of the diners surrounding them.

'I'm fine thanks, Steph. But there's hardly any cause for celebration as yet, is there?' Evie was determined to be more than cautious about her relationship with Jeremy. Things had already become a little too quick for her liking, with their embrace being plastered all over the media. 'It's early days. The offers are much appreciated, but we'll put them all on hold for now, okay?'

Steph was equally determined that no-one, not even Evie, would rain on her parade. 'Evie Merchant, when you were a struggling actress in your off-Broadway production in New York not that long ago, little lady, you'd have sold your soul to the devil if someone had said to you that one day a photo of you wearing the hottest designer underwear could be on a fuck-off billboard over Times Square. So don't tell me you're not excited about the offers, missy, because I know otherwise!'

'True enough, I would have killed for it back then, Steph.' Evie couldn't stop herself from thinking back to the time she was sharing the run down flat in New York and felt a cold shudder run through her. 'But things have changed. I'm more aware of how this business works now and we both know that when you're in my position, I can call the shots.'

'I hear you Evie, I do.' Evie's agent drained her Bellini and summoned the waiter from across the restaurant. 'Two more Bellinis please and make them strong ones, darling. Can't bear a drink to be as weak as piss.' Despite her rudeness, the waiter smiled in an obsequious manner as he took the order. Returning her attention to Evie, Steph continued. 'Just make sure that Jeremy doesn't go off you, darling, with all this hard to get bullshit.'

Evie had had enough. As much as she loved Steph's enthusiasm and go-getting nature when it came to business, there were times when she could have happily changed agents without giving it a second thought.

'Do you have to keep swearing? I'm happy to do whatever's necessary for publicity on the film, but Jeremy and I are together because we've chosen to be, not because of what our agents want, okay? I won't even be seeing Jeremy for while anyway. I'm booked on a flight home tomorrow and then I'm off on holiday for a few days with my friend Nush, who will always be my friend, too, before you start banging on about not liking her, so if you want me I'll be on some sun-drenched beach in Muscat with her, topping up my tan. As for Jeremy, well, for your information, he'll be on the beach too, but not the same one as me, so you can forget any more photo opportunities. He's told his agent to clear his diary until Venice as he wants to catch up on his surfing.'

———

As she spoke, Jeremy had indeed just finished talking on the bedroom phone to his agent, who had been congratulating him on the success of the photos from Ago being blanketed across the press. In a similar vein to Stephanie, he had also been informing Jeremy about the endless offers that had been rolling in for both him and Evie.

Jeremy had found it hard to concentrate on what his agent was saying, though. His brain was still abuzz with worry over his trip to the cruising ground. The signs were good as it had now been a couple of days since the incident and the shit hadn't hit the fan, so maybe he had escaped scandal after all, but what if …?

The other reason Jeremy was finding it hard to concentrate was the extreme pleasure his body was experiencing. As he looked down at his own nakedness stretched out on his bed, Jeremy expelled a sigh of prurient delight. He watched as a head bobbed up and down between his spread-eagled legs, lapping at the length of his manhood. Feeling his excitement rise, he fired his seed into the mouth of his partner, his entire body shaking as he did so.

'I needed that. Now, why don't you get us both a drink, Mario? There's some beer in the fridge.'

Wiping his lips as he lifted his head from Jeremy's crotch, the naked make-up artist muttered, 'Sure thing,' and scuttled out of the room. He returned a few minutes later with two bottles of beer held in one hand and an envelope in the other. 'This was by the front door. There's no stamp on it, so it must have been hand-delivered.'

As Mario slid onto the bed alongside him, Jeremy stared at the envelope. It simply had the words 'Jeremy Pinewood' written across it. Tearing it open, he removed the slip of paper inside. The colour drained from his face as he did so.

'What is it?' enquired Mario, placing his hand on Jeremy's cock once again.

Pushing Mario's hand away and climbing off the bed, Jeremy snapped back. 'It's nothing. Just get dressed and get out. I'll phone you later.' When Mario didn't move, Jeremy picked up the make-up artist's discarded jeans from the bedroom floor and threw them at him. 'I said, get out … Now!'

Mario knew not to argue. Trembling, a naked Jeremy read the slip of paper again. 'You don't know me, but we met the other night. Ring me and we can arrange to meet. Bring your cheque book. I guess we should talk money, don't you?' Below it was listed a mobile number. Jeremy knew that he would have to ring it. He had too much to lose if he didn't.

CHAPTER 50

The day of the polo match between 'Team Regan' and 'Team Grace' had started badly for Regan. She had received confirmation from Lawrence's secretary that he would see her at Kingsbury to discuss Montana. Regan had been paralysed with worry ever since.

Regan had phoned Nush to discuss her agitation. It had been a major conversation, one that had left Regan even more flustered then before. Nush had informed her that she was also staying at Kingsbury with Jake. During the preparation for the polo challenge, Regan hadn't even so much as turned on the TV or read a newspaper, so Nush's news about Mae-Ling's murder had hit Regan like a hurricane.

'Don't expect my father to be in a particularly good mood either,' Nush had warned her. 'There's something going on here. Sadie's nowhere to be seen. Dad says he's divorcing her and has changed all the locks. Have to admit I cracked a major smile when he told me that. Maybe at long last that piece of trash will be out of our lives. And I can't get hold of Harry. Dad bites my head off every time I try to speak to him about Sadie. Whatever has happened is serious shit. Dad looks like he's gone a few rounds with Mike Tyson, too. You're going to have to tread carefully, I've never seen him so angry. Do you want me to speak to him with you? Would it make it easier?'

'Would you mind? That would make it more bearable.' Regan was grateful to her friend. 'I haven't a clue what to say. I'll head up to Kingsbury after I've finished this blessed polo thing. Wish me luck.'

———

Publicity for *Wild Child* had meant that a huge crowd had come along to watch the polo match. Massive marquees had been erected containing makeshift bars serving Bucks Fizz and Kir Royals to spectators, and enormous screens showed images of the crowd, interspersed with clips from previous episodes. It would also show the live action from today's challenge. As the sun beat down, it was the perfect British summertime setting. The only thing that spoilt the idyllic scene was the flock of reporters mingling around the park, hoping to catch Regan and grab a quote about Montana's engagement. Leo had instructed his team to keep them away from Regan at all costs.

———

Just as the two teams were beginning the final chukka, a gleaming black Bentley pulled into the parking area at the entrance to the park. Clarissa was at the wheel, relishing the coolness of the inbuilt air-con on her skin. Having made the decision to wear a totally on-trend Temperley London dress, the last thing she wanted to do was overheat and ruin it in the scorching summer weather. Especially when she had such a big day planned. Clarissa had decided to strike when the proverbial iron was as hot as the sun shining up above. Checking her face in the rear-view mirror, she applied a fresh slick of fire engine red lipstick to her lips and smacked them together in preparation. *'Looking good Clarissa, if you say so yourself. Now, have I got everything I need?'*

Placing the lipstick back into her handbag she smiled at the other contents – a wad of bank notes rolled together, a memory stick, a dinky camcorder and the photo of Lawrence and Montana. 'All present and correct,' she curved her lips upwards in delight. 'Now, let's go make some more TV history.' She stepped from the Bentley and headed towards the polo field.

Minutes later, adjusting the neckline of her dress to reveal a hint of cleavage and the top of her filigree bra, Clarissa leaned across the table at the scruffy, mop-headed 20-something man sitting on the other side of it. Piled on the table between them were computer screens, decks of multi-coloured knobs and more electrical equipment than Clarissa could ever comprehend.

'Gosh, it really is so hot today,' she purred, a hint of suggestion running through her voice. 'I honestly think I might have overdressed for this weather. I'll have to slip out these things later no doubt. Still, I have to dress for the TV, my good man, can't let the public see me at anything less than my best.'

Staring directly at Clarissa's ample breasts, the man replied. 'You here with the *Wild Child* bunch? Are you one of Grace's friends? You look fit enough to be. What I wouldn't give to be one of those horses today. They normally chase foxes around here, not get ridden by them.'

'I'm very good friends with both Grace and Regan to be honest. We go way back. I'll have to introduce you to them later, if you like. Grace likes her men a little … er … rough, shall we say.' Clarissa sat herself daintily on the edge of the table as she spoke to him, allowing her skirt to rise up slightly as she did so. 'But I'm here in a work capacity today. I have to interview Regan after the match for my show in America, *Hollywood Daily*. It's all been arranged and cleared by the production team in advance. In fact they sent me over to you, handsome. I understand that you're the clever man in charge of those wonderful screens around the pitch. Is that right?' A complete lie, she'd simply asked a passing flunky with a clipboard outside one of the marquees who controlled the screens and the job was done.

Swelling out his chest with pride, the man leaned back in his chair, spreading his legs wide as he did so. In Clarissa's mind all she could think was *in your dreams sunshine,* but her gaze lingered over his body in mock appreciation nevertheless. 'That's me. Name's Mark Bancroft, the best vision mixer and visual output co-ordinator you'll find around here. Hired for the day because I can edit, switch, dissolve and pattern wipe to perfection.'

'Goodness me, Mark, what a CV,' faked Clarissa, pretending that she'd understood his technical jargon. 'Now, I was wondering if you could do me a little favour to make this interview the best it possibly can be. I'll make it worth your while of course.' She opened the clasp on her handbag and took out the wad of notes from inside. 'How much does a man of your capabilities need to shoehorn a little something extra into today's proceedings? You could use the money to buy Grace and I a drink later, perhaps.' Smiling directly at Mark, Clarissa knew that he was putty in her hands.

———

With less than two minutes left in the final chukka, Grace was a goal up, and every bone in Regan's body felt as if it were on fire. Despite all of her best efforts and those of her team, clinching an equaliser seemed to be proving impossible. A charging Grace would appear alongside her like a shadow every time Regan managed to position herself vaguely near the ball.

The clock on the scoreboard counted down. Regan kept glancing at it from under her mask. Into the last minute, forty-five seconds … surely there was no hope now.

Feeling the sweat dripping down her back, Regan watched as the ball soared into her line of vision, passed from one of her team-mates. If she could reach it first, she may have a chance of a direct hit at goal and force extra time. Spurring her horse into action, she pelted down the pitch as fast as the beast would allow. Twenty seconds left.

Swinging her right arm back in preparation, Regan could see nothing but the ball in front of her. She had to hit it, she simply had to. Ten seconds. Five seconds … As the clock counted down, Grace flew into sight, and with a final crack, the polo ball flew across the pitch and away as the final whistle blew. Grace let out a triumphant scream. Victory was in the bag. Regan let out a disappointed cry and rode to the sidelines, the cheers of the crowd ringing in her ears as she dismounted.

'Take that, bitch!' expressed an exuberant Grace, laughing with joy. 'Every bit of pain was worth it. I don't know about you, but I need to lie down for a week and, for once, I mean on my own.' Dismounting too, Grace ran over to her team mates to continue with the celebrations.

'Not your day today then, Regan? How about sharing your disappointment with the world?' The voice came from behind her. Turning around, she came face to face with Clarissa.

Taken aback, she answered, 'Looking like this? You're mad!' The sweat was still pouring down her face.

Clarissa continued regardless. 'So viewers, the race to leave their wild child days behind them continues, but there is reason for celebration in the Phoenix camp, with the news of mother Montana's forthcoming nuptials. Will you be helping mum to pick out the wedding dress for the big day?' Clarissa was facing a man carrying a camcorder as she spoke, another event flunky she had paid off to do as she required.

Realising that Clarissa had gone into work mode and that she was being filmed, Regan suddenly became self-conscious. Her gut reaction told her to tell Clarissa to fuck off, but that would not go down well with either *Hollywood Daily* or anyone on *Wild Child*, especially Leo. Taking the safe option, she decided to answer in the blandest way possible. 'I'm sure my mother has all of that sorted already. You'll have to ask her.'

Clarissa steamed on with her questioning. 'We all know that Montana is looking fabulous … especially when you actually realise how old she really is nowadays.' On cue, a press photo of Montana from *Peregrine Place* flashed up on the screens around the park. Regan stared at it, perplexed. 'I think Montana must have a few Hollywood surgeons on her Christmas card list, don't you, because she's just as stunning as she ever was. The surprise is just how little she's changed in … say, twenty or so years.'

On the screens, the press shot was replaced with the photo of the bikini-clad Montana with her arms draped around Lawrence Silvers. Regan's mouth fell open, unable to take in what she was seeing on the screens. Colour flushed into Regan's cheeks, rage mounting within her. Sensing that the photo had received the desired effect, Clarissa drew the interview to a close. 'Brad had better watch out, hadn't he, it looks like Montana has always had an eye for a good looking man. Regan, good luck for the final *Wild Child* and do give your mother our love.'

'You can turn that thing off now, I've got what I needed.' Clarissa barked the order to the man behind the camcorder.

A smug expression written all over her face, she turned back to Regan. 'Guess that's another scoop your friend Nush has missed out on honey, eh? I wonder what her daddy will say about this one.'

Puce with anger, it was then that Regan raised her fist and punched Clarissa squarely on the jaw. Before she could try to land another, Leo appeared from nowhere and grabbed her from behind. 'What the hell is going on? What's with these photos of your mother popping up everywhere?' His temper was evident.

'Why don't you ask her?' spat Regan, indicating Clarissa. But Clarissa was already dashing back to her car. She rubbed her jaw and winced at the pain as she scurried.

Just as she was climbing into the front seat of her Bentley, a finger tapped her on the shoulder. It was Mark. 'I did what you wanted, flashed up the photos from the memory stick. Can you introduce me to Grace now? I can buy her that drink.'

'Get your grubby hands off me, you little shit. You've got your money, so just piss off back to your knobs and wires, alright.' With that, Clarissa slammed the door, turned the key in the ignition and sped off across the car park, leaving a cloud of dust behind her and a puzzled and dejected Mark running his hands through his mop of dirty hair.

CHAPTER 51

'Thank God you didn't hit her on camera. Mind you, she would have deserved it. How did she get the photo in the first place?' Leo was speaking to Regan as he watched her towel-dry her hair after a bath back at her hotel room. Regan had just wrapped herself in a huge bathrobe as he'd knocked on her door.

'That I don't know. It's been with me all the time. There are only a few people that I've shown it to. Grace has seen it, Nush has seen it, but that's about it. Now, of course, thanks to that bitch Clarissa, the whole world is going to see it on her poxy show. I don't even know the story behind it.'

Leo shrugged. 'There might be no meaning behind it, just two friends having a cuddle and a laugh.'

Regan wasn't sure. 'It's too personal. They're sat on a yacht, for God's sake. You don't go off sailing with someone you hardly know. I can understand my mother forgetting to tell me that she knows my best friend's dad. She'd forget me full stop if she could, but surely Lawrence would have mentioned something over the years. I just wish I'd been able to speak to Lawrence first to ask him about it. He's going to flip his lid when he hears about this.'

'Well, you still have time. There's a blanket ban on the media letting the public know the results of *Wild Child* before each show goes to air, and didn't you say that Clarissa had started the interview by saying it hadn't been your day. She'll want to run the interview in its entirety so she can't do that until after the programme airs in a few days' time. You can tell Lawrence Silvers before he hears about it from someone else.'

'True.' Regan smiled.

'So, how are your aching bones after the polo? Too tired to celebrate?' Leo strolled towards Regan and placed his hand on her hip. With his other hand, he grabbed the towel and threw it onto the sofa.

'The bath seems to have soothed things somewhat. I am aching though … if you know what I mean?' Finishing the sentence with a kiss, Regan ran her hands down Leo's back. 'So, what are we celebrating?'

'Thanks to you and Grace, and this whole fabulous programme, my name is hotter than curry powder in the States right now. I've been offered a huge network job in Los Angeles when this is all over. I'll be developing my own reality shows. It's a six month contract but if it works out, which I am sure it will, then I could stay on.'

Regan tried unsuccessfully to hide the disappointment in her eyes. Leo was quick to spot it. 'Hey, I thought you'd be pleased for me.'

'I am, Leo, honestly. It's just that, we're just starting out with whatever this turns out to be and all of a sudden you're going to be heading off thousands of miles away to start a new life in the States. I like having you here.'

Leo couldn't help but laugh gently. 'You like having me here? Regan, whatever happens with my life, at this moment I can honestly say that I want you to be a part of it. I want to have you everywhere and I think we had better start right now, don't you?'

Undoing the tie on Regan's bathrobe, Leo pushed the garment over her shoulders and let it fall to the floor, leaving Regan naked in front of him. 'Now, didn't I promise that I would scrub your back for you?' he hinted cheekily.

'I've just had a bath, Leo, I'm clean all over already.'

Leo scooped Regan into his arms and carried her towards the bed. 'Well, in that case, we had better get dirty first then, hadn't we …?'

———

Sadie had been staying at Harry's one-bedroom Notting Hill flat ever since she had told him about the baby. The flat was too cramped for her liking, but Harry had insisted that they should be together as parents-to-be.

The only belongings she had with her were a suitcase of clothes that Harry had hurriedly packed after his fight with Lawrence days earlier. Most of her life still remained at Kingsbury.

Neither of them had heard any word from Lawrence since that day. The thought of Lawrence laying there bleeding still saddened Sadie. Despite everything, she still loved him. But now, thanks to one stupid sexual mistake, her future was mapped out.

It seemed icily tragic to her. She loved Harry, but could he provide for her and her baby? She doubted it. Lawrence's lawyer had already been in touch. Lawrence was unrepentant. According to him, the sooner the divorce papers were signed, the better.

Staring at the cartoon on the TV screen in front of her, Sadie could feel a core of sadness deep within her. She looked away from the animation as Harry entered the room. 'Here, drink this … it's elderflower cordial, like you wanted. Supposed to be good for the baby. What are you watching? *Family Guy* … cool … I love this. Let's hope our baby doesn't turn out like Stewie, he is one whacked out kid.'

Sadie didn't have the faintest idea what he was talking about and chose not to ask. Instead, she reached for the remote control and switched off the TV. 'Harry, we need to talk. I don't know how all this happened. Life has suddenly spiralled out of control. I don't know what I want anymore …'

It seemed she was talking to deaf ears. 'You're bound to feel a little confused right now, it'll be your hormones doing girly things to you,' he said dismissively. 'Drink your juice, babe.'

'No, Harry, I'm not sure what …' Her words trailed off as the doorbell sounded behind her.

Leaping from the couch, Harry went into the hall and opened the door. Standing there was Nush. Without letting him utter a word, Nush pushed past him. 'Oh, good, you're here. Harry, what the hell is going on with dad? Even for him, he's in the foulest mood. He's had the crap beaten out of him and says that he's divorcing Sadie, not that I see that as a bad thing. Never liked the bloody woman anyway to be honest, I always thought she was nothing more …' This time it was Nush's words that trailed off, as she spotted Sadie. 'Oh, hi … I didn't know you were here. Why are you here? Harry …?' Nush looked quizzically at her brother.

'I suppose I should fill you in. You'd better sit down.' Harry motioned towards the sofa. 'Fancy a drink? I suspect you're going to need it.'

CHAPTER 52

Stafford's meeting with Jeremy had been a lucrative one. It appeared that Stafford had judged the situation well.

Stafford had dwelt on the matter for ages. Twice he had picked up the telephone at his apartment to ring Nush. He was sure she would want to pay huge amounts of money for the story, but he would have to secure himself some proof first. How do you prove that one of the biggest heart-throbs in the world is in fact a gay boy who loves having his cock sucked? Without photos, there was no story.

He'd considered staking out the cruising ground every night until he saw the actor, but from the look on Jeremy's face as he fled the scene it was unlikely that he would return there.

Then it had occurred to him. The only person who knew the story was true other than him was Jeremy. The person who would want the story kept out of the press at all costs would be Jeremy. At all costs … yes, Stafford liked the sound of that. All he had to do was contact the man himself.

A few phone calls to some of his celeb-stalking paparazzi friends had provided him with an address in Beachwood Canyon. No more than an hour later Stafford had found himself waiting outside the imposing gates of Chez Pinewood.

He'd considered taping the envelope he'd taken with him to the gates. But the only problem with that would be one of the staff binning it as fan mail or a downpour of unseasonable rain

washing it off. He had to get inside the gates. Salvation had
come his way shortly after.

Having parked his car away from the gates so that it couldn't
be seen, Stafford had positioned himself behind a group of bushes. He'd been there about twenty minutes when a car pulled up
at the gates. From his vantage point, as the window wound down
Stafford could see that the driver was an Italian looking man just
a little older than Jeremy. He announced himself as 'Mario' on
the house intercom and the gates started to swing open. Stafford knew that this was his chance. As the car drove towards the
house, Stafford ran behind it as inconspicuously as he could.

Successfully inside, he hid behind a tree until he'd watched
the handsome stranger go inside the house.

'I hope you're getting a serving of what I received from Mr
Pinewood, darling,' murmured Stafford to himself. 'I certainly
know I'd like another large portion. Maybe I should insist on it
as part of my bargaining.'

Stafford was driving home after posting the letter through
the box when his mobile had rung. Number withheld. Nervously he'd answered. It had been Jeremy. The conversation had been
short and sweet. They'd arranged to meet at a coffee shop not
far from Jeremy's house. Stafford told him what he looked like
('Just in case you can't remember, I was on my knees after all,')
and said he could be there in fifteen minutes.

Sure enough, a quarter of an hour later, Stafford was grinning like the Cheshire Cat, clutching his café frappe as a peeved-
looking Jeremy sheepishly walked into the coffee shop.

'Just as gorgeous as I recall,' teased Stafford. But Jeremy was
not in the mood for humour. 'Look, let's cut to the chase shall
we. What price for your silence?'

Keen to play it cool and not undersell himself, Stafford passed
the buck. 'That's for you to decide. Just don't forget that most of

the western world knows how rich you are, so unless you want to be on the front page of every newspaper this side of Bangkok tomorrow morning then you'll make me a decent offer.'

'$80,000 and you're out of my hair for good. Take it or leave it.'

'Leave it, thank you. I'll see you on the front page.' Hoping that his bluff would work, Stafford made as if he were about to leave. It did work. A tidal wave of panic crashed across Jeremy's features.

'$100,000 …?' Stafford kept moving. 'Okay, sit back down. $150,000 and that's my final offer. You haven't even got any proof about all of this, I assume.'

'That's for me to know.' Stafford could feel that he was pushing his cockiness a little too far. Plus, the actor was right – he didn't have any proof.

'Sold. You can start writing the cheque now.' Stafford was delirious, picturing himself as some macho bargaining hot-shot in a seedy ransom flick.

'You get cash. But not here, it's too public. Give me your address and I'll have it delivered. That way, no-one sees me hand it over and then I know where you live if you fuck with me. The cash will be with you today.'

Flummoxed by how the dynamics of the rendezvous were shifting, Stafford ran out of wisecracks. 'Okay, but I want it this afternoon or else … or else there'll be trouble.' Even Stafford realised how corny he sounded. He scribbled his address down on a coffee shop serviette and handed it to Jeremy. Within seconds, the star had turned heel and left.

Two hours later, Stafford had opened the door of his apartment to find Jeremy's chauffeur, Robin, standing there, an envelope in his hand. 'Mr Pinewood says it's all there and trusts this brings the matter to a close.' Grabbing the packet, Stafford closed the door and ran to the table to begin counting it. Sure enough, it was all there.

With a holler of joy, Stafford danced around the table. 'God, if only every other blow job I've dished out paid as well. I'd be a friggin' squillionaire!'

———

'Cheers everyone, here's to the sweet billion dollar scent of the *Babylon* Glampire.' As Montana spoke, she chinked champagne flutes with Brad and Stafford. They were all being wined and dined in first class luxury on board their British Airways flight to London. 'This is the only way to fly, darlings. It's certainly put a constant smile on your face, Staffy … Seen a steward you'd like to introduce to the Mile High Club, darling, or it is just the bubbles in this fine glass of fizz?'

Stafford hadn't stopped smiling since his opening of the money-packed envelope the day before. 'First class service, first class company and the thought of all those hot boys in London and Venice. Now, why wouldn't I be smiling? Plus my best friend is engaged to one of the sexiest men in LA, isn't she?' He winked at Brad and playfully squeezed his knee.

Brad squirmed in his seat at Stafford's flirtation. 'Hands off darling,' cooed Montana. 'This chunk of manliness is for my eyes only … and my hands, and my body, and my soul, and my …'

'I can take a hint, fear not. Brad's safe,' protested Stafford. I shall be splashing the cash on some Euro-lovelies, so I've got no need for your sloppy seconds. Anyway, what's the itinerary?'

Slipping into manager mode, Brad flipped open his diary and read out loud. 'We arrive in London, have two major talk shows and a launch party booked and then we're off to the *Planet Shopping Channel* for one of their All Day Deals. It's the UK's biggest shopping channel and if we can sell out of our *Babylon* gift sets on there, then you, my dear, can pick any honeymoon you like. The TV shopping market could be massive for *Babylon*. You're going to be selling to potentially millions of homes.'

Montana's jade green eyes lit up at the prospect of both the money and the honeymoon, weighing up the likes of St Lucia and Tahiti in her mind.

'Then we've all got a few days off before heading to Venice to prepare for your *Babylon* weekend of decadence. The weekend should clash with the film festival, so it'll be big names wall to wall, or should that be canal-bank to canal-bank. I've factored in a few days spare for you and me before the weekend kicks off, darling, so that we can take in the sights. A trip over to Murano to buy some of the most gorgeous glassware in the world is a must, I feel, especially when I'm buying it for the most gorgeous woman in the world.' Brad leaned over to embrace Montana.

'Where's the sick bag in first class?' joked Stafford. 'I need one now after comments like that, Brad. Anyway, talking of glass, mine's empty … more champers anyone?'

Realising that they'd exhausted their current supply, Stafford pulled a vexed expression, mock horror dancing round his lips. 'I shall have to go and find some more bubbles. Now where is that rather beefy looking steward …'

Making his way through the first class cabin, Stafford surveyed the people around him, literally smelling the wealth in the air. First class was just as he had imagined – a grandiose melting pot of suited businessmen banging away at their laptops, affluent young music stars he'd seen on MTV dripping in bling and women of near retirement age who had obviously been under the knife far too many times in an attempt to turn back time. Letting out a wry smile, Stafford was delighted to be amongst them all.

Having located his steward and requested more champagne, Stafford made to return to his seat. It was then, across the way, that he spotted someone else he recognised from the TV. She was reclining in her chair, eyes closed. Spurred on by the alcohol running through his veins, Stafford's hunger for celebs got the better of him. He minced up to her and tapped her on the shoulder. The shock caused her to jump. Staring up at Stafford, she simply said 'Hi, can I help you?'

Beaming, Stafford started to gush. 'I really hope you don't mind me interrupting you, but I knew I recognised you from the TV. I'm a martyr to the E! Entertainment Network, I really am. Plus *Pengelly Manor* is just one of my favourite films ever. That scene where you discover you're dying just broke my heart. My name's Stafford, I'm here with an actress friend of mine, Montana Phoenix from *Peregrine Palace*, I was just wandering if you'd care to join us for a drink.' As an afterthought Stafford added. 'You are Evie Merchant, aren't you?'

Normally, Evie would have given a swift autograph and declined the offer, preferring to try and sleep, but as soon as Stafford had mentioned Montana's name, something nudged her curiosity.

Evie coyly smiled. 'You've got me, I'm the very same. I'd love to join you. I haven't seen Montana for a long while.'

When Evie and Regan had been at Farmington together, Evie had been invited to Montana's Hollywood home a couple of times. As an aspiring actress at the time, Montana was very much an icon to be admired. In fact, the first time she'd been introduced to her, Evie had hardly been able to speak, totally dumbstruck by her fame. Evie's bumbling had been something which Regan had found ridiculously amusing.

Clapping his hands together in excitement, Stafford queried the connection. 'Oh goody, so you've met before. How come?'

'One of my best friends is Regan, Montana's daughter. We were at school together. Me, her and our friend, Nush Silvers, were inseparable. We still are when we can actually get in the same time zone together.'

Stafford's ears pricked at the mention of Nush's name. 'Anoushka Silvers? Newspaper girl? Yes, I know that name as well. It's a small first-class world, deary, isn't it? Now, come on over, you can meet the man Montana's planning to marry. It's quite sickening how in love they are. He's all over her like a wasp around a toffee apple.'

Bursting with pride, Stafford introduced Evie to Montana and Brad. At first, Montana's jaw fell, a direct result of meeting anyone who possessed any association with her daughter, but then she smiled graciously, beckoning Evie to sit alongside them.

'My dear child, it's been simply ... er ... ages, has it not, since I last saw you. You were still a girl, and look at you now. Quite the big shot in Hollywood with all your lovely films. Congratulations, darling.' Montana clasped her hands around Evie's in a feigned show of warmth. Inwardly she was seething, having always hankered for major success on the big screen. 'I feel much more at home on television myself. Such a different medium, requires such unique skill sets. The nuances of emotion needed can be difficult for so many artists. But I find they come with ease.'

Regan's right, thought Evie, a smirk spreading across her face. *The line between Montana and her bitchy on-screen alter-ego is definitely a thin one.* She had to admit to still being a fan, though.

'So, what are you doing in the UK?' asked Evie, sipping her champagne. 'Are you going to see Regan? She's doing so well with this *Wild Child* show. I'm so proud of her.'

Momentarily allowing her lip to curl, Montana answered. 'We're there for *Babylon*, my new fragrance. It's divine. I'll get some over to you. Plus a couple of chat shows, spreading my joyous news about the wedding and then onto Venice for some romantic us-time for Brad and me before a weekend junket with the beauty press. We're there at the same time as the Film Festival. It will be a good chance to catch up with so many dear friends from the industry. Being such a success worldwide does keep one busy.'

No mention of either Regan or Wild Child noted Evie. *Obviously a sore point.* 'Maybe we'll bump into each other again in Venice. I'm there for the Festival this year to talk about my next film. It's a rom-com starring me and Jeremy Pinewood. It's tipped to be one of the biggest successes of the year.'

Unable to stop himself, Stafford sprayed the champagne he was drinking from his lips. It was the mention of Jeremy's name that had caused him to do so. In between coughs, he attempted to apologise. 'Bubbles went down the wrong hole, excuse me, won't you?' He wiped his mouth as he turned to Evie. 'Is he as good looking in the flesh as he seems in the magazines and on TV? What I wouldn't give to see him up close and personal. I did see him once on the red carpet outside Grauman's Chinese Theatre but he was whisked off by some odious PR before I could talk to him.' The whole story was untrue but Stafford was determined to keep the topic of conversation on Jeremy.

A giddy flurry of butterflies flitted around inside Evie at the thought of Jeremy. 'He is divine, just as good as he looks on screen. In fact, I'd say better ... but you might have guessed I'd say that after all those photos of us together in the papers, eh?'

'Sweet girl, I'm been so busy packing my outfits for this trip I haven't seen a paper in days,' said Stafford and it appeared from the prying look on both Brad and Montana's faces that neither of them knew what Evie was talking about either.

'Well, I guess you three are the only people alive who don't already know the latest Hollywood gossip.' Evie spoke with a frisson of excitement in her voice. 'As well as playing lovers on screen, Jeremy and I have let our emotions spill over into real life. We are officially together. I couldn't be happier. I wanted to keep it a secret for a little while longer, but you must know what agents are like, the cat was out of the bag before I had a chance to protest.'

It wasn't very often that Stafford became speechless, but for a split second his mind went blank. His mouth falling open wide enough not just to catch one fly, but a whole swarm. It was only another split second before a myriad of ideas started flooding his mind, popping like fireworks as he considered possibilities.

'So, you and Jeremy are an item? A good old Hollywood love story. Couldn't happen to a nicer couple,' spewed Stafford, laying on his faux delight for Evie with a trowel.

His delight was purely financial though. Money-making thoughts ricocheted inside his head. *Jeremy's coupled up with Evie Merchant. Their film is tipped for big things. I know Jeremy's dark secret. He wants to keep it a secret. I can call the shots.* Suddenly, Stafford realised that maybe the $150,000 was merely the loose change at the tip of a financial mountain that could be coming his way. He felt as if he was staring at the jackpot on a slot machine.

Clinking Evie's glass with his own, Stafford said, 'Cheers, Ms Merchant, I hope you'll be very happy together.'

He needed to hatch a plan …

———

A few hours later, as night time descended, a reclining Evie slept soundly in her chair. It was then that a nervous Stafford edged his way towards her across the cabin and masterfully grabbed her Chanel handbag from between her legs. Without stopping, he ran to the toilet with it. Searching for her mobile inside, he grabbed it, praying that his thieving had not been spotted. The phone was on flight mode. Scrolling through Evie's phone address book, he found the words 'Jeremy Mobile'. There were no other Jeremys listed. Grabbing a piece of toilet paper, he scribbled down the number as quickly as he could, wiped the phone for fear of fingerprints and dropped it back into the bag. Luckily for him, as he replaced the designer bag back between Evie's legs, she still appeared to be in a deep sleep, oblivious to his actions. Stafford knew he had taken a huge risk, but with Jeremy's number safely in his back pocket, he knew that it was one that would hopefully pay off.

Sweat trickling down his back from the ordeal, he returned to his seat.

CHAPTER 53

Regan couldn't help but smother her words with a hefty covering of mockery as she tried to get her head around recent events. 'So, let me see if I've got this right. You heard Harry cheating on Evie behind her back, somewhere along the way he's managed to knock up his own stepmother, and in the last few days he's managed to virtually kill your dad. Meanwhile, you've got the boyfriend of the loony murder victim who's been lobbing bricks through your window and threatening you with a knife staying under the same roof with you. It's like something from an episode of my mother's soap opera. Does Evie know all this?'

Regan was talking to Nush as they relaxed outside the orangery at Kingsbury sharing a jug of Pimms.

'Evie's up to date with most things. She doesn't know that I heard Harry with another woman though so let's keep that one quiet, eh? I asked Harry about it when he was telling me the sorry saga of Sadie. Despite being unable to remember much as he was so bladdered at the time, he seems to think that Evie just left him because he was being an arse. Evie's said as much to me, so I'm not going to say a word. Not that any of that matters now that Evie's with Jeremy. I trust you've seen the papers. I'm dying to grill her about it all when she gets back. She should be landing soon.' Nush emptied her glass, savouring every drop and began to pour herself another hefty measure. 'Christ, I need a drink, everything is such a bloody mess. I can't believe Clarissa's been sticking her oar in again as well. Any idea how she managed to get her hands on the photo of Montana and dad? He'll spit feathers when he sees that on her show. He's not exactly her biggest fan as it is. She still owes him a column for *The Daily Staple* from the *Wild Child* auction. He wants it all over with, but she says she's waiting for the right story apparently. Snotty bitch. I'd like to punch her lights out. I'm so glad you did, I've have paid millions to see that.'

Stirring her drink with her finger, Regan shifted awkwardly in her seat. Nush's diatribe jolted her back to her own worries and the fact that she had come to Kingsbury primarily to speak to Lawrence. 'I've got to speak to your dad before she shows the world that photo.'

'Do it tonight, the sooner the better. At the end of the day it's only a photo, so he might just laugh it off and say they used to hang out together.'

Regan wasn't convinced. 'I reckon there's more to it than that. There's something too cosy about the photo. I just have to find out from Lawrence before Clarissa starts spouting her evil gossip. I'm convinced that Grace is the one who gave the photo to her. She's the only real candidate. I don't see how it can be anyone else. I was telling Leo about it last night.'

'Pillow talk, eh?' Nush curled her lips devilishly as she enquired. Regan had filled her in on her first night of passion with the producer.

'We were too busy to talk when we were in bed, thank you,' blushed Regan, the thought of their sultry love-making still causing her skin to tingle with a craving for more of the same. 'The thing is, I trust Grace. Why would she want to give Clarissa the photo? She's one of the few people I have been able to trust … isn't she?' There was a trace of doubt in her words.

'Money, darling,' purred Nush. 'I pay thousands to my contacts around the world for a good story. If Clarissa thinks there's a story there, she'll start dishing the dosh. Even the holiest and strongest of people will sell their souls to the devil if the price is right.'

Regan hoped that her worries about Grace were unfounded. 'Anyway, talking of *strong*, tell me more about Jake. Is Mr Muscles going to be a permanent fixture? Surely he's not managed to battle his way into *your* affections.' It was now Regan's turn to curl her lips with an air of mischief.

'We'll see. He's recuperating at my family home and we're enjoying each other's company. Enough said. Plus I don't really want to get too involved with a man whose last girlfriend is still waiting to be buried, do I? It's not exactly the best way to start a relationship. He's going to the funeral later this week. Once that is out of the way, we'll see what happens. Now, another drink? You're going to need all of the Dutch courage you can muster for your chat with dear daddy tonight. Let's finish off the jug and then I'll show you to your room.'

—

Snapping his mobile shut, Lawrence paced agitatedly down one of the many corridors within Kingsbury. He'd just had yet another heated conversation with his divorce lawyer about cutting Sadie out of his life. They weren't conversations he relished, every word reminding him of her treachery and betrayal, but sadly they were necessary. But since learning that Sadie's betrayal had been with his son, the former apple of his eye, Lawrence couldn't wait to put the whole sorry affair behind him. He needed to take drastic actions. Harry's exhibition of disloyalty had hurt him far more than anything else he'd had to deal with in life. There was no turning back for their relationship. It was over, for good. He needed to make another phone call.

Pushing open the door of his Kingsbury office, Lawrence walked directly to the contacts book on his desk and started thumbing through the pages. Finding the number he required, he flipped open his phone again and dialled.

'Hello, Brian. Lawrence Silvers here. I need to meet up with you as soon as possible. I need to make some urgent changes to my will … pretty drastic ones.'

———

As Lawrence was speaking to his lawyer, on the other side of Kingsbury, Jake Saunders was sitting up in bed in one of the palatial bedrooms, with a nurse at his constant beck and call. If Jake's wound started hurting, then help was literally only seconds away.

As it was, Jake's wound was giving him a minimum amount of grief. He wanted his body back to full strength. After all, his muscles were his money-maker. He needed to be back in the gym, ready to train for the next series of *Sporting Spartans*, although he had yet to sign on the dotted line of the contract for the new season. His agent had told him to hold off until he'd explored the possibilities of work overseas. US networks had already enquired about his joining the American version of *Spartans*. If he could have just a fraction of the success in the States that he'd already had in the UK then he could be looking at enough money to set him up for life. He just hoped that the current whirlpool of scandalous publicity he was swimming around in wouldn't dash his chances.

Jake had stayed in his room since Regan had arrived an hour or so ago, giving her and Nush room to chat. He knew Regan from the papers and TV and he had heard from Nush how the bond between the two girls was strong.

Closing the notebook computer that was perched on his lap in bed, Jake yawned. The painkillers he was taking were making him more sluggish than usual and a considerable time staring at the PC screen, checking his emails and finalising his forthcoming work agenda hadn't helped. He needed to perk himself up. Easing his naked body out of the bed, he stretched his arms above his head, feeling their muscles unwind with pleasure and walked across to the en suite bathroom. Within seconds he was feeling the jets of the power shower against his skin. It felt good, awakening his spirit. He thought of Nush and his cock twitched between his legs. Even flaccid, Jake's manhood was as impressive as his entire body. Its girth and sizable head had pleasured many women in its time and as it grew to its full mighty length and stood erect, proud and glistening in the shower, Jake experienced a sensation of horniness flowing through his body. Thinking back to the sex he'd first experienced with Nush, he hoped that it wouldn't be too long until there was a repeat performance.

Towelling himself off, Jake looked down at his wound. It looked better with each day, the angry bruising around the entry point of the knife now much less noticeable. He would call the nurse from downstairs to redress it in a while.

From the bathroom he could hear the door of his room opening. It would either be Nush checking up on him or the nurse coming to see if he required any medical attention. Either way, he had no need for clothes. Both women had seen him naked, and if it was Nush, then maybe the vision of his chiselled body would put her in the mood for some kind of sexual action. Still naked, he walked back into the room.

Regan stood on the far side of the room, suitcase in hand. A squeal of surprise erupted from her mouth. 'Oh hi, I'm sorry, I thought this was my room. Nush said it was the top of the stairs and turn right. I didn't mean to … I'm so sorry.' Realising she was babbling, Regan turned on her heels and scuttled from the room, but not before she had let her eyes take in the entire length of Jake's naked torso, including the mighty sword of semi-hard flesh swaying between his legs.

'Jesus, now that's one superfit body,' she muttered to herself as she slammed the bedroom door behind her.

CHAPTER 54

Evie wasn't normally the biggest fan of flying, so she was surprised by how much she had enjoyed the flight from Los Angeles. She slept for much of it, but spent the time in between chatting and drinking with Montana, Brad and Stafford. She'd been equally surprised by how much she'd warmed to Montana. Despite the initial digs that Montana had obviously felt compelled to dish out, by the time they'd landed on the tarmac at London Heathrow, the women had discussed many different subjects and had discovered a mutual love of Hermes handbags, Spanish architecture and the history of Egypt.

The champagne had flowed freely and Evie had soon found herself laughing wildly at Stafford's bawdy tales of men he'd slept with in Hollywood and his anatomically detailed descriptions of their appendages. She'd giggled at Brad's tales of being scared of meeting Montana for the first time, saying how he'd felt like a tiny insect straying into the path of a black widow spider. 'Even after the first time we'd had sex, I was worried she'd try to eat me, like the female spiders do to their male counterparts,' he'd said.

She'd even been close to tears when Montana started telling her about Regan as a baby girl. Prompted by Evie's curiosity about her Trinity friend as a child, Montana had described how toddler Regan would spend hours making faux perfume from flower petals and rain water in the garden at their Hollywood home and how she wouldn't go to nursery until Montana or the nanny had tied pretty pink ribbons in her hair. 'She was such a girly girl back in those days,' exclaimed Montana. 'Not like now, of course. She's such a tomboy ... maybe that show will do her some good.'

Tears welling in her eyes, Evie had listened to Montana's tales of a young Regan. Dabbling her face with a tissue, Evie had told Montana how she longed for a child one day. 'I'd love a little girl I could dress up and play dollies with. Brush her hair and sing lullabies too. I'd give up all the acting to have that in the future.'

'Well, you can guarantee any child would be gorgeous with you as mom and Jeremy Pinewood as dad, wouldn't it?' offered Stafford.

Tipsy from the champagne, Evie flushed as she answered. 'Stafford, that's way down the line, we haven't even had sex yet?'

Chortling at her candid admission, Evie felt her cheeks rouge further. *You might not have had sex with him yet sweetheart, but I have* thought Stafford to himself.

Having swapped numbers with Montana and made a rash promise to make a cameo appearance on the next season of *Peregrine Palace*, Evie said goodbye to her travel companions as they passed through customs at Heathrow and waited for her driver to collect her.

As she was chauffeured from the airport, a huge billboard loomed down at her from the side of the road. It showed Regan and Grace, both wearing boxing gloves, squaring up to each other in mock battle to promote *Wild Child*. Regan had war paint smeared across her face and a plaster positioned above her eye. It was a striking, yet rough and ready look.

'Tomboy indeed, my dear friend. No pretty pink ribbons in your hair now,' laughed Evie, thinking how the image couldn't have been any further removed from Montana's description of a pre-school Regan. She was still tittering about it when she arrived home an hour or so later.

———

'Jake says he's sorry he treated you to such an eyeful, but I guess you can now see one of his major attractions, can't you?'

Regan and Nush had been sniggering for the last twenty minutes. 'I got the wrong room. Not that I regret it!' winked Regan. 'That boy sure does have hidden talents. If your TV warrior has a pugil stick like that to play with, then what are you waiting for?'

Both girls were nervously waiting for Lawrence's arrival. He'd told Regan to meet him at eight in the study. Regan had mentioned that Nush would be joining them, causing Lawrence to grunt, 'Why does she need to be there?'

It was just after eight when Lawrence pushed back the huge study door and walked in. He looked dreadful. His normally ruddy yet healthy looking skin looked washed out, his eyes baggy and lifeless. Even his hair, usually slicked into place, sprouted skywards, unkempt and unstyled.

Looking at Nush, he growled 'No bloody idea what you're here for, but you can do what you want, seeing as you're one of the few people in this family who hasn't shat on me from a great height.' His words were smothered with bitterness.

'I don't agree with what Harry and Sadie have done, you know that, don't you?' For the first time in as long as she could remember, she actually felt sorry for Lawrence. She never really liked her father – in fact there had been times when she had certainly hated him – but at that very moment she could see a deep sadness behind his eyes.

'We're not here to talk about that, are we? Those two are dead as far as I'm concerned,' he snarled. 'Now, what do you want? It's about your mother, isn't it?'

Regan reached down into her bag and pulled out the snap-shot.

'I found this photo of you and my mother and the thing is … seeing as Nush and I are best mates, I was kind of surprised that neither of you had ever mentioned knowing each other, especially as I've been here so many times.' Regan fumbled with her words, trying to formulate exactly what she wanted to say. She decided to cut to the chase. Swallowing hard, her mouth dry as she spoke, she spat her words out. 'Here's the photo. It must be from years ago. You both look happy together, so I just wandered how you knew each other. Were you friends, or …' Regan struggled to finish the sentence, not really knowing what she wanted to say.

Lawrence grabbed the photo from her hands. 'I suppose you've seen this as well, have you?' He was looking at Nush. She nodded silently.

He stared at the photo, wide-eyed, breathing out a hefty lungful of air as he did so. 'Bloody hell, that must be getting on for 25 years ago. It's even before you were born, I would say.' He motioned to Nush again.

'It's on one of the yachts. Probably St Tropez or maybe Boni-facio in Corsica. Johnny and I used to go down there all the time. Spot of fishing, take in the casinos, and doubtless a few party nights. You youngsters think you know everything about partying these days with your cocaine and your ketamine but we did it with style. Johnny and I were the playboys women wanted to be seen with. We had the money, we had the looks and we had the toys. I suppose we thought that one day our own sons would be the same. No chance of that. Mine's a cheating bastard and Johnny's got one who's weaker than a pooftah's handshake and one who's shacked up with some dumb model in America. You kids are such a disappointment.'

'But dad ...' interrupted Nush. 'Do you know Montana Phoenix or not? You do seem fairly ... er, *together* in the photo.'

Studying the photo again, Lawrence sniffed and then threw it onto the desk in front of him. 'Yes, I knew her. She was one of a group of women that used to meet Johnny and I regularly when we wanted ... company.'

Regan squirmed in her chair as Lawrence continued. She already had an inkling of what she was about to hear. 'She wasn't called Montana Phoenix back then, that's for sure. What was her name? I should bloody remember it. I wrote enough bloody cheques to her. Mind you, her and her mates usually wanted cash. What was it ... Belinda, that's it. Belinda Faye. Game girl, she was, and I don't just mean the fact she was on the game. She was always fun. She just disappeared overnight. If it wasn't for the fact that I'd be at the centre of the story, and that's the last thing I want right now, I'd have some right old tales to tell in the press about what your mother used to get up to.'

The colour had drained from Regan's face. Her mouth hung open. Nush sat there too, unable to comprehend what Lawrence had just told them. The fact that her father had admitted to using whores in the past was bad enough, but to find out that one of his favourites was her best mate's mother was mind blowing.

Regan's bottom lip trembled as she spoke. 'You used to pay my mother for sex? You're telling me she was a jet-set floozy who would jump on a plane and fly off to some exotic location to get paid for dropping her knickers? My mother is capable of many things, Mr Silvers, but I can't believe that Montana would do that.'

Lawrence was adamant with his reply. 'Well, that's just it, isn't it Regan? She wasn't Montana, was she? She was Belinda Faye ... maybe some of the cash that I put your mother's way paid for all that acting training to get her where she is today. It's simple … a woman can never be trusted. Your precious mother has let you down. So what? It's to be expected. You two will do it as well. You all let somebody down in the end, with your lies and your treachery.' Lawrence's mouth seemed to twist with annoyance and despair as he spoke, his voice getting louder with each word.

'Sadie's let me down. You've never been anything more than a disappointment to me, Anoushka. Even your mother let me down by dying on us all.'

At the mention of her mother, Nush snapped. Jumping to her feet, she started to scream at her father. 'Just shut up! How dare you even mention my mother? She died giving you your beloved son and look how he's turned out. At least she loved me. That's more than you ever have, with your years of bullying and abuse. If people let you down, then ask yourself why. You're nasty and vile and it should have been you that died years ago, not mum. Then everything would have been better.'

At that moment, the three people in the study all had something in common. They were all crying. But they were all weeping for different reasons. Lawrence cried poisonous tears of hate for those who had betrayed him. Nush cried bitter tears of sadness for the memory of her beautiful mother Lysette. Regan cried silent tears of confusion for what she had just learnt about her own mother.

CHAPTER 55

'Ladies and gentleman, will you please welcome to the UK, the sexiest woman in soap land, Montana Phoenix.'

As the familiar music of Britain's most watched live day-time chat show played in the background, Montana sashayed onto the set of *Talking Showbiz* wearing an immaculate Diane Von Furstenberg dress. Her make-up was equally flawless – her plump lips drowning in a striking shade of hot pink gloss and her Queen Nefertiti eyes outlined in symmetrical halos of jet black liner.

Outstretching her arms with mock devotion to greet the show host, she air-kissed the woman, a plumpish blonde called Davinia Brookes who was quite literally adored by the British public.

'Montana, you look … and smell divine. Am I detecting *Babylon*?' gushed Davinia.

From behind the cameras, Brad and Stafford watched in awe as Montana went into auto-pilot. She told the story of how the fragrance had been personally chosen. 'I wanted to give a little bit of myself back to my adoring public.' She followed it up with talk of her recent engagement to Brad. 'The man completes me and appreciates the women that I am. I feel truly blessed.' It was pure Hollywood schmaltz as she blew him a kiss off camera and mouthed the words 'Love you'. She enthused about forthcoming storylines on the new season of *Peregrine Palace*.

'Oh, Davinia, darling, if you think you've seen me acting my designer heels off with some of Sienna's past storylines then wait until you see what happens to my character this season. I was only saying to my dear friend and confidante Evie Merchant the other day that I really do feel that my talent seems to grow from year to year. Isn't she a marvellous actress? Such a good friend of the family, too.'

Never one to miss an opportunity, Davinia swooped upon the mention of Evie's name with professional gusto. 'Doubtless she was telling you all about her sparkling new relationship with Hollywood Dreamboat Jeremy Pinewood. How scrummy are they together? And am I not right in thinking that she is very good friends with your dear daughter Regan, star of worldwide smash *Wild Child*? How are things with you two now? You have had your difficulties haven't you?'

Keen to steer the conversation back to herself and away from Regan, Montana attempted to turn the tables on Davinia with a bit of quick thinking. In reality it was sheer panic, not an emotion that Montana normally experienced. Before the chat show host could interject, Montana made a kneejerk decision in her mind.

'In fact, I have a sneaking suspicion Evie might be watching this morning, and I'd love to ask her something live on air, if I may, Davinia. Call it an exclusive for your charming show.'

Off set, Brad was perplexed by Montana's words. 'What the hell is she up to?' he uttered. As manager, he always went through her interview answers before she went on air, making sure that every word was vital to the thrust of the interview. Had *Talking Showbiz* been pre-recorded, he would have stopped the interview to ask what Montana was doing, but an interruption on a live show with Davinia Brookes was not a good idea.

On air, Montana's face filled the screen looking pleadingly down the lens of her close-up camera. 'Evie, if you're watching, call the show's number, darling. I have a question for you. You said you'd watch.'

———

It was true, she had. Montana had told her she would be guesting on the show the day before at the airport and, true to her word, as Montana was telling Davinia about their supposedly deep friendship, Evie was at home gazing incredulously at her TV screen.

What did she have to lose by phoning up? She could always do a classic 'no comment' and move on if Davinia started asking her questions that were a little too probing. Electrified by her spontaneous decision, she picked up the phone and dialled.

The phone was answered virtually instantly. Within seconds, she was being put through to Davinia.

'Now, you sound like Evie Merchant, but you could be an impostor, of course. I do have my reputation to think of here, Evie. I hear from Montana that you were on a flight together recently. What fashionable item were you wearing on the plane?'

Evie laughed at having to prove her identity. 'A Stella McCartney top … and it is me, honestly.'

'It *is* her, Davinia, I would recognise that angelic voice anywhere.' Montana was squealing with delight, a little shocked that Evie had actually phoned.

'It's lovely to speak to you, Evie, it truly is,' gushed Davinia. 'May I be the first to congratulate you on your relationship with Jeremy Pinewood.'

'That's very kind, Davinia. Now, did I hear correctly, Montana has something to ask me? I'm a little intrigued, to say the least,' fudged Evie, moving away from Davinia's line of questioning.

An electric air crackled around the studio waiting to hear what Montana was about to ask. Even Brad, for once out of control, looked on inquisitively.

Flashing her ultra-white teeth at the camera, Montana beamed, no sign of the volcano of panic bubbling inside her. 'Evie, as you know when you shared that special time with myself and Brad, we are deeply in love. I mentioned to you that I was thinking of a huge Hollywood wedding, inviting all my admiring A-list friends. But seeing as I am from the UK, born and bred here, it seems only right that I should get married here.'

Brad placed his hand to his forehead and covered his eyes, unable to look at Montana for fear of what she might say next. Stafford on the other hand, looked on heatedly, hoping for another nugget of Montana TV gold. He wasn't to be disappointed.

Montana's story snowballed out of control. 'So, while Brad and I are here, we'd love to get married in a quiet quaint British way and who better to be our maid of honour than Britain's most famous fair rose right now. Please say you will, darling, Brad and I would be so honoured.'

Brad's skin ran cold, not because he didn't want to marry Montana, he just didn't like the goalposts being moved without discussion. Stafford, giddy from his superstar friend's actions, just muttered, 'Holy shit,' under his breath. A similar thought was going through Evie's brain.

She liked Montana but she certainly didn't want to be the maid of honour at her wedding. Shouldn't that be Regan's job? But if she said no, it would be live on air on Britain's most-watched chat show. People would want to know why she had turned down one of the most adored TV stars in the world.

Plus, Evie knew that Stephanie would be livid with any negative publicity, especially now everything seemed to be going her way. Evie cursed herself for being stupid enough to phone up in the first place. Without actually allowing herself to admit that it was her voice saying the words she answered the request. 'Of course, Montana, I'd be honoured.'

As Montana inwardly quaked at what she had just done to Brad in her abject panic, Davinia was nearly choking with the excitement of it all. After nearly 25 years on TV, it would rank as one of her most memorable interviews ever. TV gold indeed.

Watching the same TV show from her room at Kingsbury, Regan was close to choking too. From betrayal. How could Evie do it? One of the Trinity stabbing her in the back.

Reaching for her mobile and dialling Evie's number, Regan cursed. 'You bitch ... you've got some explaining to do.'

CHAPTER 56

Brad and Montana's screaming in the *Talking Showbiz* dressing room could be heard all the way down the corridor. As a result, everyone within earshot had gathered outside the door to listen. For once, though, it was Montana on the receiving end.

'So now we have to get married for the sake of the Montana Phoenix publicity machine, do we? It's not on, Montana, I wanted to marry you on our terms … you and me together … not some cheap publicity stunt.'

Montana knew that, for once, she had overstepped the mark. 'Brad, darling, calm down. I just wanted to veer the conversation away from that bloody daughter of mine and that show of hers. I got a bit carried away … I panicked, but it doesn't change how I feel.'

'I just … I just … wanted us to discuss things together, Montana, that's all.' The hesitation in Brad's speech indicated that she was winning him over. 'So, what's your big plan, then? Woe betide that we let down your public now that they think a celebrity wedding is on the cards?'

Montana knew that she had to come up with a plan. Getting married so quickly had actually been the furthest thing from her mind, but maybe the idea of a ceremony in the UK as a precursor to a more grandiose celebrity bash back in LA wasn't such a bad idea. She just couldn't let Brad know just how hasty and impulsively gung-ho the idea had really been.

With an air of total confidence, the actress replied. 'Darling, what I was thinking was that we could see about one of the sumptuous Louis XVI reception areas at The Ritz. It would be the perfect setting for an intimate wedding. It's the most exquisite summer venue and the magazines will be desperate to feature us. It's not every day that such a megastar announces her wedding on national TV after all. As for clothes, we could swing by Liberty and check out their marvellous bridal boutique. One of my friends used them last year and they had the most heavenly collections from Lacroix and Lagerfeld. If we start making some phone calls now, we could maybe arrange something for … say, tomorrow?'

Aware that even for a superstar of her stature, she had just placed the tallest of orders upon her husband-to-be, Montana slid her way over to Brad and coiled herself around him sensually. 'Brad, darling, I can't wait to be your wife. Forgive me for being a little impetuous,' she simpered, running her fingers through his hair as she spoke. 'Just think of it this way, the sooner we get married, the sooner we can celebrate with the most orgasmic wedding night.'

Brad sighed with resignation, knowing that he had lost. 'I'm going back out to the Limo, then. Looks like I have some phone calls to make. The Ritz, Liberty and the media … let's hope they can all clear their diaries for tomorrow.' As he opened the door of the dressing room, the group of eavesdroppers outside all scuttled off in different directions.

'They'll clear their diaries, darling, don't you worry … it is Montana Phoenix we're talking about here. And only consider *Hello* and *OK!*. We want a million and a front cover exclusive. I will not be surrounded by photos of some talentless bunch of scrubbers from shitty little reality shows. Understand …? And that includes my daughter and that Lazslo woman!'

Stafford had been languishing on a huge chocolate brown sofa in the corner of the dressing room throughout the entire exchange. He had been soaking up every word, loving the skilful way that Montana had managed to win over her lover. It was only when Brad was out of earshot that he dared to speak. 'You, my dear, are a piece of work,' he said, pointing his finger. 'An absolute masterpiece. Tell me that you had all of that planned in advance and I'll tell you that you're lying through your dazzling snowy white teeth.'

'I scare myself sometimes, darling. Did I sound convincing? I do want to marry Brad, I worship the ground he walks on. I just didn't want Davinia bloody Brookes to turn the whole interview into my life as Regan's mother. I'm the star in this family, remember!'

'How could anybody forget, my sweet?' sneered Stafford. 'So, a wedding at The Ritz with Evie Merchant as maid of honour. This trip gets better and better. What about Regan, though? Hadn't you better let her know that you're getting wed? You will want her there, darling … won't you?'

'I'll ring her. She can be there if she wants. But if the magazines start asking her about that bloody *Wild Child* show then they'll have me to deal with. Now, it's such a shame that Jeremy Pinewood isn't in town. He would have made up the numbers perfectly. I wander if could get a quote from his agent for the magazine feature.'

Stafford let out a grin. 'I should imagine he's a trifle busy, darling. But you could always ask Evie for his number.'

The same number Stafford had been texting while Montana and Brad had been at loggerheads. The message had read 'Guess who? I met your girlfriend yesterday on a plane – such a shame you're deceiving her. Another $150,000 should keep my silence, for now …' Stafford was still waiting for a reply.

CHAPTER 57

After agreeing to Montana's request live on TV, Evie's phone hadn't stopped ringing. Unsurprisingly Regan had been the first to phone.

'Since when did you get so bloody chummy with my mother? You're her maid of honour – how could you?' Evie needed to see her face to face.

'Look, Regan, come to my house. We can talk properly here. I don't like this situation any more than you. I just didn't know how to say no. I'm really sorry.' Regan agreed to drive to Evie's.

Next to phone was Stephanie, who had already heard about the interview from one of her London-based contacts. Her surprise at Evie's sudden friendship with Montana was coupled with her out-and-out excitement about Evie being maid of honour at the wedding. It was yet more perfect press. 'If you had said no, I would have had kittens! Montana Phoenix gets married and asks you. I couldn't have staged it better. Which magazines are covering it? I need to make sure you're on the cover with the happy couple. When is it? If it's not too soon then maybe we can get Jeremy flown over to be there too. Let me know as soon as you do.'

The questions about the time and location for the wedding were answered with the next phone call. It was Montana herself. 'Gorgeous girl, only me ... thank you a million times over for saying yes. I hope you've got nothing planned because my darling fiancé has just confirmed The Ritz Hotel for tomorrow at noon. If you do have plans, then cancel them. We're just heading off in the Limo now to check out the room and then we're heading to Liberty for an appointment with the bridal boutique. Any chance you could meet us there? The staff are pulling out all the stops to make sure that you and I are dressed to perfection. I want to look like a young Elizabeth Taylor, which is paramount since *Hello* have just agreed to splash out a cool million to feature you, me and Brad on the cover. We're quite prepared to split it three ways, Evie.'

There was no mention of Regan, so Evie got straight to the point. 'I'm not bothered about the money, Montana. It's just that I have one of my best friends, who also happens to be your daughter, driving here as we speak. She's not exactly thrilled about our on-air conversation this morning. Are you inviting her to the wedding? Because if you're not, then I'm not coming.'

Obviously a little taken aback by Evie's threat, Montana bluffed her way out of the situation. 'I've just been speaking to her. She's thrilled for Brad and me. Why don't I ring you both when she gets to yours and we can all arrange to go to the bridal boutique together. Now, clear your diary for tomorrow …' With an overly cheery goodbye, she was gone. Evie then tried to phone Regan, it was engaged.

The reason it was engaged was because a panicking Montana had swiftly dialled her daughter as soon as she'd hung up on Evie. She didn't want anything to jeopardise the money from the magazine and if Regan had to be at the wedding to keep Evie happy, then so be it.

The conversation between mother and daughter was completely one-sided. Regan, who had not been able to speak to Montana in weeks, could only listen through gritted teeth as Montana spewed words of affection down the phone. 'Darling,

Regan, it's been so hard to get hold of you, what with your charming TV show and everything. But mummy's here in the UK now and guess what, I'm getting married.'

'I know, I saw your interview. Evie's being maid of honour. That was news to me, I can tell you. I'm on my way to see her now.' Regan's sentences were clipped.

'*One* of my maids of honour, Regan. I was hoping that you would be the other. It'll only be a quiet affair, but it would be no affair at all without you.'

Regan listened, biting her tongue as Montana informed her about the wedding. 'Brad has done wonders obtaining a licence. It does pay to be a worldwide name on these occasions. People always seem a lot more obliging. So, can I count on my only daughter to be there? Any chance we could all meet up at the shop to get our outfits sorted this afternoon. The dressers are buzzing around like flies in anticipation. They've promised to work all night to get the dresses prepared.'

Regan agreed to go to the wedding with a frosty 'Okay'. Not because she wanted to see her mother happy. Not because she really wanted to be at the wedding, but because she wanted to talk to Montana about her past. She'd been dying to ask her about Lawrence's revelation, but it had not been the right time. What better way to do it than face to face at what was supposed to be one of the happiest days of her mother's life.

With a satisfied curl of her lips as she drove into London, Regan whispered to herself. 'Dearly beloved, we are gathered here today to bring together in holy matrimony Brad and Montana … or should that be Brad and Belinda? Yes, that little bit of news will make a perfect wedding gift for dear mother.'

CHAPTER 58

The morning after the fracas in the study, Nush had made two phone calls. One was to Johnny Erridge, asking if he and Ashley could come to Kingsbury. They'd agreed. The other was to Harry. She told him that Lawrence had gone out for the day and that she would like Harry and Sadie to come on over. That way, they could all talk 'as a family' and Sadie could collect some more of her things. At first, Harry was reluctant, not wanting to set foot inside 'that man's house' again, but seeing as Nush had said that Lawrence was away for the day, they would come as soon as they could.

It was a lie of course. Lawrence was going nowhere. It was just him and Nush in the house. Regan had left in a horrendous mood and Nush had instructed Jake to take one of the Kingsbury cars and make himself scarce for a few hours.

Just before midday, Nush was ushering Harry and Sadie into the drawing room. 'Let's go and have a drink before you collect more of your belongings,' she told Sadie. The look of sadness on Sadie's face conveyed the heartache she obviously felt about being there. 'I'll get some tea, unless you fancy something stronger of course,' Nush could have quite easily downed a sizable measure of whisky to calm her nerves. 'Mind if I don't. I'm pregnant you see,' deadpanned Sadie.

Harry requested a brandy and Nush left them alone, shutting the large oak doors behind her. She ran to the Kingsbury dining room where Johnny and Ashley had been seated since their arrival twenty minutes beforehand. Ashley's face lit up as Nush entered. 'Right, they're here,' said Nush, her voice breathy with nerves. 'Dad will flip when he sees them, which is where you two come in. If Lawrence starts to go for Harry, or vice versa, you need to keep them apart. Johnny, you're strong enough to prise them off each other. Ashley … you … you just do what you can, okay? I figured there was safety in numbers.' Despite Nush's putdown, Ashley smiled, eager to please. If he'd have possessed a tail, he would have obediently wagged it.

'So, where's Lawrence? He's not going to be happy,' said Johnny.

'I know. He's in his study. I just figured he can't be any less happy than he is already. Harry's still his son, still my brother, so they need to sort something out. They can't just avoid each other for the rest of their lives.'

'Well, Harry should have thought of that before he stuck his grubby little cock into your dad's wife, shouldn't he?' barked Johnny.

Nush was annoyed. 'I'm not taking sides here, Johnny, but until someone puts them all in the same room then nothing is ever going to be resolved, is it? You know how stubborn dad can be, and Harry's just the same.'

'I'll bring dad here. He'll want to see you, Johnny. Then we'll all go to the front room together. Then … let the show begin, I guess.'

Lawrence was elated to see Johnny and gripped him in a huge bear hug. 'I was just talking about our days together on the yacht last night. We'd hoped our sons might be the same one day, eh? No chance, it seems.' Lawrence eyeballed Ashley as he spoke. 'You bagged a girlfriend yet, Ashley?'

'I'm working on it,' acknowledged Ashley, shooting Nush a wishful glance.

'Jesus, Lawrence, you smell rank,' exclaimed Johnny pulling away from the hug. 'Plus you look as rough as an OAP hooker. Have you seen a razor or a bath in the last few days?'

'Let's go get a drink. Shall we go through?' ventured Nush, leading them into the front room.

For the next few seconds, everything seemed to happen at half speed. Harry was the first to spot Lawrence. His initial surprise at seeing Ashley and Johnny turned to a purple-faced anger when he spied his father. Racing around from behind the sofa where he had been standing, Harry attempted to push both Ashley and Johnny out of the way as he lunged towards Lawrence. As he did so, Sadie, seated on the sofa, opened her mouth to scream in protest.

With lightning quick reflexes built up from years fighting in the boxing ring, Johnny tackled Harry to the floor and held him down, his knee pinned to Harry's back. 'Whoa there, sunshine. Less of the hard man. What kind of son tries to attack his dad?'

'The kind of son whose dad hits his wife!' spat Harry. 'I thought you said he was out for the day, Nush.'

It was Lawrence who spoke next. He was eerily calm, his voice clipped. 'What are *they* doing here, Anoushka? Is this *your* doing?' Nush looked away, worried she'd done the wrong thing. Lawrence cast a glance at Sadie, who was balled up on the sofa, her arms wrapped tight around her. He could see that she was both scared and sad. For a second he felt a grain of pity for her … but then it passed.

'I thought I'd made it clear that you two are no longer part of my life.' He fixed his gaze on Harry, who was still pinned to the floor like a dead butterfly under Johnny's weight.

'I gave you everything, Harry.' Lawrence's voice started to crack as he spoke. 'One day, everything I have would have been yours. But you've shattered all that. You've blown it, Harry, when you chose to shag my wife behind my back.' He shot Sadie an angry look that plunged into her heart like a dagger.

'You've lost it all. Both of you. As from a few hours ago, neither of you are any longer part of this family. Your names have been removed from my will. I only have one child now, that's her,' he said pointing to Nush.

A blanket of silence enveloped the room. Harry stared open mouthed at his father's words, as if suddenly realising the cost of his actions. Sadie started to sob. Ashley moved over to Nush to put a comforting arm around her shoulders. She felt awkward but left his arm there.

Lawrence broke the silence. 'Johnny, let go of Harry, he's not worth it. Get them both out of here. You'll be hearing from my divorce lawyer.' He looked at Sadie again. 'I'll pay you what you deserve but then you're history too. I hope the two of you and your little runt will be extremely happy together.'

Lawrence turned on his heels to walk out. Seizing the moment, Harry raised himself up, pushing Johnny to the floor in the process. With lightning speed he raced towards Lawrence and launched himself onto his father's back.

'You bastard!' he roared. 'If you'd looked after her in the first place then she wouldn't have needed to sleep with me, would she?'

Lawrence crumpled to the floor under Harry's weight and the two men rolled across the floorboards, their fists lashing out. Harry was on the attack, his mind blood red with rage.

Before Johnny had time to split them up, Sadie let out a mammoth scream and ran towards the two men. Nush, too, ran forward to try and stop her brother and father.

It was Sadie who reached them first. 'Just stop it. Harry, leave him alone … please.' She was pleading through her tears. 'You'll kill him. Hasn't this all gone far enough? I'm so sorry, Lawrence.' She slumped to the floor alongside her husband. Harry raised his fist to thump Lawrence once again but Johnny caught it in his hand and dragged Harry away roughly. Nush knelt down opposite her father from Sadie, who was tenderly trying to wipe the blood away from Lawrence's face.

It was then that Lawrence lashed out, his anger passing the point of no return. 'Sorry? You let *my* son into *our* bed, you cheap whore.' He pushed Sadie away, his strength no match for her slender frame. The brute force of the push slammed her fully against an antique sideboard by the entrance to the room. Sadie lay there winded, unable to speak.

Turning to Nush, Lawrence erupted again, blood still pouring from a split lip. 'Why did you have to bring them here? To rub salt into my wounds?' Before Nush could answer, Lawrence had raised his hand and slapped her squarely across the face. 'You're all against me. All of you.'

Nush was still smarting from the blow as Lawrence ran from the room. She would have followed him, but a desperate moan from Sadie stopped her. She was still lying on the hard floor, clutching her stomach. 'I'm hurting. Something's wrong. Help me … please. I think it's the baby.'

CHAPTER 59

Having arranged with the Bridal Boutique to have their dresses delivered the next morning to Montana's hotel, the soap star and her two maids of honour eased themselves into the back seat of their chauffeur driven Limo and headed across London.

'Where to then, girls? I suppose tonight should be a hen night of sorts, shouldn't it?' Her question was met with total silence. Hardly surprising as Regan and Evie had barely spoken to each other since Regan had arrived at Evie's flat. Evie had tried to explain. Regan had chosen not to forgive. Despite it being the height of summer, the air between them was chillier than Aspen at the peak of the ski season. It was something Montana had chosen to ignore.

'How about cocktails at some chi-chi location and then dinner at The Ivy?' cooed Montana. 'Stafford and Brad can amuse themselves for a few hours while we kick up our heels and have ourselves a girlie time.'

'I think your days of being girlie are long gone, don't you, mother?' replied a poker-faced Regan. 'Give it a few years and you'll be swapping this chauffeur-driven Limo for a bus pass.' Despite her animosity towards Regan, Evie let a smile escape from her lips at Regan's cheek.

'Don't be such a bitch, dear, there's a good girl. It doesn't suit you. I thought that show of yours was supposed to be teaching you some manners.' It was the first time Montana had mentioned Regan's recent success all day. 'So, how about cocktails at The Sanderson and then onto The Ivy for something divine to eat. I am a slave to their Mascarpone Pannacotta.'

Staring at Regent Street through the window of the Limo, Evie didn't even look at the others as she answered. 'Actually, do you mind if I don't. I'm feeling jet-lagged and I could do with an early night if you want me to look good for the wedding,' she lied, much preferring a night on her own than a night of tension with Regan and Montana.

'Fine, we'll get the driver to drop you back at yours,' Regan said before Montana could even interject. 'The Sanderson sounds good. I need a drink and I think you will too, mother.'

'Why's that, dear?' Montana's curiosity was awoken. She knew that there was something on Regan's mind. 'Do you have something to share with me?' laughed Montana, a hint of nervousness in the voice.

'You'll see, mother, you'll see ...'

———

As Montana's Limo sped across London, Nush was waiting anxiously at the foot of Sadie's bed at a private hospital on the other side of the city. She was cradling a sobbing Harry in her arms. It felt like minutes since Nush had last been at the hospital with Jake. Ashley sat in the corridor outside the private room. He didn't give two hoots about Sadie and the baby, but he wanted to be there for Nush.

Sadie was asleep, having been sedated by the hospital staff. She had been right to worry about the baby. Even though it was so early in the pregnancy, she had known that the force at which she had been slammed into the sideboard by Lawrence had caused some kind of damage. It was a woman's instinct, the instinct of a mother-to-be. She could feel that something was amiss as the pain shot through her abdomen.

Tests had been carried out at the hospital and it had only taken minutes before both Sadie and Harry were informed that she had miscarried. Sadie had been inconsolable, a numbing grief sweeping across her entire body, followed by an engulfing feeling of guilt.

Whereas Sadie blamed herself, there was only one person that Harry blamed. His father. Not that Lawrence felt like a dad to him anymore. He was now the killer of Harry's child. It was something for which Harry would never be able to forgive him.

It was a few hours later that Sadie woke up again. Her tears came straight away. Nush felt it best to leave Sadie and Harry together, to share in their grief. Ashley was still waiting for her outside the room.

'Hi, how are you?' he asked feebly, stroking the poppy-red patch on her cheek.

'I'm okay,' shrugged Nush, pushing Ashley's hand away. 'Better than those two, that's for sure. I may not agree with what they've done but I wouldn't wish losing a baby on anyone. It's just not fair.'

'Neither was your father hitting you. You didn't deserve that. You were only trying to help. Your dad's a bastard, Nush. He doesn't deserve you.' Ashley moved closer to Nush and stroked her hair away from her face as he spoke. His nearness unnerved her but she said nothing.

'Yes, he is, isn't he? A really cruel bastard.'

—

'So, how are you getting on with that scrubber of a woman on that blessed show of yours? Isn't it all due to finish sometime soon?' Montana slurred her words slightly, having already downed two of The Sanderson's finest cocktails.

'We've got one more show to film. It'll decide who wins. I assume you're talking about Grace when you're referring to *the scrubber*. Your words, not mine … I actually find her pretty easy to get along with. But then you two have history, don't you? Didn't you slag me off to her at your perfume launch?' Regan reached for her own cocktail, it was still her first. She was determined to keep a clear head for when she questioned Montana about the photo.

'History? She'd be bloody history if I had my way. All of those things that were said by that awful Clarissa Thornton woman were all untrue you know. They doctored the damned tape to make me sound like a total harridan. Grace provoked me. She has as much class as a two dollar Harlem hooker. I know we haven't exactly ever seen eye to eye, Regan, but really, you know me well enough to know I wouldn't slate you to the world at large.'

'But that's just it, isn't it, mother. I don't really know you. You only ever want me when I'm of use to you. You've always had that rather spot-on knack of making me feel unloved.'

Regan was getting into her stride. She'd been waiting weeks for this moment and nothing was going to stop her now. Montana sat close-mouthed as her daughter continued.

'When was the last time you asked about *my* life? You don't. If it doesn't affect your perfect little diamond-studded Hollywood existence then you don't care. You've probably learned more about me watching *Wild Child* than you have in years.'

Montana shrugged off Regan's words. 'Oh, darling, don't be so melodramatic. And please don't think I've been wasting my time watching that excuse of a show of yours. I have better things to do. Anyway, what's your problem? You're my daughter, aren't you? God, most people would give their back teeth to have a superstar like me as a mother. Your friend Evie certainly thinks so. She's going to look divine at the wedding tomorrow, don't you think?'

'Just shut the fuck up about Evie and about how frigging fabulous you and your lifestyle are, will you!' Regan banged the base of her cocktail glass on the table as she spoke.

'It's always been about you, mother, hasn't it? What about me? How do you think I feel being the daughter that you shunted out of your life at the earliest possible convenience? The daughter who's never known her father, who's always considered herself to be someone that you never even wanted in the first place.'

Eager to calm the situation, Montana placed her hands on top of Regan's across the table and smiled through gritted teeth. 'Cool it, darling,' she hissed. 'People are staring. It's not good for your profile. Now, where is all this anger coming from? Have you got a touch of the Naomi Campbells going on my dear, a spot of inner rage? I'll be booking you into an anger management class at this rate.'

Regan was seething. 'You want to know where it's come from? Try years of teenage trauma, try years of people telling you that your mother is the best thing the entertainment world has ever seen. Try people telling me how lucky I'm supposed to be because I have a glamorous TV mother. If I'm a disappointment to you, mother, then you only have yourself to blame. You made me this way. A few more hugs and kisses, or birthday cards turning up on the right day instead of weeks late might have made me feel a bit more loved. Maybe giving me a birthday present that wasn't just a cheque to buy me off for another year. Evie and Nush used to get dresses and jewellery and flowers from their parents. Gifts that had been personally chosen. I'd get a card written by your PA and a stash of money.'

'You ungrateful little bitch.' It was now Montana's turn to seethe. 'Do you actually know what I went through to be able to earn that kind of money in the first place? The money that sent you to the best ladies' college in Britain, that gave us homes around the globe. I didn't have riches like you when I was growing up. I had to earn my money, you ungrateful slut.'

The time had come. 'Slut! How can you call me that now I know how you earned your money in the first place? It's clear where I got it from, isn't it?'

The colour had emptied from Montana's face. Even through her MAC make-up, her skin suddenly looked pale and insipid. 'What are you talking about, you stupid girl? I've always done my best for you. The millions I've accrued have come through hard work. If you look up Montana Phoenix on any website, darling, you'll see a list of films and TV shows longer than most actresses could dream of. Each and every one of them put food on the table and gave you the life I never had.'

'But I'm not talking about Montana Phoenix.' Regan reached down into her bag and placed the photograph on the table in front of Montana. 'I'm talking about Belinda … Belinda Faye. We all know how she brought in the cash, don't we? Flat on her back.'

Without saying a word to her daughter, Montana pushed back her chair, stood up and walked out of the hotel bar. It was only when she was safely inside the sanctuary of her Limo that she allowed herself to cry. They were tears that wouldn't stop.

CHAPTER 60

As weddings go, the union between Montana Phoenix and Brad Roderick was not exactly the most joyous of occasions. The atmosphere in the ostentatious room at The Ritz as the *happy* couple exchanged vows could have been cut with a knife sharp enough to slice right through even the toughest of wedding cake icing.

The only person who seemed to have a genuine air of bonhomie about them was Stafford. For him, it had been the perfect day. Kitted out in his Ozwald Boateng suit, a plump white rose attached to his lapel, Stafford felt like he'd walked into one of the dazzling plots of *Peregrine Palace*. Standing alongside Montana, Brad, Evie and Regan as they posed for wedding photos, Stafford felt he'd hit the big time. A text message earlier in the day had also assured him that another big pay packet was coming his way

Stafford had been awoken from his slumber that morning by the sound of a received text message. The interruption had been more than a little annoying. It had ripped him from the fantasy of a rather raunchy dream involving a sexual spit roasting from two of his favourite male models. The text was from Jeremy. Angry but accommodating was how Stafford would have described it.

'Look, you little shit. I'll get you the money, but that's it. No more. If you try any of this blackmail crap again then you're a dead man.'

Stafford couldn't help but smile at the alpha maleness of it all. 'Not as dead as your career if I spill the beans. Blackmail … such a nasty word.' Texting his bank details to Jeremy with instructions to wire the money immediately, Stafford leaned back in his bed and scratched his head. Reading the bedside clock, he could see it was still hours until he needed to start getting ready for the wedding. There was only one thing for it. Sex. Picking up a gay magazine he'd purchased the night before he flicked through the pages to the contacts at the back and scanned the ads. What was the point of finally having money if you didn't use it on a well hung gigolo? Now that really was his idea of room service.

The more intimate areas of Stafford's body still felt a little tender as he lined up alongside Montana in front of the wedding photographer. Professional to a fault, Montana posed perfectly, making the most of her pulchritude, working the camera to great effect. Both Regan and Evie worked the cameras too, knowing that appearing with a face like a slapped backside in print would be terrible press. Between shots, all three women let their façades slip.

Montana was still petrified with worry that Regan would delight in shoehorning her little secret into conversation with Brad. At least now the vows were out of the way, Regan couldn't stop Brad from marrying her. But Regan had hardly said a word to either her or Brad all morning and even a reptilian-thick-skinned Montana was finding the silence hard to deal with.

Evie could think of a million other places she would rather have been, and after the photos she decided to make her excuses and leave. As she tried to kiss Regan goodbye, her friend turned her head away. It cut Evie to the core.

'Look, Regan, I've explained the position your mother put me in. If you've got a problem with Montana then sort it out.

Don't bring me into it. You've been nothing but a spoilt little cow today. Just grow up.' She was shaking as she spoke, not liking the confrontation. 'Nush and I are going to Muscat for a few days to get away. She's been through the mill lately and so have I. We all have. We could all do with some time together. Why don't you come? It could be our first Trinity holiday in ages. An infinity pool and some Arabian sunsets could do us all some good, don't you think?'

Regan's response was far from sunny. 'I have a show to film in a few days, so excuse me if I don't,' she sniped. 'Or maybe you've been too busy sucking up to my mother to notice.' Evie huffed out of the room without saying another word.

'What a wonderful day it's been, darlings.' Montana was trying to be as sing-song as possible with her cheeriness, but as she watched Evie flounce out of the room without so much as a goodbye, she could sense that the atmosphere had once again plummeted to sub-zero.

'So now you're Montana Roderick, aren't you? Yet another change of name. I suppose you should be used to *that* though,' sneered Regan. 'Will that be your *working* name from now on?'

Montana shifted nervously on her heels, sensing that Regan was steering the conversation into dangerous waters. 'Regan, dear, I shall of course remain Montana Phoenix. That's how the world knows me. I'm sure Brad knows full well that inside the four walls of our house I shall be Mrs Roderick and serve him dutifully. But, to those on the outside, I will always be Montana Phoenix.'

'Serve me dutifully, eh? I like the sound of that,' said Brad, joining Montana. He pinched her bottom playfully. 'I shall look forward to some of that later tonight. It's not every day a man gets to marry the most glamorous woman in the world, is it?'

'Or indeed one who's quite so adept at serving men, eh Brad?' Regan was ready for the kill.

'Come on, Regan, I may have only been your stepfather for a matter of minutes, but I do think I'm in a position where I can ask you not to speak to your mother in such a way.' Brad's voice was stern and he placed a protective arm around Montana's shoulders as he spoke.

Softly pushing his arm away, Montana took a step closer to Regan and stared her directly in the eyes. 'Thank you, Brad, but I can fight my own battles as far as this one's concerned. I've had years of practice. Will you boys leave us alone for a moment? My dear daughter and I obviously have some things to talk about.'

Regan was adoring her audience. 'No, stay, Brad, I think you'll be interested in what I have to say. It is the perfect day for sharing after all. Let me tell you all about the woman of your dreams – the world's greatest TV star and the world's worst mother.'

'There isn't anything about me that Brad doesn't already know, Regan. We share everything.' Although an accomplished actress, for once Montana's clipped words were not entirely convincing.

'So you've introduced him to Belinda Faye then, have you? He's made her acquaintance, has he?' Brad's confused expression confirmed that he hadn't. 'Is she a friend of yours, darling?'

Montana's face was ashen grey, her eyes wide with horror. Stafford looked on, savouring every word.

Regan was now in full flow. 'You're married to her, Brad. The woman who stands in front of us now is Belinda Faye. I assume it's the name she was born with and the name she grew up with. It's certainly the name she started working under. Somewhere along the line Belinda became Montana. Much more of a Hollywood name, don't you think? Changed it by deed poll, did we, mother? Nothing in my life is certain when it comes to family.' Regan's words were becoming increasingly bitter.

'There have never been any grandparents to visit, no trips to relatives. No, just little Regan Phoenix, unwanted daughter of Montana … excuse me, let me correct myself, unwanted daughter of Belinda Faye, shipped off to school at the earliest opportunity. Why don't you tell your new husband exactly how you earned your money before hitting the big time, mother. Will you be charging him for it tonight? What's the going rate for a shag these days?'

With lightning speed, Montana's palm connected with the side of Regan's face. Both Brad and Stafford gasped audibly. Brad grabbed Montana's hand, shocked by her actions. 'Montana, what the hell is going on?' Ignoring Brad's question and shaking with rage, Montana began to speak through gritted teeth.

'Just shut up, you stupid girl. How dare you question me? What gives you the right to judge? I've earned my money, what have you ever done? You're only on this stupid show of yours because you're my daughter. If I wasn't such a star you'd be nothing, lady … nothing! Do you think anyone is really interested in you? Don't kid yourself. For your information, for *all* of you …' Montana switched her gaze between Stafford and Brad before fixing it back on Regan, still rubbing her cheek in shock. 'My real name was Belinda Faye. I did change it by deed poll. Why not? My real parents never supported me when I wanted to be an actress. My dad was a factory worker and my mother worked in a supermarket. They had no money, they had no aspirations. I did. I didn't want their hum-drum existence, scraping to make ends meet. I could see life beyond the four walls of their two-up-two-down. If that's wrong, then sue me.'

Brad, Stafford and Regan all stared at Montana as she continued, afraid to interrupt. 'You have no grandparents, Regan, you know that – they died before you came along. They left me with nothing. Every penny I have, I've earned. I took all sorts of jobs. I worked in cabaret bars, restaurants, shitty little theatre companies. Anywhere that I thought might get me where I wanted to be. I lodged with another girl and she introduced me to the glitzy world I'd always wanted to be part of. She made extra money by travelling across Europe to meet influential gentlemen, guys in the media world. People who would finally notice me and get me away from chorus-parts in touring productions in the arse-end of Britain.' Taking Brad by the hand, Montana, tears welling in her eyes, bit at her bottom lip and spoke. 'I'm sorry, Brad, I was paid for sex. I was a call girl. I'm not proud of it, but it moved me away from my poxy little life. One of my clients was the director who got me my first movie job. From there, well, the rest is history … I might not be proud of it, but I'd do it all again if I had to.'

She turned square-on to Regan, 'So, madam, if you think you have the right to lecture me about anything, then you do it, but I will not be looked down on or held to ransom by the likes of you.' As she spoke, a single heavy tear ran onto her cheek, traces of her mascara flowing with it.

Brad placed his arms back around Montana's shoulder, his action both supportive and comforting. Montana nestled her face against his chest and let her sobs run free. Her speech had been both heartfelt and draining. 'That's all history, my angel. You did what you had to do. None of us have been whiter than white along the way. It doesn't change how I feel.' Brad then turned to face his new step-daughter. 'Satisfied, Regan? Happy that you've ruined your mother's wedding day? You make me sick, just get out of my sight.'

Springing into defensive mode, Regan was determined to share her motives for the attack. 'Oh, that's just typical. Another award-winning performance from mother – she turns on the waterworks and suddenly I'm the villain. Do me a favour, Brad.

She's been turning tricks for years to work her way up the Holly-wood ladder. I used to watch her at her parties. She's never cared about anyone other than herself. She's using you like she's used every other man in her life. It just so happens that she's never managed to get any of them down the aisle before. All of this today is fake, the wedding is all about getting more good press and promotion for her rotten perfume. I don't care if you're not proud of me, Brad, I don't care at all. Look where I've learnt it from, my one and only role model – the ex-whore. I couldn't play daddy's girl because I didn't have a father. What happened with that one, mother? Couldn't narrow it down from a lengthy list of candidates? Not sure which lucrative leg-over spawned me?'

Regan's attack was the final straw for Montana. Her heart felt ready to burst. 'I know exactly who your father is, I've always known. It was an accident, a stupid drunken accident. The last thing I needed was to get pregnant. My career was just finally taking off and the last thing I needed was a brat. But something made me keep you. I knew I couldn't get rid of you. You may think I'm a heartless bitch, but I never contemplated getting rid of you. I made my choice and I did it on my own. Your father doesn't even know you exist. I chose not to tell him. He wouldn't have wanted you, he had a wife and another child on the way. I was just a bit of fun that he paid for now and again.'

After a lifetime of uncertainty, Regan knew that she had to make a snap-decision. In her mind, the decision had already been made. 'Go on then, tell me, I need to know who my father is. Maybe he'll actually want to show me the love I've obviously lacked from you. Maybe he'll welcome me with open arms and be proud of his daughter.'

Scarlet with anger and heavy with fatigue, Montana snapped. 'Try him if you like, but you'll be sorry. Your father's the man in the photo … Lawrence Silvers.'

CHAPTER 61

Nush let out a contented sigh as she lay back on her cabana lounger and took in the full beauty of the Arabian Sea across the infinity pool. 'I *so* needed this. Just to get away and unwind in sheer luxury. I'm so glad you could come, Evie.'

The girls were reclining alongside the crystal clear waters situated on the stunning Boushar Beachfront in Muscat, Oman. Their home for the next few days was the palatial hotel standing proud behind them, an oasis of Omani luxury and decadence.

It had been three days since Montana's wedding, and Evie was still spitting feathers about Regan's attitude towards her. 'It would have been nice if Little Miss Chip-on-her-shoulder could have joined us too, but honestly, Regan was a complete bitch. I couldn't pack my bags quickly enough. Thank God you were ready for a holiday. Any word from back home?'

'Mercifully nothing. I just want to switch off. The business with Harry and Sadie has been horrendous; it's torn the family apart. Are you sure you're okay about Harry? He was doing the dirty on you.'

'I'd be lying if I said that finding out that my ex-boyfriend was having sex with his step mum wasn't a shock, but losing the baby is awful. I wouldn't wish that on anyone. Losing a child must be …' Evie hesitated, her voice cracking lightly. 'It must be truly catastrophic.' Evie shivered, a band of cold creeping across her exposed flesh, despite the Gulf heat. 'Anyway. I'm with Jeremy now.'

Removing her Louis Vuitton sunglasses and placing them on top of her head, Nush swivelled to face Evie. 'Look, Evie. There's something I need to tell you. I knew Harry was cheating on you. I wanted to tell you on the phone but I couldn't and then when you said you're all happy with Jeremy I didn't want to spoil things.'

Evie was taken aback to say the least. 'You're telling me that you knew Harry was sleeping with Sadie?'

Realising the potential for confusion, Nush was quick to correct herself. 'Oh God no, I don't mean Harry and Sadie. That was a huge shock to me, too. No, I heard something when you were in Salzburg.'

Nush explained about what she'd heard down the phone line when she'd been trying to get through to Evie. Evie's mouth fell as Nush unravelled the story of Harry's adultery. A few weeks back, the words would have crushed her like a bug under a hobnail boot.

'The cheating bastard. I'm so much better off without him.'

Nush curled her lips, a wave of told-you-so forming around her mouth. 'Didn't I say as much? You were always too good for him. The boy doesn't know how to spell fidelity, let alone practise it. Now, how about another cocktail from the poolside bar?'

'Don't mind if I do. Something long, ice-cold and full of fruity goodness for me please … and crammed to the rim with vodka!' laughed Evie. 'You get them in. I'm just nipping back to the room to get my Puccis.'

As Evie walked back to the hotel along the private stretch of sandy shore that lead from the pool, the sun warmed her skin. Despite the recent mental torment of Montana's wedding, she was feeling good about herself. She glowed with happiness. She'd already been recognised by some of the guests at the hotel. She'd heard whispers about her films and the name 'Jeremy Pinewood' murmured too as she wandered around the hotel.

She'd received countless texts from Jeremy since arriving in Muscat. Some had been general loved-up mushiness and others were more specific, asking about Montana's wedding. Who was there? What was said? He'd seemed especially interested in Stafford, asking who he was and what connection he had to Montana.

She'd also received calls from Stephanie in LA. The word on the Hollywood grapevine was that Evie's performance in *Pengelly Manor* was indeed predicted to be a major contender for both the Golden Globes, the Baftas and the ultimate prize – an Oscar. Life was good.

Having retrieved her sunglasses, Evie wandered to the hotel shop to pick up some magazines to read around the pool. Browsing the shelves she saw her own face staring back from the cover of one of them. It was the one featuring Montana's wedding. The cover headline read 'TV STAR MONTANA PHOENIX GETS WED AS HOLLYWOOD DARLING EVIE MERCHANT PLAYS MAID OF HONOUR'. The cover photograph was of a group-shot ... a group-shot of three. It filled the entire page. Montana took centre stage and looked a picture of marital bliss. Brad posed on one side of her and on the other was Evie, a broad smile across her face. It gave no indication of the underlying tensions of the day. It also had no mention of Regan. She'd been cropped out of the photograph. As Evie flicked through the section of pages inside the magazine, a sense of dread filled her. In nearly every photo, except two of the smaller ones, Regan had been cropped out. Evie, meanwhile, seemed to feature in virtually every one. Evie knew that Regan would be livid.

——

Regan hated herself for not being able to resist, but when she'd seen the published magazine featuring her mother's *special day* she had been compulsively drawn to pore over the pages. What she had found had left her numb with fury. It was as if she didn't exist. Montana with Brad, Montana on her own, Montana laughing with Evie, Montana kissing Stafford on the cheek, Brad and Stafford together … all of the combinations seemed to be there. But only two small photos featured Regan. One was a shot of the five of them together, Regan not even positioned alongside her mother, that *honour* went to Evie. The other was a shot of Evie catching Montana's bouquet with Regan lurking, some would say sullenly, in the background. The article didn't even mention her much, but was laced with 'My very good friend, Evie, is my favourite actress' and 'I knew Evie wouldn't say no to being my maid of honour' quotes from Montana. Regan found it sickening.

Not that Regan and Montana were exactly on the best of terms right now. Regan hadn't spoken to her mother since Montana's revelation about Lawrence being her real father. The shock of Montana's admission had floored Regan completely. She had run from the wedding in tears. She'd always imagined that finding out her true parentage would fill her with joy, but she'd never counted on her real father actually being her best mate's dad. The only person she had told so far was Leo. She needed to share the news and Leo seemed to be the only one she could trust.

His reaction had been one of complete shock. 'Fucking hell, Regan. Your dad is Lawrence Silvers? That is so off the dial of strange it's not even funny. Are you going to tell him?'

Regan didn't know what she wanted. 'I need to get this final episode of *Wild Child* out of the way before I do anything. I don't want to let you down. You've changed everything for me and I don't want to blow things.' Regan reached out and stroked Leo's face. She was lying alongside him in the bed at his Hammersmith apartment.

'Well, for your information, according to my production crew, the final episode is one of the most hotly anticipated shows in history. Plus, you'll be pleased to know that you're the bookies' favourite to win. So, I would be eternally grateful if you didn't go off the rails.' Leo winked, hoping to alleviate Regan's worries.

'I can't believe Clarissa hasn't run that interview with me yet either. I thought that photo of Montana and Lawrence would be everywhere by now. Jesus wept, if Clarissa knew the truth she'd be smiling like a *Miss World* winner. I have to pray that nothing comes out before I've spoken to Lawrence. But what about Nush … heaven only knows how she's going to react to it all.'

Leo raised an eyebrow. 'Now that your best mate is actually your sister?'

'It's not so much that, Leo,' declared Regan. 'It's the fact that Lawrence was cheating on his wife with my mother. Nush idolised her mum and finding out that her father was cheating on her while she was pregnant might destroy her.'

———

Nush and Evie had just finished eating some of the finest Arabic cuisine they'd ever tasted. After a day around the pool, they'd both languished in the pampered luxury of the hotel spa before getting changed for dinner. It had been a perfect day for them both, except for the magazine photos of the wedding.

'I can only assume that Montana asked the magazine to crop Regan out of so many of the wedding photos. She's one of the biggest attractions on TV right now, so any magazine would want to feature her as much as possible. In my journalistic opinion, I'd say that Montana has been making some demands to the mag and they've gone along with them.' Nush dabbed the corners of her mouth with her napkin as she spoke and reached for her glass of wine.

'I think you're right. Montana was bragging enough about how much she was getting paid for it all. I guess when you can command that much money, you can pretty much make any demands you like, even if it means obliterating your daughter's presence. Maybe I'm lucky to have such down to earth parents after all.'

'Well, there's nothing run of the mill about their daughter,' slurred Nush, tipsy from the wine. 'Oscar nomination here you come … if that's not reason enough for some champagne, then I don't know what is. Your agent reckons it's in the bag then, does she?'

'It would seem so, but she does like to exaggerate. Let's get a bottle and take it down to the seafront. We can sit on the beach and watch the stars. They're so clear tonight and the water looks amazing.' Evie was right. Staring out across the garden views and the palm trees dotted across the lawns, the ocean resembled a sheet of pearlescent paper glistening and reflecting the full moon and glitter-bright stars above it.

Having weaved their way somewhat gingerly down the paths that led to the beach from the hotel, the two women threw off their shoes and walked barefoot across the soft golden sand. They giggled as they tried to steady themselves. Evie was carrying her cute black ballet pumps and two glasses, while Nush swayed back and forth, holding onto the champagne bottle and her Jimmy Choos.

'If Jake and Jeremy could see us now they would wonder what on earth was going on. On a beach in designer dresses giggling like schoolgirls. It's like we're back at Farmington. It feels good,' laughed Nush. 'Now, bring on the champers … I want bubbles, darling!'

Filling the glasses, Evie's mind swirled deliciously at the thought of Jeremy. *Maybe he's finally the one for me*, she thought to herself. 'Do you think Jake is the guy for you?' enquired Evie. 'You only slept with him for work, but look at the nightmare it's caused. A crazed stalker, a stabbing, a murder … it's not exactly a Disney fairytale, is it? More like a Hammer horror. You do seem different, though. He's got to you, hasn't he?'

Nush was unusually coy as she answered. 'I guess so … I wish I'd never written about him, but it was a bloody good story and kept daddy off my back.'

'Just let the dust settle on everything before you go giving your heart away. It's a delicate thing and Lord only knows it's been broken a few times,' advised Evie.

'Oh, you know me,' countered Nush. 'I'm a hard mistrusting woman who knows full well that any man out there will hurt me sooner or later. My defences are up and the sandbags are in place ready to fend off any unnecessary heartache.' Nush was only half-joking.

'But this time it's different, isn't it?' said Evie. 'There's something behind your eyes that gives the game away. Maybe Jake will be the one to thaw out my favourite ice queen.'

Nush was silent, her head hung down. The only sound came from the waves lapping onto the shoreline in front of them.

'Are you okay?' asked Evie.

Nush lifted her head. In the moonlight Evie could see that tears were running down her cheeks. Nush downed her champagne and held out the glass for a refill. 'I hope he's a good man. He'll be the first. I want to trust him. I want to think about the future. I know I'm falling for him, but I know he'll chew me up and spit me out.'

'Where the hell has this come from?' Evie was shocked. 'You're too young to be so sour. Jake's a good catch, but you're a better one.'

'No man has ever shown me that they can be trusted. I want to trust Jake, I do. But what if he turns out to be like every other man?'

Evie was becoming annoyed. 'Look, Nush, you've had too much to drink, we both have, and you're starting to get all melodramatic and maudlin. I'm sure Jake isn't using you. You have to trust guys or else you'll end up sad and lonely.'

Nush threw her glass down on the sand, visibly upset. 'But that's what I've been taught – a lifetime of insecurities and self-doubt. I probably will be sad and lonely.'

'Been *taught* … Nush, that's ridiculous. We all deserve love. Who told you otherwise?'

'I'll tell you. The man who has always made me feel useless and second best. The man who had always made me feel like a failure in everything I do. The man I can never please … my father.'

'Your dad …? But he loves you, Nush.'

'Maybe, but he loves Harry more. Or at least he did. I've never been good enough for Lawrence. I grew up feeling useless thanks to him. He's made me mistrust men because he's the only role model I've ever really had.'

Nush wiped the tears from her face before continuing, trying to contain her emotions. 'Do you know what, Evie? Sometimes I think Regan is lucky not knowing who her father is because she could have had one like mine. She may be completely psychotic at times but at least she likes herself. That's something I've never done … I don't like myself. Why should I? I've been taught by my father that there's nothing to like.'

CHAPTER 62

In the presenter's lounge at *Planet Shopping TV*, the UK's largest TV shopping network, the unsinkable, endlessly inventive, keep-the-ball rolling hosts were buzzing with excitement. The reason for their giddy glee was two-fold. Firstly, Montana Phoenix was due to appear later that day to promote the UK premiere of her *Babylon* perfume box set. Secondly, a meeting had just been held between Leo Weiss and the industrious presentation manager of *Planet* to finalise filming arrangements for the final episode of *Wild Child*, which would take place at the shopping network. Therefore Grace, Regan and Montana would all be under the same roof at the same time. It had left all of the presenters even more effervescent than normal.

It had also left Leo completely perplexed – something he was trying to explain to both Regan and Grace as they headed northwards to the TV studios.

'The final show is all about business acumen, ladies. You're going to be required to sell products on air. We're going to be at the station for two days. Today is day one and you'll receive individual coaching from two of the channel's show hosts. You'll be shown how to perform on air and how to demonstrate items. You will also have meetings with buyers about different products. We want you to choose which ones you want to sell. Then, tomorrow, you'll each be given a half-hour slot, which will be live TV, so no swearing. The channel says that three products should be enough for the half-hour, so try to choose something that relates to you and also relates to the audience. This channel makes millions each year and sells everything from fitness gear, DIY and kitchenware through to beauty, fashion and craft. The hosts are versatile and know how to both present and sell to the public. You're being taught by the best, so make sure you listen and learn. It's your last hurdle so don't let me down ladies.'

'Do we ever, sugar?' purred Grace. 'If there's one thing I can do it's sell. Sexalicious went on one of the American shopping networks once to sell make-up. Our sales were astronomical.' Grace looked pointedly at Regan, as if laying down the challenge.

'I'll do my best. If I'd have known we were going to be doing this I would have asked that bitch of a mother of mine for some tips. I think she's flogging her nasty perfume on one of these channels soon.'

Regan's comment caused Leo to crease his brow. 'Actually, Regan, Montana's flogging her perfume on this channel. *Babylon* perfume is *Planet's 24 Hour Perfect Purchase* slot which starts tonight. She'll be guesting countless shows over the next 24 hours. I swear I didn't know she'd be there until yesterday when I had the meeting with *Planet*. It's a complete fluke that we're all there at the same time, but it's great press.'

'And my mother really needs press at the moment, doesn't she?' Regan's comments were caustic in the extreme.

Grace was far from vexed. 'Fabulous. I get to spend some more quality time with that fork-tongued floozy. You can ask her about that photo of yours Regan, can't you?'

As yet, Regan had chosen not to share her latest news about the photo with Grace. Grace was still her number one suspect and distrust hung in the air.

—

'Screw the channel. I'll sell *Babylon* elsewhere. I will not be in the same building as that coke-snorting harlot and that disgruntled daughter of mine. Get the driver to bring the Limo round again. We're leaving, Brad. Tout de suite.'

Montana was incensed. Standing in the green room guest area at *Planet* with Brad and Stafford, the channel executives had just informed her that Grace and Regan were filming at the network during her stay. Once again, Montana could feel the spotlight moving away from her and she was determined to stop it. Brad, however, was having none of it.

'Montana, you'll go on air, be professional and sell shiploads of *Babylon*. If you pull out now, Coeur Cosmetics will be pissed beyond all reason and we might as well call off the Venice trip because Coeur could refuse to bankroll it. Just get on with it.'

Montana knew that there was no point in arguing. Brad was right. He would just have to make sure that Regan and Grace were kept well away from her at all costs.

—

'Hi Regan, I'm Derek, one of *Planet Shopping's* main hosts, and I'm going to be guiding you through the next 24 hours. Can I say what a thrill it is, I'm a huge fan ...' The camp muchloved presenter was about to add 'of both you and your fabulous mother' but stopped himself just in time, remembering a request from Leo that no mention of Montana should be made directly to either Regan or Grace. Derek was having the best week of his life. Tutoring Regan Phoenix and hosting a live show later in the day with his favourite glitzy soap star from *Peregrine Palace* was akin to the time he'd discovered that Jason Statham used the same gym as him, a fact he'd discovered by walking in just as the actor was showering. Derek was hoping that the next two days could prove a turning point in his career. An appearance on *Wild Child* would be edited straight on to his showreel and sent out to agents Stateside. If he struck while the iron was hot, it could be Sayonara Shopping Telly and Hello Hollywood in a matter of weeks.

Loving the *Wild Child* cameras pointed at him, he launched into his speech. 'The number one aim of shopping television is to sell something. If you can do that in an entertaining way then that's even better as the audience will stay with you and hopefully buy more. Engage the audience and always remember that they have invited you into their living room by switching on the TV. Even if you have no personal interest in a product, always picture the person it will be of use to and aim your pitch at them. I have sold thousands of pairs of slimming pants despite making sure that my own waistline has never strayed beyond 32 inches.' Derek giggled gaily as he talked, amused by his own patter. 'But every lady out there with a complex about her jelly belly or saddlebags will find slimming pants a miracle. So, when I sell that, I'm talking to them. You need to find the words that sell, Regan. We want positives not negatives. You must chat warmly to your audience and not bark orders at them. Also, don't lie … if you want to do that then go on *Call My Bluff*. We're all about truth here.'

Leo, who was standing behind the cameras watching Derek, chipped in. 'That's great, Derek, but we'll have to ditch the *Call My Bluff* reference. No-one in the States or under a certain age will remember that TV show. Can you change it? Just do the speech about telling the truth again. I think that's a valid point for Regan to learn.'

'Of course, no problem.' Derek was determined to impress Leo. Maybe that way he would remember him for any future presenting jobs.

'And … cue.'

Derek began again. 'You must never lie, Regan. What you say on air about a product must always be believable. This is not some fantastical storyline from your mother's glorious soap, this is real life.' As soon as he had said it, he realised his error.

'And cut!' boomed Leo.

'Oh, I'm so sorry, Leo. After all you told me and everything. Shall we do that over again? Do forgive me, Regan.'

The look on her face told Derek that she didn't.

———

Once Regan had finished listening to Derek, she was free to relax for half an hour before her meeting with *Planet's* team of buyers to discuss products. Mulling over some potential ideas in her head, she made her way back to the makeshift green room that had been set up for the *Wild Child* crew and the other shopping guests featured on the day's programmes. The usual green room had been taken over by her mother for the duration of her stay. Luckily it was at the other end of the building so hopefully their paths wouldn't cross.

The room was buzzing with activity. Cameramen, runners, assistant producers, all hovered around, catering for all of Regan's needs. There was no sign of Grace. Regan pulled a notebook from her bag and started making notes about the type of product she would be interested in selling.

'Hey, fancy seeing you here. You're the last person I expected to see.' The voice was familiar, causing Regan to look up from her notes. It was Jake Saunders. Her mind backtracked to when she'd last seen him.

'At least I have my clothes on this time,' he joked, as if reading her mind. 'What are you doing here? As if I can't guess,' he said, scanning the cameras and general chaos of the room.

'It's the final episode of *Wild Child*. We're showing our business acumen, apparently, by trying to flog things on the TV. I've got my meeting with the buyers in a few minutes. Wish me luck,' Regan flirted, unable to stop herself.

'You can sell my product if you like. I could do with a good demonstrator since I can't use it due to … er … circumstances.' Jake motioned towards his stab wound. 'Having to launch this couldn't have come at a worse time.'

'Your product? What are you selling?'

'The Jake Saunders Ab Bullet. It's a fitness machine for flattening out the stomach muscles. Not that I should imagine you have any need for that by the look of you. Both you and Nush are fighting fit.'

Regan could feel a slight blush streak across her cheeks. 'I'd love to try and sell it but I think I would get told off for favouritism. Is Nush here with you?'

'No, she's in Muscat with your mum's mate, Evie. I saw the magazine feature. Seemed quite a day.'

The association caused Regan to wince. 'She's not actually my mother's friend at all … Nush, Evie and me were all at college together. My mother just hijacked her. Be careful or she might do the same to you later. Her shows start at nine tonight.'

Jake seemed taken aback. 'Her shows? Montana Phoenix is here at *Planet*? What's she selling?'

'Her perfume, *Babylon*. Don't tell me you didn't know. The whole world has been fanfaring the arrival of her noxious concoction on these shores. Where have you been hiding yourself? Mars?'

'I haven't really had a lot of time to notice anything recently, with Mae-Ling's death and then the funeral.'

'Oh, my God. I am so sorry.' Regan noticed what seemed like genuine grief and sorrow in Jake's eyes. 'How was it? I saw the report in the paper. Are the police any clearer about who might have killed her?'

'The funeral was horrendous. I had to face her whole family and I couldn't help but feel I was to blame for it all.'

'And the police …?'

'No clues as yet, they can't even find a murder weapon. It remains a mystery.'

For such a large, muscular man, he had an air of little-boy-lost. It made Regan sad. 'Listen, Jake, if you want to talk about anything, then you can always bend my ear. It must be hard to talk to Nush as you're so close to her and she's so close to the whole Mae-Ling situation, but if you ever do need to talk, then you can always call me. Our secret.' The word *secret* made things seem a touch too deceptive and underhand in Regan's brain and she tried to correct herself. 'I mean, I wouldn't go reporting back to Nush.'

'Thanks, I appreciate it,' he replied eagerly. 'Are you staying up here tonight? I have to stop over as I have another show in the morning. Maybe we could meet up for a drink. I'm at The Plaza … you?'

'We're all staying at The Riverside. Here's my number. Call me and I'll try to swing by if I can.' She scribbled down her mobile number and handed it to Jake. Just as she did so, Leo walked into the room. He eyed the piece of paper as it passed between Regan and Jake.

'What are you up to?' Leo's voice was playful yet still spiced with a hint of confusion. 'Hi Leo, this is Jake Saunders. He's Nush's boyfriend. He's here to sell fitness gear on air.'

'Nice to meet you. I knew I recognised you. Bullet from *Sporting Spartans* and … all the stuff in the papers. I'm sorry to hear about your ex …' Leo fluffed, his words not quite hitting the right note of sincerity he'd hoped for. 'You two swapping numbers?'

'Yes, we might meet up for a drink this evening just to chat about everything that's going on. It's been a pretty rough ride lately,' said Jake.

It all seemed very innocent, so as Regan followed Leo out of the room for the meeting, why did she feel so incredibly guilty?

CHAPTER 63

'I must have had too much sun yesterday,' moaned Nush from beneath her hotel bed sheets. 'The inside of my head feels like it's been attacked by Jason Voorhees from *Friday The 13th*.' The clock on her bedside table showed that it was already heading towards midday.

'Get your naked arse out of that bed and into the shower. The sun had nothing to do with it, as well you know. It was all of that wine and champagne.' Evie was standing by Nush's bed, already dressed and ready for another day of luxury in the Arabian sunshine. She'd been ready for hours and had been knocking on Nush's door for the last twenty minutes.

'You were a total mess. If I hadn't put you to bed you'd have fallen asleep on the beach and woken up crispier that a poppadom. What was all that nonsense about your dad? Are you feeling a bit better about yourself this morning?'

The steely look in Nush's eyes as she pulled herself upright in bed was much sterner than Evie had expected. 'I meant every word, Evie. The man's a pig, one hundred per cent. Let's just leave it there.'

Attempting to lighten the mood, Evie steered their talk away from family matters. 'So, once you've risen from your pit and put your face on, what d'you fancy doing? I figure we have a few options … laze around the infinity pool, a day of spa pampering or grab a taxi and make for the world-famous Souq to buy ourselves some quality bling.'

A broad smile spread across Nush's face, her eyes blending into an avaricious glint. 'How about a mix of all three? We'll head to the Souq, buy enough jewellery to make Mr T jealous and then book ourselves into the spa back here for a reviving body polish. That way, we'll look beyond gorgeous when we hit poolside. Not that we don't already of course.'

Evie raised her eyebrows. 'You obviously haven't seen a mirror as yet. Gorgeous is not the word I would use to describe you this morning. Your face looks like someone's sat on it. Now hit the shower, get your slap on and I'll see you in reception.' She winked and turned on her heels.

—

Learning that she had lost her baby had been the most crushing moment of Sadie's life and Harry was not helping the situation. In the few days since they had learnt of their baby's death, Harry had withdrawn into himself and could barely touch her. There were no gestures of comfort and togetherness. In fact they had hardly spoken. He blamed his father for the loss of his child and his feelings towards Sadie had definitely changed since the umbilical cord of destiny between them had been severed.

Even through her depression and anguish, Sadie could see that she was losing Harry. Not that she minded. Her heart still belonged to Lawrence, despite everything. She didn't blame him for the loss of her baby. He hadn't meant to cause her any physical harm. She blamed herself. If she had been strong enough to resist Harry then she wouldn't have been in this empty mess. She had lost her husband, lost her home and now she had lost her baby.

She'd been staying at Harry's since leaving the hospital, but the close proximity between them was suffocating. The age difference between them seemed wider and deeper. She knew what she had to do. She and Harry were going nowhere. She'd never really wanted them to, but when he was the father of her un-born child there was valid reason to try and make things work. Now there was no point. Maybe he was just too immature to say. She couldn't blame him.

Harry had left his apartment an hour ago. He had told Sadie he was going out to buy food. Having seen how full the fridge and the kitchen cupboards were, Sadie knew that he was lying. He just needed to escape the oppressive atmosphere. Doubtless he would just drive around, speeding his way across London, trying to clear his head. Sadie knew that it was her chance to make the break.

Having packed the few clothes and belongings she had with her, Sadie handwrote Harry a note.

> *Dear Harry. I love you and I always will. You have been the most amazing stepson to me. I think of you as my own and that will never change. But we're not meant to be together. We never should have allowed ourselves to give in to temptation in the first place. It was wrong, and now that our little angel is gone, you should get on with your life. I shall always treasure the thought of what could have been between us, but we'd be kidding ourselves to think that there is any kind of romantic future for us. I'll always be there for you, just a phone call away. Love Sadie x*

She left the explanation on the coffee table in Harry's front room and then phoned for a taxi. It arrived five minutes later. Climbing into the back seat with her bags, her body still felt sore from its recent ordeal. But she knew she was doing the right thing. The one thing she didn't know, though, was where to ask the taxi driver to take her. She was certain she needed to end the chapter with Harry, but she didn't have a clue how the next one began.

CHAPTER 64

'Five seconds until we're live.' The clear voice of the *Planet Shopping* floor manager registered in Derek's brain as his heart pulsated wildly. Through the tiny plastic earpiece lodged in his ear, the crisp diction of the show's director spurred Derek into action. 'And cue Derek.'

Stood at the top of an impressive faux staircase which rested in a corner the main studio, Derek leapt into action, trotting his way daintily down the stairs, a broad grin plastered on his face. He wore a jet black suit caked with tiny diamante flecks. As he flittered his way down the stairs and onto the main set of the show, the music from *Peregrine Palace* bubbled in the background.

'Good evening, *Planet* people, it's 9pm and welcome to the start of yet another fantastic *24 Hour Perfect Purchase*. What a show we have for you tonight.' Derek meant it, he hadn't felt such a giddy buzz presenting a show in ages. 'Ladies, it's the night you've been waiting for. It's here, the exquisite aroma of success, the delectable and desirable fragrance of decadence, the perfume that any lady just has to have in her designer handbag this season and for many seasons to come … the fabulous *Babylon*. And the lady behind it, of course, is the doyenne of the soap we just love to dive into every single week. She's hot-footed her way from *Peregrine Palace* to be with us here at *Planet Shopping* so that we can all treat ourselves to a touch of her sheer unadulterated glamour. It's the fabulous newly-wed Montana Phoenix!' gushed Derek, spreading his arms messiah-like to greet his guest. Montana, wearing a floor-length Azzedine Alaia velvet gown, swept across the set to air-kiss him. She looked head-to-toe Hollywood glamour, her hair lifted back off her face, held in place by a diamond tiara on loan to her from London's Hatton Garden. With her feline eyes and full lips made-up to perfection, the overall look was Audrey Hepburn meets Angelina Jolie. It was a potent mix. She sprayed a liberal balloon of perfume around herself as she glided alongside the host. 'Derek, my darling. How divine to be here and to share the joy of *Babylon* with your marvellous viewers. It's been the talk of the beauty world in America ...' She turned to look directly down the barrel of her pre-arranged close-up camera. 'And now it's here for you in the UK. Enjoy.' She sprayed the perfume bottle once more with a waft of her hand and sighed, almost lustfully, in mock appreciation.

In Derek's ear, the voice of the show's producer squealed with glee. 'Like it? The viewers love it, we're got 400 phone sales already and it's rising every second. Let's work this, Derek, we've got a huge money-maker here.' Derek wasn't concentrating though. He was too excited ruminating over the fact that he'd just air-kissed his favourite TV bitch and was too busy trying to stop himself from coughing wildly as he breathed in a substantial clogging lungful of *Babylon*.

———

Regan would have seen her mother's overly dramatic entrance had she not been nervously waiting for Jake Saunders to join her in the bar of his hotel. Why the nerves? Jake seemed like good company and maybe had a real need to talk. So why was it that Regan couldn't help but worry.

Her heart fluttered as Jake sauntered into the bar. She had to admit he looked impressive, a muscle-hugging Fred Perry polo shirt stretched taut across his upper body, complemented by second-skin jeans and cowboy boots.

'Hey, I'm glad you made it.' Jake's smile was broad. 'Care to join me in a bottle of champagne. I had a sell-out this afternoon with my Ab Bullet, so I'm in the mood for celebrating. If you're anything like Nush then you'll not turn down some bubbles.'

'You know us too well.' Regan raised her eyebrows and smiled. *Was she already flirting?* She wasn't sure.

Jake bent down to kiss Regan on the cheek. It was merely a friendly sign of welcome, but Regan couldn't help but feel that his lips lingered a few moments more than necessary. 'I'll fetch the champagne.' He spoke the words while he was still in close proximity to her face and Regan could feel Jake's breath against her skin. There was definitely an air of intimacy about it. Regan squirmed in her seat, trying hard to compose herself as Jake made for the bar. She was still flushed when he returned with the bottle and two full glasses of champagne a few minutes later.

'Nush and Evie send their love. I spoke to Nush earlier. They're having a great time in Muscat and wish you were there. Sun, sand and shopping … they both seem pretty happy. Nush says she's missing me, which puts a smile on my face.'

'Well that's a first. Nush is normally a cold fish when it comes to men. You must be doing something right. But then I gather your first meeting was pretty explosive.'

Colour flooded to Jake's cheeks at Regan's comment. 'I guess she remembers more than me then as I was totally out of it for most of the night. What I can remember was … er … *explosive* though. She was sleeping with me for the story though. You do know that, don't you?'

'Nush tells me everything, Jake. She's part of our Trinity – me, her and Evie. It's what we do. You don't blame her for sleeping with you though, do you? When you have your name at the top of the most scandalous gossip column in the country it tends to make you a touch ruthless now and again in search of a great story. Anyway, you must have been good because she's come back for more, hasn't she?' Regan was enjoying the intriguing dalliance between them.

'I don't blame her at all. Things between Mae-Ling and I hadn't been good for ages. I knew what I was doing, I just didn't expect it to be all over her gossip column. It ruined my relationship, but in all honesty that was already *dead and buried* …' Jake's voice trailed off as he realised what he'd said.

'Anyway, what about you? Nush tells me that there might be a new man in your life?' He poured another drink for them both as he spoke.

Leo's face flashed into Regan's mind. 'It's early days, we'll see, but there is somebody. I've never really been the settling down kind so we'll have to wait and see what happens. He's the producer of the show. You met him today.'

'Oh right. Nush never said who it was. I suppose that's certainly one way to make sure you get more than your fair share of TV footage.'

Despite Jake's jesting, Regan could have kicked herself as soon as she'd spoken. Leo had told her to keep their relationship as quiet as possible, especially while they were working together. In an attempt to backtrack, she added 'To be honest, it's just an innocent flirtation. I'm sure he's the same with Grace.' *Why did Regan feel compelled to lie?*

'He'd be mad not to fall for you, though. You're stunningly attractive. Any man would have to be gay or mad not to tumble for your charms.' Jake placed his champagne glass on the table between them and leant towards Regan.

Regan's mind swam. Her thoughts were a cocktail of confusion mixed with quivering trepidation. Either she was reading the signs completely wrong here or Jake was making his intentions very clear. She felt appreciative, yet appalled. This was her best friend's boyfriend.

'Well it's a good job that you're mad about my best friend then, isn't it. That makes you immune, doesn't it?'

It seemed like a lifetime before he replied. 'But I'm not immune. I've been thinking about you ever since I met you at Kingsbury and, call me conceited, but I think you liked what you saw when you walked in on me.' Jake reached across the table and placed his hand on Regan's knee. She moved it away for fear of being seen.

'Now that's arrogance with a capital A if ever I heard it. I think we had better call it a night, don't you? Give me one good reason why I shouldn't phone up Nush right now and tell her that you're coming on to me behind her back?'

Breaking into his killer smile again, Jake stared Regan directly in the eyes. It was as if he was looking directly into her soul. 'Because what goes on tour stays on tour ...'

'Some women are off limits even to the most persuasive of guys,' slurred Regan, the effects of the drink hitting her. 'I think the night ends here, don't you ...?' She was adamant, but the ripple of pleasure that she felt between her legs staring at Jake made her feel that her words were far from convincing ...

CHAPTER 65

As he withdrew his condom-covered, semi-hard cock from his chauffeur's butt, Jeremy felt a heated high from the climax he had just experienced. Slumping back onto his silk bed sheets, it was a sharp contrast with the stone-cold low he'd felt transferring $150,000 into the account of a certain Stafford James earlier that day. It was money that he was being forced to part with through his own stupidity and that really irked him.

Jeremy had always been so careful. Surrounding himself with hand-picked employees who he knew could be readily paid to buy their silence. That's how both Mario and Robin had come to be in his employ. Countless interviews and high recommendations from trusted friends had guaranteed him staff members that would not only be attentive to his everyday professional needs, but also to his sexual needs. Both Robin and Mario were being paid enough to keep their lips sealed and their buttocks spread. Even Tasmina, Jeremy's trusted maid, who held no interest for him sexually, was sworn to keep his bedroom antics secret. Paying her three times the amount of her previous two Hollywood employers had assured her discretion. Money could buy anything … and anyone.

But Jeremy wasn't convinced that cold hard cash was going to buy Stafford's silence. There was something about the odious man that scratched away at him. He was like a disease, spreading his virus further and further afield. He'd spread it to within an inch of Jeremy's *new love* Evie. He'd seen them posed alongside each other in Montana's wedding photos. What worried him were the quotes from '*Montana's Best Man*' inside the pages, the '*flamboyant former photographer Stafford James*'. The cheap asides about '*How frighteningly lucky Evie was to have such a dishy catch and how both women … and men … around the world would love to get their hands on Jeremy Pinewood*'. For Jeremy, it was too close for comfort and it was making him angry and troubled.

Slapping Robin tempestuously across the backside – causing the chauffeur to emit a whimper of pain – Jeremy ordered him to get dressed and leave him alone. Jeremy picked up the magazine featuring Montana's wedding photos from the bedroom floor and stared at Stafford's face gazing out from the pages. It appeared to be mocking him. Grabbing a pen from the bedside table, Jeremy started scribbling furiously across the face. He kept going until the page tore, over and over again, the face beneath the scribbles destroyed beyond all recognition.

———

Thousands of miles away, in a hotel room in the East of England, Regan Phoenix was laying naked on a bed. Jake Saunders stood at the end of bed, his cock pendulous between his legs, his abs lined with sweat. In his hand he held an ultra-thin digital camera. Pointing it at an oblivious Regan, he clicked away. Five or six frames just to make sure that he got the right shot, the one where her face was on show, where there was no doubt as to who she was.

He'd taken the camera from the table he'd placed directly opposite the end of the bed. The camera was hi-tech and small enough to not be noticeable. Good job really. It had been filming his sexual exploits with Regan since he'd clicked the 'record' button. It had hopefully captured every last contortion.

Tossing the camera into his bag, Jake climbed back into bed alongside Regan. It was only then that she began to stir.

CHAPTER 66

The harsh studio lights at *Planet Shopping* were playing havoc with Regan's eyes. She hadn't felt this rough since her hedonistic clubbing days. She tried to focus her bloodshot eyes on the cameras surrounding her. So much had happened recently … the TV show, the truth about her mum's past, the discovery of her real father and her blossoming relationship with Leo. How could she have been so stupid to let herself down on such an important day? In just a few hours she would have to sell a series of products on live TV in order to obtain the *Wild Child* crown. All she wanted to do right now was sleep.

Regan was standing in the main studio at *Planet*, flanked by Grace and Leo. Leo had hardly spoken to her all morning, not since she'd joined him for breakfast at the hotel. She'd managed a black coffee before tearing to the toilet to throw up. Word had already spread like a bush fire among the production team that Regan had stumbled back into the hotel in the middle of the night in a complete state. She had been wobblier than Bambi on ice.

Grace, on the other hand, couldn't get enough of the situation, savouring every droplet of Regan's smothering hangover. 'Just what did you do with Mr Muscle? Isn't he with your friend Anoushka?' Her words scratched at Leo's nerves like nails down a blackboard. Regan was equally incensed.

'Just drop it, Grace. Quite frankly it's sod all to do with you. I had a couple of drinks with Jake and that's all.'

Regan could feel her cheeks rouging as she lied, unable to remember the true details of how she'd let herself wake up naked alongside Jake. *How could she have done it, betraying both Nush and Leo like that?* There was something about Jake that was mesmerising. She had regretted it from the moment she'd woken up alongside him, her head pounding, as a flood of guilt-laden thoughts had crashed through her mind. She had hurriedly dressed and fled the room, desperate to get back to her own hotel.

Grace continued. 'Whatever you say, precious. But it's certainly left you with an almighty hangover and you're in need of a little Gracie pick-you-up. I've got some painkillers back in the green room that will sort out that head of yours. You and I need to be on top form if we're to sell our hearts out later on.' She seemed genuinely sincere.

Despite her recent distrust of Grace, Regan had to admit that the thought of some heavy duty painkillers to stop the pain in her head sounded idyllic. She was also anxious to leave the studio as soon as possible. She and Grace were supposed to be there 'prepping' the format of the *Planet* shows, but having spent the last twenty minutes watching show host Derek fawning over her mother on the far side of the studio, she could feel her bile rising. A hangover she could cope with, but suffering in front of her sanctimonious bitch of a mother was just too much. Luckily Montana had been too busy enthusing on air about the supposed delights of *Babylon* to notice her daughter's appearance.

—

Or at least, so Regan had thought. Montana had indeed spied her daughter through the row of cameras lined up in front of her. Ever the professional, though, she was determined that the presence of her wayward offspring would not put her off. Things were going well for Montana as far as the show was concerned. Since launching *Babylon* the night before, she had already sold out of the stock that had been originally been planned. Frenzied phone calls overnight between Brad and Coeur Cosmetics had ensured that more stock had been drafted in. Montana was delighted, and a sparkly Derek was enthusing to anyone who would listen about his sales figures for the show. They made a happy team.

The one thought that kept streaming into Montana's mind though, as she caught sight of Regan, was the thought of Lawrence Silvers. *Had Regan told him yet? Why had she been so stupid to let the truth slip out to her daughter? How would Lawrence react if she did tell him?* Montana had never even given him the chance to know about her pregnancy. It had been a complete accident after all. One that she'd chosen to hide from him …

———

Montana Phoenix, or Belinda Faye as she was back then, had first met the dashingly handsome Lawrence Silvers at a hotel in Mayfair. She'd been invited there as part of a gang of girls she'd met through her then flatmate, a fellow wannabe actress called Leeza. A group of fun-seeking randy media types with huge bank balances and sexual appetites to match had hired a suite at the hotel for a night of debauchery. At the head of the group was Lawrence. His love of money and power was matched only by his love of women and partying. But he needed secrecy and discretion when he required company.

Lawrence was married to the stunning model, Lysette. Their happy loved-up faces had featured in many magazines and newspapers at the time. Lysette was pregnant, expecting their first child. Lawrence's public persona was that of a happily married one-woman-man, but privately he still liked to party. Alongside his best friend, the equally epicurean Johnny Erridge, they would organise licentious nights for their male friends. They would hire women who could be both sexual and secretive.

Belinda had been 'working' alongside Leeza and her friends for a few months. It had been a great way to earn some extra cash to fuel her acting ambition.

She would call them *booze 'n' schmooze* evenings, attending as many as she could in between endless nights in backwater hotels as she toured the length and breadth of the UK in some tiny unnoticed theatre production.

Through the parties she'd met, charmed and slept with film directors, script writers, authors and actors. She was paid well and Belinda knew how to play the game. It wasn't long before she was getting personally requested.

Lawrence had been attracted to her from the first moment he'd seen her. Belinda's feline features were the complete antithesis of Lysette. There was an instant magnetic connection. It wasn't long before Lawrence became Belinda's number one client. He loved to satisfy her and shower her with expensive gifts.

Lawrence would request Belinda's company whenever he could. There would be nights at casinos, snatched moments in hotels, the odd trip to the Mediterranean for a weekend on Lawrence's yacht. Belinda would be accompanied by Leeza, who was favoured by Johnny, if the two men were partying together. It was a simple and beneficial procedure. The girls would provide the glamour, the sex and the secrecy and the men would supply the cash and gifts. It was all going incredibly well. But then, disaster struck. Belinda became pregnant.

At first she had been sure that she wanted to have an abortion, but a niggling thought at the back of her mind made her decide otherwise. She may not have had the happiest of upbringings but what right did she have to snuff out a tiny life before it was born. Despite knowing that it would change everything, she chose to keep the baby.

She knew it had to be Lawrence's. He'd become her sole client. His financial generosity meant that she didn't have to look elsewhere. But she knew that she couldn't tell him the truth. His own wife was just about to give birth and what was it that Lawrence always said about Belinda? That she was his 'no strings girl', his 'bit of fun'. Fun did not equate to paying paternity for your whore's child, Belinda was sure of that.

Almost overnight, Belinda made a decision that would change the rest of her life. She would pool all of her money together, sell some of the gifts that Lawrence had showered her with and move. One of her former clients was a film director who had subsequently moved to Los Angeles to work on some low-budget sci-fi movies. He'd always had a soft spot for Belinda and when she phoned him to explain her situation, he invited her to stay with him and have the baby in the States. In a matter of days she had given notice on her flat, told Leeza she was leaving, booked herself a plane ticket and left the country. She left no forwarding address. Within weeks she was performing walk-ons as alien beauties and seductive spacewomen on her friend's movies. It was the start of her acting career in America. She changed her name to Montana Phoenix, determined to put all thoughts of Belinda Faye behind her.

Months later, Regan was born. She became a constant reminder of Montana's former life. A life to which she never wanted to return. Her arrival made Montana even more determined to succeed, to finally make the mark she'd always dreamt of.

———

Back at *Planet*, Derek was working the cameras for all he was worth. Giving his best cheeky grin, he spoke to his audience.

'That's it from myself and the divine Montana Phoenix. We'll be back with *Babylon* for our final show later today. We've got ridiculously busy lines for the entire *Babylon* range, and our *Planet* website has gone into meltdown. Montana, people just adore your perfume. What would you say to anyone who's still in two minds? Montana my darling ... what would you say ... er, Montana?'

Montana snapped back out of her thoughts. Shit, she was here to do a job and the last thing she could do was let her mind wander. Bloody Regan was putting her off. 'So sorry, Derek, I was just miles away, amazed at how much *Babylon* the lovely people at home are buying today. Can I thank them all? If I could pop round to each of their exquisite homes and thank them individually, I would. And bless you too, Derek, you are such a poppet.' She reached out and pinched his cheek like a grandmother would a toddler.

'We'll see you all later. Stay glamorous!' Derek ended the show. Montana hadn't answered his question, but he didn't care. The woman he had idolised on TV for years had just pinched his face. He was already planning where that moment would feature on his showreel.

CHAPTER 67

'So, are we feeling incredibly relaxed after a facial, a milk bath soak and a … what was it …?' Evie picked up the brochure detailing the delights of the Muscat hotel spa and started to read it aloud, '… The warm cocooning seaweed toning envelopment?'

'Relaxed? My skin feels like satin. I could do it all over again tomorrow. I haven't felt this mellow in ages.' Nush took a gulp from her cocktail and ran her hand down her mannequin-smooth leg.

'Make the most of it, lady, because we fly home tomorrow. Back to the real world,' lamented Evie.

The moon was round and silvery-bright in the Muscat sky as Evie and Nush sat at the hotel's outside bar. The night air was warm against their skin, with just a hint of a breeze wafting in from the ocean.

There was an eclectic mix of people milling around the bar area. Evie watched two young children, a boy and a girl, skipping their way around the tables. Their faces were both tanned, the freckles on their cheeks standing out proud in the moonlight. Their parents gazed on lovingly, holding hands with each other across their table. The children gave off giddy giggles of delight as they danced their way through the bar. As they passed Nush and Evie's table, the little boy stopped directly in front of

Evie. He appeared transfixed by her. Looking up from underneath his shaggy mop of deep red hair, he smiled at Evie.

'Hello, I'm Alan, do you speak English?'

Both women smiled, their hearts melted by the scamp's charm. It was Evie who spoke. 'Yes we do, Alan. Are you here on holiday?'

'Yes, my dad is doing some work here. You're very pretty, aren't you? You're like a princess from my sister's books. She loves them but I prefer monsters. See you later!' And with that, he was gone, chasing off after his sister again.

Evie and Nush couldn't help but laugh at his delectable nature. 'That boy is going to break some hearts when he is older, that's for sure,' grinned Nush. 'He's only about four now and already he's won us over.'

'He's beauty … beautiful.' Evie's voice wobbled as she spoke and as she finished the sentence, she started to sob gently. She picked up a serviette from the table to dab her eyes. 'Oh dear … sorry about this Nush.'

At first, Nush was stumped into silence by Evie's sudden air of woe, but as the tears started to flow freely, she realised her friend was genuinely upset. She reached out across the table and placed her hand on Evie's. 'Hey, what's the matter? Why the tears? That little boy was adorable. You're not feeling broody are you? It's not every day you get called a princess. He obviously thought you were gorgeous.'

'I thought he was gorgeous too, positively angelic. It just makes me wonder what might have been … that's all …' Evie's voice petered out, uncertain what to say next. The small streams of tears continued to run silently down her face.

'What do you mean? What might have been? Are you talking about Sadie and Harry losing their baby? It was probably for the best, you know. Harry is not father material as yet, far from it. He's too young and …'

'No!' snapped Evie, causing Nush to stop in full flow. 'That's not what I'm talking about.' Evie looked down into her lap, nervously playing with her hands. Despite the dryness of the warm night air, her palms were traced with a layer of perspiration. 'Nush, you and Regan have been my best friends for years now. We've shared everything … nearly. But I need to tell you something. There was a time when I did something that I'm not proud of and there's not a day goes by that I don't think about it. I was so stupid and idiotic.'

Nush could see that Evie was upset, her words uncharacteristically rambling. 'Hey, you can tell me anything. It can't be worse than anything I've ever done.'

'It was seeing that little boy,' said Evie, indicating Alan, who was now kicking up splashes of water with his flip-flopped feet at the edge of the hotel pool. 'It just brings it all back to me. My child would have been about his age now. I was selfish and couldn't handle it, thought it would ruin everything, so I made the decision. I had an abortion, Nush.'

Nush's jaw hung open wider with each and every word Evie spoke. Shocked by what she was hearing, all she could say was 'When?'

Four and a half years ago …

Evie Merchant was taking her bows at the end of yet another packed-out performance at an intimate theatre, off-Broadway, in New York. As she stared into the dazzling theatre lights and listened to the rapturous applause coming from the auditorium, she knew that this was the kind of feeling she wanted to experience for a lifetime.

Evie had arrived in New York three months earlier, pretty much fresh out of Farmington Grange. She'd had offers of work from both TV and theatre companies in the UK, but Evie had always longed to perform off-Broadway and now was her chance to do it. Many of the great actors she admired had sculpted their craft there and, for Evie, it seemed like the perfect springboard to launch her career.

She'd scanned the theatre magazines and pored over the reviews and advertisements for the productions taking place and spent hours sitting in the off-Broadway coffee shops and scanning the shop windows for ads about accommodation. Within days she'd quit her hotel, to move into a dingy apartment that she would be sharing with three other wannabe actors. All thoughts of her riches back home and her privileged upbringing were shelved as she mucked in with the others, scraping enough money together to pay the monthly rent and the utility bills. It was an escape into another world, one which allowed her to do whatever she wanted. Nush and Regan had thought that she was mad. *Why would she want to slum it in a mould-covered flat when she could afford to live in five star luxury?* Evie's answer was simple. It made her feel alive.

Evie secured a job as a waitress at a backstreet café. It was a job that she loved and the café was popular with the acting in-crowd. It wasn't long before she had found out about the auditions and castings she needed to attend. It was four weeks to the day after she'd first arrived in New York that Evie found herself being offered the job as one of the lead characters in a quirky new musical comedy full of sharp parody, irreverent humour and sinfully spectacular dancing. The salary wasn't great, the work was extremely hard, the slog of night-after-night performances draining, but Evie lapped up every second. The reviews were golden, with Evie being hailed as a major talent.

Her favourite review was from the critic who said she 'Could dance her socks off, sing her heart out and act anybody under the table'. She had photocopied, enlarged and framed the quote, and hung it in her poky bedroom.

One of her co-stars in the production was one of her flat-mates, Jerome Naylor, a deliciously masculine hunk of a man from the deep south of America. His baritone drawl and toned physique had captured Evie's attention from the moment she first went to see the apartment. The appreciation was evidently mutual as shortly after Evie moved in, the pair of them had become lovers. They would share pillow talk about common acting interests. They could lose themselves in deep conversations about the nail-biting tension of Samuel Becket's *Waiting for Godot,* or light and fluffy musings about the acting skills of Tori Spelling. Evie had found a soul mate. They had auditioned together, and Jerome had been offered a part in the chorus.

Then it happened. Evie was late for her period. At first she didn't worry as the workings of her body could be irregular at the best of times, but as the days went by, Evie knew that she had to take a test. It had confirmed her worst fears … she was pregnant.

Night after night, Evie had agonised over what to do. She had always imagined herself as a parent, a doting mother to a clutch of cherubic beauties, but all of that should come after meeting the man of her dreams, achieving her career goals and gaining the worldwide praise she'd always hankered after. Not when her career was just beginning. She had made her mind up. She would have to get rid of the baby. Evie had chosen the path to take. She wouldn't tell Jerome, she wouldn't tell Nush and Regan, she wouldn't tell anyone … this was something she had to do by herself.

Evie had scanned the internet endlessly to try and find out about clinics. One swift conversation and arrangements were made. She was to go in two days' time.

Evie's major problem would be hiding it from the people around her. How could she sing and dance her way through a musical when her body would doubtless be hurting. The websites she'd scanned had said no strenuous activity for at least two weeks after the abortion. Also, she was to have no sex as this could hinder her aftercare. How would she push away Jerome's advances? She knew that she needed to get away. She needed a story, she needed a lie.

After that night's performance, Evie asked for a private meeting with the show's producer. He had championed Evie since first meeting her and loved watching her perform. But he could tell that something wasn't right. Her performance had been missing its usual vibrant edge. When he questioned her, Evie put her story into motion. She explained that her 'dear grandmother had just sadly passed away' and that she needed to go back to England for the funeral. She added that she would never normally ask but that she would never forgive herself if she wasn't there to be at her grandma's graveside. It was a convincing piece of acting and the producer, keen not to annoy one of the lynchpins of his production, agreed that Evie's understudy could take on the role straight away. Worried that she was pushing her luck, Evie asked if she could take a fortnight off before resuming work on the show. Again, the producer agreed, albeit begrudgingly.

When she'd returned to the apartment, her flatmates, and more importantly Jerome, were nowhere to be seen. Throwing some clothes and toiletries into a holdall, she left Jerome a note and took a cab to a hotel not far from the clinic. Immediately she turned off her mobile phone. She left it off virtually constantly for the next two weeks, paranoid that Jerome or the show's producer would try to ring her and realise that, in fact, she had not left the USA.

The few hours she spent at the clinic left her with a sense of numbness. Having scrawled her signature across a consent form, she underwent the termination. Evie felt weak and wretched but it was too late for any kind of regrets.

She returned to her apartment and to the production two weeks after the procedure. Her body no longer ached, but her heart did. Every time she looked at Jerome or saw a toddler holding onto their parent's hand ready to cross a New York street she would feel a paralysing pinch of guilt. It was a reaction that would stay with her for many years to come.

———

As Evie finished telling Nush about her time in New York, both women had tears in their eyes.

'Why didn't you tell us? We'd have supported you.' Nush was heartbroken that her friend had experienced such an ordeal on her own. 'Did you ever tell Jerome?'

More sadness seemed to ebb across Evie's eyes. 'After the production finished, I was snapped up to work on a few TV movies and my career kind of snowballed from there. Jerome went on tour across the States with some play so we were hardly ever within a thousand miles of each other. We stayed in touch for a while but then I heard from a mutual friend that he'd been killed in a car crash. I still think about him now.'

The Muscat night air had become cold. Nush felt a chill run across her flesh. But her shiver wasn't from the wind fanning in from the Arabian Sea, it was the melancholy she felt after listening to Evie's story.

CHAPTER 68

'Just remember, darling, that every action is a performance. Whether you're gyrating your tushy to a sell-out audience at the Hollywood Bowl or flogging some designer trinkets on shopping TV, it has to be a crowd-pleaser. It's all about sales, because at the end of today, one of us will be the *Wild Child* winner and one will be the biggest loser.'

Grace was imparting her wisdom to Regan in the green room at *Planet*. Not that Regan was really listening. Her head was still residing in hangover hell, although she was hoping the tablet Grace had just given her would soon work its medical magic and de-fuzz her brain.

Both girls were due to 'perform' in about an hour's time. Regan had chosen to sell some faux-diamond jewellery, a hand-held cleaner and an electric wok for her show in the hope that she would come across as *normal* as possible to viewers. The last thing they would expect of her was cooking and cleaning.

'Game on. May the best girl win,' said Regan. 'Time for wardrobe, hair and make-up.' She was determined to look her best on the outside, even if inside, her brain felt like chopped liver.

———

Grace's half an hour of *Planet* airtime came first. After a brief introduction from her assigned *Planet* host, an overexcited housewife type, Grace launched into her sells. First up she promoted an air-purifying system that would 'cleanse the air you breathe'. It was basically a round glass bowl filled with fragranced water. She'd seen something similar when she'd appeared with Sexalicious on one of the American shopping networks and had been so enthralled by the way it supposedly 'washed the air' that she'd had the supplier send her a crateful. The group had taken them on tour to cleanse their dressing rooms accordingly. Grace's name-dropping tales of her touring days made for a convincing sell. Orders were placed in their hundreds. So far, so good.

Her next sell was an exercise bike - not an easy product to promote when you're wearing a knee-length Christian Dior gown. Grace had chosen total glamour for her appearance, but as she glided across the set to the bike, she pulled a master stroke. Tugging lightly at the spaghetti shoulder straps holding the gown to her body, she let the designer frock tumble to the floor. Underneath it Grace was wearing a pink skin-tight pair of buttock-skimming cycling shorts and a matching tube of pink Lycra stretched across her ample cleavage. As she kicked off her Rene Caovilla heels, replacing them with a pair of slip-on ballet pumps, and climbed aboard the exercise bike, an audible display of appreciation could be heard from the male members of the *Planet* camera crew. The phone lines lit up as Grace started to pedal, working her honed legs and showing off her ironing-board flat stomach to perfection.

Just as Grace's body was beginning to display the first faint traces of perspiration, she moved onto her third and final sell. It was for one of the core items on the channel, a kaftan. Grace was determined to make it look sexy and give it an edge of spectacular Hollywood chic.

Striding onto the set, her speech still seductively breathy from her workout on the bike, Grace eyeballed the centre of her in-vision camera and purred. 'Okay, my lovely viewers at home, my body has been shaped a little, so now it's time to drape it in something sensational. I don't know about you, but I feel ready to hit the town. Boys, I think I'm ready for my outfit …'

Right on cue, two of the male floor managers sauntered onto the set. They each held one side of a velvet, jewel-encrusted emerald green kaftan. As Grace raised her arms above her head and bent forward, the two men slipped it over her head and slid it down her body. With a model-esque flick of her hair, Grace straightened herself again and once more stared directly into the lens. 'Voila! Thanks boys … I'm feeling sexy and ready for some fun.' It was pure over-the-top theatrics, but somehow it worked. The *Planet* phone lines and website went ballistic with orders. Grace's stint as a shopping TV host had been incredibly successful and as the regular host joined her on set to wrap up the show, Grace let a satisfied smile spread across her face. As far as she was concerned, she had the *Wild Child* crown in the bag, especially when she already knew that Regan's upcoming performance would be messier than a Tinseltown divorce case.

———

Derek was avidly watching Grace's sales techniques in the green room alongside Regan. To say that he was impressed would have been an understatement. 'Have you ever seen a kaftan look so fucking sexy? You're going to have to go some to beat that. But have faith. I'll be introducing you in about fifteen minutes. You get yourself together and remember everything we've talked about.' Derek squeezed Regan's knee in encouragement.

As Derek minced out of the room, Regan stared at the TV screen in front of her. She'd been watching and listening but somehow nothing was registering in her brain. She was finding it hard to remember anything – the colours and the sounds on the screen were engaging Regan but it all seemed to merge together in a manic mess of confusion.

Regan's headache had ebbed away slightly. The cacophony of noises inside her mind had subsided and been replaced with a blank canvas. But when Derek had squeezed her knee, she had felt a rush of sensual longing run through her body. *What was she thinking?* The man was obviously dancing up the other end of the sexuality ballroom and anyway, if she wanted some hands-on action, then Leo would hopefully be at her disposal after the day's filming had wrapped. *Why was she thinking about Derek?* At the thought of her strange feelings for the camp TV host, Regan began to laugh. At first it was a sly giggle, but then, as she thought about it more, the laughter erupted from her stomach, loud and uncontrollable. Then, just as if someone had flicked a switch inside her, Regan's laughter stopped almost instantaneously and a ripple of anxious nausea flittered through her. She went from an uncomfortable frosty shiver to a clammy sheen of sweat. She could hear her teeth grinding against each other.

It was a smorgasbord of feelings that Regan had experienced before, but it all seemed out of place. She'd never had a hangover which had left her so … out of control. Regan's heart raced, the blood pumping through her body. 'I can beat that Grace Laszlo,' she bragged confidently.

Regan linked arms with the floor manager as they walked down the corridor towards the studio. She only let go when she arrived in the studio. A euphoric rush of excitement rushed through her as she saw the bright lights suspended from the studio ceiling. Derek was in position, ready to introduce her.

Derek gave Regan a cheesy thumbs-up as she was counted to air. The voices of the producer and director popped inside her head, almost seeming to sink into the mushy quicksand of her mind.

Next thing she knew, Derek had introduced her. A monumental wave of self-confidence wrapped itself around her and she rushed onto the set. The thought that potentially millions of people would be watching her didn't even seem to cross Regan's mind.

And watching her they were. Stafford and Brad were watching Regan from the plush comfort of Montana's VIP green room. Montana was having her make-up retouched for her final show and was watching the action out of the corners of her beautiful feline-like eyes. Grace watched from the *Wild Child* green room, desperate not to miss a millisecond of the action. Leo Weiss was watching it from the production gallery at *Planet*. Clarissa Thornton was watching with an avid interest from her London hotel bedroom. Lawrence was watching on his office television at *The Daily Staple,* surrounded by the junior members of Nush's editorial team. Jake Saunders was watching too, from the comfort of the Kensington home he'd shared with Mae-Ling. Harry was watching unshaven and unwashed at his apartment. Even Ashley Erridge was watching, sitting in the eerie semi-darkness of his flat.

But as millions of pairs of TV-viewing eyes looked on, the afternoon's events began to unfold ...

———

Regan felt alive with energy as she first bounced onto the set and kissed Derek on the cheek. She could hear the voices from the TV gallery coming through her earpiece, instructing her to move to the first item. It was the jewellery. The prompts came thick and fast. 'Quote the item number, Regan. Pick up the jewellery, place it around your neck. Tell us about the cut, the colour, the clarity. Who would want jewellery like this? Why do you like it?' What about the cost? Tell people how to order.'

Regan moved to the necklace laid out in front of her and placed it across her décolleté. It felt cold against her skin. Regan's mind was lost in thought and she said nothing. More urgent prompts from the producer sounded in Regan's ear. 'Give the item number please, Regan. Remember we're broadcasting live across the UK now and this will be seen around the world on *Wild Child* in a few days.'

Regan began to speak, giving details of what she saw on the monitors in front of her. Her speech seemed slurred in places and some of her words rolled into one. It could have been seen as nerves to those watching, but Regan knew that something was wrong. Her vision became blurred. Trying with all her might to concentrate on what she was saying, Regan focussed as much as she could on the jewellery. Whatever was wrong, she had to stay in control. She looked into the camera and smiled. Then she heard it. A voice in her head. It was only quiet, as if someone was talking to her from the very back of the TV gallery, but she still heard it clearly enough. 'Look at her eyes. Her pupils are massive. She's on something. She's off her tits, for Christ's sake. We need to get her off air.'

On something? With a shattering moment of clarity, everything fell into place in Regan's mind. The pill Grace had given her … it wasn't for her headache was it? It was an E … Ecstasy. That would explain her dilated pupils, the blurring of her vision, the horny rushes. Suddenly it all made sense.

Regan hadn't looked at the pill before glugging it down her throat. She'd wanted to swallow it as quickly as possible to get rid of the headache. Grace had tricked her. Now it was too late. She was on live TV and off her head. The scheming bitch had tried to shaft her, but how could she prove that Grace was the one who had given it to her? It would just be her word against Regan's. But Regan couldn't let her win, not like this.

Fired up with hatred for Grace and the situation, Regan moved to her next sell, the cleaning product. She could tell all eyes were on her, waiting to see what would happen next. At that very moment she felt alert, her senses heightened. She knew it wouldn't last and sprang into action. She blurted out the details about the handheld cleaner and gave a quick demonstration around the mock-bathroom on set. Regan attempted to keep her gaze away from the camera as much as possible, trying desperately not to draw attentions to her pupils. She repeated verbatim the dialogue being fed to her in her ear, willing the show to be over. If she could just make it to the end then maybe there was still a chance of her beating Grace.

Her sell completed on the cleaner, she moved to the final set, the kitchen, where Regan was to promote the electric wok. As the heat from the sauce bubbling inside the non-stick walls of the wok hit her, Regan felt yet another drug-induced rush run through her. It was the strongest yet and it coincided with her mother arriving in the studio. Looking around, her vision blurred again, Regan could see Derek greeting Montana with yet another batch of air-kisses. Nausea gripped Regan. As an immaculate Montana sashayed to the set of her forthcoming *Babylon* show she stared Regan straight in the eyes. Her disgust was plain to see.

It was Montana's look of disgust that tipped Regan over the edge. This wasn't her fault. She'd been tricked by Grace. How dare Montana look at her in such a condescending way?

With the sound of the producer's voice screaming in her ears, Regan snapped. Picking up a bowl of sweet and sour chicken and rice that had been placed on the kitchen counter for set decoration, a fuming Regan stormed out of the kitchen and towards Montana. Her brain swamped by the ecstasy and oblivious to the masses of people watching her, she had just one thing on her mind – dealing with Montana.

The voice in her ear continued to screech, but Regan heard nothing. The *Planet* cameras followed her as she marched towards Montana.

Her actions were quick and would be shown again on countless TV shows for years to come. People would never tire of seeing the moment when a drugged-up Regan Phoenix emptied a bowl of Chinese food all over her mother's head and Yves Saint Laurent dress, while she called Montana a slut for never telling her that her real father was Lawrence Silvers, before fainting to the floor, the drug finally getting the better of her. It was not until a hysterical Montana Phoenix marched off set in tears, still dripping with sauce and rice, that the producers of *Planet Shopping* faded the screen to black.

———

For those watching the live broadcast, the reactions to the carnival of chaos were varied. Leo Weiss just held his head in his hands, his teeth clenched, eyes wide in anger. Grace was euphoric, watching the pandemonium Regan had caused on air, the end result much better than even she, in her devious conniving ways, had imagined. As soon as Regan had dropped the bombshell about Lawrence being her father, Grace had squealed with glee and dialled Clarissa Thornton's number at once. It was engaged because Clarissa, on hearing the news, had phoned her team at *Hollywood Daily* to dictate the story. Along with the photo of Lawrence and Montana, Clarissa was convinced that she would once again have a much fuller story than any other news source. Her next phone call was to Lawrence. With Nush out of the country, maybe she could convince him to let her tell his side of the story. His line was engaged.

Lawrence's phone had sounded literally the moment his name had been mentioned on air. It was news that had caused him to choke on his whisky. *Regan was his daughter? Surely she couldn't be? Her mother was a whore, for god's sake, she must have taken dozens of men to her bed. Why would she say Regan was his? He'd have to prove her wrong.*

Johnny Erridge was the first person to get hold of Lawrence. Whilst they talked, Lawrence missed calls from Clarissa, from his secretary at *The Daily Staple* and from an angry Harry demanding to know if Lawrence had known all along.

After phoning Lawrence, Harry had phoned Nush in Muscat with the news. To say she was stunned was an understatement. If it was true, the maths made it simple … Lawrence had been cheating on Nush's dear mother. Harry had left Nush and Evie rushing off to their laptop to check out the *Planet* footage of Regan on YouTube.

Brad and Stafford had run from the *Planet* green room as soon as they'd seen Montana's upset. She would need major comforting to get over this one. When they arrived at the studio, they found her puce with anger and dripping with food. She was being comforted by a fussing Derek, who was limply offering tips on how to get stains out of her silk dress using a range of *Planet Shopping* cleaning products.

CHAPTER 69

The smile on Clarissa Thornton's face was one of Cheshire Cat proportions. Having dictated the story to her team at *Hollywood Daily*, she had activated Lawrence's number to constant redial on her mobile until he'd picked up. His gruff tone made it clear that he was not exactly pleased to hear from her. 'What the fuck do you want, Thornton? You still owe me a story, and if you're phoning up about today's TV codswallop then I have nothing to say. As far as I can work out, both Regan Phoenix and that daft bint of a mother of hers are off their rockers. If Regan is my daughter then I want nothing to do with her. I've got enough family nightmares of my own.'

Relishing the sound bite she'd just been given, a joyful Clarissa seized the moment. 'Can I quote you on that? You think she might be your daughter. It is a possibility then? You and Montana Phoenix were lovers a few years ago then ... or maybe you still are? Would you care to elaborate at all?'

Inwardly Lawrence kicked himself for his slip of the tongue. He'd already given away more information than necessary. 'Look, you infuriating woman, I've told you there is no story as far as I'm concerned. If I do have anything to say about all of this bullshit, which I don't, then I'll be saying it in my own bloody newspaper, alright. So, I suggest you take your reporter's pen and pad and shove it right up your ...'

Clarissa interrupted before he had a chance to the graphically finish his sentence. 'I have the photo of you and Montana. Put that with the quote you've just given me about you wanting nothing to do with your supposed new daughter then I have a nice little scoop for tonight's *Hollywood Daily*, don't you think?'

For the first time during the conversation, Lawrence's voice faltered slightly. 'The photo shows nothing. It's from years ago and I'll deny the quote. Your word against mine.'

'Oh, come on now. You know how these things work. I didn't get where I am today without recording every possible juicy telephone conversation I have. Modern technology is a marvellous thing. Now, the way I look at it we have two choices. I can run the story as is, with you dismissing any notion of Regan being your daughter and coming across as a nasty male chauvinist pig who doesn't give a toss, or I can make you look a little more sympathetic by getting a few more personal details. You tell me about any connections you had with Montana, what you really think about Regan's revelations and about how heartbroken you are by missing out on the last twenty years. I can make you look like the victim here. Otherwise, I could contact Montana for her side of the story. I'm sure she has a sorry tale to tell of how she couldn't face the brutal man who had got her pregnant for fear of emotional rejection. You were married at the time after all. I may not be the brain of Britain, but even I can work out that Anoushka's birth and Regan's birth were close enough to know that you were evidently doing the dirty.'

Lawrence knew that Clarissa was right.

'So, what's it to be then? Should I go and offer Montana a huge amount of cash to tell her side of the story and paint you as some kind of womaniser? Or do I run a teaser on *Hollywood Daily* tonight about how a misunderstood Lawrence Silvers will be talking exclusively to me about the heartache Regan's revelation has caused him? It can run jointly on *Hollywood Daily* and *The Staple*. Your story, your words, you as the victim. How about I drop by your office tomorrow morning where you can tell me all about it. Otherwise, your quote gets aired tonight and all of a sudden you're the most heartless bastard on earth. It's up to you …'

A crushed Lawrence barked his answer down the phone. 'I'll see you at 10am. Don't be late. And don't forget you still owe me a fucking jaw-dropping exclusive for this paper. I want it soon.'

He had hung up before an ecstatic Clarissa could answer. The smile on her face stretched even wider.

———

Having just arrived back in the UK from Muscat, Nush sunk her bronzed body into the backseat of her chauffeur-driven Mercedes. Ever since hearing about Regan's TV announcement, Nush's head had been a typhoon of torment. Thoughts of Lawrence cheating on her heavenly mother raced around her mind and the notion of Regan actually being her sister made her shudder with confusion. Her head seemed fit to burst. She thought of Jake … thank God for him. She couldn't wait to be in his arms again.

She reached for a miniature bottle of spirit from her Marc Jacobs tote bag, opened it and downed it in one. There were other bottles clanking against each other inside the bag's plush interior. What was the point of having family private jets with stacked mini-bars if you didn't use them?

She looked at her watch. It was 8.30am. Nush had tried to phone Regan constantly, but to no avail. First of all, she needed to see her father. She needed to know the truth for herself. Had he known that Regan was his all along? Did he cheat on Lysette? Was Montana just one of many?

Nush ordered the chauffeur to take her to *The Daily Staple* offices. As she did so, she reached down and took another bottle of spirit from her bag. She put it to her lips and tipped it back, feeling the warmth of its taste easing its way down her throat as she sunk further back into the freshness of the leather.

By the time the Mercedes pulled up outside the newspaper offices an hour later, Nush had worked her way through the contents of her bag. Her head felt overloaded with what needed to be said, but the potent mixture of alcohol made the task ahead seem more bearable. Confronting Lawrence had never been one of Nush's strong points. His knack of belittling her and making her feel feeble had quashed her in the past but today she needed to be strong.

Nush stumbled slightly as she exited the Merc and headed into the lobby of the *Staple* building. The clock above the reception desk read 9.42am. Lawrence should be at work by now. She headed to the lifts and pressed the button for the floor to his office. The movement of the lift as it headed upwards made Nush's legs buckle momentarily beneath her. She steadied herself by placing her hand against the elevator wall.

'I'm here to see my father,' Nush snapped at the receptionist positioned outside the glass front of Lawrence's office. The blonde teenager sat up swiftly as she motioned towards the glass. 'He's not here as yet, Ms Silvers. You can wait in there if you'd like.'

Pushing open the door to Lawrence's office, Nush headed straight to the drinks cabinet and poured another drink. Sitting herself at Lawrence's desk, Nush picked up the phone and dialled Regan's number. 'Might as well do something useful while

I'm waiting,' she slurred. She was surprised when a voice answered. It was a voice that had just woken up. 'Er … hello …?'

'Regan, it's me, Nush … we need to talk.'

Regan could tell Nush was pretty drunk from the moment she picked up the phone. Even though Regan felt like hell, the sound of her best friend's voice brought a stream of clarity to her senses. It took a moment for Regan to recognise her surroundings. As the room around her came into vision she realised that she was in her own bed, back at her London riverside apartment. *How had she arrived here?* She needed to cast her mind back …

—

When Regan had regained consciousness after fainting she had been lying across the back seat of the *Wild Child* people carrier. Leo had been driving. There was no sign of Grace, Montana, or anyone else connected with the past 48 hours.

As she stirred, Leo turned to look at her. It had been a look that said a thousand words. She knew that whatever had happened was unforgivable. Turning back to the steering wheel, staring out at the road ahead, he had begun to speak. 'You're awake, then. I'm not sure you'll remember much about what's been going on so I'll fill you in. First off, you lost the show. Grace's sales were better and she didn't go on air completely blitzed and tip food all over her mother. Neither did she call her mother a slut and tell the world who her real father was. Our viewing figures will be through the roof and you've probably just turned this show into a bigger phenomenon than even I had hoped. But personally, I'm really fucked off with you. After everything, you go and balls it up. Every human on the planet has been watching you turn from a drugged up little party animal into a talented, captivating young woman and now … well, you're back to square one. Off your tits on national TV. It's not exactly how I hoped this show would end.' Leo banged his hand on the steering wheel as he finished his sentence. His frustration was clear.

'But Leo, I was in that state because Grace gave me a tablet for my headache. The bitch sabotaged me. She must have slipped me an E.' She still felt nauseous.

'Grace says you offered her one before the show. She wisely refused. Your love of drugs is not exactly top secret is it, Regan? I know Grace has had her moments but at least she had the sense to say no to you.'

Regan couldn't believe what she was hearing. Leo's words were clipped and cold, bordering on heartless. She could feel her anger rising. 'But *she* gave it to *me*. I could have died thanks to that silly bitch.'

'That silly bitch, as you call her, saved your life. It was Grace who talked to the doctor called to treat you and showed him exactly what you'd taken. At least he knew what he was dealing with.'

'What do you mean … *saved my life*?' Regan was incredulous.

'She'd seen where you'd taken the tablet from. She showed him the bag of pills you had in your handbag. You're lucky you're not getting done for possession. We've paid off the doctor with a hefty bribe to stop him going to the police. Thanks to *Wild Child* he can now afford a two week holiday in St Lucia if he wants.'

'But I didn't have any pills. I wouldn't have been that stupid.' The back of Regan's throat started to tremble as she spoke.

'Stupid! Don't make me laugh, Regan.' An angry Leo swerved the people carrier over to the hard shoulder of the road with a screeching of the brakes. He then turned to Regan, his lips quivering with anger. 'I've been the stupid one, Regan. Stupid enough to let myself fall for you. I really thought we had something. But no, you were stupid enough to go out and get trashed the night before the show. You were stupid enough to take a class A drug before going on live TV and I was the stupidest of all … to trust you.'

'But you have to believe me, Leo, it was Grace, not me. I would never do anything to hurt you. You know I've fallen for you too.' Regan's tone was pleading.

'I'll never believe anything you say ever again. Why should I? I've had a little present, you see. It was strapped to the steering wheel when I got back to the car. An envelope with my name on the front.' Leo's eyes seemed wide and bloodshot to Regan. For the first time since she'd regained consciousness she realised that maybe Leo had been crying.

Leo reached down into his bag and pulled out his laptop computer. He slipped his other hand into the breast pocket of his blazer and pulled out a memory card from a camera. His hands were shaking with rage as he did so. 'This is what was in the envelope. Well, this and a sheet of paper telling me to *enjoy what I saw.*'

He placed the memory card into one of the computer's connections and pressed the mouse key, sparking the screen into action. Within seconds, a video movie of the sweaty tangled bodies of Regan and Jake in bed together filled the screen. After a few seconds, Leo slammed the laptop lid shut. His face was shaded with fury.

'I trust you saw the date and time on the film, Regan. It was last night. Why should I believe what you tell me about today? How can I believe a woman I know I can't trust? I'll take you home, but then I'm gone … for good. You and the steroid king can do what you like.'

Regan knew that she had been taken advantage of. Grace had plotted to make her lose the show and it had worked. And Jake

… he must have planned the film. But why would he give the evidence to Leo? Regan just prayed that he had no intention of showing the same thing to Nush.

As Leo screeched off towards London again, Regan lay back down and closed her eyes, trying to block out the trauma that was circling around her like vultures over a fresh carcass. The next thing she knew she was waking up in her own bed and answering the phone call from Nush.

CHAPTER 70

'So, it looks like we could be chips off the same old Silvers block, then. I always wanted a sister, I just never planned on it being one of my best friends.'

As opening gambits go, it was a pretty bizarre way to start a conversation, but from the upbeat tone in her, albeit slurred, voice, Regan was guessing that Nush still had no idea about her evening of passion with Jake.

'Look, Nush, I really didn't intend for you to find out like this. I was going to tell you in person. I wanted to see your dad before saying anything to see if it was true. I was out of it on the TV thanks to bloody Grace Laszlo and the whole thing is a total disaster now.'

'Listen … *sister* … that actually sounds kind of good, you know. I'm about to see Lawrence to find out if it's true or not. What pisses me off is the thought of him cheating on my mother with yours. It's a touch tawdry. How the hell did you find out?'

Regan explained about her conversations with Montana and how the story had unravelled. She told her about the wedding day and her annoyance at Evie for being there. 'Of all the people, she meets my mother on a bloody plane and then they're chumming it up like bosom buddies.'

The mention of Evie set the alcohol-soaked brain of Nush into mental overdrive. 'Don't be too hard on her. You know your mother can be a very persuasive woman at the best of times.

Anyway, Evie's had things rough along the way, so we all need to stand united for each other.'

Regan was perplexed. 'Rough? Getting paid millions for a film, shagging the backside off Jeremy Pinewood and being touted as the next British Oscar winner … that's hardly rough. She's got it easy – she'll be settling down and having babies next …'

A loose-lipped Nush couldn't stop herself. 'Well, for your information, she and Jeremy haven't slept together yet. It would seem he's the ultimate gent. So the settling down and making babies theory is totally off the agenda. Plus the whole baby thing may still be a bit … er, raw, for Evie after her loss before.'

As soon as the words had thoughtlessly tumbled from Nush's lips, Regan sat bolt upright in her bed. 'What loss, you're not telling me Evie lost a baby … when?'

As Nush recounted Evie's New York nightmare, Regan's mouth hung open in disbelief. It was only when Regan had soaked in every word that she dared to speak.

'Jesus. The poor cow. She should have told us, we could have been there for her.' There was a moment's silence before a hesitant Regan continued. 'Look, Nush, you are sure about this aren't you … you're going to hate me for saying this, but you've obviously had a fair amount to drink. Have you not got this whole baby story a bit … er … confused?'

An indignant Nush was swift to answer. 'Evie told me in Muscat. Yes, I've had a drink or two, but coming from someone who got trashed on Class A on national TV and poured food all over her mother, you're hardly in a position to criticise about overindulging are you? And anyway, I'm about to meet *our* father so I need all the Dutch courage I can get. I think a good drink and you girls are the only things that keep me going sometimes. Oh, and the very horny Jake of course …'

A stab of guilt lacerated its way across Regan's body at the mention of Jake's name. It caused Regan to panic. How had she allowed herself to be so stupid? 'Look, Nush, I need to sleep. Let me know what Lawrence says, and tell him I'm coming to see him as soon as my head doesn't feel like it's been run over by a juggernaut.' There was a wavering in her voice as she continued. 'Nush … you know I love you, don't you … no matter what? I'd never hurt you. Your friendship means the world to me.'

In her inebriated state, Nush was not in the mood for any soppiness or padded birthday card sentimentality. 'Jesus, Regan, you're not getting all slushy on me, are you? Sleep that off straight away,' she replied dismissively.

As Nush hung up the phone, a noise sounded behind her. Swinging round on her father's leather chair, she saw a figure at the door. It was Clarissa.

'Oh, it's you, what are you doing here? Haven't you got better things to do, like pissing off back to Hollywood.' Nush spat the words out.

'For your information I'm here to see your father … Regan's too it would seem. We have a pre-arranged meeting.'

'He doesn't deal with trash like you. There's only one person he'll tell his side of the story to and that's me.'

Teasing the collar of the silk Fendi blouse she was wearing between her fingers, Clarissa smiled complacently. 'Actually, honey, *he* called the meeting and *he* wants to talk to me. So I think it's about time you got your facts right. But, to be honest, my dear, I think he'll be much more interested in what *I* have to say to *him*. I'm a mine of information …'

Clarissa let the words tail off. Before another word was said by either woman, Lawrence Silvers marched into the office. He fixed Nush with a stare that signalled a mixture of anger and fear. He knew he had some explaining to do. It was obvious that now was not the time, though.

'Anoushka, get out … I have some things to discuss with Clarissa. Whatever you want will have to wait …'

Nush was not ready to be brushed off. 'I've just got here from Muscat and we need to talk about you supposedly fathering my best friend. I think I take priority over this skank, don't you?'

'Right now, you don't … We'll talk later, when you're sober, for one.' His manner was brusque. Placing a hand on a protesting Nush's arm, he grabbed her, lifting her from the chair and guided her to the door. Within a few seconds she had been ejected from the office with the door slammed behind her. Nush knew that it was fruitless to argue. She would have to see him later. She looked back into the office as she walked towards the lifts. A grinning Clarissa ostentatiously waved at her through the glass.

Inside the office, Clarissa felt like the cat that had not just got the cream, but stumbled across the whole dairy. Lawrence motioned her to sit down. 'Right … I want to make this quick. I'll tell you what I know about Montana. You write the story, I approve every word to make sure that I come across as Mr Nice Guy and you get the by-line you want. I'll even film an interview for your Yankee show. You double cross me on this and I will personally make sure that you never write another story again because you'll have ten broken fingers. And I meant what I said about you still owing me a story.'

Raising her eyebrows and staring Lawrence straight in the eyes, Clarissa leant back in her chair as she spoke. 'Oh I've just discovered a story that your readers will lap up. Let's just say that it's all about a potential Oscar winner, the baby she sacrificed and the late father-to-be who never knew what a heartless bitch his lover was.' Even Clarissa wowed herself with how fabulous it sounded. She went on to tell Lawrence all about the exchange she'd heard Nush having on the telephone. Unbeknown to Nush, Clarissa had been eavesdropping at the door of Lawrence's office, devouring every word of her conversation to Regan.

CHAPTER 71

Stafford was reading his Venice guide book as he sipped his red wine in one of the softly-lit dining cars of the Venice Simplon-Orient-Express. Languishing across from him were Brad and Montana. 'It does all sound wondrous ... the magical atmosphere of the Carnival, the rich tapestry of art and architecture, the decadence of the Film Festival and of course the romance of the waterways and gondolas. I need to find a swarthy gondolier to prod his oar in my direction. I've always found those Italian boys just *delizioso*.'

Stafford was ecstatic to be heading towards one of the most opulent cities in the world in the zenith of style. His travelling companions appeared not to be sharing his delectation, especially Montana.

'Oh, just *shut up*, Stafford. All you've done for the last hour is bang on about bloody Venice. I'd rather be back in LA, hiding from the world. Do you know what it's like to be a laughing stock?'

Nothing was going to dampen Stafford's spirits. 'No raining on my palazzo, if you please. The TV incident may have been a little bit ... *unexpected,* shall we say, but it was your crazed cuckoo of a daughter who ended up with egg on her face, darling. Your blissful *Babylon* sold out and made you a small fortune. The Glampire grows ever bigger.'

'She may have had egg on *her* face, Stafford, but I ended up with sweet and sour sauce all over mine. Plus this business about the identity of her father going public is not good press. What will my adoring fans think about me being a working girl back in the day? I'm supposed to be classy not brassy.'

Taking her hand in his, Brad tried to calm Montana's worries. 'To be honest, it doesn't look like it's done you any harm whatsoever. My phone hasn't stopped ringing since the show aired. The producers at *Peregrine Palace* have said your job is safe. They reckon the whole scandal of how Regan was conceived gives you an air of gritty reality that the viewers will adore. Virtually every paper in the world wants to interview you and I've had approaches from at least three Chinese food firms offering you megabucks to be their next campaign celebrity face … and *yes*, I turned them down, my angel.'

'I'm going to have to pull off some of the best acting of my career in Venice if I'm to schmooze the beauty press. I just hope the whole thing dies down before they arrive. When are they expected?'

'We have a good few days before you have to do any meeting and greeting. The only thing you need to worry about for now is checking out the Basilica Di San Marco and what glassware to buy in Murano.'

Stafford peeped with excitement. 'Oh, those lovely glassblowers. Now if ever there were men who knew what to do with their lips, then it's those boys. They can blow me anytime they like …'

Brad and Montana spoke in unison. 'Stafford … just shut up!'

———

The unique city of Venice was on the mind of a few other people as well. With the Film Festival just over a week away, Stephanie Love had already packed her suitcase and insisted that her first class flight be confirmed.

At the Beachwood Canyon home of Jeremy Pinewood, his imminent departure for Venice left him with mixed emotions. He would be pleased to see Evie again. They could play out their picture perfect coupling for the world to see. As far as Evie was concerned, their relationship was more or less perfect. It was Jeremy who had cause for worry … one man could upset everything, Stafford James. He was the one weak link that could show Jeremy's relationship with Evie for what it really was – a polished Hollywood lie.

Stafford's financial greed was now beyond irritating. It was becoming a major migraine. He'd thought that two hefty deposits into Stafford's account would be sufficient. An insidious text message that morning had proved otherwise.

'Jeremy – am heading towards Venice as I text. Shall be there for the Film Festival. Know you will be too. Such an expensive city I hear. How I'll make my Euros last I'll never know. Maybe you could help with my expenses.'

Jeremy knew what he had to do. If he kept bowing down to Stafford's demands then he would never be free of him. He would need to show Stafford that he would never get the better of him. Replying to his blackmailer's text he typed 'Shall ring you in Venice and arrange to meet to give you what you need'.

When Stafford had read the text in the sanctuary of his compartment on board the Orient Express, he had assumed that Jeremy's text meant that he would be the recipient of yet another financial reward from the film star. His avaricious mind immediately started planning what he could spend the money on. If he'd have scrutinised the message again he might have realised that, in fact, Jeremy actually planned on giving Stafford something completely different and a lot more sinister.

———

Evie knew that she had to dazzle in Venice. She'd spent endless hours when she was younger watching coverage of the Film Festival, marvelling at how the actors with their chiselled features and the starlets with their perfect smiles won over the critics and fans.

It had been a spectacle that had always enchanted her. She'd seen vintage footage of Katherine Hepburn from the 1930s and Laurence Olivier from the 1940s and been hypnotised by their flair. It was a place that Evie had always dreamt of and this was going to be *her* year. In just a matter of days she would be taking her rightful place as a cinematic icon outside the Palazzo Del Cinema on the Venetian Lido. As well as the red-carpet appearances throughout the Festival, there were press junkets, TV interviews, parties to attend … and every one of them required a differently dazzling designer gown. Evie knew that she would look nothing short of chic perfection. She would make Jeremy proud …

———

Lawrence watched the screen of the immense plasma TV mounted to his office wall flicker into high-definition life. It had been a full and arduous day and he needed to unwind. He'd spent the morning being grilled by Clarissa about his past 'affair' with Montana. The entire story was due to run in the next day's paper. It was not something he relished hitting the newsstands.

At least his tabloid notoriety would be short-lived. Clarissa had left to do some serious digging about Evie's abortion story. She reckoned that it would be easy enough to hunt down the details of the termination and the whereabouts of Jerome's family. Evie had killed off their grandchild without them even knowing. Clarissa was sure that she could clinch the juicier details of the story within days and give Lawrence the exclusive he hankered for. For Clarissa, it would be the ultimate comeback. Her name above the biggest story of the year in the newspaper that had fired her. How bittersweet.

Lawrence had already instructed his deputy editor that the story would be coming and that he should drop whatever was scheduled for the front page that day. To quote Lawrence, 'I don't care if the fucking Prime Minister suddenly announces he's a cross-dressing serial killer, you make sure this story gets the biggest splash this paper has ever given. And don't breathe a word until this comes in. Not to my daughter, not to anyone. If this gets leaked, then I know it's come from you and I'll have your bollocks for cufflinks.'

Flicking through the digital channels on his TV, he stopped as Evie's face filled his screen. The voiceover was announcing that she would be appearing at the forthcoming Film Festival. Stock footage of previous red-carpet appearances from Evie and snapshots of her and Jeremy together rotated before Lawrence's eyes. Venice was just days away … the timing was better than even he had realised. If Evie was to be the toast of Venice then the story couldn't explode at a more perfect moment.

He made another call to his deputy, instructing him in no uncertain terms that the story was to run on the day of Evie's big appearance at the Film Festival. He then made a call to Clarissa telling her that she was to do 'whatever it takes' to have the story ready for publication in just a few short days. Clarissa assured him it would be and that she would take great pleasure in personally delivering it to Evie. Lawrence may not have liked Clarissa but he had to admit that the little madam had a certain style.

Lawrence smiled for what felt like the first time in weeks. He'd had enough of the office and wanted some fun. He'd take his car and drive to Johnny's for a boys' night out. They'd talk about the old days, before life had become so bloody complicated.

His Audi was stationed in its usual spot in the secluded car park at the back of the offices. Lawrence took the elevator to the building's parking lot. It was a warm evening, the sun still radiant in the late summer sky. Lawrence looked up at the sun and became momentarily blinded by the light.

It was an action that cost him dearly. If he hadn't have been so distracted, maybe he would have seen the gloved hand come from behind him and swiftly run a razor-sharp knife across his throat. Maybe he could have been alert enough to fight off his attacker. As it was, it was too late. He could feel the blood bubbling from the hairline slice across his throat. He could feel his vision blurring and the bright sunlight around him fading from his eyes. Then it went dark. Darker than he'd ever known before.

CHAPTER 72

The morning edition of *The Daily Staple* detailed Lawrence's version of the Montana Phoenix scandal in scintillating detail. Under a smiling, some would say smug-looking, photograph of Clarissa Thornton, an image of a faux-heartbroken Lawrence stared out. Accompanying it was the straight-to-the-point headline 'MONTANA HAS BROKEN MY HEART'. The story portrayed Lawrence as the innocent victim. The only mention of Lawrence's infidelity came in one of the end paragraphs of the four-page story. To quote Lawrence, cheating on Lysette was 'a foolish, weak-willed action that I bitterly regret' but 'at least, if Montana proves that Regan is indeed mine, I may have gained a daughter ... even if Montana has made sure that I was ignorant for so many important, precious years'.

It was this quote that had caused Nush to angrily spit a mouthful of her cereal across the table at her London apartment. She'd been in a rage ever since she'd seen the paper. Clarissa's face peering out at her, taunting her failings, coupled with Lawrence's mock-misery, was not the best start to the day. She needed to speak to Lawrence, but his mobile went straight to voicemail. She decided to corner him at work. Yes, she would say what she needed to say to Lawrence and then she would arrange to see Jake. It would be a day for sorting out the men in her life – the one she currently loathed and the other who she was falling in love with.

——

Regan too, had been poring over every word of Lawrence's dejection in the paper. It left her confused and feeling empty. *Would Lawrence be able to fill the father-shaped gap that had always been so apparent in her life?*

She knew better than anyone not to believe everything that she read in the newspaper, but Lawrence's story had touched a chord inside her. Maybe she and Lawrence could learn to love each other and maybe it wasn't too late to forge a family bond. Everything that Regan had touched recently had crumbled like decaying brickwork. She'd lost *Wild Child*, attacked her mother live on worldwide TV, argued with Evie, somehow let herself sleep with Nush's boyfriend and lost the one man she really cared about in Leo. Her success rate was deflating quicker than a pin-pricked balloon, but at least all of that was in the past. *Wild Child* was done but, even though the outcome was not as she'd hoped, it had turned Regan into something she'd always desired. It had moved her out of her mother's shadow.

It was Montana who had caused the ill-feeling between her and Evie. Regan could see that. The mess with Evie could easily be sorted with a slice of humble pie. Besides, after Nush's revelations about the baby, Regan knew that she had more important things to discuss with Evie. The business with Leo was Regan's own fault. She had been weak. It had cost her Leo's love and she ran the risk of it costing Regan her friendship with Nush.

Regan knew what the day ahead involved. She would go to Lawrence's offices to speak to him about the paper and then she would go to see Nush to tell her the truth about Jake. Neither were tasks she relished, but she knew that both of them were highly necessary.

——

'It's great to have you back, angel. I can't wait to see you. How about I meet you at your work and we can have a cosy catch-up. Sound good? Right, I'll see you then.'

Jake Saunders clicked off his in-car phone as he sped across London and glanced in the rear-view mirror at his handsome features. He liked what he saw. A man in control. Today was going to be a good day, he could feel it. He'd been talking to Nush. He hadn't seen her since her return from Muscat. She'd wanted to meet the day before but he'd chosen not to. He'd been busy promoting his fitness gear and talking with his agent about a possible move Stateside. Things were definitely on the up. But before he could concentrate on his next career move, Jake knew that he had a few loose ends to tie up at home ... which was why he needed to see Nush.

—

Knowing that she would be seeing Jake in a matter of hours gave Nush a feeling of inner strength as she walked into *The Daily Staple* offices to corner Lawrence. She would say her piece. If Regan was her sister then so be it. Celebrity sisters ... it could be a winner. Kylie and Dannii Minogue, Jessica and Ashlee Simpson, Kim and Khloe Kadashian ... celeb siblings seemed to merit a double whammy of column inches in the worldwide press. No, on that front she could forgive her father ... what she couldn't forgive was the betrayal of her mother. She would never understand how he could sleep with another woman behind the beautiful Lysette's back.

'I'm here to see my father.' Nush barked at the receptionist outside Lawrence's office.

'Well, best of luck because nobody's seen him all morning. I have a list of people as long as my hair extensions waiting to get hold of him.' The receptionist held up her notepad with names scribbled across it.

Her manner vexed Nush. 'Well where is he, *sweetheart*, because I need to speak to him urgently?'

'If I knew that, I would have told this lot, wouldn't I? When he comes in, if he wants to see you, I'll ring you at your desk, shall I? Can I ask what it's about?'

'Just make sure you do. As I said, it's important … and no, you can't ask what it's about, that's my business, not yours … okay?' Nush flounced out of the room, the receptionist shrugging behind her as she went.

The same receptionist was having a virtually identical conversation with Regan some forty minutes later, but in a much cheerier tone. She ran her eyes up and down Regan's combo of skinny jeans, blazer and Louboutin heels as she spoke to her, completely in awe.

'I've not seen him all morning, Miss Phoenix,' she blustered. 'If he does come in I'll be sure to let you know straight away. Not even his daughter knows where he is, she's been after him too. It's great to meet you. You must be so busy right now …'

Regan cut her short. 'Did you say Nush's been here too? I was just about to ring her.'

'No need, take the lift to her office on the second floor.'

Heaving a sigh, heavy with trepidation at what she needed to say to Nush, Regan walked away from the reception, her heels clicking loudly against the polished floor. If she was any kind of friend to Nush, let alone a sister, she knew that she had to tell her the truth.

When she arrived at the door, she could see Nush inside scanning the pages of the day's *Daily Staple* yet again.

'Makes for interesting reading, eh?' Regan quipped.

Nush's face lit up as she turned to greet Regan. 'Hey there, lady cakes, looking good … nice heels, sweetie. Great to see you've inherited the family taste in high-end fashion.' Nush laughed and clicked her own pair of Yves Saint Laurent ankle boots together on the table. 'You here to see *dear old daddy* too?'

'Except he's nowhere to be seen, is he? Have you heard from him at all?'

'Not a dickie-bird. It seems that all of this headline-making has turned him into a bit of a hideaway. He's scared to face the music. I'll just wait until he turns up. Now give me a hug, it seems ages since I've seen you.'

Nush gripped Regan close to her, her arms tight around her. Regan hugged back, squeezing hard. She wanted to savour their moment of friendship, scared of what she knew she had to say.

'You'll crush me if you keep hugging like that, Regan, not to mention creasing this Jonathan Saunders silk dress. I want to look as delicious as possible for Jake when we meet.' She freed herself from Regan's embrace and twirled around, as if working the end of a catwalk.

Regan shivered inwardly at the mention of Jake and started to answer. 'Look Nush, we need to talk …'

A voice, masculine and deep, erupted from the office door. 'Well, look at this, two of my favourite ladies in the one room. Could things get any better?' It was Jake.

Nush ran across the office with a squeal and threw her arms around him, kissing him. Jake let the kiss continue for a few seconds before pulling away.

'C'mon, Nush, not in front of other people,' he laughed. 'We don't want Regan getting jealous, do we?' With that he winked at Regan. She shivered inwardly again. It may have been a summer's day outside, but inside Nush's office, Regan thought that the air had turned decidedly wintry.

CHAPTER 73

It had been relatively easy for Clarissa to slot together the pieces of the jigsaw puzzle about Evie's abortion. An internet search of Evie's past credits had given her the name of the off-Broadway production, which in turn had given her its cast list. Jerome Naylor's name was there loud and clear along with his career history and education details. A few probing conversations with a couple of the drama teachers at his old acting school and the offer to donate a fee towards the financing of the year's end of term production had secured the home address for Jerome's family.

Clarissa had then interviewed Jerome's mother and father, informing them about the termination. Despite their severe shock at learning about the potential grandchild they had lost and how they would have been linked to one of the most famous actresses in the world, a relatively small amount of money bought Clarissa the quotes she needed. Jerome's family were farm folk from the deep south of America and with times being hard, the promise of enough money to ease their financial worries for the year was eagerly accepted.

She'd arranged for a local photographer to take photographs of the 'woeful grandparents'. A little more than a day after she had first eavesdropped on the scandal, the story was complete. Even for Clarissa the process had been remarkably quick. As she finished the article, she phoned through to Lawrence to spread the good news. Clarissa was perplexed to find there was no reply.

—

As Jake walked into Nush's office, he turned to shut the door behind him. It was an odd thing to do and it didn't go unnoticed by Regan. It made her feel even more uncomfortable. He leant forward to kiss Regan on the cheek, said 'Hello' and then followed it with a whispered 'again' in her ear. The sound of his voice in such close proximity spooked her. Eerily he added 'Did you enjoy the Rohypnol, Regan?' Suddenly it all made sense … she'd known that she'd have never consciously slept with her best friend's man. Jake had obviously planned the whole thing – but why?

In her head, Regan was willing herself to speak. It would have been easy to just open her mouth and allow the words 'Nush, I'm sorry, but I was stupidly duped into sleeping with your boyfriend,' just tumble from her lips, but something was stopping her. Fright fused with confusion. She wanted to pummel her fists into Jake and blame him for her break up with Leo, but she knew that now was not the time. Like Leo would believe her anyway – professing that she'd been drugged by both Grace and Jake. It hardly seemed real to her and she knew it was the truth.

Jake appeared to have a swagger about him. He sat down at Nush's desk, leaving the two women standing. He seemed to possess an air of cockiness. Reaching into a holdall he'd been carrying, Jake pulled out a pink envelope and handed it to Nush. 'Here you go, babe. Here's a little something to say welcome back home. It'll tell you how much I've been missing you.' There was almost a sneer in his voice.

Nush's eyes lit up as she picked up the envelope. 'See, do I not have the best man in the world?' she said, turning to Regan and beaming a carefree smile. Regan herself could feel beads of sweat forming on her neck as Nush tore at the envelope. Everything told her that there would be more than just a schmaltzy loved-up Hallmark card inside the pink paper. She was right.

The front of the card was white, the only thing printed on it was a large black question mark, filling virtually the full length of the card. Nush's eyes narrowed quizzically as she stared at it. She'd been expecting hearts, flowers and teddy bears. Looking at Jake she grinned and said 'My international man of mystery, eh?' Jake stayed silent but raised one eyebrow.

The split second that it took Nush to open the card and watch as a photograph tumbled from it and glided onto the floor seemed like an eternity to Regan. She heard Nush saying 'What's this?' as she bent down to retrieve the photo. She was aware of Jake saying 'I thought you'd like to know what I've been doing while you've been away …' but it all happened in slow motion inside her brain. Her mind snapped back into normal time as Jake finished his sentence. 'Or should I say … *who* …'

Nush's face appeared to drain of all colour as she took in the details of the photograph. A naked woman in bed. A crumpled, freshly-vacated space alongside her. The face, eyes-closed, seemingly still deep in sleep – the face of her best friend, part of the Trinity, the face of Regan.

Finally finding her tongue, Regan attempted to speak, her words broken and stuttering. 'Look, Nush, this shouldn't have happened, it was him. I didn't mean to hurt you.' She knew her words were futile.

Nush felt all strength leave her legs, her knees buckling beneath her. The realisation of what she was seeing finally hitting her. Looking through teary eyes at both Regan and Jake in turn, all she could say was 'How could you?'

It was Jake who spoke, his words cold and full of spite. 'It was easy. Your so-called friend was gagging for it. She has been ever since she feasted her eyes on me at your dad's house. When she was appearing on that shopping channel and I was there selling my sports gear … well, the opportunity seemed too good to miss. She gave me all this crap about wanting to be a shoulder to cry on if I needed to talk, but all she really wanted was for me to crawl inside her knickers. Obviously not getting it from your own boyfriend, were you? Or should that be your ex now? Did your producer like his film show?'

Regan knew she was defeated, crippled by her own fragility. All she could say was 'Why?'

'There was only one thing I wanted … and that was revenge. Revenge against the piece of trash who tried to ruin my career with her cruddy little gossip column.' He looked directly at a sobbing Nush. 'You may strike fear into most celebrities' hearts, darling, but not me … not the invincible Jake Saunders. You messed with the wrong person this time. Did you honestly believe for one second that I'd be falling for the nasty piece of work that slept with me and then decided to splash it all over the papers? I'm supposed to be a role model and all I was to you was another cheap and tacky scoop for your daddy's rag.' Despite the venom in his voice, Jake remained seated at the desk, eerily calm in his explanation.

As Jake's words smashed into her like a clenched fist, a confused Nush spoke through her tears. 'But you said you enjoyed that night, that you wanted to be with me and not Mae-Ling.'

'The sex was great. I'd be lying if I said otherwise. God knows I needed it. My relationship with Mae-Ling was over long before you stuck your grubby little oar in, trying to crucify me in public in your pathetic column. You thought you'd get the better of me? No chance. I'm the victor – it's how I'm trained. You wrote your own downfall the moment you wrote about me. I'd planned to dump you publicly, let the world see what a malicious bitch you are, but Regan made it so much easier and far more painful for you than even I'd imagined. This way you lose me and your best mate. Diddums.' Jake's words were childish and mocking. 'At least you can run back to daddy, eh? Oh no, he's always treated you like shit too, hasn't he, and made you feel second best. Well get used to it, because that's all you'll ever be.'

A bewildered Nush could only whimper. 'I thought you wanted me …'

The robotic calm in Jake's voice melted and was replaced by malice and anger. 'I wanted you to feel how I felt when I read your seedy little column. You didn't give a damn about me, my career and what I had with Mae-Ling. You didn't know that our relationship was already on the rocks. As far as you were concerned, you just wanted to prove yourself as *the big I-Am* again to your daddy. You bang out your low-rent scoops and don't think about who you're hurting. Well, now you know what it's like to be hurt and to lose those you care about.' Jake pointedly looked at Regan as he said the last sentence.

'Mae-Ling would still be alive if it wasn't for you. She only went off the rails because of your story. I may not have loved her anymore but she was still Famke's mother. My daughter will grow up without a mum because of you … how does that make you feel?' He was silent for a few seconds before delivering his final verbal blow. 'Stupid question, really. You know how that feels, don't you? You lost yours at an early age after all. Every time you think about your mother in the future, think about my daughter too … because her mother's blood is on your hands. I hope you can live with yourself.'

Grabbing his holdall, Jake pushed his way past the desk towards the door, shoving Regan roughly as he did so. She had never been more distressed. To watch one of her best friends being emotionally crushed in front of her was awful.

Regan knew that she had to make the first move. Without saying a word, Regan wrapped her arms around Nush and held her tight. She was half expecting Nush to push her away, abhorred by the contact. Instead Nush just placed her head against Regan's chest and wept. To Regan it signalled that maybe she and Nush could actually survive what had just happened. It was only then that Regan dared to whisper, 'I'm sorry'.

CHAPTER 74

At 6.51am two days later, the body of Lawrence Silvers was found by the bin men emptying one of the dumpsters in the car park at his offices. It was clumsily buried under a pile of bin bags. According to the police, who cordoned off the area straight away, his body had been there about 60 hours. One of the first officers to arrive on the scene was DS Cole, the man who had investigated the murder of Mae-Ling. The brutal murder of Lawrence Silvers led DS Cole to believe that the two murders may be linked. The first person he called upon was Nush. The news had shocked and saddened her, leaving her with a feeling of numbness. Her father was gone for good. Someone had killed him.

Nush had spent much of the last 36 hours trying to contact Lawrence. She'd wanted to know the depth of his betrayal to Lysette and his thoughts about Regan. Regan herself was with Nush when DS Cole had broken the news about Lawrence. She'd been with her friend ever since the showdown with Jake.

Nush had wanted to hate Regan for what she had done but strangely she couldn't, especially when she told her about the Rohypnol. Jake was to blame and had taught her a lesson that she would never forget. It was one that would hopefully strengthen her for the future. The women knew that they would have to try and put the whole sorry episode behind them if they were to remain friends, to remain sisters.

During his interview with Regan, DS Cole brought up the subject of Montana. 'What about your mother? We'll need to speak to her about Mr Silvers. Do you know where she is?'

'She's in Venice. She left straight away after the … er, altercation we had on TV. She hasn't seen Mr Silvers … *my father*, in years, as far as I'm aware.'

As DS Cole talked to Nush, He enquired about Jake, Harry and Sadie. Nush explained that she and Jake were no longer together, but that she had no reason to believe that he would want to kill her father. On the subject of Harry and Sadie, however, she couldn't be so sure, and filled the policeman in on the story of Sadie's unexpected pregnancy and the subsequent changing of Lawrence's will.

'So Harry would have nothing to gain from Lawrence's death?' probed DS Cole.

'No, if you're looking for someone who would gain financially then I would imagine you'll be looking at me. Although my father hadn't divorced Sadie before his death, so she might be entitled to something as his wife … albeit a cheating one.'

'What about any business acquaintances? Had your father made any enemies on that front?'

'My father was one of the most ruthless men in his field, DS Cole. I am sure he must have made more enemies than Adolf Hitler, but I wouldn't know who. You should speak to his right hand man, Johnny Erridge. He knew my father better than anyone. I'll get you his number.'

By the time DS Cole had left Nush's a few hours later, he had a list of numbers of people he needed to speak to. He just hoped that one of them could lead him to the murderer of Lawrence Silvers and maybe even to the person behind the killing of Mae-Ling Ch'en.

—

Johnny Erridge had been crying all day. The last time he had cried was when he had watched his beloved Tottenham Hotspur being beaten during extra time by Coventry City in the FA Cup Final. Grown men didn't cry. Not unless they had good reason. But Lawrence's death had dealt him a cruel blow. To Johnny, Lawrence had always been there, like a sparring partner to learn from. It was hard for Johnny to grasp that he was now gone for good. Johnny knew that it was his duty to tell his boys. He'd phoned his pride and joy, Seth, in the States already. Now it was time to inform Ashley.

Knocking on the door of Ashley's apartment, Johnny could feel tears welling up again as he thought of Lawrence lying dead at the city morgue. He rubbed his eyes squarely with the back of his hand to try and compose himself. There was no answer from behind the door.

Johnny left it a few moments and then knocked again, this time louder. Maybe Ashley was asleep. Perhaps he'd heard the news and had left to comfort Nush. *He'd always had a soft spot for that girl.* When there was still no answer after several minutes, Johnny decided that he should let himself in and leave a note for Ashley to ring him.

Reaching into his jacket pocket, he pulled out a set of keys. Even though he hadn't been to Ashley's flat in years, he was sure that he still had a key from when he first moved his son in there. He tried a few keys in the door. It was the third attempt that was greeted with a satisfying click as the door swung open. Removing the key, Johnny stepped into the darkness and called Ashley's name.

There was no response. Johnny flicked on the light. He gasped sharply as light flooded the room. Every wall was covered with newspaper cuttings featuring Nush. Photos of her as a child, playing alongside Seth and Ashley, were peppered in between the cuttings.

As if the newspaper cuttings weren't chilling enough, something caught Johnny's eye that disturbed him even more. In the corner of the room, placed neatly on an armchair, were a pair of gloves and a knife. Alongside them was a large chunk of metal. They were all stained with blood. It was as though they had been displayed with pride. An avalanche of dread and horror pulverised its way through Johnny's body at his discovery.

'What are you doing here?' Ashley's voice sounded cold and callous as he entered his flat, surprised to find his father there. 'You never come here.'

'I wish I'd never come now. Look at this place, Ashley, what are all … all of these …?' He indicated the cuttings on the wall, his voice full of horror at his own offspring.

'They're all for my Anoushka, so that I can see her every time I open my eyes. She belongs to me. You know as well as I do that Anoushka and I should be together. It's all I've ever wanted. It's our destiny.'

Johnny could see a madness in Ashley's eyes. He'd always considered Ashley to be something of a misfit, but this was beyond his comprehension. Johnny fixed his gaze back to the armchair and the objects placed there. 'And those …?'

Ashley's answer was again matter of fact. 'My trophies – they allowed me to do what I had to do. Now if you don't mind, I'd rather you leave.'

Johnny didn't need to be asked twice. He pushed past his son and ran out of the apartment. He knew exactly what he had been looking at and he knew exactly what he had to do. It would be the hardest thing he had ever done, but he would do it … in honour of Lawrence.

CHAPTER 75

It was the kind of moment that Evie had always dreamt of – a solid wall of paparazzi flashes greeting her as she stepped from a private shuttle boat onto a docking platform at the back of the famed Westin Excelsior Hotel at Venice Lido. Evie angled her body to perfection, making the most of each and every camera lens and working her couture Marios Schwab dress to its full potential. She couldn't imagine anyone on earth being happier than she was at that instant. It was her perfect moment.

As Evie sashayed into the reception of the hotel she didn't utter a word, but her fashionable entrance, complete with a smile on her face and the raising of her hand in acknowledgement of those around her was to be the image that would be splashed across newspapers and magazines the next day.

———

Jeremy had arrived in Venice six hours beforehand. By his own choice, his entrance had been more low key than Evie's. Determined to avoid any press, Jeremy had instructed his agent to arrange for a car with blacked-out windows to take both him and Mario, on hand for make-up duties, from the airport to a remote dock where he could then catch a private boat to another hotel on the Lido. He'd chosen the Hotel Des Bains, located just five minutes from the Westin and featured in his favourite Dirk Bogarde film, *Death in Venice*. Once there, Jeremy had changed into tattered jeans, a T-shirt and baseball cap and walked to the Westin. As he casually strolled through the back doors of the hotel, none of the press or any of the legions of fans gathered there recognised him.

Staring out at the Adriatic through the enormous window of his suite, Jeremy contemplated the hours ahead. He would have to meet up with Evie that night and make sure that photos of them dining romantically together were made available to the world's media. What he didn't want made public was his other planned rendezvous for the night. He had an appointment with Stafford. It was the meeting that he hoped would finally get the parasitic Stafford off his back.

Stafford himself was just closing his own hotel room door after seeing off his 'trade' for the afternoon, a lissom and flexible deity of a gigolo named Rodolfo, whom Stafford had hired by the hour. Having waved off Montana and Brad to entertain the world's press on the final day of their *Babylon* junket, Stafford had wanted to kill some hours partaking in what he enjoyed most – sex. To Stafford, it was hundreds of Euros very well spent.

Not that he needed to worry on the finance front. A text from Jeremy a few hours before had informed Stafford that they were to meet that evening. Jeremy had given him the name of a small bistro-cum-hotel on the outskirts of Venice. According to Jeremy, it would be 'wonderfully private and cater for their every need'. Stafford had the feeling that maybe Jeremy wasn't just going to reward him financially and that perhaps a repeat sexual performance of what had happened between them in LA was in order. He was to be there at 10pm. That gave him five hours. Just enough time for a catnap, a power shower and a dose of Viagra before playtime. He figured the little blue tablet might come in very handy with Jeremy – it certainly had with Rodolfo.

———

Men were supposedly the last thing on the minds of Nush and Regan as they checked in at reception at the Hotel Des Bains. No, the two women were not in Venice to find partners. They had both learnt their lessons in love recently. They were there to support Evie, the Trinity coming together to put on a united front.

It had been an awful week for Nush and Regan. Lawrence's death and the subsequent funeral had been difficult for Nush and her new sister. It had pushed both of them full throttle into the headlines once again.

It had fallen on Nush to arrange the funeral. It had been held in the chapel at Kingsbury, where Lawrence had married Sadie years earlier. Sadie herself had chosen not to attend, preferring to stay in the States where she had decamped after leaving Harry. Harry had come but had stayed silent throughout the service and left without a word afterwards, his grief at his father's death and the preceeding rift between them etched onto his face.

Apart from Regan, who would never now get to speak to Lawrence as her father, his work colleagues and a garrulous Clarissa, who had managed to gatecrash the ceremony at the last minute, the only other person of note in attendance was Johnny Erridge.

One man who was definitely not in attendance was Johnny's son, Ashley. He was unable to attend. He would be unable to go anywhere for a very long time to come. He was facing a double-murder charge for the deaths of both Lawrence and Mae-Ling. It had been Johnny who had informed DS Cole of the grim discovery of the murder weapons at Ashley's flat.

A crazed Ashley had been arrested and kept at Her Majesty's pleasure ever since. His confession to the police had been covered in every national paper. He was proud of his actions and didn't regret either of the killings. He'd slaughtered them both because of his loyalty to Nush, the woman he had always idolised. In Ashley's warped mind he was certain that one day he and Nush would be together. Having read about Mae-Ling's threat to Nush's life, Ashley knew that there was only one answer … to dispose of her for good. He knew he had to dispose of Lawrence too, after he'd witnessed his brutal treatment of Nush at Kingsbury. How could one man be so malicious? The slap had sealed Lawrence's fate. Ashley just had to pick his moment. The act itself was an easy one. Ashley knew where Lawrence parked, he knew that the car park was secluded. He knew that all he'd have to do was lie in wait. He'd seen the *Staple* buildings a thousand times with Johnny. Hide behind the dumpsters, use the knife wisely and dispose of the body. Simple. The only thing he hadn't planned for was his own father's betrayal.

Ashley's confession made it an open and shut case. Double murder would equate to two life sentences. In his messed-up mind, Ashley knew that Nush would wait for him.

—

'I've spoken to Stephanie. She knows we're here, but Evie doesn't have a clue. She's dining with Jeremy tonight for the necessary photo opportunities and no doubt for a romantic catch-up. Then they'll just chill before the teaser screening and press conference tomorrow. I reckon if we swing by to the hotel as they're hitting the dessert then we could share a nightcap or two with them before Steph imposes a curfew. Apparently she's monitoring Evie's actions like an army general.'

Nush was directing her words at Regan in their hotel suite. Regan was busy hanging a selection of expensive designer dresses into the room's armoire.

'It'll be good to see her in the flesh again. I haven't seen her since the debacle of Montana's wedding. That seems light years ago now. So much has happened in between.'

'You've spent hours on the phone to Evie recently, apologising for your behaviour at the wedding, and you've listened to her reasons for not telling us about the baby. It's obvious that Evie still loves you dearly. I just want you, me and Evie to relax together, as only best mates can. You and I can chill and Evie can do what she does best … give another dazzling public performance …' Nush started to grin as she finished her conversation … 'And she can finally tell us what Jeremy has got hidden down his trousers, because I'm hoping tonight's the night we can find out if he's hung like a Grand National winner … and I mean the horse, not the jockey!'

Shutting the armoire doors, Regan began to laugh. 'They still haven't *done it*, have they? Maybe this Venetian air will be just the aphrodisiac they need.'

CHAPTER 76

The opulence of the Westin Excelsior has been famed as one of the most decadent hot spots for the European in-crowd for over a century, but even by its own prestigious standards the buzz of expectation as Evie and Jeremy walked into the domed grandiosity of its restaurant was electrifying. Evie had chosen a floaty Miu Miu dress, accessorised with opal earrings. He looked matinee-idol-delicious in a coal-black double-breasted Hugo Boss suit. A day's worth of designer stubble speckling his face gave him an extra air of heart-throb machismo.

Evie had hoped that she and Jeremy would have had a few idyllic moments together in their hotel suites. But with Stephanie bombarding her with her Italian itinerary and Jeremy insisting on *getting over his jet lag with an early evening sleep*, any notions of romance had been thwarted. The ripple of desire that had been running through Evie had now turned into a stream of frustration.

A wave of applause rippled around the restaurant as they both took their places at their table, Jeremy gallantly holding out Evie's chair as she seated herself. It was a table for two, Stephanie had insisted on it, despite the fact that she was at the next table, alongside Jeremy's agent, the film bosses behind *The Bouquet Catcher* and a sulky looking Mario. The make-up artist still found it niggling to see Jeremy acting out his romance with Evie, despite having satisfied his employer with a frenzied bout of sexual manoeuvres of porn star expertise just hours before.

'You look magnificent, Evie.' Jeremy squeezed Evie's hands across the table as he spoke, 'I trust the finest champagne for the finest lady in all Venice will satisfy?'

'Sounds good to me. I want the next few days to be as special as possible. This is all I've ever dreamt of and to be here with you … well, I couldn't ask for a better partner to share it with. I honestly believe we could be perfect together. I know we started off a little shakily but isn't it true that sometimes the rockiest of roads can lead to the most beautiful of places?'

Evie was sure that the evening ahead was going to be a pivotal one in their relationship. The seductive feel in the air, the majesty of their surroundings, the connection between them both … for Evie, it all augured well for the hours that were to follow.

———

Or so she thought. Swallowing her last mouthful of amaretto truffles at the end of her meal, Evie picked up her napkin and dabbed the edges of her lips. 'That was one of the most delicious things ever. Shall we order more champagne … my glass appears to be empty?'

Evie's head felt blissfully frothy and bubbly from the champagne she'd enjoyed throughout the meal. Between her and Jeremy they had managed to finish two bottles, although it had occurred to Evie that Jeremy certainly seemed to be filling up his own champagne flute a lot less than he did Evie's. Not that she minded. Jeremy had been the perfect dining companion. They had laughed, posed for photos, held hands throughout the three courses and they'd even indulged in a few flirtatious kisses, causing comment from an increasingly drunken and loud Stephanie at the next table. Her comment of 'Get a room, lovebirds,' after their last tender kiss had caused laughter around her table. To Evie, though, it was just what she desired. Holding Jeremy's hand she made her suggestion. 'Shall we get a bottle to go and take it …' She gave a momentary pause before finishing the sentence '… upstairs'.

Jeremy looked at his watch. It read 9.40pm. Placing his other hand on top of Evie's, he looked her squarely in the eyes. Evie could sense that something was troubling him. She already knew that his answer was not going to be what she wanted to hear. 'I'd love to, Evie, but our disappearing off together is not exactly the image I want to project. Especially in front of *that* lot.' He motioned to the film people sitting with Stephanie and his agent. 'We both need to be on fine form tomorrow for the press conference. You keeping me up all night would not exactly get me in the right frame of mind, would it?' Jeremy leant in and kissed Evie, sensing her disappointment at what he was saying. 'We've both got a busy day ahead, so I'm going to quit. I adore you, Evie … you know that don't you?'

All Evie could think was *so much for the perfect evening*. Her brain told her that Jeremy was right. It was better for them to get a good night's sleep before the furore of the next day. But she knew from the deep longing within her that she craved for Jeremy to carry her upstairs and make love to her. But as Jeremy stood up from the table and moved over to bid goodnight to Stephanie and the others, Evie knew that tonight was not to be the night. 'Look after Evie for me, will you? The jet lag is kicking in and I need an early night.'

Jeremy moved back to where an increasingly dejected Evie was sitting. 'I'm sorry, but if we went upstairs, I'd be asleep in seconds and that's the last thing I want to do with a beautiful woman like you. I'll see you in the morning. Goodnight, my love.' Jeremy leant over to kiss Evie fully on the lips. He rested there for a few seconds. Evie closed her eyes. Despite her annoyance at his protestations, he still felt good … amazingly so.

As they kissed, a voice alongside them chipped in. 'Goodnight? You're not leaving on our account, are you? We were hoping we could crash the party and we've both been desperate to meet the man who's putting a smile on our Evie's face.'

Evie opened her eyes to see Nush and Regan. Her mouth fell open in joyful shock at seeing her friends. Pointing towards the bar Regan said, 'There's a bottle of shockingly expensive bubbly on ice over there and four glasses … care to join us?'

As Regan refilled Evie's glass half an hour later in the hotel bar, there was still one of the four glasses that had remained empty and dry. 'I can't believe he's gone to bed for an early night. Three beautiful women, some of the finest champagne on earth and the world's hottest actress desperate to slip between his sheets, and he still bails out.'

'I know, it's totally annoying,' agreed Evie, 'but Jeremy is just being sensible. He's flown here from the States, he's jet-lagged and we do have a busy day tomorrow. He needs his sleep. I guess when you're that sexy and gorgeous you need a lot of beauty sleep. Bless him … doubtless he'll be dozing like a baby as we speak.'

———

Stepping from his water taxi and into the night air, Jeremy pulled up the collar of his overcoat and pulled his baseball cap further down his forehead. Thankfully the early September night air was chilly enough to suit his disguise. If ever there were a night when Jeremy didn't want to be recognised, then this was it.

Having made his excuses, albeit rather pathetically, to Evie, Nush and Regan about needing his bed, Jeremy had returned to his room and changed out of his suit. Then he met the taxi that he'd had Mario pre-order for him earlier in the evening at the side entrance to the hotel. That took him to catch a water taxi, which dropped him close to the bistro at which he'd arranged to meet Stafford. Again it had been the ever-loyal Mario who had chosen the rendezvous, knowing it to be away from the crowds of the city.

As Jeremy stood outside the bistro he took a sharp intake of breath and surveyed the scene through the window in front of him. The inside was dimly lit, just a few candles in bulbous bottles burning on every table. Wooden arches between the tables appeared to be draped with faux bunches of grapes, and framed scenes of Venice through the ages hung on the walls. Jeremy was grateful that there only seemed to be a handful of people seated at the tables. Checking his watch he could see that he was late, it was nearly 10.35pm. But he knew that Stafford would still be there. Pushing open the front door, Jeremy entered the bistro.

Moving to the bar, Jeremy ordered two glasses of red wine and took one in each hand as he walked to the back of the bistro. It was there that he saw Stafford, sitting smugly at one of the tables. Looking at the time on his mobile phone, he smirked, 'Evening. I hope you're not normally this tardy on set. I was about to give up on you … but I knew you'd come.'

Placing the drink on the table, Jeremy sat down opposite Stafford and whispered, careful that no-one could overhear their conversation. 'I've got you a red wine. In fact I've got everything you need. You're an expensive little shit, but it ends tonight. €500,000 and you're out of my hair for good.' Jeremy patted the breast pocket of his overcoat, indicating that the cash was concealed inside. 'You've had more than your fair share but it's over. You take your sorry little arse and scurry off into the distance, okay?'

It was Stafford's biggest payday to date, but he still wanted to push his luck further. If he was to leave Jeremy alone in the future, then he wanted to go out with a bang … literally.

'You enjoyed sex with me, didn't you?' Stafford fixed Jeremy with a lascivious gaze as he spoke. 'Loved seeing me down on my knees in front of you. Well I want more … and I think you do too. Why meet me in some seedy hotel otherwise? You could have transferred money to me if you wanted to. No, I reckon you wanted to see me again. Why don't you plough my sorry little arse before I disappear for good? One last shag for the road?'

Without saying a word, Jeremy downed the wine and stood up, ready to leave. All he said was 'Shall we go?' To Stafford, it was the green light he'd hoped for. Knocking back his own glass of wine, Stafford slid out from behind the table and followed Jeremy across the bistro. He'd expected him to head upstairs to the bedrooms. Instead he walked back out into the night air. A perplexed Stafford marched behind him.

Without looking back at Stafford, Jeremy spoke. 'Let's go down by the canal. It's quieter there.' As he walked, unnoticed by Stafford, he slipped a pair of black leather gloves onto his hands.

'Of course, you like getting your kicks alfresco, don't you? That is where we met after all. Why not, it's a bit chilly but I'm game if you are.' Stafford naively scurried along behind Jeremy, thoughts of money and sex swirling through his mind. They walked for about five minutes in silence, Jeremy working out where he wanted to go. Eventually he found a small path that snaked downwards, with steps leading to a secluded area underneath a bridge spanning the canal.

'This looks perfect … shall we?' Jeremy gestured. 'I'll give you exactly what you want here, away from prying eyes.'

Once underneath the bridge, Jeremy and Stafford were hidden away from the world. The only light came from the moon reflecting on the water.

'What comes first ... cash or cock? I'm easy either way. Tell you what, take this and you can give me the money afterwards. That'll make it nice and seedy.' He handed Jeremy a condom. It was only as Jeremy took the little silver packet from him that Stafford noticed that Jeremy was wearing the black leather gloves. A moment later Jeremy tossed the condom to the floor and in one swift move placed both of his gloved hands around Stafford's neck. He placed his thumbs together at the front of Stafford's throat and pressed down hard on his Adam's apple, causing Stafford's eyes to bulge and his mouth to open in horror.

Jeremy spoke in a raspy whisper. 'I could kill you now, snap your neck into a thousand tiny pieces and leave you to rot under here for the rats. Or you could do the sensible thing and quit while you're ahead. There's no more money and no more sex. You get it?' He pressed his fingers down harder against Stafford's neck as if to emphasise the point. 'We are through. If I ever hear from you or see you again then I will kill you, or I'll get someone else to do it for me. You'll spend your life looking over your shoulder, dreading the moment when someone will be there to finish you off. What's it to be?'

Stafford's hands were desperately trying to claw Jeremy's fingers away from his neck, but the actor's strength was too great. He could feel his head becoming fuzzy, his blood pounding in his brain as he stared into the eyes of his would-be killer.

'Had enough, have we? Is this where you die or do you give up?'

Stafford nodded feebly, knowing he was beaten. No amount of money was worth losing your own life for. A dead man couldn't spend.

The pressure around his neck decreased as Jeremy removed his hands. Stafford fell to his knees, trying to take in a lungful of air as he did so. Jeremy punched him to the ground and reached into Stafford's coat pocket to remove his blackmailer's mobile phone. He then turned and threw the phone into the canal, the machine making a plopping sound as it fell into the water. 'You won't need that again … and I meant what I said, if I hear from you again, you'll be wishing I'd killed you here.'

Stafford gazed blankly out across the canal from his position on the ground as Jeremy disappeared out of sight into the Venetian streets.

CHAPTER 77

The Laguna Room at Venice's Palazzo del Casino had been a whirlwind of activity since the early hours of the morning. Metre after metre of red carpet had been laid. Security guards with sniffer dogs had covered every inch of the building. Diligent staff members had cleaned the walls and high ceilings, positioning the beautiful drapes and polishing the wooden furnishings. By the time the world's movie press arrived late in the afternoon, everything was spotless.

Evie and Jeremy had spent the morning on the Pompeiana Terrace at the Hotel Des Bains giving interviews for various TV shows around the world. Evie revelled in the attention, changing into as many outfits as possible throughout the morning. It was a blessing she was on great form as Jeremy seemed to be agitated. When Evie questioned his bad mood, he blamed it on too much sleep. The truth was that he'd tossed and turned all night unable to sleep after his encounter with Stafford.

The interviews were all fairly identical, following the same line of questioning – wanting to know when the couple had realised that their love affair had moved from on-screen to off, whether they planned to make further movies together and what the secret of their chemistry was. It was fairly standard stuff and easy for Evie to autopilot her answers next to Jeremy's surliness.

Once the interviews were over, Evie and Jeremy were whisked back to their hotel by Stephanie to prepare for the press conference. Outfits were picked, hair was styled and make-up applied. It was only later, as Evie and Jeremy stood behind a huge silk curtain at the front of the Laguna Room waiting for their introduction, that a sudden bout of nerves hit Evie. Her legs felt as if they would give way from under her. Sensing her anxiety, Jeremy placed one of his arms around her and pulled her gently towards him.

'What if people don't like the film, Jeremy? We could be the laughing stock of Venice. A bad launch here and the movie will be pretty much doomed. They're only seeing part of it, but if they don't like it then nobody will bother coming to see the rest. I want this movie to really work … for both of us.'

She turned her face upwards to stare into his and stood on tiptoes to allow their lips to meet. Jeremy held her in his arms and they continued to kiss, his tongue exploring her mouth. It was only when they heard their names being announced that Evie allowed her lips to be parted from his.

The curtain lifted in front of them both and applause filled the room. The room was wall-to-wall faces. She spotted Nush and Regan at the front of the room. Nush raised one of her hands and formed her thumb and forefinger into an O.

The film's producer walked onstage to greet the couple and directed them to where they would sit to take questions. He then introduced the rushes of the film on a huge screen above Evie and Jeremy's heads. From the natural and genuine laughter that filled the room it soon became evident that Evie needn't have worried. Even the harshest of critics seemed to like the movie. As the rushes came to an end, the crowd rose to their feet, applauding the performances they had seen on screen. Evie felt close to joyful tears and turned to look at Jeremy. He, too, seemed overwhelmed by the reaction and leant forward to kiss Evie on the cheek. As he did so, he whispered in her ear, 'They love it'.

For the next forty minutes, both Evie and Jeremy answered the questions thrown at them. As the conference came to a close, the film's producer asked for any final questions. It was then that a voice erupted from the back of the room.

'Excuse me, excuse me … I do have another question. If I may say a little something before your stars disappear.' The voice belonged to Clarissa Thornton, who was striding down the centre aisle of the room. In her hand she held a folded newspaper.

Both Nush and Regan could feel their blood start to boil as Clarissa waltzed to the front of the room. 'Does that bloody woman never tire of making a last minute entrance?' seethed Nush.

Clarissa was basking in her moment in the spotlight. 'Clarissa Thornton, *Hollywood Daily* and *Wild Child* winning bidder for the accolade of writing a story for the UK's *The Daily Staple*. I believe Regan Phoenix from *Wild Child* and Anoushka Silvers from *The Daily Staple* are both here somewhere.' She looked straight at them both, a sideways grin emanating from her lips. 'It's nice to see them both enjoying themselves so soon after the funeral of their father. Poor Lawrence, barely cold in the grave and both daughters living it up. But so be it. I have news that would thrill Lawrence if he was still around today.'

There was an air of anticipatory hush that clung to the air. Had it not been for the fact that the world's showbiz press were literally gathered together in one room, Nush would have rugby tackled Clarissa to the floor to shut her up.

'Shortly before Lawrence's death I gave him the story that I owed him from my bid on *Wild Child*. It was a story that he was incredibly fired up about. Better than any story he'd been given by his own staff members lately, it would seem.' Again Clarissa made a point of staring at Nush. 'It's a story that he insisted should be published in tomorrow morning's *Daily Staple* to coincide with this Festival. It's such a pity that he never got to see the story that only a few days ago he was so excited about. The story of an actress from a privileged background who early in her rise to fame fell pregnant by accident. She then decided to abort her baby because it just didn't fit into her career plan. And what's more, she did it without even telling the father about it. It would make a heart-wrenching movie, don't you think … who would you want to play *you*, Evie? Care to comment?'

As Evie listened to Clarissa's words, it was as if the earth stood still. She could feel the sweat starting to form on the back of her neck. Jeremy's hand slipped away from hers as Clarissa held the newspaper in her hand aloft. But she could say nothing, any clarity in her mind shattered into pieces.

'Nothing to say, it appears. Not to worry, the world can read about it in tomorrow morning's *Daily Staple*, under my by-line of course. If anyone wants a comment from me about it, I'm staying at the Dona Palace.'

As Clarissa turned and marched back up the aisle and out of the room, a numb and weeping Evie felt herself being ushered offstage by Jeremy and a furious Stephanie. Just before Evie disappeared behind the curtain she looked over at Nush and Regan. They both had tears in their eyes too.

CHAPTER 78

Taking the sheets of paper from Evie's trembling hands, Regan read the copy of the article from the following morning's *Staple*. It had been faxed to them at the Excelsior on Nush's orders. 'Can't you stop the newspaper from being printed? You must own it by now, seeing as Lawrence is dead. We can't let that bitch of a woman ruin Evie's career.' Regan's voice was raised and soaked in desperation as she spoke to Nush. The two women, along with a shell-shocked Evie and an appeasing Stephanie, were all pacing around Evie's suite. They had been there ever since Clarissa's shattering announcement at the press conference over an hour ago.

Nush had spent the last twenty minutes on her mobile to Lawrence's solicitor back in the UK, desperately trying to find out if there was any way the story about Evie could be halted from going into publication. It had been a fruitless conversation.

'It appears not,' Nush explained, 'Father's will left everything to me ... except the newspaper. He left that to Johnny Erridge. I suppose it was his final blow to me, not that I'm particularly bothered, Johnny is welcome to it. I only ever worked there in the first place because Lawrence forced me into it. Rightfully, it ought to have gone to Harry. All of that business with Sadie changed that of course. According to the solicitor, my father figured that the newspaper was a man's domain, which is ridiculous. How god damned Dickensian can you be!'

'So what does Johnny say? Can't he stop it?' begged Regan.

'No, apparently Johnny thinks it's what Lawrence wanted. He left strict orders with his deputy that the story should run tomorrow as soon as Clarissa broke it to him. Johnny's guilt over Ashley means that there's no way he would disregard anything my father wanted.'

'It's too late now, anyway. The damage is done. Everybody knows. It'll be the talk of Venice, probably the entire planet by now.' Evie seemed resigned to her fate. 'This is a storm that I have to ride. It's the truth. I tried to hide it, but now the secret's out. I just wish it hadn't happened like this …'

'Look, Evie, I am so sorry, I didn't know Clarissa was standing behind me when I told Regan. There's no way on God's earth I would have ever let such a secret slip to her.' Nush had already told Evie exactly how she thought Clarissa had come to learn about the story. At first Evie had been scarlet with anger, but soon the feelings of exasperation had been replaced with an aura of contemplative calm.

'It's Jerome's family I feel sorry for. To find out now that they had the chance of a grandchild and I took it away from them is unforgivable. I should have talked to Jerome. I was scared … scared I'd done the wrong thing. But I'm not the first woman to have aborted a baby and I won't be the last. We can't turn the clock back and change things. It's in the past, but we need to sort out the present. Stephanie, we need to formulate a plan of action for the press. I will not let this spoil everything.'

It was the moment Stephanie had been waiting for. Ever since the shocking news had broken, Stephanie had been metaphorically sitting on her hands and biting her tongue, waiting for Evie to ask for her opinion. A good agent could always deal with the bad news as well as the good. In her mind she had already worked out exactly what was necessary.

Clasping her hands together as if in prayer and placing them to her mouth, Stephanie verbally sprang into action. 'Honey, you did what you deemed necessary back then in New York and there are a million women out there who have found themselves in a similar situation. You can be their voice. There's no shame in what you did, as far as I can see. It's deeply tragic, and there are things that need to be rectified … we'll have to arrange for you to meet Jerome's family, for one. There's a huge amount of face-saving we need to do there, but I honestly believe this is not going to affect your career. Every decent actress out there has had some kind of upset along the way and they still come back, stronger and as inspirational as ever.'

Stephanie was on a roll, her business mind speeding into overdrive. 'Drew Barrymore and the drug hell years, Mischa Barton being sectioned, Halle Berry's hit 'n' run, for God's sake … need I go on? The public like their stars to have a rough time now and again. Makes you all seem real. Even way back when you girls were mere twinkles in your mummys' eyes, Jane Fonda was kicking a cop and getting into all sorts of mischief, and people still adore her. If you're going to get through this, Evie, and you will, then you don't run away from it. You're still the most talented actress on the planet, in my opinion, and people love what you do. I'll call a press conference here tomorrow and you need to hold your head up high throughout it. I'll get you on the best chat shows around the world to explain what was going through your poor mind at the time you were pregnant. And then we all pray that a new bombshell is around the corner for some other Hollywood starlet to cope with … one who's not on my books! That way, you and the story about the baby will be off the front page of *The National Enquirer* before you know it.'

'God. She's good …' Regan was genuinely impressed by Stephanie's plan. 'I'd keep her if I were you …'

Evie's lips formed a semblance of a smile. 'Well, if you're looking for an agent I would recommend her. She may roar like a lion, but she's a pussycat really.' Evie turned to her agent. 'Go to it. What's done is done, and I'll answer whatever I have to. Also, I want to do a follow-up article in the *Staple*, my side of the story. They're the only newspaper I'll talk to, okay?'

Nush looked at her friend. 'You don't have to, Evie ... I caused this mess, you don't have to be loyal to the newspaper just for me. If I'm still working there then it's for a new boss. It's not a family affair anymore. I've got to decide what I want to do.'

'Well, before you make any rash decisions about your career, I want you to help get mine back on track. I'll give you the full exclusive, no-one else. You get to print it before I do any TV and I'll let people know that at the press conference tomorrow. Why I went through with the termination in my own words. Written by you and sod all to do with Clarissa Thornton. That woman gets nothing from me in the future ... get that, Steph? And I'll make sure that Jeremy feels the same.'

Stephanie nodded her head. 'Sure thing. Where is that hunk of a boyfriend of yours anyway? Surely he should be here giving you a bit of support?' As she finished talking there was a knock on the hotel suite's door. 'Talk of the devil, no doubt, I'll let him in and go organise the conference for tomorrow. May I suggest you girls bin any notion of heading off to the Festival parties to-night and stay here away from prying eyes. I can recommend the room service ... the ricotta spaghetti is button-burstingly divine.'

'Will do. Funnily enough, I'm not in the mood for partying,' replied Evie. 'Now let Jeremy in.' Another knock at the door signalled his impatience.

Stephanie headed to the door and pulled it open. She greeted the person standing there with curt execution. 'Oh, can I help you? I thought you were someone else? I'm afraid we're all some-what busy in here right now?'

Standing behind Stephanie, a chorus of female voices from all three women emitted the same word. 'Stafford …?'

CHAPTER 79

Whenever Stafford phoned Nush with his tales of LA tittle-tattle she was used to hearing his upbeat camp little voice on the phone, spilling the beans with lashings of glee and relish. As soon as he appeared at the door of Evie's suite, she knew that something was seriously wrong. His mood was decidedly sheepish.

Regan and Evie were equally perturbed. Evie had last seen him all dolled up in his designer finery at Montana's wedding, and Regan's last vision of him was running past her into the *Planet Shopping* studios to find Montana covered in Chinese food. Both times there had been a grin on his face. This time his face looked etched with worry. His eyes twitched between the three women. It was Evie who spoke first.

'Stafford, how lovely to see you … er, what are you doing here? If you've come to see me it's not really the best of times.'

Stafford seemed uncertain what to say. He genuinely liked Evie and suddenly his seedy little tryst with Jeremy seemed a lot more reprehensible than ever.

'N … n … no … thanks, it's not you I've come to see. It's Nush. I saw coverage of the conference on TV so I knew you were in Venice. The people on reception said you were here. Can we talk?'

Nush narrowed her eyes in confusion. 'It's as Evie says, this isn't the best time, we could meet up later for a drink, if you fancy. If you've heard what's been going on today then you'll know the three of us have some urgent things we need to sort out.'

'I need to talk to you … alone if possible. You'll want to hear what I've got to say.' Nush could see that Stafford was sweating, two droplets running down his face from his hairline. It wasn't really surprising as he was wearing a thick coat on top of a chunky roll-neck sweater which rose up to just underneath his chin. It may have been a cool September evening but inside the hotel the centrally-heated air was comfortably warm.

There was something about Stafford's manner which rang alarm bells with Nush. 'Why don't you come in? We can talk in the bedroom. It'll be private. Regan and Evie can wait out here. Besides, Evie's expecting Jeremy to arrive any moment. I think she needs some serious comforting after today.'

A twitchy Stafford looked from side to side, as if checking the space around him. He seemed disoriented. 'Oh God … of course … Jeremy. I'd better go … I don't want to spoil anything. Can I see you later, Nush? Not now … definitely not here.'

Nush scribbled down her hotel details. 'This is where I'm staying. Meet me in the reception there tomorrow morning.'

Stafford snatched the paper from Nush's hand. 'I'll be there, say 11am. I'm fine … but can you keep it to yourselves that I was here. I don't want anyone to know. Nobody at all.'

'Like who …?' quizzed Regan and Evie together. 'Would anybody actually care?' But Stafford was gone, running as quickly as his aching body would carry him down the hotel corridor.

'Oddball,' said Regan. 'It's no wonder he hangs out with my mother all the time.'

CHAPTER 80

Jeremy didn't like to be linked to any kind of controversy. It was not good for his image. The press conference had not gone to plan and Jeremy was worried that his so-far spotless reputation was about to be tarnished by association. The news about Evie's abortion was not what he needed in the run up to their film being released.

That was why he'd been holed up in his hotel suite ever since. He knew he should be there for Evie, but what if the movie-going public turned on her? He couldn't afford to be tainted and risk less bums on seats at his films. But, on the other hand, if the public did still back Evie then it wouldn't hurt Jeremy to be seen as the supportive boyfriend, there for his damsel in distress. He would have to wait and see.

The evening after the press conference Jeremy had slipped on another designer suit and headed off to one of the many industry parties taking place across the city. He and Evie had originally planned to go together, as guests of honour, but he felt it best if he showed his face alone … just in case.

An increasingly irked Mario, overjoyed to see Evie sidelined for once, had begged Jeremy to take him to the party. The response he'd received was brutally frank. Although the heavily endowed make-up artist was of use to Jeremy in the bedroom, escorting Jeremy to a fashionable industry party was not part of the deal.

Before heading out, Jeremy handwrote a note and slid it under Evie's suite door. It read 'What a day, in more ways than one! Hope you're okay. Decided to leave you to chill. Am off to one of the parties to big up our film. Shall see you tomorrow, love J x'.

It seemed a touch harsh and pragmatic, even uncaring. But Jeremy really didn't care. Had he delivered the note thirty minutes earlier, however, he certainly would have cared about seeing a very unwelcome visitor at Evie's door …

Evie had not exactly been thrilled to receive Jeremy's note. If ever there had been a time when she needed his strong arms around her it was now, but it seemed that playing the industry game and schmoozing came first in his book. She texted him twice, but received no reply. Eventually, annoyed by his lack of response, Evie switched off her phone.

She spent the night with Regan and Nush in her suite, picking at room service and flicking through the television channels. They hardly spoke, there was no need. It felt good to Evie to have them by her side. Sometimes words were surplus to requirements. The fact that they were in Venice at the most famous Film Festival in history was insignificant. They could have been anywhere. All that mattered was that they were together. They eventually all fell asleep in front of the TV watching *Pretty Woman*.

There was another note alongside Jeremy's when Evie awoke the next morning. It was from Nush. 'Girls, am off to the hotel to see Stafford. Let me know where and what time you're speaking to the press, Evie, and I'll be there for you. You can get through this. Love you girls. Nush x.'

Evie checked her watch. It was 8.45am. Letting her eyes adjust to the daylight streaming into the room, she saw that Regan was still asleep on the huge armchair opposite her. She started to stir as Evie began to brew the kettle. 'Cup of tea?'

'Please. What time is it? Where's Nush?' yawned Regan.

'Just before nine.' She handed Nush's note to Regan. 'She's back at your hotel to meet Stafford. Why don't you stay here? I can lend you some clothes, there's enough stuff here to fill Bloomingdale's and I could do with the support.'

'How are you feeling? Ready for the press conference?' Regan stretched as she spoke.

'Bring it on. All I will be saying is that my side of the story will be announced in *The Daily Staple*, written by Nush. I meant what I said yesterday. I have nothing to be scared of, there are no more secrets to hide. Milk with your tea?'

Somehow, Regan knew that Evie was going to be alright…

——

Stafford was wearing the same overcoat and high-necked sweater when he walked into the reception at Hotel Des Bains just before 11am. Nush was waiting for him. He seemed just as sheepish as he had done the day before.

'Are you not boiling in that outfit? It's warm outside and you're dressed up like it's mid-winter. Plus the same clothes two days running? That's not right for a fashionable gay man?' Nush needled.

'Can we go to your room now, please? I don't want to be seen.' Stafford hissed the words. Nush marched up the stairs to her room, Stafford right behind her. Once inside, she got straight to the point.

'Stafford, what's going on, who are you scared of? If you've got some juicy morsel of gossip about somebody that's in town for the Festival, then don't worry, I never reveal my sources. As long as it doesn't affect Evie then that's all that matters, she's got enough on her plate. Her press conference is at two. You should come along and lend your support.'

Fidgeting on his chair, Stafford fired his answer straight back. 'There's no way I'm going. He might be there. He might see me … he'll kill me.'

Confusion flooded Nush's face. 'Who, Stafford? You're not making any sense.'

'The person who did this …' Taking off his overcoat, Stafford laid it on the floor. He then carefully rolled down the neck of his sweater and tilted his head back. Either side of his neck were dark patches of bruised skin. It was clear that someone had tried to strangle him.

'Oh, my God, Stafford, who did this to you?' Nush reached forward and placed her hand on Stafford's knee, reassuring him of her trust.

Total amazement registered on Nush's face as Stafford revealed the answer. 'It was Jeremy Pinewood. I need to tell you the whole story.'

Stafford started right back at the beginning when he had first encountered Jeremy in LA and unravelled the entire story to a speechless Nush. As he finished detailing the violent encounter under the bridge, Nush already knew what she had to do and how she intended to do it.

———

Twenty four hours later, the Venice Film Festival had come to an end and the visitors who had collected there, all for different reasons, had left.

Stafford was the first to leave. As soon as he'd finished speaking to Nush, she'd arranged for one of the family private jets to fly to Venice. It transported him back to London, where he connected to a long-haul flight to LA. Given the time difference, he was back at his own house the same day. He then did as Nush had instructed him and packed as many of his personal belongings into an extra set of luggage, phoned a cab and drove to Burbank airport to catch the first internal flight he could. It took him to San Francisco… he figured he'd be out of harm's way there. It would be easy for him to lie low until things became safe.

Montana and Brad had been bewildered by Stafford's last few days in Venice. They had hardly seen him. But they figured it was his groin leading him astray, and, after all, it did mean that the newlyweds had more time to themselves. Stafford left them a note saying that he was leaving early and that he'd be in touch. Montana and Brad themselves left the following morning. They had come to Europe as lovers, as business partners, as equals, but they returned to LA as all of that and also as a married couple. The *Babylon* press trip had been a success. Not without incident, for sure, but sell-outs and good reviews spoke for themselves. But Montana was keen to put it all behind her. She had other fish to fry back home. High-profile interviews about Lawrence and a new season of *Peregrine Palace* loomed on the horizon. There was also the matter of bridge-building between her and Regan. She had just lost her father after all … so shortly after finally finding him. Surely she deserved some love from her one remaining parent?

—

Stephanie and Jeremy were seated alongside each other on their flight back to America. The hastily arranged press conference for Evie had worked out just as Stephanie had hoped. She'd been amazed at Evie's strength throughout. Stephanie had asked Jeremy to appear for moral support, but the actor had declined. 'This is something I know Evie should do for herself,' he'd bluffed. 'She's exorcising a demon.'

It was only after the press conference, when Jeremy had realised just how forgiving the press seemed to be, that Jeremy had finally re-established contact with Evie, kissing her cheek as she left the stage. Her reaction to him was warm, but not as loving as she'd been the day before. Her warmth was in stark contrast to the ice-cold reception he'd received from Nush. She'd not even replied to him when he'd asked her to make sure she did a good job on the exclusive about Evie's side of the baby saga.

Evie, Nush and Regan jetted back to the UK together. So far, only Nush knew the dark secret that Jeremy was concealing from Evie. There was no way she could tell her as yet. It would crush her. Besides, there were more pressing issues, such as making sure that her version of the events surrounding the termination hit the newsstands as soon as possible. The article that Clarissa had written for that morning's *Daily Staple* had been a one-sided rampage attempting to portray Evie as a calculating conniving bitch. Nush wanted to redress the balance as quickly as she could. She owed Evie that.

Both Nush and Regan had noticed something different about Evie. There was an air of serenity about her. She appeared calm, collected, in control … traits that normally neither woman associated with the actress. It was Regan who questioned the change as they touched down on a private runway back in Britain.

'Are you sure you're okay about everything, Evie? You seem detached … stoic even. I thought you would have been a blubbering mess about all of this.'

Evie, who had been staring out of the window at the light September rain falling against the jet window, turned to look at both girls. Her lips curled upwards into a smile and she spoke. 'I am okay, I've surprised even myself. I've lived with this secret for the last four years and there hasn't been a day when I haven't thought about what my baby would be like now. But it's out in the open for everyone to judge, and that means I don't have to worry about it anymore. Those people at the press conference yesterday weren't ready to crucify me, were they? They just wanted today's bit of gossip. They're still the same people who enjoyed the screening of *Bouquet* the day before, the same people who gave me wonderful reviews for *Pengelly Manor*. But I honestly believe that the people who pay to come and see my movies will still do so. They're the important ones. Stephanie was right, I just have to hold my head up high. So I've made mistakes, who hasn't? Look at the three of us ... how many have we made? Too many ... doubtless we'll make more. Who knows what's around the corner ... I don't ... but I do know that with you two alongside me then I'll be alright ... whatever happens.'

After all the three women had been through, maybe it had made them stronger, both individually and as a unit ... as a Trinity.

'Well, the feeling's mutual, girlfriend. Plus, on the baby front, there's always the thought that one day you and Jeremy may be adding to the world's population. If ever beautiful babies are guaranteed then it's with you two,' said Regan.

Evie's smile faded somewhat. 'Well, our *relationship* is another thing that I'm seeing with less blinkered eyes. Jeremy's not exactly supported me over this, has he? He chose to party in Venice when I needed him most and left you two to pick up the pieces. And anyway, you have to have sex to make babies, or at least you did last time I read up on it. Jeremy's not exactly throwing me to the floor and ravaging me, is he, more's the pity. In fact he seems to make any excuse to avoid it. We'll be more or less in different time zones for the foreseeable future, which won't exactly help. I'm not sure that Jeremy and I are as together as I'd hoped. But I'll live.'

Nush couldn't help but muse that maybe her news wouldn't crush Evie as much as she'd previously thought.

CHAPTER 81

The storm about Evie and the baby blew over as quickly as it had erupted. Under the masterful orchestration of Stephanie, Evie had been honest with the world about the pregnancy and the world understood. Even a private meeting with Jerome's family had ended amicably, with his parents telling Evie that Clarissa had distorted their words beyond belief.

Evie's interview in *The Daily Staple* telling her side of the story was, for Nush, the most satisfying thing she had ever written. It had made her feel worthwhile, something that her daily column had always failed to deliver. As a result, she went to see Johnny Erridge to quit her job. She would no longer work full-time for the paper. What she suggested was that she would still write the odd exclusive. She would keep her showbiz ears to the ground and if she could see a story that would benefit those around her then she would write it. With Johnny as her new publisher, the immense pressure Nush had always felt under Lawrence seemed to disappear. She could believe in herself and her talents. Johnny agreed to Nush's request, even listening to her one condition … that her old job was never given to Clarissa Thornton.

With the money that Lawrence had left her, Nush became a very rich woman overnight. In time she would give portions of it to Harry and Sadie, but for now it was all hers, to do with as she pleased.

Regan found herself besieged with work offers on her return to the UK. Her dramatic exit from *Wild Child* had given her cult status and she became the epitome of underground cool. Within weeks she was writing a fashion column for a glossy magazine and lined up to host a trendy music programme. Offers flooded in from the States to host her own lifestyle show and she was even offered Clarissa Thornton's old job on *Hollywood Daily*. After her recent bouts of publicity, Clarissa had quit her job to front her own prime-time talk show, eponymously called *Clarissa*. But, after her cheap expose on Evie, the public seemed to turn on her and the ratings on her new show halved after three weeks on air. Six weeks later the debut series of *Clarissa* was canned, leaving her jobless.

Regan chose to stay in Britain. Leo was Stateside, based in LA with his new show. It was doing well and she didn't want to overshadow him or invade his new international success. She felt she owed him that. Regan made the odd trip to LA to see her mother. Things seemed better between them than they'd ever been. If Lawrence's death had taught her one thing, it was that it was easier to try to sort out problems with the living rather than leave it until it was too late. They still argued and screamed at each other until their faces were cherry red with anger, but they were finally beginning to understand each other.

Jeremy went to work on a film in his native Australia, a sun-drenched epic set in the outback. He phoned Evie every day of the four months he was there, telling how much he missed her and longed for her touch. In the run up to *The Bouquet Catcher's* release Evie flew to Australia twice to join him on set. Stephanie had said it would be good press for them both. They were photographed together, laughing and smiling, even sharing the odd kiss. To the outside world, the flame of romance seemingly still flickered between them. Jeremy told Evie how much he loved her but they still never slept together. Evie didn't expect them to. It would have been awkward because he was sharing his on-set Winnebago with Mario, the ill-treated make-up artist he insisted on taking everywhere with him. Then there was the *small* fact of why Jeremy would want sex with her anyway ... she knew his secret after all.

Oh yes, Evie was playing the role of being Jeremy's girlfriend with considerable aplomb. When Nush had gathered the Trinity together and informed both her and Regan of Stafford's story, Evie's immediate reaction had been one of hysteria. Then everything fell into place in her mind. Why he'd been so uninterested in her at first, why the 180 degree turnaround had come when people had seen how good they were together on-screen, why Mario was constantly at his side and why she and Jeremy had never had sex. Jeremy was merely working their so-called relationship for the good of their film. What would happen when it was released in just a few short months? Doubtless, Jeremy would then make his excuses and run straight into the hairy arms of the querulous make-up artist, and the world's press would be full of tales of how 'the pressures of work' had driven him and Evie apart. It was classic modern Hollywood and she'd fallen for it hook, line and sinker.

'So, what do I do?' Evie had asked the girls when Nush had told her. 'If we break up before the film, Stephanie will go ballistic. This whole film relies on the chemistry between Jeremy and me.'

'When does it hit the cinemas?' pressed Nush.

'Two weeks before the Oscars. The film company want to coincide its release with what they hope will be my Oscar nomination for *Pengelly Manor.'*

Nush grinned, a soupcon of delicious revenge spreading from her lips. 'That's just perfect. Just make sure you blag Regan and me into the Oscars because the three of us are going to make it an affair to remember.'

Nush unravelled her plan to a spellbound Evie and Regan ...

EPILOGUE

Oscar Night

'Our thanks to Grace Laszlo for presenting that last award, and now we move onto the category for Best Actress in a Leading Role. Here, to present the award, will you please welcome the charismatic Zac Efron…'

Evie watched from her front row seat as the actor took to the stage. Alongside her sat Jeremy. Tonight was the first time they'd seen each other in weeks. He'd flown in from Australia especially for the event. The two of them were still the talk of Hollywood after the success of *The Bouquet Catcher*. Two weeks at the box office and it was still sitting pretty at number one. It was the same story around the world.

Nush and Regan sat further back in the auditorium, alongside them was Mario, whom Jeremy had insisted on bringing along for the night. Regan's seat was directly in front of Grace's, which had pleased her enormously. She and Grace had not spoken all night.

The three women listened as Zac read out the list of nominations. 'Evie Merchant for *Pengelly Manor*.' At her name the cameras focussed on her. Jeremy attempted to squeeze her hand supportively. Evie let it rest there without turning to look at him.

After clips of the five nominated actresses had been shown, the cameras returned to Zac Efron on stage to announce the victor. The silent pause that followed seemed to last for an eternity inside Evie's brain. Then it came. 'And the winner is … the totally stunning Evie Merchant!'

The camera panned back to Evie just as Jeremy leant in to try and kiss her. He was too late. She'd already risen and his lips smacked thin-air. Regan and Nush leapt to their feet, hollering their delight.

Gliding swan-like onto the stage in her ivory Dior gown, Evie knew that the night belonged to her. It was her turn in the glow of the Oscar spotlight.

'Wow, there are so many people I would like to thank. Where to begin? First off, to the entire crew of *Pengelly Manor*. To my co-stars and everyone who went to see it. I'd like to say thank you to my parents for always believing in me and to my agent, Stephanie Love, for being fabulous and guiding me through everything. Also to my two best friends, who are here with me tonight, Nush Silvers and Regan Phoenix. You girls are simply amazing and I love you both. Especially with all the support you've given me over the last few months …'

Evie took a deep breath before continuing. 'Can I say as well, that my latest film saw me starring with one of the most handsome guys on the planet. Suave, chiselled, totally romantic … yes, I'm talking about you, Jeremy…' Evie pointed down to the front row where a frowning Jeremy, worried that he wouldn't actually get a mention, suddenly beamed at hearing his name. 'And he's also, as us Brits like to say, a bloody top actor. Jeremy's made such an impact on my life. If this Oscar has been awarded to me by people who believe that it is what I deserve then, Jeremy, I truly hope that *you* get what *you* deserve one day soon too. I am certain you will. Thank you everyone, you have made a little girl from Britain the happiest women alive tonight.' Evie giggled and held the golden statuette aloft.

Turning to the crowd and blowing a kiss to an elated Regan and Nush, Evie turned to walk offstage. As she did so, she looked down to the front row and winked at Jeremy. He was on his feet, clapping wildly, his chest pumped with pride, delighted at being a focal point in Evie's speech.

Before reseating himself, he turned round to stare at Mario, Nush and Regan. The three of them were staring directly at him. Again he felt the intense rush of being the object of their attention. His cock twitched as he looked Mario directly in the eyes. It was going to be a memorable night all round, he could feel it.

Offstage, an elated Evie made her way back to her seat. The ceremony was nearly over and then the night would truly commence. It would be time to party …

———

Nush, Regan and Evie surveyed the room at the *Vanity Fair* post-Oscar party. Situated on the ground floor of one of Hollywood's most prestigious hotels, it was a mass of designer frocks, dazzling diamonds, and Hollywood heart-throbs. Jeremy, who had accompanied the three women to the party, was working the room with skilled accuracy, pin-pointing the directors and producers who were known to be planning the next big thing. Every so often, he would make his way back to the Trinity, who had spent most of their time at the party giggling with Mario at the bar. For Jeremy it was perfect. It kept them all out of his way while he schmoozed the room.

As the party started to thin out, the five of them grouped together, champagne glasses in hand. It was the perfect moment for the women to roll their plan into action.

Evie, who had flirtily been caressing Jeremy's buttocks with her free hand, turned to face Jeremy and kissed him full on the lips. It was a lusty, hearty kiss. As she did so, she moved her hand from the round firmness of his buttocks and weaved it up his back as sensuously as she could, letting it rest at the nape of his neck. Sensing the eyes of those around upon him, Jeremy reciprocated by pulling Evie towards him.

'Time for someone to get a room, don't you think?' coaxed Regan. 'Looks like you two lovebirds should be celebrating Evie's win with a little horizontal performance of your own.'

Evie made it evident to all around her that she was not prepared to take no for an answer, certainly not tonight. Vixen-like, as if playing a seductress from one of her movies, she pressed herself against him. 'I'd like that, Jeremy. We haven't had much time together recently and our suites are upstairs after all. That's why I asked Stephanie to book us all adjoining rooms here. I was hoping you and I might make my Oscar winning night pure perfection.' Evie leant in to whisper in Jeremy's ear, 'Physically perfect'. As she spoke, her 'whisper' clearly audible to those around her, she playfully squeezed Jeremy's crotch.

Nush feigned mock-horror. 'Okay, you two, I've seen and heard enough. It's definitely time we left you alone. Regan … you and I should head to Elton's party. I promised him we'd make an appearance. Mario, you're coming with us, my friend, because you may be staying in Jeremy's suite next door to ours but something tells me that you should be sharing with me and Regan tonight. I think we should all give these two some privacy, don't you?'

The make-up artist swayed, somewhat exaggeratedly, as Nush spoke, apparently a little worse for drink. 'I think I'll give Elton's a miss. I don't think I could drink any more. I'm a little *ubriaco* as we say in Italy – the room is spinning and I need to get out of these clothes and lie down. I could do with getting to bed. You girls go and have fun at Elton's party and knock on the door of the suite when you get back. I'll let you in, since these two will obviously be celebrating with a slice of *passione*.'

As Mario left the group, he kissed the women goodnight and hugged Jeremy, allowing the growing erection in his pants to press against Jeremy's leg. Without saying a word, the look between them spoke volumes.

As Mario departed, Jeremy began to protest to the women. 'Maybe we should go to Elton's party too, Evie. It's bound to be full of people we need to speak to. We've got a lifetime of happiness ahead of us ... we could go there for an hour or two ... what do you think?'

It was Regan who playfully shouted him down. 'Are you mad? You're being offered a night of rapturous intimacy with the most celebrated woman in Hollywood right now. You two are heading upstairs straight away. Nush, don't you leave without me. I'll be down in a minute when these two are safely *tucked up* for the night.'

Pushing herself between Evie and Jeremy, Regan linked her arms into theirs and whisked them across the party, towards the hotel lobby where she found the elevators. Within minutes she was ushering them into their palatial suite on the fourth floor. Evie giggled constantly at her friend's cheery forcefulness. Jeremy stumbled along, for once at a loss for words.

Finally letting go of Evie and Jeremy, Regan moved towards the door. 'We're off to Elton's then. You two have this place to yourselves 'til morning. We'll be next door,' tittered Regan. '... if we make it back tonight of course ... We won't disturb you though, that adjoining door over there between our suites will remain locked.'

Just as Regan was about to shut the door, she bobbed her head back around it. 'And keep it down with the screams of passion, eh? Mario will be trying to sleep off the champers next door. Poor little love.' With that she was gone, leaving Jeremy and Evie alone.

Turning her back to him, Evie asked an increasingly flushed Jeremy to undo the zip at the back of her Dior dress. As she did so, she let it slip to the floor, revealing a matching lace bra and panties set. She grabbed Jeremy's hand and guided it to her breasts. 'I've been waiting for this moment, Jeremy … for what seems like forever.'

Moving his hand away from her chest, just as she had expected, Jeremy was as quick as ever to make his excuses. By now, she could pretty much recite his pleas by heart. 'Look, Evie, I'm a little tired, it's been a lovely evening, but I really think I might call it a night. You don't mind, do you? Why don't you join your friends at Elton's party? This is your night. You should be out there showing your beautiful face to the world.'

Evie didn't protest, she had no intention of doing so. 'You get yourself to bed next door, my sweet handsome man. I'll catch up with the girls and have a few more celebratory drinks.'

Jeremy took Evie's face in his hands and kissed her lips. 'I don't deserve you, Evie Merchant …'

As he walked out of the suite, leaving Evie standing in her lingerie, Evie couldn't help but reply. 'No, you truly don't …'

———

Rushing next door, Jeremy couldn't wait to get inside his own suite. He'd been feeling horny ever since Evie's Oscar speech but there was only one way he planned to get his rocks off tonight and it certainly wasn't with the soft, slender form of Evie. Jeremy wanted to get to grips with the doting Mario. He wasn't disappointed as he let himself into the suite and swaggered into the bedroom to find a naked Mario on all fours on the bed. *Good to see that Mario knows his place*, thought Jeremy. He'd obviously been expecting him.

Throwing off his clothes, Jeremy climbed onto the bed behind Mario, his erect cock bouncing in front of him. Picking up a condom from the bedside table, he unwrapped it and rolled it onto his shaft. Without a word, he eased himself into Mario and began to pump back and forth.

Observing their carnal actions from her hidden vantage within the huge wooden closet on the other side of the room, Nush rang Regan's mobile phone. It was the pre-arranged signal that Evie and Regan were waiting for in the suite next door. Opening the adjoining door, which had been conveniently left unlocked for them by Mario, they burst into the bedroom. In Regan's hands a camera clicked, time and time again, capturing the image of the two men joined together. At the same time, Nush jumped out of the closet to complete the Trinity.

The three women stood together united, seeing Jeremy's face erupt into sheer terror as he attempted to pull himself away from Mario and cover himself in the sheets. As he did so, a calm and collected Mario got off the bed and wrapped himself in a hotel bathrobe.

'What the fuck are you doing?' screamed Jeremy to the trio.

It was Nush who spoke. 'It's called revenge, Jeremy. You mess with one of our friends, you mess with all of us. You've been stringing Evie along ever since you two became an item. Gay men make fabulous friends and shopping partners for a woman, but dreadfully deceitful boyfriends. I've come out of your closet, so that you can finally come out of yours.'

A defensive Jeremy felt backed into a corner, his worst fears suddenly a realisation. 'I'll deny it, you stupid bitches' he cried.

Evie, still just wearing lingerie and high heels, seized the moment. 'Just how are you going to do that then, Jeremy? These photos might just happen to find themselves all over the internet come the morning. And I could be sorely tempted to tell my story since Nush is so experienced at reporting celebrity scandal.'

Without pausing for breath, Evie continued relentlessly. 'I really did think you and I were the perfect couple. But the fact that you can turn down offers like this,' she said, indicating her semi-naked form, 'made me realise that you were lying to me. When I discovered the full extent of your deception, I knew it was time to expose you for what you are. I don't care that you're gay, Jeremy, far from it … I just care that you lied to me. Nush, Regan and I have been planning this for weeks now and luckily Mario was more than willing to join us in our revenge. It's funny how megabucks and the promise of a job as my permanent make-up artist can persuade even the most loyal of employees. You're lucky I didn't out you at the Oscars. I was incredibly tempted. I've been forced to explain my own secret recently and it's actually not that hard, you know. In fact, it felt kind of good … you should try it.'

Grabbing the camera from Regan, Evie took one last shot of a deflated Jeremy cowering on the edge of the bed. 'I'll keep that one for posterity, it must be the most honest photograph of you in existence.'

Turning on their heels, the three women, along with a grinning Mario, walked back through the adjoining door into Evie's suite and locked it behind them. As they did so, Nush smiled at Mario. 'Thanks for your help. We couldn't have done it without you. Now, your tuxedo's hanging up in the wardrobe, so get yourself dressed and let's head on out. We all have Hollywood parties to go to …'

—

The Trinity walked the red carpet into Elton John's party together, arm in arm, their heads held up high. Having surveyed the wealth of male beauties buzzing around the room, the three women reached for glasses of champagne from a passing waiter's silver tray. As they did so, Regan noticed flashing blue lights outside the venue. She could see that it was an ambulance. Her curiosity aroused, she asked the waiter, 'Excuse me, what's going on outside ... nothing serious I hope.'

'Oh that.' The waiter excitedly looked around, making sure that he couldn't be heard and gathered the three women around him. 'Well, I shouldn't really say anything, but according to security, it's for that Grace Laszlo woman. They've just found her flat out on the bathroom floor. She's had a little bit too much of the old nose candy and lord knows what else apparently. She's in a total state, vomit everywhere. They're carting her off to have her stomach pumped. Classy, eh?'

Turning to Evie, he smiled before sauntering off to service another celebrity's thirst. 'Congratulations on the win, by the way. You're my favourite actress. It made my night.'

Raising their glasses in toast, the Trinity let them clink together. Regan allowed herself a wry smile. 'And that news about Grace has just made mine. Right then, ladies ... let's mingle.'

LETTER FROM NIGEL

Hi there everyone! I really hope you enjoyed the highs and the lows, the mayhem and the madness and the secrets and the sauciness you've just experienced with Evie, Regan and Nush. I love the Trinity girls and hopefully you did too. It was quite a ride.

Trinity is the first blockbuster novel that I have written and I really loved weaving a web of intrigue for the three young women to become involved in. I suspect that all three of them might pop up again in future books. In fact I am sure they will as doubtless they will be friends for life, even if they do have the odd disagreement! What true friends don't? I just need to decide which stunning locations I'll send them to next time.

If you enjoyed the book I would LOVE you to leave me a review on Amazon. Hearing what readers think means everything to us storytellers. Who was your favourite character? Did you like Regan and her wild child ways, Nush and her hard-hitting headline-grabbing nature or the romantic Evie and her dreams of Hollywood stardom? I love them all equally, but I'd love to hear what you think. Who was your favourite Trinity man too? Fill me in.

And, if you liked this book, perhaps you'd like to read some more of my blockbusters! I'd love to talk all things glam on Twitter, Facebook and Goodreads. I'm never happier than when I'm discussing a cracking story – bring on the thrills and let's dare to share!

To keep right up-to-date with the latest news on my new releases just sign up at the following page:

www.bookouture.com/nigel-may

Here's to more glamorous reads with a whole host of fantastic characters – there's a huge amount of danger and sparkle coming up!

Keep it gritty and glam, Nigel x

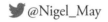 @Nigel_May

www.nigelmay.net

ADDICTED

Move over Jackie Collins, there's a new blockbuster star in town.' *New!* Magazine

Fame, fortune and five-star luxury. Meet four *fabulous* women – all of them hold a dark secret… one of them won't live to tell the tale.

Nancy Arlow – the fading entertainer determined to gamble and charm her way out of a mountain of debt.

Laura Everett – behind the façade of the perfect politician's wife lies a woman with an outrageous past and a spiraling drug habit.

Portia Safari – the world famous opera diva, adored by millions, has it all, but could her secret drinking problem cost her everything?

Martha Éclair – The millionaire wine heiress whose appetite for kinky sex could bring down her father's business empire.

Each woman must face their own addiction before they pay the ultimate price…

Switch off your phone, grab a glass of bubbly and escape into an outrageous word of thrills, glamour and passion. You'll be addicted…

'Packed full of sauciness, darkness and intrigue, this lively romp of a story takes you on a colourful journey through the world of showbiz, from the ultra-highs to the face-planting lows. If you're looking for a sexy, racy, riotous read for your sun lounger this summer, this is the perfect choice.' *Heat* Magazine

'ADDICTED is a sexy, dark, thrilling celebrity whirlwind that lifts the curtain on some blistering superstar scandal. It's the most fun you can have between two covers. I need more!' Victoria Fox

**Read on for an exclusive extract from Nigel May's new novel,
Scandalous Lies, coming soon…**

Hell's Canyon, California

Daytime

The heat was intense. The sun, still burning lava-bright in a
one-colour tapestry of the purest idyllic blue despite the late
hour of the afternoon. Clouds non-existent as a monotonous
heat continued to blur the lines where horizon introduced itself
to sky. The ground, shouting a natural desire to be quenched
by the waters of the heavily depleted river nearby had its request left unanswered as its skin began to crack, an aging process no imminent meteorological surgery was likely to repair.
Shriveled plants, those who had survived the brutal heat of one
of the fiercest summers on record so far, were only moments
from oblivion, a death that would be a welcome one to their
moisture-searching veins. Any furry inhabitant that had once
scurried across the canyon floor was either long gone in a hunt
for food, or showed the idiocy of their tardiness by now remaining as now more than a skeleton. Mother Nature was a bitch
and despite the beauty of the canyon and the surrounding area
for most of the year, at that precise moment the globe of raging
white embellished above the canyon was a dangerous one. A
lethal one. Nothing could survive.

Unless, of course, you were currently opening the heavy, curved door of a floor to ceiling fridge freezer combo within the confines of your air-conditioned RV and reaching for a chilled bottle of Moet & Chandon Bi Cuvee Dry Imperial, one of six housed within the confines of the chiller. At a cost of nearly a grand each these were diamond-dipped bubbles. And fizz that could extinguish even the most barbarous of sunshine. In that case, then survival was easy.

'A sneaky peak to put you in the mood?' asked Foster Hampton, pushing his blond surfer-dude curls, pure Bondi Beach even though it was pure Brit blood that ran through his veins, away from his eye line as he reached for the bottle. The whirl of chilled air from within the fridge enveloped his naked skin as he stood, bottle in hand and faced his lover, lying on the double bed on the other side of the road vehicle.

'You should turn back around and show me that peachy backside of yours again. I was enjoying the view from over here,' answered Mitzi Bidgood. 'It's something I will never tire off. It should be added to every British female tourist's itinerary for a road trip across America. Mount Rushmore, Dollywood, Golden Gate Bridge and Foster Hampton's bubble butt. A pink, glowing spectacle of an ass. A wicked wonder of the world. The tourist board could make a fortune in ticket sales. Not that I'm keen to share it with any passing Yank though to be honest. That rump is mine all mine. The view from this angle is totally appetising,' remarked Mitzi, pointing towards the sizable pendulum of meat currently rising to attention between Foster's legs. 'And what, to answer your question, makes you think for one orgasmic moment that I am not already in the mood?'

Foster smiled as Mitzi spread-eagled her naked legs and dipped the finger she'd been pointing at his cock with into the fleshy, wet folds of her pussy. The weapon between Foster's legs

rose to its full length, blood flooding through it with anticipatory desire.

'Now, pop that cork, pour me something beautiful and bring
that body of yours onto this bed right away. Mitzi needs some
loving after that long drive today. I assume we have all night?'

'We are going nowhere until dawn,' Foster replied as he poured
the champagne, a flow of frothy bubbles rising to the rim and cas-
cading down the body and stem of the glass and onto the tiles below his feet. 'I did not drive the entire length of this canyon in this
monstrosity to just turn around and head back out again. There
aren't many cars that can make it this far, so we might as well
make the most of our surroundings and the fact that we're the
only ones around for miles. Not that I'm going out in this heat.
The dashboard thermometer says it's about 113 degrees Fahren-
heit. That's way too hot, even for a beach-loving boy like me.'

It was true, the road they had driven on to reach the secluded
spot at the far end of the canyon was impassible by most vehi-
cles. It was only top of the range RVs like the one Foster and his
girlfriend of three years, Mitzi, had hired for their month-long
USA vacation that were able to cope. The camper was outwardly
perfectly equipped to deal with even the rockiest of terrains and
its lavish interior was equally custom built for sheer luxury while
travelling with its satellite system, surround sound, DVD player,
huge TV and wireless internet. On the few occasions they had
used the internet during the previous three weeks of their journey it had only been to check emails from their lives back home
in the UK. As a professional dancer on one of her home country's top TV shows, Mitzi needed to find out what the next season of the hot show held for her when she returned in just over
a week's time. The rumour mill was circling with the notion that
Mitzi's celebrity partner for the next six months would be a fellow reality TV star from Surf *N Turf*, the same show which had

seen Foster rise to fame four years ago. The show, about a group of Cornish surfers who also ran their own landscape gardening business at the same time, had been a huge hit and Foster had been the breakout star, securing a spot as Mitzi's dancing partner after only one season on *Surf*. Viewers loved his relationship with Mitzi, which quickly spilled from the ballroom and into the bedroom. Their Barbie and Ken blond perfection meant that when the two of them lifted the glitter ball trophy aloft at the end of the series, the offers came flooding in for them both. Sponsorship deals, lucrative cruise tours to showcase their dancing prowess and a massive pay increase for Mitzi to stay on the show, saw both their kudos and their bank balances snowball. Foster's latest project, a documentary in which he would put his gardening skills to the test to turn a downtrodden Cornish council estate into a thriving oasis of green shrubbery and happiness, was due to commence on his return to Britain.

But for now, all that was on the cards for the next few hours was a nerve-tingling, gymnastic, symphony of love-making, something their sporty, supple dancer's bodies allowed them to indulge in as often as possible and in positions most sexual partners could only dream of.

'I'll show you what's hot,' moaned Mitzi deliriously as she moved her finger faster inside her, the body arching with pleasure as crests of desire snapped through her inner core, spreading from the heat between her legs. Shift that six-pack of yours over here now and ride me like a Texas rodeo athlete.'

Foster didn't need asking twice. Moving to the bed, he emptied his own glass of champagne and handed the other to Mitzi. As she placed the glass to her lips, Foster pushed his face deep into the open layers of joy between her legs. The feel of her wetness thrilled him, encouraging him to force his face deeper. It was only once his mouth was completely enveloped by the flower of her pussy that he allowed his lips to open and the pouring of champagne to icily flow from his mouth into the sexual cavity of her vagina, swirling around his tongue and Mitzi's finger as it did so. She let out a squeal of joy and dropped her now virtually empty glass onto the sheets alongside her. The remaining droplets of champagne dribbled onto the material underneath her body.

Foster looped his tongue around Mitzi's finger and felt an increase in the ferocity of her excitement as she moved her finger faster and more pressingly inside her. The fusion of the sweet champagne and her own natural womanly flavour washed across Foster's tongue as her finger rubbed against his taste buds. Mitzi's breathing became more urgent. Beads of sweat formed on her forehead and she felt them run down her face and weave down between her round, cherry-peaked breasts. Only Foster could turn her on so quickly, his love-making as pleasing now as it had been when they had first given in to temptation years before. If there was another skill that Foster could add to the many that he already possessed it was his cunnilingual technique. She wriggled with pleasure as his tongue seemed to reach places that her finger could not.

She felt the three-day old stubble on his chin graze over her tender flesh and a hunger gnawed within her. It was a hunger that only one action could assuage. She let out a whimper, a gasp as the roughness of his feasting centred on her clitoris and reached her hands down to move his head away.

A smiling Foster looked up at her from between her legs, his face shiny with sweat and Mitzi's juices.

'Why don't you fuck me' she stated. It wasn't a suggestion.

Foster flicked his tongue along the thin line of hair decorating her pussy, circled it around her belly button and feather-kissed his way up to her breasts, taking her to the edge of bliss. He maneuvered himself into position and, as he bit down onto one of Mitzi's erect nipples, allowed his erection to plough into her. Firm, long and proud, his dexterous crescent of flesh caused her to bite down of her bottom lip as he thrust faultlessly into her. She could feel her euphoria rising. No lover had ever made her feel like Foster. There had been many, but he was unique.

A scream escaped her lips but volume control was unnecessary. Who would hear her? Only the man causing her to ride the waves of joy in the same skilled way Foster himself could ride those on the ocean. She was ecstatic for him to hear her appreciation. But no more words came as she pressed her mouth onto his and kissed him deeply. A knowing look from deep within his eyes, one of trust and shared love, told her what was to follow. Mitzi's eyes blurred, her vision smudging as she felt him unleash his liquid into her and her own orgasm climb to its perfect peak. She wrapped her arms tightly around him, attempting to coax him even deeper. He kept his cock, still semi-stiff in his post denouement delirium, inside her. Foster and Mitzi were still in the same position, united in their love, half an hour later.

—

Nighttime

'This has been the best holiday ever, Foster. Both sexually and otherwise,' giggled Mitzi, somewhat tipsy from the third glass of champagne she'd drunk, accompanying the Caesar salad Foster had prepared her for dinner. 'I mean it. The places we've seen have been amazing and it's wonderful to just spend so much time together without cameras and press interviews and people screaming for autographs. Just to be you and me, us, together. Doing whatever we want, whenever we want. I have loved it so much, and I love you so much.'

'I'll have to make you drink champagne more often,' said Foster, 'if it makes you this mushy. You weren't such a softie when you were barking dance moves at me when we first met, were you? Are you becoming softer with age?' He winked playfully.

'You were my professional partner then and I was doing my job. Now my job is to let you know how much I love you. Do we have to go back home?'

'Not for another week or so, there are plenty of adventures to come yet. It's not over til the gorgeous lady starts dancing, and that's not until we reach UK shores again.'

'Actually, I was thinking of putting on a bit of a show for you now? I love this song!' said Mitzi rising to her feet from their table outside their RV. It was late evening and the air was finally cool enough to be outside, where they had eaten. The sky had moved from blue to almost black, only a moon and a dotting of stars illuminating the air. She ran inside the camper van, and moved to the sound system which had been playing some of their favourite tunes all evening. It was Beyoncé's *Drunk in Love* that had just started. Turning up the volume, Mitzi sashayed back to the doorway of the camper van and let her body sway seductively to the beat. Silhouetted by the light coming from behind her in the RV, her actions were a perfect mix of flirty and dirty. The beat of the song throbbed as she moved, her timing perfect.

Just as Foster could feel his cock rising to attention again in his sweatpants, a sudden flash of light further across the canyon startled him away from Mitzi's gyrating. Staring out into the darkness he could see a flicker of bright orange. What was it?

'Stop the music will you, Mitz. What is that over there?'

Mitzi paused the music and silence fell around them. Joining Foster again, Mitzi too gazed out into the night.

'It's a fire?' There was questioning in her tone, but there was no doubt.

'But I didn't know there was anybody else out here,' said Foster. 'Maybe the sun started it earlier. We should take a look. It could be blocking the road out of here. And you never know it may have been some dirty old men watching us through the RV windows earlier. We put on quite a show.' The thought didn't displease Mitzi, she was a showgirl after all. And their afternoon sex session had certainly been a spectacle to behold.

Foster was sure that he could hear something in the air. The sound of music. Was the champagne playing tricks on him? He didn't think so.

'Shall we go take a look?' he asked.

'Why not?' giggled Mitzi, 'maybe it's another hot young couple out here just like us. And maybe they're just as adventurous as us...and just as horny.' She gave Foster's ass a playful squeeze as they ventured off towards the bright orange glow.

The sky was pitch black yet the air seemed clear as they stumbled, a little giddy on bubbles, in the direction of the light. Mitzi kept losing her balance slightly on the pebbles and loose rocks beneath her feet. Foster took her hand to steady her. 'We can't have you twisting an ankle before dance season, can we?'

Mitzi found the whole situation borderline erotic. Her and the man she loved, miles from anywhere, in the pitch blackness of the Californian wilderness. Alone and wild.

Except they weren't alone.

Narrowing their eyes to try and scan the glow, the couple blinked until the crackle of orange came into focus. What they saw made Foster gasp. If Mitzi's gasp earlier during their lovemaking had been one of total rapture, Foster's was the complete antithesis.

'What the fuck...?' His words petered out.

'What is it, Foster, what's going on?' It didn't look like they were going to run into an amorous couple interested in a bit of fireside alfresco shagging. As she focused, a chill ran through Mitzi's body and she let out a slight shiver.

'Holy shit.

Dancing around the fire, which they had obviously built themselves, to a heavy tribal musical beat, were a series of figures. They were all dressed in head to toe outfits obscuring their faces. They looked like robes, heavy, maybe made of hessian, almost monk like in appearance, all topped with wide hoods. There must have been about six of them. As the flames flickered higher, one of the figures stripped off the hood and untied the robe allowing it to fall to the floor. It revealed a naked woman, Mitzi guessed about the same age as her, mid-20s. She possessed full, round breasts and a small dark triangle of hair between her legs.

'What the fuck is going on?' Mitzi whispered, reconsidering the alfresco sex theory. Maybe they were just about to witness some kind of outdoor dogging scene with a difference. Mitzi always thought dogging was a load of dirty old men whacking off in a lorry park with some rough old housewife. Maybe the Yanks did it with glamour and lit by a naked flame.

The sound of the beat became louder and more frantic in the air. Foster and Mitzi could see that the other figures surrounding the young woman had stopped, but all bar one of them remained with their hoods in place. The one who revealed his face was a man of about 50 with what looked like a head of salt n pepper hair. It was hard to work out his features exactly as the flickering of the firelight distorted the air.

From one of the sleeves of his robe he pulled out a long, wide-bladed knife. The blade caught the firelight and reflected shards of colour shot into the air.

All of the other figures around the fire held their hands aloft. The music stopped almost instantly. Silence filled the air. 'What's happening, Foster? This is beginning to freak me out' stammered Mitzi. The atmosphere had turned from daring to deadly.

Foster was unsure what to say.

Then it happened.

The man holding the knife, drew it aloft and brought it swiftly across the woman's throat. Even from their somewhat distant position, as the female clutched her hands to her throat, the spurt of deep crimson blood that flowed from her neck before she fell to the floor could be seen by Foster and Mitzi. Disbelief and fear stuck in their throats, threatening to choke them.

For a moment, time stood still, nothing daring to move. Then the full horror of what the couple had just seen hit them. Before she could stop herself, Mitzi screamed. A loud, terrified, blood-curdling scream. 'They've killed her.' It was all she could shout. Her voice pierced the air. Sensible it wasn't, but the noise had escaped from her lips before any semblance of rationality could form.

Once again for a second it seemed like all movement halted, nobody sure what their next action should be. Then as Mitzi and Foster watched on in horror, the figures turned to face the direction of the scream. A sense of anger and panic wrapped itself around the group.

Moving away from the fireside and the body on the floor, the figures began to run in their direction.

'Fuck, they've heard us, they're coming this way. Foster, we need to get out of here now.'

Foster and Mitzi raced towards the camper van, the sound of footsteps and shouts coming from a mass of directions behind them. They needed to get back to the van and drive away from the canyon. Neither was in any fit state to drive, both over the limit, but fear and abject terror spurred them into sobriety. This was a race to survive.

Mitzi could feel her heart burning within her chest as she fumbled her way towards the van. The flip flops she was wearing slid beneath her feet on the loose canyon floor. As one fell off, she jettisoned the other leaving her barefoot.

Foster ran beside her, his panting just about audible alongside her own. A cacophony of voices sounded behind them. They seemed to be getting closer.

The light of their camper van, guiding them to hopeful safety, didn't seem to be getting any nearer. They hadn't walked for more than a few minutes towards the fire, had they? Maybe it was further than they realised.

Mitzi was suddenly aware that the sound of Foster's breathing behind her had disappeared. Where was he? She called his name, her voice dry with fear. There was no answer. She didn't dare stop and look back. She kept running towards the light. She'd soon be there, soon. Maybe Foster was there already, he was stronger than her.

A voice sounded behind her. Was it Foster? She couldn't tell above the sound of her own heartbeat. Turning to glance, her ankle twisted beneath her as another loose rock slid beneath her toes. She fell to the ground. As she did so, she bit down into her tongue as the force of the canyon bottom slammed into her face. The coppery taste of blood filled her mouth.

She had to keep going. The light was brighter, she was nearly there.

Dizzy from her fall, she tried to stand up and keep running. She felt wobbly, a stabbing of pain from her leg. Had she broken something? For a second all she should think about was her dancing career. The bright lights of the dance floor filled her head. Would she ever see it again? Would she ever escape the darkness?

Still on her hands and knees as she tried to stand back up, Mitzi felt the brushing of hessian against her skin before feeling hands either side of her neck. She didn't even have time to scream before a different kind of darkness took her.

———

The next morning as the sun rose over Hell's Canyon and remorselessly beat down onto the arid land, there was no sign of life again. No animals scurrying, no lush green vegetation thriving, and no sign of the RV or the two famous Brits who had been there the night before.

9 781910 751053